MOUNTAIN DEVIL

A commotion erupted, and Nate heard much thrashing and flailing. The scuffle was punctuated by the low growl of a beast and the strangled cry of a man. Suddenly, quiet descended once more.

He must put distance behind him or find a hiding place. One moment he was adroitly weaving among the trees; the next, someone hurtled out of the night and slammed into him from the rear. He was knocked to his knees, and when he frantically twisted to see his attacker he saw a tall warrior armed with a knife—a knife that streaked at his face.

BLACKFOOT MASSACRE

At any second Silver Hair would spot Nate. He turned to the cliff and saw numerous spots where the rock face had crumbled. Climbing the rock wall was his only hope. If he could get high enough, the grizzly wouldn't be able to get him. Wedging his fingers into a narrow cleft, he rose a few inches. He dared not glance over his shoulder.

Five feet he climbed. Then seven. His fingers hurt, his toes too, but he couldn't slow down. He expected to hear the monster closing in on him, but he heard nothing. Then, as he grabbed for a hole formed where some of the stone had eroded away, he heard a rumbling growl from directly below, and peering between his legs, Nate saw Silver Hair at the base of the cliff. That very instant, the bear lunged upward, it's huge forepaw reaching up to rip him from his perch....

MOUNTAIN DEVIL/
BLACKFOOT MASSACRE

WILDERNESS DOUBLE EDITION
DAVID THOMPSON

LEISURE BOOKS   NEW YORK CITY

A LEISURE BOOK®

November 1997

Published by

Dorchester Publishing Co., Inc.
276 Fifth Avenue
New York, NY 10001

ISBN 0-8439-4327-0

Printed in the United States of America.

MOUNTAIN DEVIL

Dedicated to Judy, Joshua, and Shane.
The best family a man could ever have.

Chapter One

Someone—or *something*—was watching him.

Or so Nathaniel King believed, and he turned from the fine black stallion he had been rubbing down with a handful of soft green grass to survey the rugged countryside surrounding his remote cabin in the central Rockies. He was a big, broad-shouldered man with penetrating green eyes and a mane of black hair, and his brow furrowed as he searched for any sign of life, for any movement at all.

To the southeast a bald eagle soared, hunting prey. To the north an irate squirrel chattered. East of the cabin lay a lake teeming with ducks and other fowl, and on its southern shore stood four black-tailed deer, a buck and three doe.

Nate saw nothing to arouse alarm and allowed himself to relax. He resumed stroking the stallion, the buckskins that covered his supple frame flowing with the motions of his muscular arms and shoulders. Angled across his powerful chest was a powder horn and a bullet pouch. In a beaded sheath on his left hip hung a butcher knife, while tucked under his wide brown leather belt were two flintlock pistols, one on either side of the buckle. An eagle feather had been tied at the back of his hair with the quill jutting upwards.

As Nate worked, the nagging feeling persisted that he was being observed. He repeatedly glanced over his shoulders, wondering each time if his nerves were getting the better of him. Not that he didn't have cause for being concerned. Living close to Ute country as he did, he never knew when the resentful Utes might decide to pay him a visit and try to wipe out his entire family. The Utes despised whites, and they went out of their way to exterminate any mountaineers they found.

Nate finished rubbing down the stallion and tossed the grass aside, then turned to exit the stout corral attached to the south side of his cabin. Nearby, milling about, were the five other horses he owned. He paused at the rails to retrieve his prized Hawken rifle, then climbed out. A cool breeze from the northwest stirred his hair. Inhaling deeply, he smelled the tangy scent of pine and the dank odor of the rich earth that carpeted the lush valley he'd staked out as his own.

The cabin door opened and out came his lovely wife, Winona. A full-blooded Shoshone, she had long dark hair and matching eyes. A buckskin dress clung to her shapely figure, and cradled in the crook of her left arm was a basket.

"Where are you going?" Nate inquired in English.

"To gather eggs for our supper," Winona answered, closing the door behind her. She smiled and headed for the lake.

The thought of a savory omelet made Nate's mouth water. He gazed at the sunny sky, grateful winter had ended. The early April weather had been exceptionally mild, and soon he must leave to get some trapping done if he hoped to take a large number of prime beaver pelts to the annual rendezvous held in the summer. "Is Zachary sleeping?" he thought to ask before Winona went too far.

She halted and pivoted. "I thought he was with you."

"What?" Nate said, stiffening.

"He went out to help you with the horses a while ago," Winona explained, retracing her steps, her tone betraying a hint of anxiety.

Nate looked every which way. "He never came near the corral," he said, keeping his voice calm, telling himself there was no need to become apprehensive . . . yet. Their three-year-old son was notorious for wandering off without a word to either one of them. Unfortunately, what with the many predators in the area, not to mention the ever-present prospect of the Utes showing up, wandering off could prove fatal.

"Not again," Winona said.

"You go north, I'll go south," Nate proposed. "Keep yelling until he replies."

"I hope he doesn't hide from us."

"He'd better not. I warned him what would happen if he did that one more time."

They separated, Nate skirting the corral and entering the dense trees. "Zachary!" he bellowed, startling sparrows in a thicket. "Where are you?"

From north of the cabin came Winona's voice. "Zachary! Zachary!"

For several minutes Nate hiked and shouted. The boy didn't respond. Worry battled with anger for supremacy in Nate's mind. There were times, he mused, when being a parent tried his patience to its limits. On several occasions he'd been strongly tempted to apply his belt to his son's backside, and only the promise he'd made to Winona shortly after Zach was born had stopped him. They'd agreed to raise the boy in the Shoshone fashion, which meant never striking him no matter how badly he misbehaved. Instead, they tried to influence Zachary's behavior by always exhorting him to do what was proper and good and by setting ideal examples themselves. Talk about difficult tasks. Nate often marveled that Indians resorted to such exacting child-rearing practices when a good spanking would be so much easier to apply and would bear more immediate fruit. How well he recollected the many spankings his father had given him, and he'd turned out okay.

He wondered if Zachary was playing at being an Indian warrior again. Sometimes the boy would pretend to be a mighty brave on a raid, and during this play Zach would only answer to his Shoshone name. "Stalking Coyote!" he called out. "Time to come back to your village."

The forest mocked him with its silence. All his shouting had caused every living creature within hearing distance to become quiet.

"Young man, this is your father!" Nate yelled angrily. "If you're listening, I demand you answer me this instant."

A bee buzzed past him.

Nate halted at the base of a knoll, the Hawken in his left hand. Far off Winona still shouted. He couldn't imagine the boy straying so far, but he decided to climb to the top of the knoll for a look-see before returning to the cabin. Hastening upward, he stopped on the crest and made a complete revolution, idly noting the towering ring of snow-capped peaks rimming the valley even as he probed the underbrush. Not so much as a rabbit stirred. Convinced he was wasting his time, he turned to depart, and his gaze landed on a boulder-strewn hill approximately a hundred yards to the southwest.

A diminutive figure marched resolutely toward the top.

"Zachary!" Nate thundered, and ran in pursuit. Promise or no promise, the boy's breach of discipline deserved harsh punishment. Time and time again, Winona and he had warned Zachary about going more than a few feet from the cabin when unescorted. The boy simply couldn't get it into his inexperienced head that there were great dangers lurking in the woods. Just once Nate would like to see Zachary have a serious scare that would bring the boy to his senses. Just once—

Something else moved on that hill, something big and long and tawny, something creeping down the slope toward the unsuspecting child.

It was a panther.

Some trappers called them mountain lions. Some referred to them as cougars. Nate used the term favored by the majority of trappers. However they were known, the big cats were renowned for their stealth and their ferocity when aroused. And the sight of one stalking his son sparked a ripple of stark fear down Nate's spine.

"Zachary!" Nate bellowed, and raced toward the hill. His son stopped, turned, and waved. "Come down!" he yelled, motioning with his free arm for the boy to descend, but Zachary resumed climbing.

The panther, 20 yards above the child, paused and glanced at Nate. Then it effortlessly vaulted onto the top of a large, flat boulder and crouched at the lip where it could see the slope below and mark the progress of its intended victim.

Such a bold cat was exceedingly rare. Usually mountain lions fled at the sight or scent of humans. This one, Nate speculated, must be famished, or else believed Zachary to be such easy prey that it wasn't about to stop stalking him just because another person had shown up. He saw Zachary wend among some boulders and opened his mouth to scream. "Zach! Come back! There's a panther above you."

The boy kept going.

Nate knew he wouldn't reach the hill in time to prevent the cat from reaching his son. He must act, and act now, if he hoped to have Zachary grow to a ripe old age. Accordingly, he abruptly halted, snapped the Hawken to his right shoulder, and cocked it. He sighted along the barrel, fixing the bead on the panther's head. It would be a long shot and he couldn't be certain of scoring, but it was his only hope. To compensate for the distance he elevated the barrel to where he instinctively felt it should be, then held his breath and steadied the rifle.

Crouching low, the panther fixed its hungry gaze on Zachary and coiled to spring.

Please let me hit it! Nate prayed, and squeezed the trigger. The Hawken blasted, belching smoke and lead, and on the flat boulder the cougar suddenly recoiled and twisted sharply to one side as the ball nicked its left shoulder, causing blood and flesh to spray outward. Snarling, the cat stared balefully at Nate.

Appalled that the shot hadn't killed it, Nate sped onward. He wouldn't waste time reloading the rifle. If he could get close enough, he'd employ both flintlock pistols.

Little Zachary had halted at the loud retort and now stood watching his father approach. Beaming, he waved happily.

"Come here!" Nate cried on the run. "Come here this instant!"

Finally the boy obeyed. His slender shoulders slumping in resignation, he headed down the hill.

Nate's eyes were locked on the big cat. The panther glanced at Zach, then vented a loud, angry growl. It took a tentative step, as if about to leap from the boulder and attack, but its head turned toward Nate once more and, with remarkable alacrity, it whirled and went up the hill covering 15 feet in a bound. In moments it was gone over the crest, back into the heart of wilderness from which it had emerged.

"Zachary!" Nate cried in relief. The boy stopped at the base of the hill and waited for him, and when he got there he sank to his knees and impulsively gave his son a firm hug. He closed his eyes and held Zachary for almost a minute, overwhelmed with gratitude for the child's deliverance.

"Pa?"

Nate drew back and coughed to clear a constriction in his throat. "Didn't you see the panther?" he asked gruffly.

"Where?" Zachary responded excitedly, and looked all around for the beast. "Show me."

"It ran off," Nate said. "But if I hadn't shown up when I did, it would have eaten you."

Zachary giggled at the prospect. "Panther not eat me. Me hit it," he declared, and swung his tiny right fist at an imaginary cougar.

Under different circumstances Nate would have laughed at the comically determined expression his son wore. But this was serious. The boy had nearly been slain. He maintained a stern face and said, "You can't stop a panther with your bare hands."

"Me could. Me strong."

"You're not strong enough," Nate said harshly. "Anyway, the panther is not the main issue here. Going off by yourself is. Why did you wander away from the cabin when you've been told time and again not to do so?"

"Me saw a butterfly."

"A butterfly?"

Zachary nodded and used his right hand to mimic

the flapping motion of a butterfly's wing. "Yes. It flied past the cabin and me try to catch it."

"Oh," Nate said, and sighed. The boy had been intensely interested in bugs for the last six months or so. Every bug Zach saw, he had to catch and examine. Nate could well imagine how hard it would be for Zach to resist the fluttering temptation of a colorful butterfly, but he still couldn't let the violation go unpunished. "So you ran after it and didn't bother to tell your mother or me."

Zachary, in his youthful innocence, answered promptly and honestly. It never occurred to him to lie. "Yes, me did."

"Say '*I* did,'" Nate corrected him.

"You did?"

"No, you did."

"But you said—"

"Never mind," Nate declared, and took the boy into his right arm. Rising, the Hawken in his left hand, he pivoted and headed for the cabin. "You can't keep doing this, son. One of these days we won't realize you've gone off and a panther or a grizzly or something else will get you."

"Me not scared," Zachary stated.

"I know. And that's part of the problem. You'd be better off if you *were* scared."

"Me *should* be scared?" Zachary asked in amazement.

Nate nodded. "A man who claims he's never been scared is either a liar or a fool. Fear can be good for you if you don't give in to it. It teaches you to be cautious, to play it safe instead of being reckless and getting yourself killed. Do you understand?"

Zachary shook his head. "Me never scared. Me just like you."

"I've been scared plenty of times."

"You have?"

"More times than I care to remember," Nate admitted. "And I'm here today because I learned how to cope with my fear and do what had to be done anyway."

"Tell me some of the times," Zachary requested.

So Nate did, detailing his several terrifying encounters with grizzly bears and his battles with hostile Indians. He told about the time a rattler nearly bit him, and the time he was attacked by a savage wolverine. His son listened intently, eyes agleam with the thrill of adventure. Nate concluded his narrative as they came up on the rear of the cabin. "So you can see that I've been scared many times and it's nothing to be ashamed of. Just don't let your fear stop you from doing whatever has to be done."

"Me won't, Pa. Me chase butterflies anyway."

"That isn't what I meant," Nate muttered, angling around the south end of the corral while racking his brain for a way of getting through to his son, of making his meaning clear. Engrossed in his thoughts, he didn't realize they weren't alone until he stepped in front of the pen and glanced up to discover three mounted men near the front door.

Chapter Two

"Look Pa!" Zachary cried in delight. "Peoples!"

The boy was excited because visitors to their remote cabin were few and far between. Nate didn't share his son's enthusiasm. From bitter prior experience he knew that sometimes visitors spelled trouble, deadly trouble, and the moment he laid eyes on the trio he gently deposited Zachary at his feet and straightened, deliberately hooking the thumb on his right hand in his leather belt close to the right flintlock. He'd foolishly neglected to reload the Hawken after shooting at the panther, but he had two good pistols and a butcher knife he could employ to decidedly lethal effect should these strangers prove to be unfriendly. "Howdy," he said, keeping his tone reserved, his features impassive.

Zachary started to move toward the men.

"Stand still," Nate ordered severely, and the boy stopped and glanced up at him in startled surprise.

The three men were all armed, but they made no

move to bring their weapons into play. All three wore buckskins, the typical attire of mountaineers and Indians alike. Two of the trio were whites; the third was an old Crow warrior whose hair was almost white from age and whose face resembled a craggy bluff. The nearest white sat astride a black gelding and wore a blue cloth cap of the type initially popular with Canadian *voyageurs*, Canadian trappers, and now worn by many of their counterparts in the lower Rockies. He was tall and lean and sported a full black beard. The other white man was on a bay. He was stocky and clean-shaven and wore a string of bear teeth around his neck. Both whites were showing teeth.

"Howdy, friend," the tall one said. "My name is Milo Benteen." He nodded at the stocky man. "This is Tom Sublette. We're both from Pennsylvania and we came out here to do some trapping a year ago."

Nate simply bobbed his chin. He was thinking about Winona, wondering what had happened to her, and no sooner did the thought cross his mind than she emerged from the cabin casually holding a rifle in the crook of her left arm. She looked at him and smiled, then stood still and faced the men.

All three newcomers glanced at her, at the rifle, then at Nate.

"Are you folks expecting trouble?" Milo asked.

"You never know," Nate responded.

Milo cast a shocked expression at Tom, then turned to Nate and said, "Are you referring to us? Hell, man, we don't mean you any harm. We came all this way searching for you to offer you a proposition."

"Oh?" Nate said, not yet ready to accept them as friendly. Some years back he'd taken a stranger into his home, fed and sheltered the man, and when the stranger's companions later arrived they had abducted Winona and left him for dead. He wasn't ever going to make that mistake again.

"That is, if you're Nathaniel King," Tom Sublette threw in.

"I am."

Milo beamed. "At last. Do you have any idea how hard it was for us to track you down? We heard about you at the rendezvous last year. They say you're one of the best, as good as Jim Bridger or Shakespeare McNair. They say you brought in over six hundred pelts one year."

"Six hundred and forty-two," Nate said.

"They also say you're honest to a fault and as dependable as they come," Tom mentioned. "We were told we could trust you with our lives."

"How did you find my cabin?" Nate inquired. So far as he knew, only his good friend Shakespeare McNair and two other trappers knew its exact location. It wasn't wise to advertise where one lived; enemies might find out and pay you a visit.

"Once we decided it was you we wanted, we asked around," Milo said. "Ran into a man named Cumberland who is a close friend of McNair's. Cumberland told us he believed you lived in this general area but he couldn't pinpoint where. So for the past two weeks we've been traipsing all over this stretch of mountains looking for you."

"Why?" Nate asked.

Milo shifted in his saddle. "We've been riding for hours. Do you reckon we could light and sit a spell?"

Nate hesitated, thinking of the consequences for Winona and Zach if he made the wrong decision. But these men seemed sincere. All three had rifles, but they had studiously refrained from so much as touching the long guns resting across their thighs. If they'd meant to harm him and his family, they could easily have lain in ambush and gunned him down when his back was turned. He suddenly recalled the feeling he'd had earlier of being watched and gazed up at Benteen. "Were you watching us earlier?"

Milo blinked. "We first saw your cabin from across the lake yonder. I took out my telescope for a look-see. Cumberland gave us a description of you and I wanted to see if we'd lucked out and found you. How did you know?"

"I knew," Nate said, and let it go at that. He took Zach's small hand in his and walked to the door. "Why don't you climb down and tie your animals at the corral? My wife will fix us a pot of coffee and you can explain the reason you've sought me out."

"Thanks," Milo said.

Winona took Zachary inside while Nate watched the three men move to the corral and dismount. The old Crow had not said a word. Nate studied the warrior's face, trying to determine the man's character in the many lines and creases. For such an oldster, the Crow held himself erect and displayed remarkable vitality. Nate knew quite a few elderly Indians who could hold their own with 20-year-olds, and suspected their out-standing longevity and physical prowess was attrib-utable to the Indian way of life, to drinking only pure water and eating the freshest of foods and breathing the clear mountain air. He remembered how it was back in New York City and other cities and towns, where the smoke from burning coal and wood in the winter would form heavy clouds that made a person cough and stung the eyes, and how food served at home or at eating establishments would be steeped in salt and invariably overcooked. It was a wonder white men lived to be 60, let alone 80 and older as did many Indians.

He waited and allowed them to go in first, then followed and leaned the Hawken against the wall to the left of the doorway. The cabin was comfortably furnished. A large table near the center of the spacious single room was ringed by four wooden chairs. Off to one side against the wall sat the bed. A stone fireplace was directly opposite the door and a new bearskin rug lay in front of the hearth. Beaded leather curtains covered the one window, compliments of Winona. Her feminine touches were everywhere, from the flowers in a clay vase to the decorated parfleches hanging on one wall. It was her handiwork, Nate reflected, that had transformed the cabin into a home.

"Nice place you have here, Mr. King," Milo Benteen commented.

"Call me Nate. Why don't you gents take a seat?"

All three sat down, leaving empty the chair facing the entrance. Nate walked over, turned it around, and straddled it so he could rest his forearms on top of the crest, leaving his hands free to draw the pistols if need be. He still wasn't taking any chances.

"We're glad we found you at home," Tom said. "We were afraid you'd be out doing your spring trapping."

"A few more days and I would have been," Nate said, glancing to his left where Zachary was playing with a toy rifle he'd whittled from a tree limb. Winona was busy preparing the coffee.

"We'll get straight to the point," Milo Benteen stated, leaning forward on his elbows. "Tom and I came out here with the hope of catching enough beaver to provide both of us with the stakes we'd need to buy homesteads for the families we hope to have one day. We know that an average trapper makes about two thousand dollars selling his hides at the annual rendezvous, which is quite a bit of money considering a mason or a carpenter only makes about six hundred a year."

Nate listened patiently, well aware of the economic facts of life for trappers and laborers alike.

"But we'll be honest with you," Milo went on.

"We've tried trapping for a year and had a darned hard time of it. Between the two of us we've only made three hundred dollars so far."

"Trapping can be rough," Nate said to hold up his end of the conversation.

"And we've heard that it's getting harder every year," Tom interjected. "The old-timers tells us there aren't as many beaver around as there used to be. The best streams, those easiest to get to, have all been pretty much trapped out. To find prime pelts nowadays a person has to go deep into the remote valleys."

"I know," Nate agreed. He never would have believed it was possible, but beaver were becoming harder to find with each passing year. When he'd first ventured to the Rockies, there had been so many beaver that he'd scoffed at the idea the critters would ever be trapped out.

"We became discouraged," Milo confessed, "and we were considering heading back to Pennsylvania when we bumped into Red Moon here." He indicated the Crow with a jerk of his thumb. "He told us about a valley where the beaver are as thick as flies on a rotting buffalo carcass, where three or four men could go in, spend three or four months trapping, and come out with five hundred pelts or more *apiece*."

Nate looked at the old warrior, trying not to let his skepticism show. He'd been all over the region and he knew of no such valley. He wondered if Red Moon was a drinker. Some of the Indians became addicted to alcohol and were prone to telling tall tales when they were under the influence. For that matter, many of the whites were the same way.

"Tom and I want to trap this valley," Milo said, excitement in his tone. "Red Moon has agreed to take us there in exchange for ten percent of our profits."

Nate performed some hasty mental calculations. If the beaver were as thick as the Crow claimed, and if

Tom and Milo each made about two thousand dollars, that would give the Crow four hundred in pocket money, which was more than most Indians saw in a lifetime. He wondered what the warrior wanted with so much currency. Generally speaking, Indians had little use for the white's man scrip.

"But Tom and I know our limitations," Milo stated. "We're pretty green. We figure we need someone else to throw in with us, someone who has trapped for years and knows the profession inside out, someone who has a reputation as being one of the best in the business." He paused and bored his eyes into Nate. "Someone like you."

So this was the reason for their visit. Nate saw all three men gaze expectantly at him and leaned back, stretching, buying time to think. He preferred to trap alone. Most trappers did, simply because each had favorite areas and didn't want anyone else moving in and taking pelts away from them. Then too, most trappers were loners, highly independent men who could go for months without seeing another living soul and not be bothered by it in the least.

"Would you be interested?" Milo asked hopefully.

Nate had to admit to himself the proposal was intriguing. If the valley was rich in beaver, if no one had ever laid a trap line there before, then every one of them stood to earn top dollar for their peltries. He might make more money than he would trapping alone. "I'm interested," he said, "but I have reservations."

"What are they?" Tom Sublette inquired.

Twisting, Nate stared at the Crow. Since the warrior had told Benteen and Sublette about the valley and neither of them had been in the mountains long enough to learn much of the Crow tongue and likely weren't greatly proficient at sign language, he figured the oldster must know English. "I've lived in these mountains for some time," he noted. "Why haven't I heard of this valley before?"

Red Moon answered in a soft voice, his English clipped and precise. "No whites have ever been there."

"What about your people?"

"My people have not gone there in many, many winters."

The disclosure struck Nate as peculiar. "Is it located in Crow country?" he asked.

"Yes. Far to the north."

"Which means it's close to Blackfeet country," Nate said.

Benteen glanced from the Crow to Nate. "Is that important?"

"Haven't you heard about the Blackfeet? They're the scourge of the Rockies. They despise whites and kill every one they find. More trappers have lost their lives to those devils than to any other tribe. I've tangled with them a few times and I'm lucky to still be wearing my hair."

"I'm willing to take the risk," Tom Sublette said.

"Have you ever fought the Blackfeet?" Nate asked.

"No," Tom answered.

"Then don't be so eager to lose your scalp," Nate cautioned, and turned to the Crow again. "Tell me, Red Moon. Do the Crows stay away from this valley because they don't want to run into the Blackfeet?"

"No."

"When was the last time the Crows were there?"

"Twelve winters ago one of our bravest warriors, Crooked Nose, went there. He never returned."

"The Blackfeet must have got ahold of him," Milo Benteen commented.

"No," Red Moon said.

Nate lightly drummed his fingers on the table, pondering. He was convinced the brave had not revealed everything he knew about the valley, perhaps deliberately. But what? And why? "You sound as if you know what happened to Crooked Nose. Do you?"

"Yes. He was killed."

"If the Blackfeet weren't responsible, who was?"

"Not who. What."

"An animal killed him?" Nate asked. Even Indians, with their wealth of woodlore and their ability to move silently and unseen through the forest, occasionally fell prey to grizzlies or panthers or other predators.

"No," Red Moon said, and sighed. "Crooked Nose was slain by the thing that lurks in the dark."

Chapter Three

For a full five seconds no one said a word. Milo Benteen and Tom Sublette wore amused expressions, as
if they thought the statement had been some sort of
joke.

Nate knew better. He'd lived among Indians long
enough to be able to pick up subtle nuances of behavior and intent other whites often missed. Red
Moon had been deathly serious; his eyes had regis-
tered the faintest hint of deeply buried apprehension
when mentioning the "thing" that had slain Crooked
Nose.

"What is this?" Milo broke the silence. "What kind
of critter are you talking about?"

"I do not know," Red Moon said softly.

"But you Indians know everything there is to know
about the animals in these mountains," Tom noted.
"Was it a bear or a big cat or what?"

"It was none of those," Red Moon said, staring at

each of them in turn. "It was . . ." and then he used a Crow word with which Nate was unfamiliar.

"Say it in English," Milo said.

"There is no English word for the thing that lives in the valley," Red Moon replied. "So I just call it the *thing*."

"You're not making any sense," Tom stated. "What's this thing look like?"

"I do not know. No one has ever seen it and lived to tell what he saw."

Milo laughed. "Oh, come now, Red Moon. Is this another of your silly Indian superstitions like all those demons and other spirit creatures your people believe in?"

"The thing in the valley is not a spirit. It is flesh and bone, like you and I. It can touch and be touched. It can kill and has done so many times."

Insight flared in Nate and he cleared his throat. "Your people stopped going into the valley because of this creature?" he inquired.

"Yes," Red Moon confirmed. "Even though the valley has much game, with deer and elk and beaver everywhere, we no longer go there to hunt. Crooked Nose was the last to do so, and he suffered the same fate as have a dozen warriors over the years."

"How many years are you talking about?" Milo asked.

"The creature has lived there for over seventy winters, so far as we know. Perhaps it has been there much longer. Perhaps it has lived there since the beginning of all things."

Both Milo and Tom laughed.

"Have you ever heard such nonsense?" Tom said, addressing no one in particular. "It must be an old grizzly, and the four of us can handle any bear that rears its ugly head."

"Why didn't you mention this critter sooner?" Milo asked the Crow.

"I did not want you to change your minds about going," Red Moon answered.

Tom chuckled. "You were afraid this spook tale of yours would scare us off? Red Moon, you don't know us very well. Milo and I aren't scared of anything, and that especially goes for Injun hokum." He paused. "No offense meant."

Nate was speculating on the implications of the warrior's comments. Why, if Red Moon firmly believed this mysterious creature existed, was the Crow willing to brave its wrath by venturing into a valley that was shunned by the entire tribe? Did Red Moon need the money so badly he was willing to risk his life to get it? And if so, what did he want with the money anyway? Indians invariably traded for whatever they wanted. They had no need for money.

"Hold on a second," Milo said. "I've been doing some figuring. You say Crooked Nose was killed how many winters ago?"

"Twelve."

"Hell, man. That's twelve years. For all you know, the grizzly or whatever killed him is long dead by now."

"The thing that lurks in the dark will never die," Red Moon said.

Milo looked at Nate. "Have you ever heard tell of critters like the one he claims is in this valley?"

"No."

"I have."

The declaration came from Winona. She was standing to one side, holding two tin cups in each hand. Now she placed them on the table and gazed meaningfully at her husband. "My people have known of such creatures too. We call them the Giants of the Night. They lived in this land before my people came, and our legends tell of how our brave warriors drove most of the Giants away after great battles." She paused and glanced at the Crow. "I did not know there were any still around."

"Giants?" Tom Sublette repeated, and snickered. "Ma'am, there have been mountaineers in these parts ever since Lewis and Clark set foot out here. That's well-nigh thirty years. You'd think that if there were strange critters running around, most of the trappers and such would know about it by now."

"I know what I know," Winona said, and went to the hearth to retrieve the coffeepot.

Milo turned to Nate. "I hope you won't let this foolishness get to you. It must be a bear, nothing more. We were told that your Indian name is Grizzly Killer, that you've killed more grizzlies than any other trapper alive, so the idea of facing another shouldn't worry you none."

"Facing any grizzly worries me. They're not to be taken lightly," Nate said, thinking back to that distant day when he'd killed his first silver-tip while crossing the plains with his Uncle Zeke. Since then he had been through several horrifying encounters with the fearsome giant bears and nearly perished on each occasion. If there was an old grizzly living in the valley, he didn't relish confronting it. Nor did he view the bear as reason enough to put off trapping there when they each stood to make a couple of thousand dollars from the enterprise. They would have to remain alert, and if the bear showed, kill it. It was as simple as that.

"Will you throw in with us?" Tom asked bluntly.

"Your offer is intriguing," Nate told them. "I'm definitely interested, but I need some time to think about it and discuss it with my wife." He gazed at the window. "How soon were you fixing to head on out?"

"Any time you're ready," Milo responded. "Our pack animals are down by the lake in a clearing. They were plumb tuckered out after the long climb up to this hideaway of yours so we left them there to rest and came on ahead."

"How about if you let us know in the morning?" Tom proposed. "Would that give you enough time to make up your mind?"

"More than enough," Nate said. "I'll give you my decision at dawn, then."

Winona brought over the coffeepot and poured each of them a full cup of the steaming brew. Over an hour was spent in idle conversation, with Nate eliciting information from the two Pennsylvanians about the latest news in the States and sharing information about his years in the Rockies and the trapping business in general.

He learned that a new religious group calling themselves the Mormons had sprung up and were causing quite a stir. They had been driven out of New York after being relentlessly persecuted by those who regarded them as blasphemous. He heard that a slave named Nat Turner had instigated a revolt in Virginia. The insurrection was speedily crushed and many innocent blacks slain by the outraged whites. And he also listened to a fascinating story about a new hotel in Boston that was the talk of the East. Apparently this hotel had installed elegant imported indoor water closets that were all the rage. Folks would travel hundreds of miles and take a room just to be able to use the newfangled bathroom facilities.

"And did you hear about the *Fulton I*?" Milo asked.

"No. What about it?" Nate replied. The *Fulton I* had been designed and constructed by the famous inventor Robert Fulton. It was Fulton who had built the first commercially successful steamboat, the *Clermont*, back in 1801. The *Fulton I*, authorized by Congress in 1814, was the world's first steam-powered warship and had been put into service specifically for the defense of New York Harbor.

"It went and blew up," Milo related. "Caused by some kind of breakdown in the engine, I think the newspapers said."

Tom Sublette took a sip of coffee. "And I guess you've heard about the trouble brewing down Texas way?"

"No, I haven't," Nate admitted. Texas was a province of Mexico, and all he knew about it was that it was terribly hot in the summer and took a man forever to cross on horseback. Or so many of the tall-tale tellers claimed.

"There might be a shooting war down thataway in the next couple of years," Tom mentioned. "A lot of Americans have drifted to Texas to live, and by all accounts they're none too happy with the way Mexico is running the province. Our government is interested in buying Texas like we did all that land in the Louisiana Purchase, but when an envoy was sent down to Mexico City to make the Mexican government an offer, they sent him back with his tail between his legs."

"A lot of folks back in the States are riled by the whole affair," Milo added. "The former governor of Tennessee, Sam Houston, has gone there to see about bringing independence to the province, and the Mexicans aren't likely to sit still for any meddling in their country."

"I wish those folks luck, whatever they decide to do," Nate commented, "but it doesn't concern me."

Then the two Pennsylvanians plied him with questions about the state of affairs among the various tribes. He knew little they didn't already know. How the Blackfeet, the Pagans, and the Bloods were still united in a confederacy that controlled all of the northern plains region and most of the northern Rockies. How the Kiowas were giving travelers on the

Santa Fe Trail a hard time. And how the Nez Percés and the Flatheads had sent delegations all the way to St. Louis to request religious instruction for their respective tribes.

At that remark Nate saw Milo Benteen glance thoughtfully at Winona, and he could deduce the man's thoughts. Benteen was wondering what it must be like to have an Indian woman for a wife, and how the differences in cultures were reconciled. To Benteen's credit, the man had been in the Rockies long enough to know not to pry into the personal affairs of other folks and he didn't voice any of the questions filtering through his mind.

"Well, I reckon we should go check on our horses," Milo said, rising. "Ma'am, the coffee was delicious."

"Thank you," Winona said.

Nate also stood. "You can keep your animals in our corral for the night, if you wish. They won't wander off and you won't need to fret about prowling panthers so much."

"We're grateful," Milo said. "We'll bed down under the trees and await your decision come morning."

"Fair enough," Nate responded. "And we'd be happy if you'd join us for supper. My wife can make the best venison stew this side of the continental divide."

Tom beamed and licked his lips. "Home cooking! Why, I haven't tasted a home-cooked meal in a coon's age. Be sure and have Winona make extra."

Nate laughed. "We'll fill the pot to the brim," he promised, and escorted them out to their mounts. The trappers waved, Red Moon nodded, and off they rode.

"They're nice men, Pa," Zachary said at Nate's side. "Me like them."

"Me too," Nate absently replied, and instantly regretted it.

"See? You say 'me,'" the boy pointed out.

"Yes, but it's not the same. You're supposed to say 'I' most of the time when you're talking about yourself."

"Then why is there a word called 'me'?"

"Because you use that at times too."

His smooth brow knit in confusion, Zachary shook his head and declared, "Me no understand when me is I and I is me."

"We'll sit down and go over your English after I get back," Nate said, turning toward the cabin. Winona stood in the doorway, and she gave him a troubled look, wheeled, then went in. He picked up Zach and carried the boy inside, setting him near the table. Winona was at the fireplace, adding a few small limbs to the flames. "I take it you don't think I should go?"

"I do not like the idea, husband, no."

"If what Red Moon says is true about all the beaver in this valley, I could collect three times the amount of pelts I ordinarily would in half the time. I can be home from trapping that much sooner."

"If you live," Winona said, her shoulders held stiffly. "Do you believe his story about the thing that lurks in the dark?"

"I would not take it lightly."

Nate sat down and rested his feet on the edge of the table. "All right. Let's talk this out. Let's accept for the moment that there is some kind of strange critter up there, something few Indians have seen and fewer white men even know about." He paused to get her attention and she faced him. "Didn't you tell us that long ago your own people fought these Giants and drove them out of your country?"

"That is the legend the old men tell."

Nate shrugged. "Then I don't see where we have much to worry about. Your people used bows and lances back then. We'll have four rifles among us and pistols besides. Even if this critter is as hard to die as a grizzly, we can kill it."

"Didn't you say grizzlies should not be taken lightly?" Winona asked softly.

"Yes. And you know me well enough to know I'm not about to take any reckless chances. If we find any grizzly sign in this valley, I'll track it down and we'll dispatch it right off so we can run our trap lines in safety. And you know I'm a damn good tracker thanks to Shakespeare."

"You are one of the best trackers alive, Indian or white," Winona agreed.

Nate rose, walked up to her, and put his hands on her shoulders. The concern in her eyes touched him deeply. "Dearest, I'm only thinking of us. We could use a good haul of peltries. And I like the idea of getting my trapping down well before the end of the season. It means I'll have more time to spend with Zachary and you."

"So you have made up your mind?"

"Not yet, but I'll confess I'm leaning toward going," Nate said, and tenderly embraced her. He kissed her lightly on the lips and smiled, trying to cheer her up. "Don't worry. I'm not about to let some old legend stop me from coming back to you. And I'll swing by Shakespeare's cabin on the way out and ask him to check on Zach and you every now and then. Knowing him, he'll probably ride on over and move in until I return. So you have no need to get all bothered. Everything will be fine. You'll see."

Winona made no reply, but Nate swore he felt her tremble slightly in his arms.

Chapter Four

The four men rode out the next morning two hours after sunrise.

Nate had agonized all night over whether he should go. He tried to sleep but caught only snatches now and then. Beside him Winona slumbered fitfully, tossing and turning more than she normally did and mumbling words in the Shoshone tongue occasionally. The only word she said loud enough for him to understand was "beast."

The determining factor in his decision to go was his family. He simply couldn't afford to let such a golden opportunity pass. They could use the money. And, as he'd told her, he liked the idea of completing his trapping season early so they would have more time together.

Shortly before dawn he slipped out of bed, donned his buckskins, wedged his pistols under his belt, and went outside. Red Moon was already awake, seated quietly at the base of a tall tree and gazing thought-fully at the gradually brightening eastern horizon. Nate informed the Crow he would go, and Red Moon said he would tell the two Pennsylvanians when they woke up.

Tiptoeing back inside, Nate found Winona sitting up. There was no need to tell her his decision. He knew that she knew from her troubled expression and the hint of anxiety in her lovely eyes. She didn't protest, though, or complain. She simply got up, got dressed, and began preparing breakfast. Then she helped him pack the supplies and trapping gear he must take along.

There was a lot of it. Not only must he take enough flour, jerky, coffee, and other foodstuffs to tide him over for an extended period, food he would naturally sup-plement by killing wild game as needed, but he must tote a dozen Newhouse traps, each of which weighed about six pounds, two skinning knives and fleshing tools, a heavy axe and a light tomahawk, extra fire steels and tinder boxes, blankets, assorted small tools, and odds and ends.

Most of the trapping gear was stored in the south-west corner of the cabin where it was handy for pack-ing. Since they knew the routine by heart, they had the pair of packhorses Nate wanted to take fully loaded within an hour. Zachary helped, carrying small items when requested and repeatedly dashing outside to give Benteen and Sublette status reports on their progress.

The Pennsylvanians were mounted and patiently waiting when Nate loaded the last pack and went in-side to get the Hawken. Winona stood to the left of the door, out of sight of the three men. Her eyes said everything.

Nate enfolded her in his arms, their cheeks touch-ing, her warm breath on his ear. She hugged him tighter than she ordinarily did, much tighter, almost as if she expected it to be the last time she would do so, but her eyes were dry and her face proud when he stepped back and smiled. "Take care of yourself."

"I will."

"I'll miss you. You know that."

"And I you."

"I will carry you with me always, right here," Nate said, and tapped his chest above his heart. He kissed her then, a lingering kiss, savoring the feel of her lips and tongue. When he straightened, small arms looped around his left leg and he glanced down.

"Me miss you, Pa."

Nate lifted Zach and hugged him. "I'll think of you every minute I'm gone," he said. "You're the man of the house while I'm away, so you be good and help your mother. Listen to her at all times."

"Me will."

"And don't wander off like you did yesterday."

"Me won't."

Feeling a constriction in his throat, Nate kissed the boy, then laughed and said, "Me love you, little one."

The Pennsylvanians had their mounts turned to the northwest when he emerged and climbed onto his black stallion. "I'm ready, gents," he announced. "And if you don't mind, I'd like to stop by the cabin of a friend of mine and ask him to keep watch on my family during my absence. He's my nearest neighbor. Lives about twenty-five miles north of here."

"Fine by us," Milo said. "Who is he?"

"Shakespeare McNair."

"*The* Shakespeare McNair?" Tom blurted out.

"Yep," Nate said. He looked at his wife and son, standing rather forlornly side by side in the doorway, gave a little wave, and forced himself to face forward and ride off, the lead to the two pack animals in his left hand. Twenty yards from the cabin he twisted in

the saddle and looked over his shoulder. Winona and
Zach both waved and he did likewise. Leaving them
periodically to go off trapping taxed his self-control
to its limits. He hated leaving them alone. But he had
to make a living. He was a free trapper, and since the
beaver weren't about to march up to his front door
and lie down to be skinned, he must go where the
beaver were. Still, thinking of all the grizzlies and
panthers in the Rockies and the constant threat of the
Utes didn't make departing any easier.

"We've heard McNair is a good friend of yours,"
Tom commented.

"The best I have," Nate admitted.

"They say there isn't a mountain man alive who can
hold a candle to him, except maybe Jim Bridger," Milo
said.

Both men were clearly eager to meet McNair, and
Nate couldn't blame them. Shakespeare was a legend
in the Rockies, a man who had ventured into the unknown region decades ago, long before wearing beaver
became so fashionable and trappers flocked to the
mountains in droves. Shakespeare was one of the original white inhabitants of the territory, a man whose
knowledge of the wildlife and the Indians was unsur-
passed, who knew how to hunt and trap better than
any man alive, and who spoke a dozen Indian tongues
fluently and could converse adequately in six or seven
more. The trappers in general looked up to him as a
model of what they could achieve if they tried.

Provided they lived long enough, of course. Every
mountaineer was acutely aware of the odds. Every
trapper knew that for every ten men who trekked to
the Rockies, less than half would make the return trip
one day to civilization. Most wound up slain by hostiles or animals. Many simply decided to stay. There
was something about the Rockies, an indefinable quality of majesty and wonder combined with the alluring

appeal of the wild and of untrammeled freedom, that touched deep into their souls and held them as firmly as the strongest magnet held iron in its grasp.

Nate had proven susceptible to the same allure, and he didn't regret his decision to stay at all. His sojourn in the wilderness had tempered him much as a sharpening stone tempers a keen blade, dashing his boyish beliefs and his Eastern illusions on the hard rock of reality. He'd learned early that the only law that mattered in the wild was the law of the survival of the fittest. Nature played no favorites. Men and beasts must always be alert, always on their toes for trouble and ready to take advantage of situations as they developed. Those who blundered gravely seldom lived to commit the same mistake twice. If a deer didn't run fast enough from a panther, then that deer became panther food. If a man neglected to keep his rifle loaded and handy at all times and then encountered a grizzly, that man became grizzly food. It was as simple as that.

Yet despite all the latent savagery in the wilderness, despite the constant hovering overhead of the grim shadow of death ready to claim its next victim, he loved the mountains with almost as much passion as he loved Winona. He loved the regal, towering peaks crowned with snow; he loved the lush, green valleys packed with trees and verdant meadows; he loved the constant ebb and flow of the wild creatures inhabiting the Rockies, the constant swirl of life, the vibrant vitality that reached into the core of a man and made him feel truly alive.

So it was that as they rode northward, he immersed himself in the mountains, admiring the breathtaking scenery, alert for animals, keeping his mind active to take his thoughts off Winona and Zachary. They would be all right. He must trust in the Good Lord, keep his fingers crossed, and get back to them as soon as he could.

There was plenty to observe as they rode. Hawks soared by. Eagles sailed high in the sky. Ravens and mountain jays flapped overhead now and then, while smaller birds flitted about in the trees. Squirrels chattered in the high branches while chipmunks scampered on the ground. Occasionally they saw larger wildlife. Black-tailed deer were numerous. Twice they passed herds of huge elk grazing not far off. And once they saw a small herd of mountain buffalo in the brush. An enormous bull strode into the open and watched them go by but made no move to charge.

The air was crystal-clear, digging deep into the lungs with each breath and invigorating the whole body. The sky was a tranquil azure blue. A few pillowy clouds floated eastward.

"I can understand why you stay out here," Milo Benteen remarked when they were halfway to McNair's place. "If there wasn't a certain young woman waiting for me back in Pennsylvania, I'd be tempted to build a cabin and stick permanently."

"I feel the same way," Tom said. "You're fortunate, Nate, that you didn't have a woman back in the States when you came out to the frontier."

But Sublette was wrong. Nate had been close to a woman, and the statement provoked memories of the lovely Adeline Van Buren, the wealthy, prominent woman he'd intended to marry. What was she doing now? he wondered. It had been a long time since last he saw her. He'd departed New York City back in April of '28, and here it was April of '32. She must be married to a rich businessman or lawyer or politician and have children. Well, he wasn't so sure about the children, but he knew beyond any doubt that Adeline had married someone as wealthy as or wealthier than she was. Her whole life had revolved around money, no doubt because her rich father had spoiled her from childhood, had pampered her with anything and everything she wanted.

In part, Adeline was responsible for his current happiness. It had been to please her that he'd joined his Uncle Zeke and headed West. Zeke had promised to share a treasure with him, and falsely assuming Zeke had struck it rich in the fur trade or even by finding some of the vast riches in gold rumored to exist in the Rockies, he'd left New York in the expectation of returning a wealthy man and being able to marry Adeline as her social equal instead of her inferior.

Strange, sometimes, how fate worked out. The treasure his uncle had promised to share turned out to be the most precious and basic of all: simple freedom. And instead of going back to the States penniless, he'd stayed in the mountains and met a woman who surpassed Adeline in every respect, an Indian maiden who was more real woman than Adeline could ever hope to be.

He thought of Adeline from time to time. He imagined she despised him because he had gone off at such short notice with no more than a brief note of explanation. Often he wished he'd taken the time to write, to explain. But somehow he'd never been able to put his thoughts on paper.

Not even to his own family. Nate thought about them a lot too. His father, a hardworking, stern man who had not spoken about Zeke after Zeke went West, would probably never forgive Nate for doing the same. As far as his father was concerned, living in the wilderness was for fools and men who were no better than the savages they associated with.

It saddened Nate to recall his father's attitude toward the Indians. Many Easterners shared it. They regarded all Indians as savages who deserved to be driven off their lands and exterminated. Even the

President of the United States, Andrew Jackson, had publicly declared the Indians were an inferior race and should be organized as the white race saw fit.

The memory made Nate's features harden. He'd learned the truth about Indians, and he would confront any man who dared insult them in his presence. By and large, the Indians were a fine, noble people, living in harmony with the wild, and they deserved to live as they saw fit, not to have their lives dictated by those who justified bigotry in the name of patriotism.

Oh, there were bad Indians, just like there were bad whites, but the vast majority of Indians wanted much the same things longed for by the majority of whites: a family, a home, and a long life. Unfortunately, the way things were shaping up, it appeared the government wasn't going to let the Indians exist free and unmolested. Already a number of tribes living east of the Mississippi River had been forcibly uprooted and relocated. If the day ever came when the tide of white migration flowed westward past the Mississippi, the same fate might well await the Indians living on the plains and in the mountains.

Nate believed such a day was far off, if it ever occurred. Most folks in the States regarded the vast wilderness beyond the Mississippi as the Great American Desert, a name bestowed on the territory by Major Stephen Long after Long had completed a survey expedition for the government back in 1820. Except for the beaver that drew adventurous trappers to the mountains by the scores, the vast plains and the imposing Rockies held no allure for the many millions who believed the land was inhospitable and conditions unspeakably dangerous.

How wrong they were.

Nate was glad that few knew the truth. If more did, if word of the marvelous wonders and beauty to be found in the well-nigh limitless region was widely publicized, settlers would flock westward in hordes. He shuddered to think of it ever occurring. The Indian way of life, and his as well, would come to a speedy end.

Engrossed in his thoughts, he skirted a low hill and started to cross a meadow beyond. The stallion suddenly lifted its head, its ear pricked forward, and he glanced up. Hair at the nape of his neck tingled at the sight of a huge animal coming straight toward him.

It was a grizzly.

Chapter Five

Of all the wild creatures in the untamed Rockies, none were more generally feared by both whites and Indians alike than grizzlies. The mighty bears were the lords of the mountains and the plains to the east, fierce beasts that could crush the skull of a man or horse with a casual blow. Justifiably, grizzlies had earned the reputation of being extremely "hard to die," as the mountaineers liked to say. A grizzly might be shot repeatedly at close range and seemingly be unfazed by the balls or arrows.

Captains Meriwether Lewis and William Clark, on their famous expedition to the Pacific Ocean, encountered the great brutes on a number of occasions. In one particular instance, six of their best hunters decided to slay an old grizzly lying on open ground about 300 paces from a river. They snuck up on it and four men fired balls into the beast. The enraged grizzly then attacked and was shot by the other two hunters.

Unstoppable, the bear kept coming and pursued them all the way to the river, at which point it was shot again and again. When finally slain, it was on the verge of ripping one of their men to pieces. Later, when they dressed it, they found eight balls had pierced the bear, including two that had passed through the lungs and one that had broken its shoulder. Yet not until a lucky shot scored in its brain did the grizzly expire. As Lewis wrote in his journal, "These bears, being so hard to die, rather intimidate us all."

And they weren't the only ones. Nate's breath caught in his throat as he drew rein and the grizzly before them now halted, regarding them balefully. The bear was less than 50 yards away. Typical of the breed, it stood four and a half feet high at the shoulders, which were further accented by a prominent hump. This hump distinguished grizzly bears from the black variety. A large male, it easily weighed over a thousand pounds, and was capable of overtaking a horse at full gallop over a short stretch. Its brownish hairs had white tips, which gave the bear its distinctive grizzled appearance.

"Oh, Lord," Milo said softly.

Nate placed his thumb on the hammer of his rifle and waited for the bear to make the first move. If sheer savagery was their foremost trait, then being unpredictable was a close second. No one ever knew when a grizzly might charge. Sometimes a bear would spot a lone man and flee as if its hind end was on fire. At other times, a bear might encounter a party of ten or more and tear into them in unbridled fury.

This bear now reared on its hind legs to study them, its massive head swinging ponderously from side to side as it sniffed loudly. Its four-and-half-inch claws gleamed dully in the bright sunlight.

"What do we do?" Tom whispered.

"Sit tight and hope for the best," Nate advised in a low tone. "If it comes at us, scatter."

"But what about the packhorses? They can't outrun a bear loaded as they are," Tom said.

"If we scatter, it might not be able to make up its mind which one of us it wants and it will go off without chasing any of us," Nate explained, having heard of the strategy working before for the Shoshones. "If not, if it comes after any one of us, the rest can turn and help out."

The grizzly took a few lumbering strides forward, its muscles rippling under its hide.

Nate raised the Hawken. The bear had the look of one about to attack, and he wanted to get off a shot before he raced away. It would buy time for the others to put some distance between the bear and them, and might draw all of the bear's attention on himself.

Suddenly, Red Moon rode a few yards toward the bear, then stopped. His rifle resting across his thighs, he lifted both arms skyward, titled his head back, and began chanting in the Crow tongue at the top of his voice.

What was he doing? Nate wondered, watching the grizzly. Was it Red Moon's death song? He knew that warriors sometimes experienced strong premonitions of their own deaths and would sing to the spirit world before engaging in battle with enemies they believed would slay them. But he'd never heard of a brave doing so before a fight with an animal.

The grizzly cocked its enormous head back and forth, listening to the song. Then, after a minute, it sank to all fours, turned, and made for the forest at the west edge of the meadow, walking slowly, clearly unafraid yet also uninterested in conflict. In moments the murky shadows under the trees swallowed the great bear up.

Red Moon stopped chanting and took up his reins.

"Thank goodness," Tom breathed. "I thought we were in for it, there."

"Why did the bear just go away?" Milo asked.

"Who knows?" Nate responded. "Just be thankful it didn't want us for a meal." He glanced at the old Crow. "What was the song you sang, Red Moon?"

"I asked the Great Medicine Spirit for help in making the bear leave us alone," the Crow replied. "Every time I have met a grizzly, I have done the same thing and it has always worked." He paused. "My father taught me how to do it. A grizzly has not attacked anyone in our family for more winters than my people can remember."

Interesting, Nate thought. Maybe the singing had a calming effect on the bears, or maybe the grizzlies were bewildered by the songs and wanted no part of the strange singers. He goaded the stallion into a walk, pulling the pack animals behind him. "Let's go. And keep alert. Sometimes grizzlies travel in pairs."

"Hey, Red Moon," Tom said as they got underway. "If we run into the critter in this valley of yours, why don't you try singing to it to drive it off?" He winked at Milo, who chuckled.

"It would not work on the thing that lurks in the dark," the Crow answered somberly. "Nothing will."

Nate stared at the warrior. "If you're so convinced of that, why are you taking us there?"

Red Moon hesitated. "No one has ever tried to shoot the creature with a gun," he said at last. "I am hoping a ball will stop it where an arrow cannot." He gazed westward and sighed. "If not, I am an old man and have lived more winters than I should have."

"What the dickens is that supposed to mean?" Milo Benteen inquired.

"I am ready to die. There is one more task I would like to do, but if it is not meant to be, I am ready."

Milo shook his head, his eyes glittering in amusement. "No one ever *wants* to die. That's a crazy notion."

"When a man has outlived his usefulness, then it is time to go on to the spirit world," Red Moon said firmly.

"Not me," Milo said. "Death will have to take me screaming and kicking every inch of the way. I'm not about to stop breathing without a struggle."

Tom grinned, his gaze on the Crow. "I swear, if I live to be a hundred I'll never understand you Indians."

"Many of us feel the same way about you whites," Red Moon responded.

Nate laughed, although deep down he was bothered by the old warrior's attitude. There was more to Red Moon's visit to the valley of mystery than he was letting on, and Nate didn't like having the question hovering over his head, as it were, like a shadowy harbinger of trouble to come. He wanted to come right out and ask, but he'd been ingrained with the unwritten frontier edict that no man should ever pry into the personal affairs of another. He must wait until the Crow broached the subject, then take it from there.

He was extra cautious for the next mile, aware that grizzlies occasionally circled around to come at their intended victims from another direction. Only after two miles had fallen behind them did he relax completely and resume enjoying the magnificent scenery and the abundant wildlife.

They entered a long, winding valley running north and south and bore ever northward. A stream meandered on their left, gurgling softly. Now and then a fish would leap out of the water and splash down.

"Lord, these mountains are beautiful, aren't they?" Milo commented, breathing deeply.

"That they are," Nate concurred.

Tom Sublette abruptly drew rein. "What the devil

is that?" he asked, and pointed at the slope of a mountain beyond the stream.

Nate halted and looked, and right away he spotted the black shape high up on a barren part of the mountain. It was an animal, obviously, and on all fours, but the distance was too great to note specific details.

"Looks like a black wolf," Milo said. "I didn't think there was such a thing."

"No wolf," Red Moon declared. "It is a dog."

"A dog?" Tom repeated skeptically. "Where did it come from? What is it doing up there all by itself?"

"It might have strayed off from an Indian village," Nate speculated, searching the slope in the dog's vicinity. "Happens sometimes. Or there might be someone up there with it, perhaps an Indian out hunting."

"A friendly Indian?" Milo asked, shifting in his saddle and placing both hands on his rifle.

"There's no way of telling," Nate said. He clucked the stallion into motion, his eyes on the black canine. It suddenly ran into a patch of trees and was lost to view. For over a minute he watched to see if it would reappear lower down, but there was no sign of it.

"Maybe it's a stray and it will follow us," Milo said hopefully. "I wouldn't mind having a dog around. I've always liked them. Had a big hound dog when I was a kid and that critter was as loyal as could be. Saved me from a black bear once."

"If that mutt does join us," Tom stated, "you'll be the one responsible for feeding it. I'll be damned if I'm going to go out and bag game to feed a mangy, flea-ridden mongrel."

Milo gazed at him in surprise. "Don't you like dogs?"

"I'm not much on pets, period. My ma cottoned to cats and we have seven of the rascals. They were always getting their hair all over everything and none of them ever was completely housebroken."

"Cats," Milo said, and snorted. "No wonder you feel the way you do. If the Good Lord had wanted us to have cats as pets, he wouldn't have given them claws. Cats are for folks who don't know any better."

On they rode, the hours passing uneventfully. They would not reach McNair's until the next day. When there was only an hour or so until dark, Red Moon stopped once again.

"We are not alone."

Nate turned, and there was the black dog about a quarter of a mile to the rear, just standing there and staring at them. "It must be a stray," he remarked. "Milo, you might get your wish after all."

"Hold on a minute while I try to make friends," Benteen said. He started to ride toward the dog, but no sooner did he do so than the black dog whirled and darted into dense undergrowth. "Well, I'll be!" he exclaimed, reining up short. "Why did it go and do that?"

Tom chuckled. "Cats have claws and dogs don't have any brains. We'd be better off having fish as pets."

"Don't be ridiculous," Milo said. "Who ever heard of such a thing?" Reluctantly, he brought his mount around. "Well, I tried. If that dog wants to join us, the next move is up to it."

Nate glanced at the Crow, whose face was thoughtful and vaguely troubled. "Is anything wrong?" he asked.

"That dog is bad medicine. We must shoot it if we can."

Milo Benteen reacted as if he'd been slapped in the face. "What the dickens are you talking about, man?" he demanded angrily. "It's a dog, not a grizzly, and it's probably lost and hungry. I won't stand for having it shot."

Red Moon shrugged. "As you wish. But I have

warned you." He continued northward, his shoulders squared, his back stiff.

"Now you've done it," Tom groused at Milo. "You've gone and got his dander up."

"What do I care?" Milo responded. "I'm not going to let him kill an innocent dog because of some Injun drivel about bad medicine. Hell, Tom. You know as well as I do that Indians are the most superstitious bunch of people there are."

"I'll grant you that," Tom agreed. "But you shouldn't get him mad. He's the only one who knows how to find the valley. If you antagonize him, he might up and ride off one night before we get there. Then where will we be?"

Milo pondered a moment, then sighed. "All right. I'll apologize. But it galls me because I know I'm in the right." He rode faster to catch up with the old Crow.

"Yes, sir," Tom said softly more to himself than anyone else. "We can't let any harm come to that Injun until after we strike the valley."

"Or any other time," Nate said harshly. "He's in this with us all the way. And it doesn't matter if a man's companions are white or Indian, he should stick by them no matter what happens."

"Of course," Tom declared. "I didn't mean otherwise."

"I hope not," Nate said, wondering. A tiny doubt trickled into the back of his mind. Perhaps there was more to these men than met the eye. Perhaps they weren't to be trusted after all. But he promptly shook his head, discarding the suspicion as a product of his wary nature. Tom simply wanted to reach the beaver rich valley at all costs, and considering the money they stood to make from their enterprise, his attitude was understandable. Nate faced front, noting landmarks he recognized and seeking a game trail that would take them to a clearing where they could camp for the night.

"Damn. There it is again," Tom muttered.

Nate looked over his shoulder. The black dog had reappeared, still a quarter of a mile away, still following but keeping its distance, a spectral canine shadow determined to haunt their tracks for the time being. Why? What did it want? He concentrated on finding the trail, the skin between his shoulder blades itching terribly. First a grizzly, now the black dog. It was a good thing he wasn't superstitious himself, or he might be inclined to regard the two beasts as bad omens and give up on the idea of going to the valley. But the thought of all those beaver spurred him on. Nothing was going to make him change his mind: not a passing bear, not a stray dog, and certainly not an ancient legend about a creature that lurked in the dark, a creature undoubtedly long since dead.

Or so he hoped.

Chapter Six

Shakespeare McNair's cabin was situated in a pristine valley at the base of a knoll and only 50 yards from a rushing stream. To the north of the sturdily built structure was a horse pen, to the south a small storage shed. Ancient pines bordered the homestead to the rear and on both sides, while a narrow strip of ground in front of the cabin had been stripped of all vegetation. The home blended in perfectly with the surrounding vegetation. Unless one knew exactly where to look, a man could ride almost right past it without knowing it was there.

Nate wasn't certain how the mountain man would take to having three strangers show up. Nate had a standing invitation to visit any time he wanted, but Shakespeare might be upset at him for bringing the others. Many of the mountaineers were tight-lipped about the locations of their homes because they didn't want the information getting to potential enemies.

And many of the mountaineers did have bitter enemies, usually in the form of an Indian tribe that wanted the trappers killed.

He saw no indication of activity as he approached the closed cabin door. Maybe the grizzled codger and his wife had gone off to visit her people, the Flathead Indians. He scoured the ground, seeking clues, and spied tracks that had been made within the hour. Reining up 20 feet from the cabin, he cupped a hand to his mouth and shouted, "Shakespeare! It's me, Nate. Don't shoot!"

There was no reply from within.

"Perhaps he isn't home," Milo said.

"Shakespeare!" Nate repeated. "Do you hear me?"

"I hear you."

The low, gruff voice came from directly behind them. Nate swung around, beaming happily at discovering his mentor and best friend not a dozen feet off.

As with most men who had spent any great span in the Rockies, Shakespeare McNair look every bit as rugged as the mountains in which he lived. Fringed buckskins covered his muscular frame. On his head perched a brown beaver hat, and from under the hat spewed bushy gray hair. His beard and moustache were the same color, testimony to his age and resourcefulness in lasting as long as he had. He wore the ubiquitous powder horn and ammunition pouch and carried a large butcher knife on his left hip. In his hands and pointed in the general direction of Benteen and Sublette was a cocked Hawken.

"We've come in peace, Mr. McNair," Sublette blurted out. "Honest."

Nate was staring at the woman beside Shakespeare, a statuesque Flathead named Blue Water Woman. She wore a buckskin dress and held a rifle trained on Red Moon.

"Howdy, Nate," the mountain man said cheerily, and then sobered as he regarded the pair of Pennsylvanians and the old Crow. "Where did these fellows come from?"

"They're with me," Nate explained. "My trapping partners."

"Do tell," Shakespeare said, but he made no effort to lower the gun. "I've never met any of you gentlemen before," he said to the trio. "Mind telling me your names?"

They did so, the Pennsylvanians rather nervously, the Crow smiling at some private joke.

"Obviously you know who I am," Shakespeare said, advancing slowly. Blue Water Woman stayed right by his side. "Since you're friends of Nate's, you're welcome to share my hospitality. But be forewarned." He paused and gave Benteen and Sublette long looks. "I'm a cantankerous old cuss and there are certain rules I go by. Obey them, and you won't have any trouble while you're here."

"What kind of rules?" Tom asked.

"I won't be insulted. I won't be laid a hand on. And any man who treats my wife with disrespect will be shot right then and there."

"We'd never treat your wife shabbily," Milo said indignantly. "Nor would we think of insulting you, sir. We've heard a great deal about you since we came to these parts, and we think you're one of the greatest mountaineers who has ever lived."

"Really?" Shakespeare said, a twinkle in his eyes. "Then we should get along just dandy." He lowered the Hawken, his wife lowered her rifle, and together they walked around the horses to the cabin. "Light and make yourselves to home," Shakespeare said.

Nate dismounted, ground-hitched the stallion and left the pack animals standing behind it, and walked up to his mentor. Smiling, he gave Shakespeare a clap on the shoulder. "It's good to see you again."

"Why don't you put your horses in the pen?" Shakespeare suggested.

"We're not staying that long, unfortunately," Nate responded, and squinted up at the sun, which hung high in the afternoon sky. It had taken them the better part of two days to make the journey from his cabin to McNair's. There were still five or six hours until nightfall, and he wanted to travel as far as possible before they bedded down. "The main reason I stopped by was to ask if you would check on Winona and Zach every so often until I get back."

It was Blue Water Woman who answered in her crisp, precise English. She had learned the language years ago from McNair. "We will be delighted to go see her."

"Thanks. I'm in your debt," Nate said.

"You have it backwards," Blue Water Woman responded. "It is I who am in your debt. I have not talked with another woman in over two months, and this gives me the perfect excuse to get this lazy bear to leave our cabin for a while."

"Who are you calling a lazy bear?" Shakespeare demanded.

"She'll be happy to see both of you," Nate predicted.

The mountain man watched the Pennsylvanians and Red Moon tie their animals to nearby trees. "So how did you hook up with these gents?"

Nate briefly detailed how he happened to be with his newfound acquaintances, and as he did they joined him. When he mentioned the mysterious valley ripe with beaver, Shakespeare's lake-blue eyes narrowed.

"Where is this valley?"

"Only Red Moon knows," Nate answered.

Shakespeare glanced at the Crow and addressed Red Moon in that tongue. They talked for several minutes, a frown deepening on Shakespeare's face the whole time. At last the mountain man turned to Nate.

"If you want my advice, you'll stay clear of this valley you're heading for. Going there will only bring trouble."

"Why?" Nate asked.

"It's a long story," Shakespeare said. "Why not stay for one cup of coffee at least and I'll tell you everything I know."

There was a telltale edge to McNair's tone, an edge Nate had never heard before. Was it apprehension? He nodded and said, "It's all right by me if it's all right with the others."

Milo gestured at the entrance. "Lead the way. A cup of coffee would do fine about now."

They entered, Blue Water Woman moving off to prepare the pot while the men sat down at a large round table. Shakespeare leaned back in his chair and gazed coldly at Red Moon. "I've heard about this valley before, and about the creature that supposedly lives there. These critters were common ages ago. Now they're rare."

"You know what it is?" Tom Sublette inquired dubiously.

"Not exactly," Shakespeare admitted. "There have been stories about these critters making the rounds of the camp fires for as long as I've lived in these mountains. And practically every tribe has legends about them."

"Have you ever run into one?" Milo asked.

"Nope. Thank goodness. By all accounts, you run into one and you wind up dead."

Milo smiled politely. "No offense, McNair, but my partner and I aren't given to believing every tall tale the Injuns tell. And we don't take at face value those fireside stories that are usually exaggerated ten times over."

"No offense, Benteen," Shakespeare mimicked him,

"but you haven't lived out here as long as I have. When you do, you can tell the difference between when an Indian is talking about some spirit being and when it's a real animal. And these monsters are as real as you and me."

"Monsters?" Milo repeated, and snorted. "Now I get it. You're trying to put one over on us. There are no monsters except in the minds of those fiction writers. I can read, Shakespeare, and I know about some of the books that have been so popular over in Europe and in the States. There's that strange one called *Frankenstein* by that poet's wife, and the one they made the play out of, *The Vampyre*, by that doctor. And there have been stories about those wolf-men, those werewolves, too."

Tom Sublette grinned, nodding knowingly. "And don't forget all those tales about those sea serpents off the coast of New England, and the newspaper stories about the monster that lives in Lake Erie."

"I almost forgot how you old-timers like to pull the wool over the eyes of us greenhorns," Milo said, and chuckled.

Nate saw exasperation in his mentor's eyes. He knew Shakespeare better than any man alive, and he knew when the mountain man was telling tall tales and when he was telling the truth. This bizarre business about the thing in the valley was a true story, not a whopper.

Shakespeare drummed his fingers on the table for a bit, then look at Nate. "If these two want to go off and get themselves killed, that's their business. But I've spent a lot of time teaching you everything I know, and I'd hate for you to be torn to pieces and never get to use that lore." He paused. "Are you bound and determined to go to this valley?"

"I gave them my word," Nate said.

"Damn. I wish you hadn't."

"Tell me everything you know about these critters."

"All right. The first story I know of concerns a man who explored a sizable chunk of Canada some years back. I can't recollect his name, but I know he wrote a narrative of his travels. And back in 1810 or 1811, while he was near the Athabaska River, he came on some peculiar tracks in the snow. Huge tracks, these were—"

"Probably a grizzly's," Tom interrupted.

"Since when does a grizzly have *toes*?" Shakespeare said testily, then went on. "And about fifteen years ago three men went trapping to the northwest of here. Frenchmen, they were, down from Canada. I met them at a Flathead village. They were nice enough and excited about all the game in these parts." He stopped, his gaze straying to the open door. "No one ever heard from them again, and I forgot all about them until about six years ago when I was out trapping with a gent named Rogers. We came on this old cabin, not much more than a bunch of logs set crosswise. One of the walls had been knocked down. We found old utensils and traps and such scattered about."

Nate leaned forward, fascinated. Milo and Tom were also hanging on every word.

"We found an old cap of the kind French trappers favor, about rotted through, and it reminded me of those three Frenchmen I'd met years ago. We got to poking around, and under a corner of that downed wall I noticed a bunch of bones. Wasn't much to them, but from what there was I could tell they'd been broken into bits."

"An animal, most likely," Milo said.

"No," Shakespeare stated. "These bones had been broken up when the man was still alive. Something had busted him to pieces."

No one said anything. Nate pursed his lips, pondering his course of action. He believed his friend and he believed the legends of the Indians, but he wasn't fully convinced that whatever inhabited the valley years ago still did so now, and he couldn't see breaking his word to the Pennsylvanians and calling it quits when he stood to benefit so handsomely if there were abundant beaver in the valley.

Tom coughed. "Well, let's suppose there was some kind of creature in these mountains we don't know about. What are the chances of the thing still being alive?"

Shakespeare shrugged. "Who can say?"

Milo rested his forearms on the table. "Is that all you know? Just those two stories and the Indian tales?"

"That's it," Shakespeare replied.

"We appreciate the warning, McNair, but we're not going to change our minds. We have plenty of guns. Red Moon knows the territory. And since Grizzly Killer here can kill grizzlies like most men swat flies, we don't have a blessed thing to worry about."

Nate didn't like Milo's condescending tone. Shakespeare was sincerely trying to do them a favor by emphasizing the danger and the Pennsylvanians were making light of it. "All it takes to kill a bear is a good rifle and a lot of luck. These creatures might be another story entirely."

"Now don't tell me you believe all this nonsense," Milo said. "We're counting on your experience, Nate, to help us bring in more damned beaver than most men see in two years of trapping. If you back out, we're stuck."

"I never said anything about backing out," Nate declared. "I gave you my word, and I'll stick by it."

Both Milo and Tom seemed vastly relieved. Red Moon's face was a blank stone.

Blue Water Woman brought over tin cups for each of them, then carried the pot of coffee to the table.

She poured for Shakespeare first, then for Nate.

"I am glad I heard this talk. Now I know I must stay with Winona for a long time," she commented.

"Why's that?" Nate inquired.

"I want to be there to comfort her if you do not return."

Chapter Seven

Nate pondered over the discussion at McNair's for the rest of the day, and was still contemplating his friend's words when it came time to picket the horses for the night. The four of them had ridden hard after leaving the cabin, and had not stopped until about an hour after the rosy sun sank out of sight beyond the western horizon. Since it was his turn to handle the stock, he watered the animals at a nearby stream and then found a suitable spot at the edge of the meadow where they had camped to tie the horses, allowing enough slack in the ropes to permit each horse to graze to its heart's content.

He wasn't much given to believing in spooks and goblins and such. Nor did he lend much credence to the idea of monsters existing. Unknown animals, however, were another matter. He'd seen stories back in New York about the strange creatures found by explorers in deepest Africa and in remote regions of

South America. So there probably were creatures remaining to be discovered by science, but he felt it unlikely that anything on the North American continent could still be unknown in light of the fact that adventurers, explorers, and the trappers themselves had penetrated into the heart of the Rockies and had never reported encounters with unknown beasts.

Still, there were the Indian tales and legends and they couldn't be discounted offhand. The Indians knew the land better than the whites ever would, and if the Indians believed certain creatures existed, then the odds were long that the creatures were alive or had once been.

Despite McNair's advice, he wasn't about to abandon the idea of trapping the valley. Always he came back to the same thought, that he could gather all the pelts he'd need in a short time and be back with his family much sooner than he ordinarily would at trapping season. So he decided to forge ahead and not let himself start jumping at every sound in the night.

Just as he reached his conclusion, as he turned from securing the last horse and headed for the camp fire 20 yards to the south, he heard a twig snap in the inky forest off to his right. He promptly halted and held the Hawken in both hands, peering intently into the night. The edge of the trees lay the same distance away as the fire. There was no hint of movement, but something was out there.

Nate waited, speculating it was most likely a skunk or a raccoon or some other small but harmless critter that would hasten off once it detected his scent. The large predators tended to shy away from fires, all except for wolves, and he hadn't seen any sign of a pack in the vicinity before halting to make camp. But a man could never be too careful.

Was it his imagination, or had something moved among the trunks near the meadow? He leaned forward, his thumb cocking the rifle, his finger lightly touching the cool trigger. If attacked, he must make the shot count and not fire until certain of hitting whatever came at him.

A tense minute dragged by.

Benteen and Sublette were joking and laughing by the fire, Red Moon seated across from them and not saying a word. None of them were looking in Nate's direction. He hesitated to call out and warn them for fear of appearing foolish if no threat materialized.

Another minute went by. Nate shrugged and started toward his companions. Apparently there was no cause for alarm. He took several strides, then abruptly halted as the hairs at the nape of his neck prickled and an overwhelming feeling that he was no longer alone seized him. Intuitively he sensed there was something close to him, even though he'd not heard a sound, and he swung his head around, hoping he was wrong, but knowing from prior grim experience never to discount his instincts.

Behind him, not a yard away, stood the black dog.

Startled, Nate spun and began to bring the rifle barrel up. But in his haste he tripped over his own feet and went down hard on his buttocks, the Hawken ending up in his lap. And no sooner was he on the ground and momentarily helpless than the dog closed on him.

Nate's eyes involuntarily widened as the canine stepped right up to him and stared him right in the eyes. He hadn't quite realized how big the dog was; it was immense, and even in the dark its rippling muscles were prominent. The head was huge and shaped like a box, the ears short and flopped over. The brute's eyes were uncanny, with the right one blacker than coal and the left one an unnatural shade of ivory, as if covered by a white film.

The brute's warm breath tingled Nate's nostrils and he tightened his grip on the rifle, preparing to surge to his feet and fight for his life if necessary. He was amazed the thing had been able to sneak up on him unheard and unseen, and he marveled at its prowess even as he tensed his leg muscles to stand.

Suddenly the immense dog moved, flicking its head closer and opening its gaping mouth to reveal its large, tapered teeth.

Nate flinched and tried to draw backward. He began to swing the stock, intending to bash the dog on the head. But the swing was only half completed when the animal did the unexpected.

The dog licked him.

At the clammy sensation, Nate froze, flabbergasted. He'd expected the brute to attempt to tear him to ribbons. Instead, the dog was showing him it was friendly. Again it licked him with a great roll of its wet tongue, slobbering over his face in the process. Flooded with relief, Nate began to smile and that dripping tongue slapped across his lips. He raised his right hand and wiped his sleeve across his mouth, grinning at the ridiculous situation. "That's enough, boy."

The dog recoiled at the sound of his voice, then relaxed and sat on its haunches.

Nate slowly stood. He didn't want to make any abrupt movements that might frighten the dog off, although on second thought he doubted the dog knew the meaning of fear. It was big enough to handle practically anything that came after it, standing four feet high at the shoulders and being half again as wide. He'd never seen its like anywhere and he wondered again where it came from. He'd forgotten all about it since they hadn't seen it after that first afternoon, and he'd assumed it had gone elsewhere, perhaps to an Indian encampment. "So you want some company, do you?"

The dog cocked its head and elevated its ears.

"I'm Nate King and I'm pleased to meet you," Nate

said, speaking softly to show the dog he meant no harm and could be trusted. Animals, particularly horses and dogs, usually responded remarkably well to the sound of the human voice. He'd seen a soothing tone calm the most agitated horse and pacify the most aggressive dog. So he kept talking simply to establish a rapport with it.

"I don't know where you're from or what you're doing here, but you're welcome to stay as long as you like. I like dogs myself. Had one once when I was a little boy. I reared it from a puppy and we went everywhere together until it was eight years old. Then it was run over by a wagon and killed." He stopped, saddening at the memory. "I cried for days."

The dog uttered a low whine and shifted its legs.

"Would you care for a bite to eat?" Nate asked. "We shot a buck earlier and we have plenty of meat to spare. Why don't you come along and I'll introduce you to the others." He turned slowly and motioned for the dog to follow. To his delight, the animal rose and walked on his left side, its steady gaze directed at the trio beside the fire.

Red Moon had shifted and was watching Nate and the dog approach. Sublette and Benteen had their backs to Nate and were talking about Pennsylvania.

"Gentlemen," Nate announced as he halted behind them. "We have a visitor."

"What?" Tom said, casually glancing over his left shoulder. The dog's huge face was inches from his own, its eerie eyes unblinking and hard, and he yelped in astonishment, leaping to his feet. "What the hell!"

"Well, I'll be!" Milo exclaimed, smiling and rising. "I never expected to see you again, boy," he said, extending a hand to pat the dog on the head.

To Nate's surprise, the dog uttered a rumbling growl, its lips curling back from its teeth. For a moment he thought the dog would snap at Milo's fingers and he quickly said, "No! Behave yourself!"

The dog glanced up at him, then ceased growling and stood still.

"He seems to have taken a liking to you," Milo observed, slowly withdrawing his hand.

"I hope you don't intend to keep it," Tom stated. "We'll have enough to do without having to take care of a dumb mongrel."

"I suspect this dog can take care of itself," Nate commented, stepping up to the fire to take a seat. The dog stayed by his side and sat down when he did.

"Well, I don't like it," Tom persisted. "And since I have a one-fourth interest in this enterprise, I think I have a say in whether the dog stays or goes. And I vote it goes."

"Be reasonable, Tom," Milo said. "What harm can it do to have the dog come along?"

"That thing just growled at you and you still want to keep it around?" Sublette responded.

"I like dogs. You know that. And I vote the dog can stay if it wants," Milo said.

Nate looked at the old Crow, recalling what Red Moon had said about the dog being bad medicine. "How about you? What do you say?"

The warrior stared silently at the dog for a full minute before finally answering. "Our paths are now joined for better or for worse. Do as you want."

"What the hell is that supposed to mean?" Tom asked.

"It means the dog stays," Nate declared, and reached over to scratch it under the chin. The dog didn't growl or make any threatening moves. "Since I'm the one it has attached itself to, I'll be responsible for it."

Tom scowled, moved a few feet away, and sat down. "Next we'll be taking in stray grizzly cubs," he grumbled.

Leaning forward, Milo whispered to Nate. "Pay no attention to him. He's just in one of his moods. By tomorrow morning he'll have a whole new disposition." Straightening, he joined his friend.

The buck slain earlier had been butchered by Red Moon and chunks of roasting meat were now suspended over the fire on a crude spit. Nate drew his butcher knife and sliced off a small section that was still quite rare, then offered it to the dog. Although he held the meat right next to its nose, the dog showed no interest.

"That's odd," Milo remarked. "I never knew a dog to refuse meat before."

"Maybe it ate a while ago and isn't hungry," Nate speculated, placing the morsel at the dog's feet in case it should change its mind. The dog rose, took a step sideways, and laid down with its head resting on its forepaws. The flickering firelight played over the animal's sleek black coat, and when Nate gazed at its back he noticed a series of long, jagged lines crisscrossing its hide from the top of its neck to well past its shoulders. Curious, he placed his right hand on its neck and the dog flinched and raised its head to give him a quizzical stare. He suddenly realized what the lines were. "This dog is covered with scars."

Milo came over and studied them. "It looks as if someone beat him with a whip clear down to the bone. Not once, but a lot of times." He shook his head in disgust. "No wonder this dog isn't too fond of people."

The scars were old. Nate guessed the whippings had taken place well over a year ago, if not longer, and he reasoned that a white man must have been responsible. Indians rarely beat their dogs. Oh, they might smack one with a stick if it misbehaved badly, but if a dog was a chronic troublemaker they simply ate it.

"Maybe he was with another party of trappers and ran off after being mistreated," Milo said.

That could well be, Nate reflected. Trappers, by and large, were drinking men. And when under the influence of demon alcohol, their tempers could flare mightily. Men who wouldn't hurt a soul when sober might turn into hateful brutes when drunk. He'd once seen a drunken trapper beat a fine horse to within an inch of its life, and when the man had sobered up he'd bawled like a child over what he'd done.

"What do you figure to call it?" Milo asked.

"I don't know," Nate said. He hadn't given a name much thought.

"How about Blackie?"

Nate gazed at the dog, at its powerful build, and said, "How about Samson?"

"Samson?" Milo repeated, and glanced at the animal. "Why not? It sure fits him. He's got more muscles than any dog I've ever known. I like it."

"Who cares what you call it?" Tom Sublette said, and looked at the Crow. "Let's discuss something really important. I, for one, would like to know how long it will take us to reach the valley."

"It was agreed you would not question me about the valley before we get there," Red Moon said.

"I'm not asking for a detailed map," Tom said sharply. "But it would help if we knew how long the trip will take."

Red Moon pondered a bit. "Very well. It will take nine sleeps, possibly ten."

Ten days of hard riding? Nate scratched his chin. That would put them close to Blackfoot country, all right. And if the Blackfeet found them, their scalps might end up hanging in a warrior's lodge. He thought of Winona and Zach and hoped he wasn't making the biggest mistake of his life.

Far off, a wolf howled.

Chapter Eight

For five days they pushed in a generally northwestern direction, skirting ragged peaks and high country lakes, wisely staying off of ridges and hills and any other elevated points where they ran the risk of sky-lining themselves. Twice they saw the smoke of camp fires, but uncertain of the identity of those who made the fires and the reception they might receive should they venture too near, they shied away from making contact.

Wildlife was everywhere. Majestic elk and alert deer, shaggy buffalo and lumbering bears, soaring birds of prey and chattering chipmunks.

The sky was a deep blue, the clouds fluffy and white as they drifted overhead. The air invigorated the lungs.

Nate drank in the sights, sounds, and smells, as he always did, his soul vibrant with the pulse of life. He'd watch mountain sheep perched on narrow trails thousands of feet up leap from one precarious foothold to another and marveled at their dexterity. He'd watch a bald eagle execute a lightning dive to snatch an unwary rabbit and had been amazed at the eagle's speed and accuracy.

This was the life for him. No matter how long he stayed in the rugged Rockies, he would never tire of the beauty and wonder all around him. Occasionally he would think about New York and his parents, and he knew deep down that he would never return there to live. A visit, though, might be in order, if only to let his folks see his son and meet his wife. But that was a matter to ponder at length later, after trapping season.

His newfound canine companion stayed by him nearly all the time. The dog never barked. It never displayed the slightest fear of the horses, nor did it display concern when they sighted wandering grizzlies. And it never begged for food. When they stopped for meals the dog sat silently besides Nate and refused meat and drink.

"It's downright spooky the way this critter behaves," Tom mentioned on the fourth day. "I've never heard tell of a dog that didn't eat before."

But Nate knew better. Two or three times a day the dog would dash off into the brush and be gone for anywhere from thirty minutes to an hour. Eventually, inevitably, it would catch up with them again and take its position near his horse. Where it went he could only guess. Several times he noticed drops of dried blood or bits of fur on its chin, and he deduced it was going off regularly to hunt its own game and drink. For whatever reason, the dog would accept food from no man.

Sublette complained now and again about the dog being along. He would sarcastically remark that they could always eat it if they ran short of provisions.

Milo tried to befriend the dog, but was rebuffed every time.

And Red Moon neither made comments nor tried to get the dog to like him. Often, at night, he would sit and watch it, his brow furrowed, never revealing the trail his thoughts were following.

Then, on the fifth night, an incident occurred that drastically changed Tom Sublette's opinion.

They had camped at the base of a cliff where the towering rock wall shielded them from the wind and a convenient spring provided cold water. That afternoon Nate had shot a black-tailed deer, and he was roasting juicy steaks over the fire while Milo took care of the horses, Tom gathered wood for the fire, and Red Moon stood and stared at the sky.

"There will be heavy rain tomorrow," the Crow announced after a while.

"Shouldn't slow us up much," Nate said conversationally, and flipped over one of the steaks in the pan. Beside him, as always, was Samson.

"We are making good time," Red Crow said. "Four more sleeps and we will be at the valley."

Nate saw an opening and took advantage. "I hope there are still plenty of beaver there. My wife and I could use the money from the sale of our peltries to take a trip back to the States. How about you?"

Red Crow was silent for a bit. "I need my share of the money for my grandson."

"Planning to buy him a whole herd of fine horses?" Nate joked.

"No. I want to take him to a white doctor in St. Louis."

About to flip another steak, Nate stopped, the knife poised in his right hand. "A doctor? What's wrong with the boy?"

"He was climbing a tree fourteen moons ago when he fell and landed on rocks. Since then he has not been able to walk. Our medicine men have tried every cure they know but nothing has worked. They say the boy might never walk again."

The sorrow in the old warrior's voice touched a responsive chord in Nate. "You must love him very much."

"Little Sparrow is the joy of my life. I want him to grow to be a great warrior," Red Moon said softly. "All my other grandchildren are girls." He shook his head in disappointment. "My sons must not be living right."

The idea of an Indian visiting a doctor was a new one to Nate. He knew many tribes sent members to St. Louis to trade or to meet with the Superintendent of Indian Affairs. Where medicine was concerned, though, Indians preferred their customary treatments to the strange practices of the whites.

"I was told about your doctors from a trapper friend," Red Moon revealed. "He said they know very little of the many plants that can heal the sick and they never use a sweat lodge, but somehow they still manage to cure those who come to them. It is most puzzling."

Nate turned the second steak over.

"I do not know if a white doctor can help my grandson, but I will take him there to find out. I must try every way I can," Red Moon said. "My friend told me white doctors take money for their treatments, much money sometimes. Now you know why I need my share, and why I will work very hard to make sure we catch as many beaver as we can."

Indeed, Nate reflected. And he knew much more. Such as why Red Moon was willing to violate a tribal taboo and take them to the remote valley, even though the Crow must be deathly afraid of encountering the creature his tribe so dreaded. The trip to St. Louis was

an act of desperation on Red Moon's part, his last hope
to cure his grandson.

Milo walked up. "Got the horses settled down for
the night," he mentioned. "What were you two talking
about?"

"We were making small talk," Nate said, and saw
Tom approaching with broken branches for the fire.

Samson growled.

Nate glanced at the big dog, thinking it was growling at Tom. Instead, Samson was peering into the
forest to the southeast, his lips trembling in anger, his
eyes narrowed.

"He must hear something," Milo said.

Rising, Nate stood with the knife in one hand and
the pan in another, listening to the night sounds. Or
trying to. Because he suddenly realized the forest ringing their camp had grown totally silent. Even the insects were still. Not so much as a cricket chirped.

Tom edged backwards toward the fire. "What is it?
What's out there?"

Before Nate could answer, Samson streaked into the
vegetation, gliding like a living shadow into the Sty-
gian darkness of the wilderness. "No," Nate said, to
no avail. Placing the pan down, he slid the knife into
his sheath and scooped up his Hawken. Fixing on the
point where Samson had entered the trees, he trotted
toward it.

"Wait! Where are you going?" Milo called out.

"To see what's out there," Nate responded. "Stay
here until I get back."

"Don't—" Milo objected.

But Nate had already plunged into the murky realm
that constituted the forest at night. He went several
yards, then halted and crouched to get his bearings
and listen. What had the dog heard or scented? A bear?
A panther? Wolves? Or other men? He doubted it had
been Indians since Indians rarely were abroad after

the sun set. Few raids were conducted at night, for the simple reason that many tribes believed the souls of those slain at night were fated to aimlessly wander the earth and never attain the Indian version of heaven.

He heard nothing himself, but that meant nothing. The dog's hearing undoubtedly was much sharper than his. There must be something in the woods nearby to account for the dog's agitation, and he wanted to find whatever was out there before whatever was out there found them.

Then, from the southeast, there came the faintest whisper of sound.

What had it been? Nate strained his ears, trying to identify the vague noise. More than anything else, it had sounded like the tip of a limb brushing against buckskin clothing. He went deeper into the woods, staying low, using every bush and tree for cover, his moccasins making no noise as he moved. His years spent in the wilderness had honed his woodsman skills to perfection. In many respects he was much like an Indian, and some might say he was more Indian now than white. Which wouldn't bother him in the least. He'd take it as a compliment.

After traveling 40 yards from the camp, he still saw no reason for the dog's behavior. He stopped beside a wide tree, gazing in all directions, and detected movement at the limits of his vision. Sliding behind the trunk, he held the rifle firmly and waited.

Soon he heard them: Indians, sneaking toward the campfire, making barely any noise, but enough for him to tell who was approaching. The pad of stealthy feet, of men moving quickly in the direction of the fiery glow at the base of the cliff, alerted him to the fact there were at least four or five and they were on both sides of him.

His back flush to the tree, crouching as low as he

could, Nate placed his thumb on the hammer and froze. Could they be Crows? This was Crow territory. If so, they would probably be friendly and he didn't want to shoot them without provocation.

To the right a black form materialized, then a second. To the left appeared three more. They were concentrating on the fire to the exclusion of all else and none, evidently, looked in Nate's direction. He saw them advance less than ten feet and halt. One of the men whispered to another, the words barely audible.

Was that the Crow tongue? Nate wondered. He didn't think so but he couldn't be certain. Peering through the trees, he saw Milo and Tom near the fire with their rifles in their hands. Red Moon was not in sight. If these Indians were hostile, and if he let them get any closer to the camp, they'd be able to easily pick the two Pennsylvanians off before Benteen and Sublette knew what hit them. He couldn't let that happen.

Easing lower, hoping his figure would be indistinguishable against the background, Nate spoke clearly. "Who are you and what do you want?"

His words sparked swift reaction. An Indian on the left wheeled and a rifle boomed, the muzzle spitting flame and lead.

Nate heard the ball smack into the tree above his head. The other Indians were scattering. He sighted on the one who had fired, who seemed to be trying to reload, and let the Hawken show how much he appreciated being shot at. At the retort from his gun, the Indian shrieked in pain and fell. Instantly, Nate dived to the right, and it was well he did.

Two other guns spoke, and two more balls struck the trunk of the tree.

Rolling to one knee, Nate held the rifle in his left hand and drew one of his flintlocks with his right. He cocked the hammer as he drew so he was set to fire when his arm reached full extension. Only there were no targets to shoot at. The four remaining Indians had gone to ground.

Realizing they would be out for his blood, Nate crept to the right. A stationary target was a sitting duck. He must keep constantly on the move if he hoped to partially counter their numerical advantage.

Off to the left there was an abrupt screech, then total silence.

What had that been all about? Nate mused, easing flat in the shelter of a low thicket. He crawled to his right, wishing he could reload the Hawken but knowing he increased his risk if he did. If they converged on him he had his two pistols and his butcher knife, and they would learn the hard way that a King was as hard to kill as the mighty bears after which he had been named.

A commotion erupted and Nate heard much thrashing and flailing. The scuffle was punctuated by the low growl of a beast and the strangled cry of a man. Suddenly, quiet descended once more.

Had that been Samson? Nate continued to crawl, scouring the ground. He hoped Benteen and Sublette would have the good sense not to blunder into the forest bellowing his name. By now they should have taken cover.

A second commotion ensued, much louder than the first, and the growling was much more ferocious. No one screamed, but a few seconds after the noise stopped, someone groaned in acute agony.

What the blazes was going on out there? Nate wondered as he skirted the end of the thicket, trying to outflank the Indians on the right. His elbow struck a thin dead branch lying on the ground and it broke with a sharp crack.

Fuming at his stupidity, Nate rose into a crouch and dashed to the right. The Indians were bound to have heard and would easily pinpoint his position. He must put distance behind him or find a hiding place.

One moment he was adroitly weaving among the trees, the next someone hurtled out of the night and slammed into him from the rear. He was knocked forward, onto his knees, and when he frantically twisted to see his attacker he saw a tall warrior armed with a knife—a knife that streaked at his face.

Chapter Nine

In sheer desperation, Nate threw himself to the right. He felt the tip of the blade dig into his left shoulder, felt a clammy sensation as blood spurted over his skin, and then he was on his back with his attacker looming above him in the dim light, ready to stab again. His right arm jerked the pistol straight out and he fired at close range into the Indian's abdomen.

The force of the ball made the warrior stagger backwards and the man doubled over, let go of his knife, and clutched at his stomach.

Nate pushed off the ground, stuck the spent pistol under his belt, and drew his second flintlock. It wasn't needed, though. The warrior was doubled over, his forehead resting on the grass, groaning pitiably. The knife lay at his feet.

Taking no chances, Nate backpedaled a few feet and covered the man. Suddenly, from out of nowhere, appeared Red Moon. The Crow slipped up beside Nate and stared at the downed warrior, who had tilted his head to peer at them.

"Blackfeet," he commented.

"This far south?" Nate responded absently while gazing anxiously around for sign of the rest.

"They go where they please, when they please. These must have been looking for a village to raid when they saw our fire."

"There were five in all," Nate informed him, looking over his shoulder.

"I know. Now there is just this one."

The man on the ground spoke, uttering his few words defiantly.

"He speaks my tongue," Red Moon said. "He says all Crows are cowards and fit for the buzzards."

Nate was worried about the remaining Blackfeet. He expected one of them to charge or open fire at any second. "What about the others?"

"Dead."

"All of them?"

"Yes," Red Moon said, and tapped the knife he wore on his left hip. "I killed one. You shot one with your rifle and then this one. And the dog sent the last two to meet their ancestors."

"Samson?"

"Is there another dog around here?"

Nate turned in time to see the big black beast advance out of a tangle of vegetation nearby. Samson strolled over to him and stood at his side, staring wickedly at the wounded Blackfoot brave. He thought the dog might tear into the man and said sternly, "No. Leave him alone." He had no idea if Samson understood, but the dog made no move toward the warrior.

Crashing in the underbrush heralded the arrival of Benteen and Sublette, who hurried over with their rifles at the ready.

"Who is he, Nate?" Milo asked, gesturing at the brave.

"What happened?" Tom added. "We heard shooting and growling and such."

"This here is a Blackfoot," Nate informed them. "He and his friends were fixing to take our scalps."

"Blackfeet!" Milo exclaimed. Like every other trapper in the Rockies, he'd heard all about the many white men slain by the fierce tribe. "How many were there?"

"Five."

Tom glanced at Samson. "Well, I'll be damned! This mutt of yours saved our bacon by hearing them before they could get close enough to put an arrow or a ball into us."

"That he did," Nate agreed.

"If you want to keep him, I won't raise a ruckus," Tom said.

"What about this one?" Milo inquired, jabbing his rifle at the brave at their feet. "Shouldn't we finish him off?"

As if the Blackfoot understood, he came up in a rush, his bloody arms flashing out with the knife clutched in his right hand. He tried to stab Red Moon in the neck, but the wily Crow was a shade faster and sidestepped.

Nate pivoted, bringing his flintlock to bear, but before he could fire there was a tremendous snarl and Samson sprang like a pouncing panther. The big dog didn't bother going for an arm or leg as would others of his kind. Samson went straight for the throat, his momentum and weight enabling him to sweep past the Blackfoot's knife and knock the brave over. They went down, Samson on top, his teeth sunk deep in the Blackfoot's soft neck.

Still game, the Blackfoot drew back his knife arm to stab Samson in the side. Nate saw the movement and tramped down hard on the brave's forearm with his foot, pinning the arm and the knife in place. He held his leg firm as the Blackfoot gurgled and thrashed, listening to the slurping sounds made by Samson as the dog's teeth shredded the Blackfoot's throat. A whine rent the cool air, not the low whine of a dog but the terrified whine of a man who was dying, a man who fought and struggled with all his waning strength but was no match for the massive brute chewing his neck to bits.

Abruptly, the Blackfoot lay still.

Samson moved back, blood dripping from his muzzle. Tiny pieces of pale flesh dotted his cheeks and lined his mouth.

"If I ever forget myself and try to kick this mongrel," Tom said softly, "I want somebody to shoot me before it can get to me."

"Consider it done," Milo said, grinning.

Red Moon drew his knife. "I claim the scalp of the man I killed, but the rest are yours, Grizzly Killer."

"Mine?" Nate repeated distastefully. Of the few Indian practices he disliked, scalping was at the top of his list. He'd taken the hair of a few foes since arriving in the Rockies, but he couldn't reconcile his conscience to the horrid practice.

"You shot one and your dog finished off the rest," Red Moon stated. "So, by right, four of the scalps are yours."

"I don't want them," Nate said.

"You're passing up four fine scalps?" Milo asked in astonishment.

"When you've taken as many as I have, what's one more?" Nate said as nonchalantly as he could.

"I'd hate to see them go to waste," Milo said, looking down at the last Blackfoot.

"If you want them, they're yours."

"What about me?" Tom interjected. "I've never taken a scalp either, and I wouldn't mind having the hair of a Blackfoot hanging from my belt."

"Divide them, then," Nate proposed. "Each of you can have two."

"You really mean it?" Milo responded eagerly.

"Yes."

"You're all right in my book." Tom beamed, drawing his knife. "It takes a big man to share scalps. Wait until we tell everyone about this. You'll be the talk of the mountains."

"I'd prefer if you didn't tell a soul," Nate said.

"If that's what you want," Tom said, and knelt to grip the Blackfoot's shoulder-length black hair.

Nate didn't stay to see the scalps removed. He started toward their camp, appalled by the attitude of the Pennsylvanians. Then he reminded himself that many trappers shared the same attitude, and some could boast of having a dozen or more scalps in their possession. For that matter, the Indians were no better. Every male in every tribe prided himself on his bravery in battle and the number of coups he'd counted. Owning a string of scalps conferred great prestige on the warrior who did, and Indian men entertained no qualms about lifting hair.

He was pouring hot coffee into his tin cup when the others drifted back. Red Moon had the fresh scalp attached to his thin leather belt. Milo held two in his hand and was examining them critically. Tom Sublette was swinging his and chuckling like a giddy child who had just received a new toy.

"Wait until I show these to the folks back in Pennsylvania," Tom declared happily. "Why, they'll think I'm the greatest Injun-fighter since Daniel Boone."

"But you didn't kill those Indians," Milo noted.

Tom laughed and winked. "We know that, but my friends in Pennsylvania won't." He swung the scalps again and grinned.

"Boone would roll over in his grave," Milo said.

"He'd understand," Tom countered. "After all, Boone was born in Pennsylvania just like we were." He paused. "Besides, it's just in the nature of a practical joke. I'm not trying to hurt anyone."

Nate had heard all he could abide. "A man should never claim credit for a killing that isn't properly his," he commented, and took a sip of the delicious, steaming coffee.

"It's easy enough for you to criticize me," Tom said resentfully, "when you already have a reputation the likes of which most men only dream about." He snorted. "You're the mighty Grizzly Killer who can slay grizzlies with his bare hands. You can track and shoot as good as any Indian who ever lived. Beaver drop dead at the mere mention of your—"

"That will be enough!" Nate snapped, rising.

The others froze. They all knew there were certain things a man never did when in the company of others. A man never asked prying questions because many men had left the States to escape pasts they would rather forget. A man never made fun of another man's woman because there was no surer way of getting a fist in the face. And a man never, ever insulted another man or treated others sarcastically unless he was ready to back his foolishness with a knife or a gun.

"We're trapping partners, but that doesn't give you the right to treat me like a green pilgrim," Nate said sternly. "Any reputation I have, I've earned the hard way."

Tom glowered for a full ten seconds. Only when Milo said softly "Tom" did he glance at Benteen and then sigh. He faced Nate. "All right. I was wrong and I admit it. Sorry, King."

"No harm done," Nate responded, and squatted in front of the fire. In his heart, though, he was developing a dislike for Tom Sublette. The man had a high regard for himself and a low regard for others, a dan-

gerous combination in any person. Nate almost
wished he'd had the presence of mind to turn down
their offer, but again he thought of all the furs he
would collect and of getting back to the cabin much
earlier than he normally would. He would just have
to put up with Sublette's behavior for a few months.

Milo, who was tying his scalps to his belt, suddenly
looked up. "Say, I just had a thought. What if those
shots were heard by other Indians?"

"They might have been," Red Moon said.

"We'll act on the assumption someone did hear
them," Nate said. "And since we're avoiding other
company for the time being, we'll saddle up and cut
out of here before first light. If someone comes to investigate tomorrow morning, we'll be long gone before
they find where we've camped."

"I will keep first watch," Red Moon volunteered.

"I'll go second," Nate said, and drank more coffee
while listening to Milo and Tom argue over who
should pull guard duty third and fourth. At times they
were more like bickering boys than full-grown men.

He sipped again, pondering. What had happened to
him? he wondered. There had been a time when they
wouldn't have bothered him in the least, not even
Sublette. There had been a time when others could
tease him and he would have merely laughed and gone
about his business. Why, now, was he so different?

All of the old-timers he knew were the same way.
By old-timer, he meant anyone who had lived in the
Rockies for more than two or three years. In comparison to the number of men who flocked to the Rockies
to trap, very few stayed on for long. Most died, either
from Indians, beasts, or accidents. Men like Shakespeare McNair and Jim Bridger were the exceptions
rather than the rule. And they too were touchy about
being offended.

Why? And when had he changed and become like them? What had done it?

Was it because living in the wilderness, where a person encountered the majesty of creation on a daily basis, conferred a profound sense of inner dignity on those who did so? A dignity above reproach, but not above reprimanding those who belittled it?

Was it because living in the wilderness, where survival was often won by superior wits and endurance, made a person appreciate his or her own uniqueness that much more, made a man realize he was special and had a place in the greater scheme of things? Consequently, he was unwilling to abide the insults of those who didn't know any better?

Or was the cause simpler than that? Was it because the wilderness took a man and molded his soul in its own hard image? Nature, after all, was never forgiving or compassionate. Everywhere, the strong prayed on the weak. The slow deer fell to the panther, the weak elk was taken by wolves. And men who were weak seldom lasted out a year in the wild Rockies. Only the hard ones lived on. Those who were living reflections of the life-and-death spectacle surrounding them.

Nate shook his head, clearing his mind, and smiled at himself over his train of thought. He was starting to think in circles, just like Shakespeare often did. Give him another five years and he'd probably wind up as crotchety as that cantankerous old cuss!

"I hope we don't run into any more Blackfeet before we reach the valley," Milo was saying.

"The valley is very close to Blackfoot country," Red Moon reminded him. "Very close. We must be on our guard at all times. But if we are careful, we will have much money when it is all over."

"Now you're talking, Injun," Tom said. "I can't wait to hold a couple of thousand dollars in my hand. I've never had that much money at one time."

"Do not forget a share goes to me," Red Moon said.

Tom glanced sharply at the Crow. "I won't forget, old man. Don't you worry none. And don't you forget that for you to collect your money, we've got to make it back alive."

Nate took a long swallow and peered at his companions over the rim of his cup, speculating on how many would actually make it back.

Only time would tell.

Chapter Ten

"The valley," Red Moon said, and pointed straight ahead.

Nate placed a hand on the pommel and leaned forward to survey the land before them. They had reined up in a small clearing on a pine-covered ridge, and it became immediately apparent why few knew the location of the valley.

The old Crow had led them into stark, rugged country rarely visited by human beings. Regal mountains were everywhere, most craggy peaks over ten thousand feet high. Between and among the mountains were deep gorges, steep ravines, and occasional verdant valleys. Many were dead ends. The whole area was like a gigantic maze carved by the erratic hand of the whimsical elements.

The ridge on which they had stopped bordered an isolated series of jagged spires and rocky heights that formed a seemingly impassable barrier. Situated as it was so close to those heights, the ridge cut off from view whatever lay at their base. And there, nestled between two mountains looming over 12 thousand feet above the ground, was the opening to a lush valley.

"Well, I'll be damned," Milo commented. "We're finally here."

"Where the hell are we?" Tom wanted to know, and shot a questioning look at Nate.

"It's a branch of the Rockies, but I don't know which one," Nate said. "I've never been this far northwest before." He paused. "Very few have."

"What are we waiting for?" Milo asked eagerly, and nodded at the valley entrance. "Let's get down there and set up camp for the night."

Nate took the lead, squinting up at the late afternoon sun. There were about four hours of daylight remaining, enough for them to find a suitable spot to bed down. Bright and early tomorrow morning they could scout the valley and see if the beaver were as abundant as Red Moon had claimed.

He glanced over his shoulder at the warrior, who was riding at the rear of the line, and noticed Red Moon cast an anxious gaze toward the two mountains flanking the valley. Was the Crow thinking about the thing that lurked in the dark? Or about the Crow braves who had gone into the valley and never emerged? Facing front, Nate placed the Hawken across his thighs so he could lift it quickly in an emergency.

All around was wildlife. There were hawks high above them, ravens and jays in the trees. Chipmunks darted from under rocks and squirrels chattered from the treetops. Elk and deer prints were plentiful.

Nate saw no reason to be alarmed. With so much game there must be few predators in the area. Once, at the bottom of the ridge, he spied a bear track, but it was that of a black bear and not a grizzly.

They rode to the opening, a relatively narrow gap between the mountains, no more than 50 feet wide. Pines grew in profusion on both sides of a broad stream that flowed out of the gap and angled abruptly to the left, to the west. The stream flowed along the base of the peaks for hundred of yards, then disappeared in deep forest. From the ridge the stream had not been visible because of the high grass and weeds that grew along each bank and the overhanging branches of the many trees bordering the slowly flowing water.

"This is right pretty," Milo said.

Nate nodded in agreement. The countryside was picturesque. If the valley wasn't so close to Blackfoot territory, it would be an ideal spot to build a cabin and raise a family. He goaded his stallion through the gap, sticking to the east bank of the stream, listening to the gurgling water and the soft wind whispering in the branches.

"Say, look there!" Tom exclaimed, pointing.

At that moment Nate saw it too: a large beaver dam constructed from reeds, saplings, sticks, and branches all woven into a compact mass and caulked with mud. Past the damn, in an oval pond, was the beaver lodge, a dome of similar construction well over seven feet high and 30 feet wide, average size. There were no beaver in evidence, but it was still early. Mainly active at night, beaver usually made their appearance in the early evening.

"That's a good sign," Milo said. "Where there's one lodge there might be a lot more."

Similar thoughts inspired Nate. They had barely entered the valley and already found a lodge. It had been his experience that the farther up a valley a trapper went, the more lodges and beaver he would find.

And so they did. They passed dam after dam, lodge

after lodge, and twice saw beaver swimming. The animals paid no attention to them, which in itself was promising because it meant the beaver had had few dealings if any with hunters or trappers and would be easier to catch.

The valley stretched on for mile after mile, widening out as they advanced, winding between magnificent peaks to the east and the west. At its widest the valley covered five to six miles. Occasionally it narrowed to only two miles or less. Small herds of elk and black-tailed deer were frequently spotted. At various points they came on tributaries of the main stream, creeks branching off to the right or the left, and they saw beaver dams and lodges up those too.

Milo laughed lightly. "I think I've died and gone to trappers' heaven."

"I've never seen so many beaver in one valley before," Tom said. "How about you, Nate?"

"Me neither," Nate admitted.

Tom looked at Red Moon. "I've got to hand it to you, old man. You were right. You knew what you were talking about."

"We will catch many beaver," the Crow predicted.

They hadn't gone more than a third of the way into the valley when Nate decided to call a halt. The sun perched low on the western mountains and would soon drop from view, plunging the valley into deep shadows and eventual darkness. He studied those jagged peaks, realizing they cut off the sunlight much earlier than would normally be the case. He estimated night fell in the valley a good half hour before it did, say, at his cabin.

Nate picked a spot where a meadow bordered the main stream as their campsite. While Tom got a fire going and Red Moon gathered dead wood, Nate and Milo stripped the horses and took them to the stream to drink. Samson stayed near Nate.

"This valley is better than I'd dare dream," Milo mentioned, beaming as he surveyed the expanse still before them. "If all goes well, I'll return to Pennsylvania with enough money to put down on a sizable farm. Maggie will be so happy. I gave her a ring before I left for these mountains. Hope she hasn't grown tired of waiting for me."

"I wish the two of you the best."

They tethered the horses in the meadow, then strolled to the fire, where a pot of coffee was already boiling. Red Moon had taken a seat and was chewing on a piece of jerked meat.

"I can hardly wait to start trapping," Tom said as he poured coffee into Nate's cup.

"We have a few things to do before we trap," Nate told him. "We should go to the end of the valley and see if there are a lot of beaver farther up. Then we can pick our first camp and begin to set traps."

"First camp?" Milo repeated.

"This valley must be twenty-five to thirty miles long," Nate said. "If we were to set up a permanent camp near the center, whoever went out to check the traps couldn't possibly make it back by dark and would have to bed down in the brush. It's too far to cover from end to end at one time. So I propose trapping one section of the stream at a time and working our way down the valley until we're done. We can move our camp farther down as we go along so each of us won't have as far to travel when we check the trap lines."

"Makes sense to me," Milo said.

"Me too," Tom added.

Red Moon, who was bearing more wood to the fire, halted and said, "There is more to this valley."

"What do you mean?" Milo responded.

"The valley forks far up. There is another part as long as this one."

"Does it have as many beaver?" Milo asked.

"More," the Crow answered, and deposited his load of wood.

Tom laughed and slapped his thigh in delight. "This is too good to be true. We don't have enough pack animals for all the pelts we'll collect."

"When will we reach the fork?" Nate wanted to know.

"Well after the sun is straight overhead we should be there," Red Moon informed him.

Because they had not shot any game, they had to make do with jerky and biscuits Milo made from the flour in their provisions. Hot coffee capped off their meal. Then they settled around the fire and discussed their trapping plans.

"Should we take turns standing guard?" Tom inquired at one point.

"There is no need," Red Moon said.

"What about the Blackfeet?" Tom mentioned. "You keep telling us that we're close to their country."

"The Blackfeet do not come into this valley."

Nate, about to take a sip, stopped and studied the Crow's impassive features. "Why not?"

"For the same reason my people no longer come here," Red Moon said.

Milo snickered. "Are you saying the Blackfeet are also afraid of this thing that lurks in the dark?" He shook his head in disbelief. "The Blackfeet don't know the meaning of fear."

"They do not come here," Red Moon reiterated.

Swallowing more coffee, Nate gazed into the inky night. Like Milo, he was skeptical. The Blackfeet deserved their reputation for being indomitable warriors. They fought everyone and everything. Even grizzlies didn't intimidate them. So why would they shun this valley when it was a hunter's paradise?

"Now don't start with that nonsense again," Tom

grumbled. "We haven't seen anything unusual since we got here. And I don't recollect any of us seeing so much as a strange track."

"Once the creature knows we are here, it will come," Red Moon stated. He removed a piece of jerky from his pack and took a bite.

"There is no damned creature," Tom insisted. "And I don't want to hear you talk of it again."

"As you wish."

A nervous whinny suddenly issued from one of the packhorses, and a moment later several others had chimed in with loud whinnies of their own.

"What the hell?" Tom blurted.

Nate grabbed his Hawken, rose, and hurried toward the stock. Perhaps because of the fireside conversation, his every nerve was on edge. On his left was Samson, not displaying any agitation whatsoever. Red Moon and Milo were on the right. Nate reached the tethered animals and saw them staring intently to the northeast with their ears pricked.

"There is something out there," Milo whispered.

But what? Nate wondered, his thumb on the hammer of his rifle. They couldn't afford to lose any of their animals. They only had one riding horse apiece, and the eight packhorses would be sorely needed to transport the furs.

Then, from perhaps half a mile away, a piercing shriek rent the cool air, a shriek resembling that of a terrified woman in agonizing torment. The horses fidgeted anxiously, a few tugging on their ropes.

Milo lowered his rifle and snorted. "It's just a panther. The stock must have picked up its scent."

"What if it tries to get one of our horses?" Tom asked from behind them.

"Perhaps we should post guards after all," Nate suggested. "I'll take the first watch if no one has any objections."

No one did. They walked back to the fire. Nate finished his coffee while standing and gazing at the horses. The flickering firelight played over their sleek forms. Some had already gone back to grazing. A few had lain down. None appeared concerned about the big cat, which meant they no longer smelled the panther and it must be prowling in another direction.

"Maybe that's it," Tom said. "Maybe there's a real whopper of a panther in these parts, a man-killer. Maybe it's responsible for killing that Crow brave and scaring everyone off."

"The thing is not a panther," Red Moon stated firmly.

"If you say so," Tom said sarcastically. "But if anything shows up, and I don't care if it's one of them Frankenstein monsters or one of those vampyres, I'm going to give it a little surprise." As he finished speaking he reached out and patted his rifle, propped on his saddle beside him.

"There are no such things. All of that is make-believe," Milo said while chewing on a biscuit.

For another 30 minutes they talked. Then the Pennsylvanians and the Crow turned in and Nate started his watch. The Hawken cradled in his left arm, he strolled into the meadow and walked around the horses, Samson sticking with him all the time. The horses were bedded down and quiet.

In the near and far distance arose typical wilderness sounds: the hoots of owls, the howls of wolves, the yips of coyotes, and occasionally the snarls and growls of predators. Stars filled the heavens, a dazzling celestial spectacle that took the breath away.

Nate munched on jerky and took a seat close enough to the fire to be warm, but with his back to it so his night vision wouldn't be impaired by the bright flames. The hours passed uneventfully. When the time came, he awakened Milo and gratefully crawled under his blankets to get some sleep. His last thoughts before drifting to sleep were of the legendary creature. They had been in the valley for hours and it hadn't shown up. Red Moon must be wrong. The Crow was letting the old tales get to him. There was nothing to worry about.

Nothing at all.

Chapter Eleven

The next several days were jammed with activity.

On their second day in the valley they traveled to where the stream forked, debated a bit, and finally decided to go up the right fork first simply because they spied a huge beaver lodge up it, bigger than any of them had ever seen or heard of, and the sight drew them like a magnet. They rode until they could ride no farther, until they found themselves at the base of a steep mountain and saw where the stream came down off that mountain from a high country lake Red Moon said was up near the summit. The water was runoff from the snow that perpetually crowned the surrounding peaks.

Eagerly, they established their first camp. The gear was stripped off the packhorses. All four of them pitched in and constructed a sturdy lean-to that would adequately shelter them from the elements. Their food supply, stored in parfleches and packs, was hung by ropes from high trees limbs to discourage bears and other varmints that might wander by while they were off trapping. Their traps and tools were stored in a corner of the lean-to, but only until the next day, when they began trapping in earnest.

They started out when the sun was still below the horizon, working in pairs. Nate and Red Moon crossed the stream and worked along the west side, exploring up each tributary they discovered. Milo and Tom did likewise on the east side.

Since Red Moon knew little about how to properly set a trap, Nate did most of the work that morning. His traps were all Newhouses, manufactured by Sewell Newhouse of Oneida, New York, from whom they got their nickname. Newhouse sold every type of equipment a trapper needed, and even published a useful manual on the trade that many a beginning trapper carried with him into the vast Rockies.

Laying a trap line was cold, hard work. They hiked from dam to dam. At each, Nate would search for a runway or other likely spot to set his trap. Then he would place the Newhouse flat on the ground, stand on the leaf springs until the jaws dropped open, and adjust the trigger on the disk until the proper tension held the disk in place.

Next the trap was carefully carried into the frigid water and positioned on the bottom so the surface of the water was no more than a hand-width above the disk. This was done because beaver, being short-legged, had to step right on the disk to spring the trap. If the trap was placed any lower, they might swim right over it.

A stout length of wood was then inserted through the ring at the end of the chain and pounded into the bank using the blunt end of a hatchet. Pulling on the chain verified the beaver would be unable to yank it loose.

The last step in setting a trap concerned the bait. Usually contained in small wooden boxes that were frequently sold at the annual rendezvous, the bait consisted of the musky secretion beavers used to mark their territory, and was collected from the glands of dead ones before they were skinned. A thin stick was dipped into the box and then the other end was jabbed into the bank above where the trap had been placed. Once a passing beaver smelled the scent, it would come to investigate, step into the trap, and be caught in rigid steel jaws. Inevitably it drowned, unless the beaver chewed its own foot off to escape, which happened quite often if the traps weren't checked regularly.

Nate took until well past noon to set his 12 traps, and then returned to camp. The two Pennsylvanians had finished much earlier and were already there.

"How did it go?" Tom asked.

"We'll know this evening when we check our lines," Nate replied.

"This evening?" Tom repeated. "But we've always checked our traps in the morning."

"Only once a day?" Nate inquired.

"Sure. What's wrong with that? Many trappers only check their line once a day."

"And they're the ones who lose a lot of beaver. When you only check once a day, it gives any animal you've caught more time to chew its leg off. By checking twice you seldom have one get away on you," Nate said. "Shakespeare himself advised me to check twice and I've always done so."

Milo had been listening attentively. "So that's why we've lost so many. Okay, Nate. From here on out we check twice each day."

"That's a lot of work," Tom grumbled.

"Which would you rather be?" Milo retorted. "Rich or lazy?"

Tom grinned. "Rich, of course. But I hate going into that icy water. It pains my legs something fierce."

"Quite a few trappers have the same complaint," Nate noted. "If you sit by a fire for a while as soon as you're done checking the line, your legs won't hurt half as much."

"I know," Tom said, and shrugged. "You know how it is. We don't always do what is best for us even when we know better."

Red Moon took his bow and quiver from his gear and went off to hunt, leaving his rifle behind. Everyone knew why. Using a gun often spooked game from an area and they wanted to keep the game close so they wouldn't have to spend as much time securing their fresh meat. Over an hour later he came back with a large doe draped over his shoulders.

The sun was close to the western horizon when they went off to check their lines. Nate didn't expect to find many beaver in his traps since the line had been in place for such a short time. To his delight, though, he found three.

At each sprung trap he had to wade into the water and haul the 40-pound carcass onto the bank. After removing the dead animal, he reset the trap in a different spot. Since Red Moon accompanied him, they lugged all three back to camp instead of skinning them on the spot as he would have done had he been alone.

Milo and Tom had not yet returned. Nate placed the three beaver near the fire, obtained his curved skinning knife from his pack, and set to work removing the hides. Many a pelt had been ruined by a man who cut rashly and pierced the soft fur, so he took his time. The better the condition of the pelt, the more money he would make for it.

He had been done for quite some time and darkness was descending when Milo and Tom came back. Five beaver had been snared in their traps and they had removed the hides beside the stream.

Milo glanced at Nate's skins and beamed. "Eight already! I tell you, this venture will pay off handsomely."

Over the next two days his words were borne out. They caught a grand total of 71 beaver, and were kept busy skinning when not checking their lines. They were so busy there was barely time to eat.

By the morning of the fourth day they were all fatigued but elated at their good fortune. Chewing on a flapjack, Milo looked at them and chuckled.

"If we keep going at this rate, we'll have the valley trapped out in a month."

"The sooner, the better," Tom said.

Nate inwardly agreed and was pleased. Between all the beaver along the two upper forks, the dozens of tributaries, and the lower body of the stream, they should each take back between four and five hundred pelts. Not a bad haul at all considering that most trappers took in three or four hundred pelts during an entire year. There were exceptions, of course. Jed Smith had caught close to seven hundred one year. But it was Nate's mentor, Shakespeare McNair, who held the all-time record for a twelve-month haul: 827 pelts.

For three more days they trapped using the same base camp, until the beaver at the head of the fork were almost depleted, and then Nate proposed moving the camp a bit farther down the stream. The move was accomplished in one morning, and by the afternoon they were again working their trap lines.

Red Moon expressed an interest in learning to trap and Nate took it upon himself to teach the old Crow. The warrior's keen mind easily grasped the essentials, and before long Red Moon could trap as well as any of them and skin beaver a lot faster.

On the sixth day in the valley, as evening descended, Nate and Red Moon walked along a narrow creek feeding off the stream, checking their traps. They reached a beaver pond surrounded by high lodgepole pines and worked along the north shore toward a spot where they had placed a Newhouse that morning.

"We caught one," Red Moon said.

A moment later Nate saw the dead beaver submerged in the cold water. He handed his Hawken to the Crow and put his left foot in the pond, idly listening to the nearby chatter of squirrels and the chirping of playful sparrows.

Abruptly, the noises ceased.

Nate had not spent almost five years in the wilderness for nothing. He knew animals never fell silent like that without reason, and the reason invariably was either a roving predator or passing humans. Since there were no other people in the valley except for Benteen and Sublette, who were both over by the fork, the cause for the sudden silence must be a predator.

Visions of a hungry grizzly flitted through Nate's mind and he reached out and took his rifle. The Crow was gazing into the forest, his expression one of questioning curiosity.

Samson uttered a low growl.

Nate looked down at the dog and saw it peering into the wall of vegetation, its nostrils working as it tried to pick up a scent. He cocked the Hawken to be prepared in case there was a grizzly close at hand, then waited for a telltale sign, the crashing of underbrush or the characteristic gruff rumble of a bear in a killing mood.

Time seemed to stand still. The wind had died and not so much as a single leaf fluttered.

As unexpectedly as the interlude began, it ended with the chirp of a robin. The wildlife resumed its normal rhythm of living and the forest was filled with the songs of birds and the buzzing of insects.

"Must have been a bear," Nate speculated.

"No bear," Red Moon said.

"Then what was it?"

"I do not know."

Nate gazed into the Indian's dark eyes, eyes rimmed with wrinkles and reflecting a profound wisdom born of a lifetime spent in the wild. He had the impression Red Moon did know, or had guessed. A possibility occurred to him, but he promptly discarded it. Couldn't be, he told himself. The thing that lurked in the dark only came out at night according to the Indian legends. And besides, there was no such animal.

"I will keep watch while you get the beaver," Red Moon offered.

In half the time it ordinarily required, Nate had the trap out of the water and the beaver out of the trap. His hand fell on his knife, but he paused. If there was a grizzly in the vicinity, perhaps it would be wiser to remove the hide at their camp.

"What about the last trap?" the Crow inquired.

Nate stared off up the creek, remembering the small pond a hundred yards farther on where they had discovered a recently constructed beaver lodge. "I'll go. You take this one back to camp," he proposed.

"We should go together."

"I can manage," Nate insisted. He hefted the Hawken and walked off, Samson beside him as always.

"We should go together," Red Moon insisted, and quickly caught up with them.

Nate glanced at the warrior's impassive features and tried to ascertain the reason the Crow was being so persistent. As if Red Moon knew his thoughts, he met Nate's gaze and spoke softly.

"Perhaps you are right, Grizzly Killer. You have killed many grizzlies, so you must known them well. Perhaps there is a bear out there."

Was Red Moon poking fun at him? Nate wondered, but said nothing. He noticed the Crow had not brought the dead beaver and now held his rifle firmly in both hands.

The last pond in the creek was only 40 feet in circumference, the dam barely five feet high but growing higher every day as the beaver occupying the pond behind it worked continuously at improving the size of their barrier.

Nate walked rapidly, seeing the long shadows all around them and realizing the sun had almost disappeared over the far western horizon, spearing the western sky with vivid streaks of red and orange and pink. The beautiful sunset, which ordinarily would stir his soul mightily, failed to impress him.

The trees were farther back from this pond than the previous one, allowing them to hike around to the opposite side without having to push limbs aside or forge through brush.

Above the surface adjacent to where the stake had been imbedded jutted the rounded tip of a beaver tail.

"Another one," Red Moon said. "We are very fortunate."

"Yes," Nate responded, although secretly he would have been just as happy to find the Newhouse empty. Had it been, they would be on their way to camp. Now he must go into the pond and fetch the carcass.

The frigid mountain water soaked his moccasins and the bottom of his buckskin leggings as he waded in. He grunted when he lifted the beaver, and no wonder, for it was an exceptionally large specimen weighing between 45 and 50 pounds. Once on the bank, he stepped on the leaf springs and yanked the crushed leg out, then stepped aside. The jaws snapped shut with a loud metallic snap.

"We'll skin both at camp," Nate proposed. "I'd like to get back and have a cup of coffee."

"I also," Red Moon said. He pulled the stake out of the ground and dangled the trap from his shoulder by the chain.

As they retraced their steps, Samson between them, Nate mentally chided himself for his nervousness. There was no logical excuse for him to be so jittery. Winona would be ashamed of him if she knew. Not to mention Shakespeare. He squared his shoulders and whistled as they worked their way around the larger pond to where the other trap and beaver lay. But when they got there, he drew up short in surprise.

The trap was exactly where they had left it.

The dead beaver, however, was gone.

Chapter Twelve

"A panther must have taken it," Tom Sublette stated an hour later as they sat around their roaring fire. He squatted beside it, preparing their evening meal.

"That would be my hunch," Milo chimed in.

"I suppose," Nate reluctantly agreed, although deep down he was bothered by an uneasy feeling that a panther had not been responsible. Nor had a grizzly. He couldn't explain the feeling and that worried him even more. There were plenty of tales of mountaineers who inexplicably lost their nerve after two, five, or even ten years in the Rockies and were never the same men again. Day after day, year after year, these men contended with hostile Indians and marauding beasts without batting an eye. Then one day they changed, and they were unable to explain the change to their own or anyone else's satisfaction. But they would pack their belongings and head off for the flatlands never to be seen west of the Mississippi again.

"You don't think so?" Milo asked.

Nate shrugged, unwilling to mention his unfounded anxiety for fear of their ridicule.

"I know!" Tom exclaimed, and laughed. "I'll wager Nate thinks it was the thing that lurks in the dark!"

"I do not," Nate responded, a bit too harshly.

Milo, who had been stretching a hide, stopped and appraised Nate as if he was examining a bug under a microscope. "Did you see any tracks?"

"None," Nate replied. "There was some crushed grass where a heavy foot had pressed, but not a clear print anywhere."

"A heavy foot would mean a bear," Milo mentioned.

"It could have been a bear," Nate said in the hope they would drop the subject. No such luck.

"A bear or a panther, what difference does it make?" Tom stated. "If it has filched a carcass once, it'll be tempted to try taking another. We'll have to be on our guard and keep our rifles handy at all times."

"I intend to do that," Nate said.

Milo devoted his attention to the hide he was working with. "The damnedest thing happened to Tom and me today," he commented offhandedly.

"Oh? What?" Nate asked.

"There we were, walking between traps and talking about the land we want to buy back in Pennsylvania when this is all done with, and all of a sudden the woods became as quiet as a cemetery at midnight. The woods were like a tomb."

Nate exchanged glances with Red Moon.

"Must have been the same critter that stole your beaver," Tom guessed. "It came near us and scared everything within half a mile."

"Must have been," Nate said.

Milo chuckled. "We should count ourselves fortunate the worst we must deal with is a bear or a panther. At least the Blackfeet don't know we're here, or we'd really be in trouble."

Hours later, after Tom and Milo had fallen asleep, Nate lay on his back on his blankets and listened to the horses grazing. Red Moon was on guard and he should have felt safe and comfortable, but he felt neither. Try as he would, he couldn't dispel the odd premonition that all was not well.

A thought struck him with the jolt of a lightning bolt. What if the premonition concerned Winona and Zach? What if they were the ones in danger? He rolled on his side, his forearm under his ear. By now Shakespeare and Blue Water Woman were at the cabin with his wife and son, and there wasn't a man alive who could protect them like McNair.

For that matter, Winona was perfectly capable of looking after herself and their son. She wasn't like many of the refined women Nate had known back in New York City, women who could flash a pretty smile and knew which dress to wear on which occasion and how to dance and curtsy and flutter a fan in the summer heat. A few could cook and fewer could sew, but they all detested the so-called drudgery of maintaining a home. They'd much rather have servants handle such menial work. They didn't seem to realize, as Nate's grandmother had one expressed it, that taking care of a home and rearing a family was the most noble type of work both men and women could hope to perform. And it was only a drudgery if a woman let it be so. His grandmother had often asserted that the three qualities a wife and mother needed most were ingenuity, persistence, and the patience of a rock.

How different Winona was from those pale, spoiled women in New York. She could sew, cook, and butcher an animal with consummate skill. She could hunt, when need be, and she knew scores of edible plants. She knew more about medicinal herbs than any doctor. And, as she had demonstrated time and again, she possessed as much raw courage as any Shoshone warrior.

Lord, she was a woman! He smiled, thinking of the last time they'd clasped one another in a passionate embrace. His lids grew heavy and began to droop, and he was on the verge of falling asleep when the stillness of the night was split by the sound of a branch breaking in half.

Nate sat up, thoroughly awake, and looked in all directions. Some of the horses were feeding, others were lying on the ground. None appeared disturbed. He placed a hand on his rifle, and in doing so brushed his palm against Samson. The dog was gazing to the south but not in the least agitated.

Perhaps it had been Red Moon, Nate decided. He listened for a minute longer, until satisfied there was nothing out there that posed a threat. Then he eased down and closed his eyes. He must stop being so jumpy. By tomorrow his uneasiness would have evaporated like the morning dew and he would feel like a fool for having gotten so worked up over nothing. Despite his assessment, it took him a long, long time to finally drift off.

The next morning he felt remarkably invigorated. As he'd supposed, his anxiety was gone. During the morning hours he diligently checked his traps, retrieved beaver, and repositioned some of the traps where they would do more good. By noon he had ten new pelts to add to their swiftly accumulating haul. That night, eight more.

One busy day after another went by. A week elapsed. Two. Two and a half. They worked their way down the right fork and camped at the junction.

"Tomorrow," Milo said in anticipation as they sat around the fire shortly after sunrise, "we start up the left fork. And if there are half as many beaver as there were up the right fork, we'll be rolling in prime furs."

Nate nodded and sipped at his steaming coffee. Their camp lay in a clearing nestled among the pines where they were sheltered from the often chilly night winds. Northwest of them, picketed in a field, were the horses.

"We should have toted more traps in," Tom remarked.

"A man can only do so much, can only check so many traps in a single day," Nate said. "We have all we'll need."

Red Moon, who sat with a blanket draped over his shoulders, suddenly straightened, letting the blanket fall, and pivoted in the direction of the valley entrance. "Listen," he said.

Nate did, and heard nothing out of the ordinary. "What is it?"

"Someone comes. One man on horseback."

Tom stood. "The hell you say. I don't hear a thing."

"Grab your guns and take cover," Nate directed, scooping up the Hawken. He ran to the trees bordering the stream and leaned his shoulder against a tree trunk. From where he stood he had a clear view of the stream for hundreds of yards.

A second later a lone rider appeared, proceeding up the east bank.

Nate studied the man, immediately seeing it was an Indian. From the way the warrior wore his hair, swept back on either side with a large eagle feather attached to the top of his head, and from the style of his long buckskin shirt and leggings, Nate recognized the tribe the man belonged to. His stomach muscles involuntarily tightened.

He was a Blackfoot.

The brave carried a lance in his right hand and had a bow and quiver slanted across his back. He was leaning low, concentrating on the ground.

Nate glanced at Milo and Tom, hidden nearby, and saw the anxiety on their faces. With good reason. That Blackfoot was following the trail they had made when they first entered the valley weeks ago. It had only rained once, briefly, in all that time, so the hoofprints of their horses were undoubtedly still evident.

Nate shifted and glanced to his left, where Red Moon stood behind a pine tree. The Crow, as always, did not betray his feelings. But he had his rifle cocked.

The Blackfoot reined up two hundred yards off and surveyed the valley. Then he swung down, dropped to one knee, and ran his hand over the tracks.

Nate could imagine what the brave was thinking. The Blackfoot would know that white men were in the party because the horses ridden by Benteen and Sublette were shod, as were their pack animals. Nate had long since stopped bothering to shoe his horses, preferring to ride them unshod as did the Indians.

From the heavier tracks of the pack animals, the Blackfoot would be able to deduce exactly how many men were with the group. He would probably suspect there were two Indians and two whites, and he would be greatly perplexed. What was such a mixed group doing in this valley so close to Blackfoot territory? Since the Crows occupied the region to the south, he might suspect there to be a Crow encampment somewhere farther up the stream.

Nate watched, debating whether to shoot. He refrained because he doubted very much the brave was alone. The warrior might be part of a war party heading into Crow land, and if so, the rest of the band might hear any shot and come to investigate. Had he been closer he would have tried to get the man with his knife. Under the circumstances, there was nothing he could do.

At length the Blackfoot rose and scanned the forest. Gripping his mount's mane, he vaulted onto the animal and yanked sharply on the rope reins. Using his feet and his quirt, he urged the white horse into a gallop and raced back the way he had come.

"Damn!" Milo fumed.

"He'll be back with his friends," Tom snapped. "Now we're in for it."

Nate led them to their camp. The Pennsylvanians were sullen and silent. Red Moon moved to one side and folded his arms across his chest.

"Well, I'll tell you now," Tom declared. "I'm not about to pack up and run off with my tail tucked between my legs because of the rotten Blackfeet. This valley is a gold mine in furs, and I'm not giving up my chance to go home with my pockets filled with money."

"I agree," Milo said. "We've worked too hard to call it quits at this stage. I say we stick it out."

Nate swung toward the Crow. "And you?"

Red Crow grinned. "I like to kill Blackfeet."

"Then it's settled," Nate said. "We stay and keep trapping."

"You haven't told us how you feel," Milo noted.

"I'm not too keen on tangling with the Blackfeet," Nate answered. "But I'm like you. I want to get as many peltries as I can before we leave."

"Good," Tom said, and wagged his rifle. "If those devils show their faces, we'll make their squaws widows."

"There's bound to be a shooting scrape," Milo commented, and frowned.

"From now on we must do things differently," Nate told them. "We can't leave our camp unattended at any time. So we'll take turns in the morning and evening checking our trap lines. One day Red Moon and I can go out first and then the two of you can go after we get back, and the next day we'll switch and you two can check your line first. Sound fair?"

"Sounds perfect," Milo said.

"We must also select our campsites with more care," Nate recommended. "We can't camp in the open and we must always build our fires under trees so the smoke will thin out as it rises."

"And never use our guns," Red Moon said.

Nate looked at him. "Since you're the best with a bow and arrow, you'll have to do the hunting from now on."

"I will," Red Moon said, and walked across the clearing toward the horses.

"Where are you going?" Tom asked.

"I will find out how many Blackfeet there are," Red Moon replied. "Do not expect me back before dark."

"Be careful," Nate cautioned.

"Always."

They watched the Crow mount his horse and ride off bareback, his long hair flying, man and horse one.

"I'm glad he's with us," Milo said.

Nate gripped the Hawken in his left hand. "Since I doubt the Blackfeet will be paying us a visit in the next hour or so, I'll go on up the left fork and see if there are as many beaver there as we've found elsewhere."

"Alone?" Milo said.

"I'll have Samson," Nate reminded him, and started off, the dog so close to his leg he had to be careful not to accidentally bump into it. He stuck to the inner bank and came on a large pond with a huge lodge within minutes. The vegetation pressed right up to the water's edge and he had to fight his way through to the high dam. Beyond lay another pond, another lodge.

Onward he went. As with the other fork and the lower branch, beaver sign was everywhere. He also saw the tracks of deer, elk, and smaller critters in the mud along the stream. Raccoons, skunks, bobcats, and more all came regularly to drink, and he was able to determine when they had done so and their approximate size and weight from the impressions they'd left.

Four more lodges he discovered, and then he paused beside another dam and absently gazed at the bare earth near its base. For several seconds he stared at a peculiar depression, thinking it must have been made when a large rock was dislodged. But there were no rocks anywhere near the dam, and suddenly he realized what the depression really was. His breath caught in his throat and his eyes widened in amazement.

It was a huge footprint.

Chapter Thirteen

Nate dashed down the slope toward the base of the dam and slipped on the slick ground. His left leg flew out from under him and he wildly flapped his arms to retain his balance. He reached the base upright, halted abruptly, and slowly sank into a crouch so he could study the marvel before him.

The track was unlike any he'd ever seen. Roughly square in shape, the heel being only slightly tapered, it measured approximately 15 inches in length and seven inches in width at the ball of the foot. Unlike bear tracks, which invariably gave some evidence of the bear's nonretractable claws, this one displayed the distinct impressions of five large toes, toes very humanlike in shape and arrangement.

Awed by the dimensions, Nate whispered in awe, "What in heaven's name is this?" He placed his right hand in the center of the track and saw how the track dwarfed it. Then he stood and placed his foot beside the track; his foot seemed like that of a small child's in comparison.

He cast around for more tracks but found none. Mystified, he walked back to the print and then noticed his own tracks. Where he'd walked in the mud, his moccasins sank to a depth of less than a quarter of an inch. But the huge print, by contrast, was a good inch and a half deep, which meant whatever made it had been extremely heavy.

Nate stood over the strange print and pondered. He thought of every animal that inhabited the Rockies and their tracks. None came close to resembling this one, not even the tracks of grizzlies. Either the impression had been produced by natural circumstances, by a means he could not fathom, or a totally unknown animal had made it.

The thing that lurked in the dark!

Unbidden, the Crow legend sprang to mind. He glanced up and scanned the surrounding forest, but saw nothing out of the ordinary. Birds were singing in carefree abandon. Had there been anything unusual in the area they would fall silent.

He walked in a circle around the track, inspecting it from every angle, mulling his course of action. If he went back and told the Pennsylvanians, they would be skeptical. Even if he showed it to them, they might not be willing to believe the creature behind the Crow legend had been responsible for making it. Considering how badly they wanted to acquire stakes so they could buy land in Pennsylvania, they certainly wouldn't be willing to leave the valley simply because a peculiar track had been found.

Nate halted and scratched his chin. If he was right, and the creature had made it, then what did it mean? Had the creature bothered them in any way since they entered the valley? No. Had they seen hide or hair of it? No. Had their trapping been affected? No.

Suddenly he recalled the missing dead beaver. What if the creature had taken it? Had it been watching them? Had it seen him pull the beaver out of the pond and then go off, leaving it unattended? Had it been hungry and decided to venture from concealment and grab the tempting meal? He had no way of knowing for certain, but the supposition made sense.

It also troubled him. If the creature did exist, and if it had stolen the beaver, then it meant the creature ate meat. It was carnivorous, a predator like a panther or a lynx. Or maybe it was more like a grizzly, which would eat practically anything under the sun. Grizzlies not only ate anything they could catch, including small and large animals, but they would also eat certain roots, sprouts, berries, and insects. Not to mention their fondness for fish. And grizzlies would kill and eat a man just as readily as they would a trout.

Did this creature have similar eating habits? If so, why hadn't it attacked any of them yet? Was it afraid of them, the Crow tales notwithstanding? Or was it because they nearly always worked in pairs?

He shook his head and sighed. There were too few facts to go on and his suppositions were meaningless. He held the Hawken in his left hand, trying to decide whether to go back to camp and inform Benteen and Sublette or continue scouting the fork. His eyes fell on Samson, who was lying a few yards away. The dog's eyes were on him. They seldom left him nowadays, and he knew Samson had developed quite an attachment to him.

An idea occurred to him. What if the creature was shying away from them because of Samson? Large animals such as grizzlies and panthers were naturally wary of one another, and this might be the same case.

On second thought, Nate discarded the notion. The thing that had made the huge footprint must be incredibly big and extraordinarily powerful. Such a brute would have no reason to fear a dog, or humans for that matter.

"Samson," he said softly, and Samson lifted his head. "Come here, boy."

The black dog rose and padded over.

"Here," Nate said, touching the track. "What do you think?"

Samson lowered his head and touched Nate's hand with his nose. Then he stiffened and sniffed loudly, not once but several times, while moving his head around the edge of the track. Stepping back, he vented a short growl.

"I feel the same way," Nate said. Facing up the stream, he resumed walking. He wanted to go farther, to check for more beaver. If, along the way, he happened to find another such track, so much the better.

For the better part of an hour he hiked, finding a series of lodges and dams just like on the other fork. Once he saw a large beaver swimming out near a lodge, but the beaver paid no notice to him. Twice he saw elk back in the brush.

He found no more huge tracks, which disappointed him. The single impression had been insufficient to tell him much about the creature. He could guess at its size and weight, but he would have a better idea of both if he could find a set of tracks and determine the length of its stride. Competent trackers, by taking account of the distance between two tracks, could accurately gauge the height of the animal or person making them.

He would also have liked to trail the beast to its lair. If he could get to it before it got to them, he could judge for himself whether the thing deserved to be shot or whether it was actually a harmless animal. Given that they had been in the valley for weeks without being bothered, he inclined to the opinion the Crow stories were greatly exaggerated.

At last he turned back and retraced his route to the camp. Halfway back he stopped, bothered by a vague feeling of being watched. He scoured the undergrowth but saw no reason for the feeling. Since Samson was not acting as if something might be out there, he ascribed his jitters to another case of bad nerves and continued on.

"How does it look?" Milo asked as soon as Nate appeared.

"There are as many beaver up the left fork as there were up the right, if not more."

Tom, who was near the rekindled fire and busy repairing a small hole in his left moccasin, nodded and beamed. "I can almost feel that money in my pocket. Red Moon has done us a big favor by bringing us here."

"Maybe we should pay him a little extra," Milo suggested.

"Are you crazy?" Tom rejoined. "He's earning enough to keep him in whiskey for the rest of his life. Ten percent is plenty. A bit too much, in my estimation."

"Ten percent is what we agreed on and ten percent is what we'll give him," Milo said.

Nate was tempted to tell them the reason Red Moon wanted the money, until it hit him that the Crow might not care for them to know. Red Moon had been with Milo and Tom for many weeks before they showed up at the cabin, and in all that time the warrior had not bothered to let them know about his ailing grandson. Why Red Moon had told him instead of them, he didn't know. But he wasn't about to violate the Crow's confidence. If Red Moon elected to tell them, that was his business.

"You're too soft, Milo," Tom was saying. "He's just an Injun. What does he know about money?"

Resentful of the disparaging comments about Red

Moon, Nate elected to change the topic of conversation and did so by announcing, "I saw a strange track."

They stared at him, both puzzled by the declaration.

"A what?" Tom said.

"A track bigger than any I've ever come across," Nate elaborated.

"Do you mean a bear print?" Milo asked.

"No. There was no sign of claws. I have no idea what made it. I'd like to show it to you so you can see for yourselves and give me your opinion."

Tom snickered. "Perhaps it was the thing Red Moon is so scared of."

"Perhaps," Nate said.

"You're joking, King," Tom stated.

"No, I'm not."

"Where did you find this—" Milo began, then fell silent when the drumming of hoofs sounded from the south.

Instantly on his feet, Nate spied Red Moon galloping toward their camp. The Crow was using his quirt as if trying to ride his horse into the ground.

"Trouble," Milo said, clutching his rifle.

"Damn it all," Tom muttered, hastily slipping his left foot into his moccasin even though he hadn't completed the repair.

Nate advanced to the edge of the clearing. He gazed past the Crow, seeking any sign of pursuing Blackfeet, but there was none. The Crow arrived with a clatter of hoofs and jerked hard on the reins.

"A Blackfoot war party is coming."

"How many and how far off are they?" Nate inquired, suppressing a swell of anxiety. Rare was the trapping party that didn't run into some sort of grave difficulty. They'd been exceptionally lucky so far and hadn't lost a single man or animal. All that might be about to change.

"There are ten warriors, all well armed," Red Moon

disclosed, and slid to the grass. "I saw them when I climbed a tree to see how close I was to the man I followed. From a high branch I saw him riding toward a group waiting down the stream."

Nate didn't need to be told the rest. That lone brave, who had been sent on ahead to scout the trail, would rejoin the other Blackfeet and the whole group would head on up the valley with dreams of counting coup on white men foremost in their heads. And once the war party reached the spot where Red Moon had turned around and ridden back they would know the brave had been seen and the white men were forewarned. They would press on swiftly, eager to take scalps.

"I say we make a stand right here," Tom declared.

Nate studied the lay of the land. They were ringed by trees, but there was plenty of cover for the Blackfeet to creep right up on them before they knew it. And they would be unable to adequately protect the horses. "They'd overrun us in no time," he said.

"What do we do?" Milo asked.

In his mind's eye Nate reviewed the course of the right fork and remembered a point where the stream curved to the northeast. There were large boulders flanking the east bank, not many but enough to hide behind and ambush the Blackfeet when they showed up. He voiced his idea.

"Sounds fine to me," Milo said, and stooped to pick up his saddle and blanket.

"That spot is half a day's ride away," Tom groused. "Isn't there somewhere nearer?"

"None that are any better," Nate said, "and we'll need the most defensible position we can find if we're to hold off ten Blackfeet."

In silence they worked, rapidly loading their traps, food, and gear onto the pack animals and saddling their horses. When they were all mounted, Nate took the lead and cantered along the bank. Samson padded on his right.

"Nate, you've done more Indian fighting than we have," Milo said. "What are our chances against this bunch? Realistically, I mean."

"Not very good."

"If they gain the upper hand and it looks as if we'll be taken prisoner, promise me you'll put a ball in my brain before they get their hands on us."

Nate shifted to glance at the lean Pennsylvania.

"I've heard about the tortures those red devils inflict," Milo said. "They stake a man out and do all sorts of hideous acts. They poke out eyeballs, cut off noses, and slice off tongues. They've been known to rip a man's guts out while he's still alive. And I heard about that Frenchman they skinned alive." He shuddered. "I don't want any of that to happen to me. I couldn't take it."

"I promise," Nate said.

"Those heathens won't get us if I can help it," Tom asserted. "I'll fight until I drop, and I'll take as many of their black souls with me as I can."

The sun climbed steadily higher. They slowed every now and then, saving their mounts in case a burst of speed should be needed. Several times Red Moon left them and rode back to see if the Blackfeet were gaining. Each time he caught up again and informed them the trail was clear.

Except for taking brief breaks to allow the horses to drink, they didn't stop. By late afternoon the boulders came into view.

"We made it," Milo said in relief.

Beyond the boulders was a field where they tied the horses, leaving both their saddles and the packs on for the time being. Nate took his rifle and took up a post behind the boulder nearest the stream. Samson reclined nearby and dozed, unaffected by their tension.

"Now all we can do is wait," Milo remarked.

Nate leaned on his left shoulder, tucked the Hawken in the crook of his arm, and settled down for a possibly long wait. The Blackfeet were experienced, canny fighters, and once they believed they were close to overhauling their intended victims they would slow down and proceed cautiously. He didn't expect them until near dark.

Warmed by the sun and feeling a bit fatigued after the long ride, Nate gazed at the stream and considered taking a drink. He forgot about his thirst the next moment, however, when he saw something that prickled the short hairs at the nape of his neck.

Another enormous track.

Chapter Fourteen

Projecting into the stream from the bank was a finger of land around which the water flowed at a slow rate. On that narrow strip was the footprint, the same size as the one found on the left fork, the toes pointing downstream.

Nate was tempted to run out for a closer look, but the Blackfeet might show up at any minute. A disturbing insight struck him. What if the creature had been shadowing them? What if that track had been made as the thing trailed them toward the junction? The only way he could know for sure was to closely examine the track later.

The gurgling water provoked another train of thought. Both tracks he'd discovered were located near water. Was it possible the creature preferred to travel along the streams and creeks so it wouldn't leave many clues of its passing? Trappers, when chased by Indians, often resorted to riding along a watercourse in an attempt to lose pursuers. But he'd never heard of an animal adopting a similar practice.

He glanced at the others. Milo was staring intently to the south. Tom was sharpening his butcher knife. Red Moon was staring at the track. The Crow looked at him and neither of them spoke. There was no need. They both knew what had made it—at least they knew the creature existed and was aware of their presence in the valley. At the moment, however, it was the least of their worries.

Slowly the glowing sun sank toward the western horizon. The shadows lengthened and the depths of the forest became dark and foreboding.

"Where the hell are they?" Tom muttered.

"Are you in a hurry to be killed?" Milo whispered.

"No, but if we're going to be in a shooting scrape I'd rather get it over with now than wait," Tom responded.

Nate shared those sentiments. As the minutes crawled past with all the speed of sluggish earthworms, he became increasingly restless. It was apparent the Blackfeet had no intention of launching their attack before dawn since they rarely if ever fought at night. When the sun had dipped so low that only a rosy rim remained, he straightened. "They plan to try for our hair tomorrow," he stated.

"Why are they waiting?" Milo asked.

"Why should they rush things and lose more men than they have to?" Nate rejoined. "There's only one way out of this valley, and they must know it. They have us boxed in." He moved toward their horses, Samson walking in his footsteps. "No, they'll rest up tonight and tackle us tomorrow, probably after they spy on us a while. They'll pick the time for our fight, and there's not a blessed thing we can do about it."

"Grizzly Killer is correct," Red Moon said. "The Blackfeet will attack when they are ready and not before." He paused. "Maybe they have sent someone for more warriors."

Nate hadn't considered that angle. It worried him profoundly. If there were more Blackfeet in the general area, and if another ten or more joined the first bunch, the likelihood of escaping from the valley was almost non-existent.

"Do we stay put or move elsewhere?" Milo inquired.

The encroaching veil of night allowed only one answer. "We stay right where we are," Nate said. "It would be useless to go traipsing around in the dark searching for a better spot."

Milo nodded in agreemnt. "Can we have a fire?"

"A small one, if you build it behind the boulders where the glow can't be seen and keep it small so there isn't much smoke," Nate instructed him.

For the next half an hour they were busy tending to their stock. The horses were watered and picketed to graze. Since they weren't anticipating an attack, the packs and saddles were removed. Milo got a fire going and made a pot of coffee and cooked venison steaks carved from a buck Red Moon had shot with an arrow the day before.

None of them were talkative. Each ate quietly, immersed in his thoughts. Every so often Tom Sublette would turn to the south and glare into the darkness, his thoughts transparent.

Nate dwelled on their predicament and tried to devise a way out. Trying to sneak past the Blackfeet at night would be impossible since they were bound to post braves at various points across the valley floor until morning. He weighed the merits of sneaking down to the Blackfoot camp and shooting as many as possible, finally deciding the risks were greater than any prospect of reducing the odds.

When the meal was over, Milo took the utensils

down to the stream to wash them. Tom went along as escort.

No sooner were they out of hearing range than Red Moon swiveled to face Nate. "None of us may leave this place alive."

"I know."

"The Blackfeet will find us. Then they will surround us and close in on us when our guard is down."

"I know."

"I am a warrior, Grizzly Killer. I have counted twenty-seven coup in my life. I have fought the Blackfeet, the Bloods, the Utes, and the Cheyennes. I have killed men with my knife, my tomahawk, my bow, and my rifle. It is not in me to sit by and let my enemies pick the time and place for me to die."

Nate lowered his coffee cup. "What do you propose?"

"Before the sun rises we must be awake and have our horses ready to ride. Then we must sneak down the valley, past the Blackfoot camp, and head for the valley entrance," Red Moon proposed.

"They'll probably spot us."

"Would you rather sit here and wait to die?"

"No," Nate admitted. "I like your plan." He leaned against the boulder and let the fire warm his feet. Although once he would have scoffed at the notion, he was a fighter. Repeatedly he'd been thrust into life-threatening situations where he either had to resist or die, and each time he'd chosen to struggle with all his might to live. Yes, he was a fighter, and it galled him to contemplate defeat. He had a wife and a son who loved him. He fully intended to see them again, and he would fight tooth and claw to preserve his life.

The two Pennsylvanians returned. Nate outlined the ploy they would use, then offered to take the first watch while the others slept. They spread out their blankets at the edge of the firelight so they wouldn't be easy targets should a Blackfoot creep up on them, leaving Nate alone at the boulder.

He tried not to dwell on the war party. Instead, he mused on the whims of circumstance that often dictated the course of a person's life. A man or woman never knew from one day to the next what subsequent days would bring, and each was at the mercy of a capricious fate that held no regard for anyone. How many trappers had he known, good men who worked hard, who were honest to a fault, but who had perished at the hands of marauding Indians? How many decent trappers had lost their lives through a freakish accident, never to see their kin back in the States again? What had those men done to deserve deaths? Nothing. And yet they went to meet their Maker ahead of their allotted time.

A month ago he had been comfortable and safe in his cabin. Now he was on the verge of battling bloodthirsty Blackfeet and might well lose his life. And all because of a series of circumstances over which he had no control. Had the Pennsylvanians never gotten it into their heads to enlist his help, he would still be comfortable and safe in his cabin.

Still, the decision to come with them had been his. When a man got right down to the bone of the matter, decisions determined a man's fate more than circumstances. Decisions were reactions to circumstances, and it was those reactions that determined whether a man lived or died, grew rich or poor, lived happily or miserably.

Lost in reflection, he didn't realize how much time elapsed until with a start he saw the fire had burned down to glowing embers. He rose and gathered more wood, then fed the embers until a crackling fire again brightened the night. Walking to Milo, he shook the lean trapper.

"What?" Milo mumbled, his eyelids fluttering.

"You agreed to take the second watch," Nate said. "Spell me."

"Oh. Yes," Milo said sleepily. Rousing himself, he pushed to his feet, wiped his eyes with the back of his hands, and took his rifle over to where Nate had sat. "Anything?"

"Nothing. Keep your eyes skinned."

"You don't need to tell me twice," Milo replied, and stretched.

Nate spread out his bedroll and lay on his back, the Hawken at his side. Samson claimed the left side of the blanket, his back pressed flush against Nate.

"Did you see this fire?" Milo asked.

"What's wrong with it? I just gathered more dead branches," Nate answered.

"No, not *our* fire. This other fire."

Milo was standing out past the boulder when Nate joined him. In the far distance to the south, flickering faintly, was another camp fire.

"The Blackfeet," Milo deduced.

"Yep."

"How far do you reckon they are?"

"It's hard to judge at night," Nate said.

"I'm surprised they'd let us know where they are," Milo said.

"They're not afraid of us. The Blackfeet are the most murderous lot of Indians this side of the divide, but there is no denying their courage. They don't care if we know where they are. If we should attack them, so much the better. They won't need to come looking for us."

Milo cocked an eye. "You give me the impression you admire these savages."

"I admire courage in any man, Indian or white," Nate responded, and rotated. He took a stride when his ears caught a fluttering sound, so indistinct as to make him believe he had imagined hearing it. Pausing, he turned and listened.

"What is it?" Milo inquired.

"I don't know," Nate said, and then he heard a slightly louder sound, a long, high-pitched, wavering cry.

"Dear Lord!" Milo exclaimed. "What in the world was that?"

From behind them came the clipped voice of Red Moon. "A scream," he said, walking forward.

"The Blackfeet must have captured someone else," Milo speculated. "Perhaps another trapper."

The wind, which had been wafting from north to south, chose that instant to die completely and the air hung still as death around them. Without the wind to stir the trees and grass, an eerie silence ensued. In that silence, from the direction of the speck of light to the south, there came a hair-raising series of terrified screams and screeches attended by the boom of gunfire. Once, as clear as a church bell on a Sunday morning, a horse whinnied as if in abject fright.

"What's happening over there?" Milo breathed.

The frantic screams and screeches rent the night interminably. Their own horses neighed and stamped in nervous agitation.

Milo cast a bewildered gaze at Nate. "It's like they're in a war or something."

"Or something."

"Now it begins," Red Moon declared solemnly.

"What begins?" Milo asked.

The Crow didn't answer.

Every time Nate heard one of those horrifying cries, a twinge rippled along his spine. His skin crawled as if of its own volition. There could only be one explanation in his estimation, and the knowledge created an icy chill in the depths of his soul.

"What the hell is happening?" Tom Sublette demanded as he stepped past the boulder. "Why are the horses—"

"Shhhhh," Milo hissed. "Listen!"

The distant din went on for another minute or two before diminishing in volume and tapering off on a single plaintive note of raw despair.

"What *was* that?" Tom inquired.

"The Blackfeet," Nate said. He moved to the fire and squatted on his heels to pour coffee into his tin cup.

"I don't understand," Milo said. "Why would the Blackfeet be carrying on that way?"

"It was a trick," Tom stated. "They want us to ride to their camp to investigate so they can spring an ambush on us."

"You didn't hear as much as we did," Milo disputed him. "It was no trick. Those devils were fighting for their lives."

"Against who?" Tom demanded.

Nate let some of the warm coffee trickle into his mouth and swished the brew with his tongue before swallowing. "We must go find out."

"Are you touched in the head? It's a trap, I tell you," Tom insisted. "Go there and some buck will be showing your hair to his sweetheart when he gets back to his village."

Red Moon knelt and commenced folding his blanket. "We must go."

"You too?" Tom responded. "What's gotten into the two of you? At least wait until morning when we can see."

"Now," Nate said, and swallowed once more. He spilled the rest of the coffee on the grass and stood.

Milo frowned and stepped closer. "What is it? What do Red Moon and you know that we don't? What will we find down there?"

"I don't know," Nate said. But he did. He knew,

deep within the well of his being. He knew, and he cursed himself for being the biggest fool who'd ever lived.

Tom made an angry gesture. "Will someone please tell me what the hell is going on? Since when do we go riding around in the middle of the night?"

"If you don't want to tag along you're welcome to stay here by yourself," Nate told him.

Glancing to the south, Tom took less than five seconds to reach a decision. "No thanks. Where you gents go, I go. I just hope you know what the hell you're doing."

So do I, Nate thought. So do I.

Chapter Fifteen

A crimson hue tinged the eastern horizon when Nate drew rein and tilted his head to sniff the air. He smelled the lingering scent of wood smoke and something else, a revolting stench that nearly made him gag. Hundreds of feet away, rising sluggishly on the slight air currents, was a thin column of gray smoke.

"The Blackfoot camp," Milo said softly.

Nate nodded and attached the lead rope to his pack-horses to a low branch. The Crow was already moving to the right to approach the site from a different angle. He looked at the Pennsylvanians and pointed to their left.

Tom promptly tied his pack animals to a tree limb and waited for Milo to do likewise, and together they started circling.

The feel of the invariably reliable Hawken in Nate's left hand, which usually inspired him with confidence when he confronted danger, failed to assuage his growing uneasiness. Placing the rifle across his thighs, he glanced down at Samson and rode onward. The nauseating smell grew stronger and stronger with each stride his stallion took, forcing him to breathe shallowly to keep his stomach from tossing.

He was within 25 yards of the wispy tendril of smoke when the stallion suddenly shied from an object lying directly in their path, an object he'd assumed to be a broken limb. Stopping, he bent forward and involuntarily gasped.

The limb wasn't from any tree. Lying in the shadow of a pine, the skin bronzed from constant exposure to the sun, was a human arm. The fingers were locked like claws. Ribbons of severed flesh dangled from the top of the upper arm where it had been violently torn from the shoulder.

Nate skirted the grisly legacy of the nocturnal battle and made for the smoke. He hadn't gone another five yards when he came on the body to which the arm had once belonged.

The Blackfoot lay on his back, his lifeless eyes fixed blankly on the canopy of limbs above him. A puddle of blood had seeped into the ground from his ravaged shoulder. Torn leggings covered his legs.

Nate stared at the man's face and scowled. The Blackfoot wore an expression of stark terror, his features contorted in a grotesque mockery of a human visage. What had the warrior seen in those last moments of life that provoked such terror?

He prodded the stallion with his heels. Soon a clearing opened up before him. All that remained of the fire were flickering coals and the ascending smoke. Littering the area around that fire in all directions, sprawled in postures of gruesome death, were more Blackfeet.

Nate stopped at the edge of the trees and tucked the stock of the Hawken against his side, his thumb on the hammer. He surveyed the clearing and bile rose in his throat. With an effort, he swallowed it. Never had he seen such carnage. Never would he care to view such unspeakable slaughter again.

The clearing might aptly be termed a battlefield. That a tremendous fight had occurred was evidenced by the many dead and the many pools of drying blood, by the arrows and lances and guns scattered about, and by the torn parfleches, the ripped blankets, and the occasional articles of scattered clothing.

There were 17 Blackfoot warriors in all, young and old alike, most splotched with bloodstains. Quite a few had dried blood ringing their parted lips. Every one bore evidence of having received a vicious beating. Bruises marred their faces and torsos. There were bite marks on nearly each brave, and over half showed several spots where their flesh had been ripped from their bodies. Many had broken arms or legs, as displayed by the unnatural angles at which the limbs were extended. One warrior was on his stomach but his head had been twisted completely around so that his wide-eyed gaze was fixed on his heels.

Nate heard retching and glanced to his left. Milo was hunched over a bush, his back to the clearing. Sublette, still on horseback, seemed pale. Nate swung to the right and saw Red Moon walking among the fallen. Easing from the saddle, he stepped into the open.

A husky brave nearby had been gutted, his abdomen ruptured. A pile of pale, pulpy intestines rested on the crushed grass beside him. Another warrior had a caved-in chest. His ribs and sternum curved sharply inward and jagged tips of busted rib bones poked from his taut skin. A third brave had lost half of his forehead and his left cheek.

A fly flew close to Nate's face and he swatted it aside. It recovered in midair and flew to a corpse, where it settled on the warrior's smashed nose. There were more flies on the same man, and gazing over the clearing Nate spotted scores if not hundreds of flies flitting about on the bodies.

"Who could have done this?" Tom Sublette asked.

"Who?" Nate said.

"Which tribe? The Utes don't range this far north, or so I've been told," Tom mentioned. "Could it have been the Crows?"

Red Moon heard the query. "My people did not do this."

"Then who? Are there tribes to the west I don't know about who can lick the Blackfeet so handily?" Tom inquired.

"This was not done by men," Red Moon informed him.

Sublette halted, blinked, and grinned. "You're not going to try and convince me that the goblin who supposedly lives in this valley was responsible, are you?"

"See for yourself," Nate said, halting near the fire where there was bare earth. Next to the shattered leg of a Blackfoot was the outline of a by-now-familiar track.

"See what?" Tom said, and walked over. Consternation lined his countenance and he squatted. "This can't be what it looks like."

"It's the same sort of track I saw up the left fork," Nate stated.

"There must be a logical explanation for it," Tom said, his tone lacking much conviction. "Maybe it's a bear print."

"Then where are the claw marks?"

"I don't know. Maybe it lost its claws in an accident."

"You know better."

The stocky Pennsylvania touched the track, then

stood. His eyes were troubled when he faced Nate. "The creature did all of this?" he asked, sweeping the clearing with an emphatic wave of his arm.

Red Moon walked toward them, and for the first time his emotions were plain for anyone to read. He was profoundly upset, as his strained tone confirmed. "Yes," he answered Sublette. "There are not many tracks of the thing that lurks in the dark, but the sign is clear enough to know what happened."

"Tell us," Tom urged.

The Crow nodded at the west side of the clearing, the side nearest the stream. "It came up out of the water and stood for a long time watching the Blackfeet. They did not know it was there. Knowing them as I do, I would say they were busy getting ready for their attack on us. They must have talked until late about their plan. Then, when their weapons were all in order, most of them went to sleep. They would have wanted to be rested when morning came."

"And then?" Tom said when the Crow paused.

Red Moon scanned the ground, pointing at specific points as he talked. "The beast made some noise to draw the guard into the forest. His tracks lead off that way," he said, indicating due north.

"I found him," Nate revealed. "His arm had been torn from its socket."

"With the guard dead, the thing was free to do as it wanted," Red Moon said. He motioned at four Blackfeet lying in a row, each with his throat crushed. "It came into the camp and killed those four before the Blackfeet knew what was happening. Another must have woken up, seen it, and shouted the alarm."

Nate scoured the vegetation, wondering if the thing was still lurking nearby or whether it had gone off to its lair, wherever that might be.

"The rest were awake in no time and fighting for their lives," Red Moon continued as Milo shuffled up to them. "They fought bravely but they were confused and very, very scared."

"What do you mean by they were confused?" Tom inquired, hanging on every word the aged warrior spoke.

Red Moon walked to a corpse and flicked his right foot out to touch an arrow jutting from the Blackfoot's chest. "This one was shot by another member of the war party," he said, and swiveled. "There are more, warriors who were slain by arrows or lances or were shot by a gun."

Nate looked and saw several examples. He'd missed it before because he'd been concentrating on finding evidence of the creature. But Red Moon was right. The scene must have been sheer chaos. Mental images of the frightened Blackfeet fighting valiantly for their lives in the frantic jumble of whirling companions made him see how easily the accidents must have happened.

"The horses ran off, leaving the men on foot," Red Moon detailed as he moved in a circle, his alert eyes missing none of the sign underfoot. "A few ran. The rest stayed. They would not desert their friends."

"But there were twenty or more Blackfeet and only one creature," Tom said in exasperation. "How could one animal lick them?"

Red Moon nodded at a brave whose head had been split open, exposing the brain. "The beast must have knocked many down, breaking their bones or cracking their heads, and then gone around later and finished them off."

"But they must have hit it!" Tom asserted. "They couldn't all miss! Why didn't it die?"

"I do not know," Red Moon said. "But I do know it went from man to man, killing them in its own sweet time. Look there." He pointed at a Blackfoot whose neck and face had been gnawed down to the bone. "It ate parts of them."

"Oh, God," Milo said. "Oh, God."

Tom kicked at the dying fire. "Damn it all! There's no way one animal could have killed so many Blackfeet and gotten off without a scratch. The thing must be lying in the brush, about dead from its wounds."

"Perhaps," Red Moon said.

Milo pressed a hand to his stomach, his mouth curling downward. "You say a few got away?"

"Three. They ran toward the valley entrance."

"Maybe they will come back with others," Milo said.

"No. They have learned their lesson. The only reason they entered the valley was to take our scalps, and now they will never enter again," Red Moon stated.

Milo gave each of them a quizzical glance. "What do we do? Stay or leave?"

"How can you even ask?" Tom rejoined. "We can't give up now, not when there are so many beaver left."

"I don't much care about the beaver anymore," Milo said.

"And I suppose you don't care about the stakes we've been counting on to buy the land we want?" Tom snapped. "If we leave now, we may never raise the money to have our own farms."

With an air of haunted indecision, Milo regarded the bloody carnage. "Is it worth risking our lives for?"

Nate rested the stock of his Hawken between his feet and lightly gripped the barrel in both hands. "Since you've brought it up, Tom, we should decide now whether we stick this out or mount and get out while we still can."

"I vote we stick," Tom replied.

"Milo?" Nate asked.

"Can I talk to Tom in private?"

"Of course."

The Pennsylvanians moved to the east and began arguing in harsh whispers.

"They will decide to stay," Red Moon said.

"I know," Nate responded.

"We are fools if we do."

"I know."

"And I am the biggest fool of all because I will not leave until they have all the hides our packhorses can carry. I need my share of the money for my grandson."

Nate grinned. "You're no bigger a fool than they are."

"How about you?"

"Do you think the thing will leave us alone?"

"No."

"Tom could be right. It might be wounded."

"Yes, but that will not stop it," Red Moon said. "The thing that lurks in the dark hates men. It will not rest until every one of us is dead or gone."

"Why hasn't it come after us? Why attack the Blackfeet first when there were more of them?"

The Crow looked at Samson. The dog was sniffing a corpse. "I do not know."

"But you think it has something to do with Samson?" Nate asked, and included the clearing in a sweep of his hand. "The creature can't be afraid of him." He frowned. "The creature can't be afraid of anything."

"It is not fear. Something else."

"What?" Nate probed, but the Pennsylvanians chose that moment to return.

"We've settled the issue," Tom declared.

"Yes," Milo agreed hesitantly. "We want to continue trapping."

"I too will stay," Red Moon stated.

Nate was suddenly the focus of attention. If he had any smarts he would tell them so long and ride as if the Devil himself was hot on his heels. But he'd given these men his word that he would trap the valley with them and they were counting on him to do his share of the work. If he left now, it would take them twice as long to do it all.

"What do you say, Nate?" Milo inquired.

"Yeah, King," Tom added. "I never took you for a quitter, but a man never knows. How do you vote?"

An invisible ghastly specter seemed to tug at Nate's soul and he felt a stab of cold deep within himself, but he ignored the disquieting sensation. In the certain knowledge of the sequence of events that would ensue, and with a full awareness of the implications for his future, Nate sighed and gave them his answer. "We keep trapping."

Chapter Sixteen

Somber and silent, the four men rode from the scene of slaughter to the junction of the forks in the stream. Each one of them rode with a rifle in hand, senses primed, eyes constantly in motion.

Milo and Tom were most affected. Where before they had frequently joked or sang or related outlandish tales they had heard, they were now grim, their lips compressed, the very postures of their bodies testifying to the nervous tension permeating every pore.

Before leaving the clearing, Red Moon had tracked the creature into the stream where the flowing water had erased its prints on the bottom. So they had no idea in which direction it had gone. Nor, from the few tracks found, could they determine if it had been wounded in the battle with the Blackfeet.

Nate, riding in the lead, noticed Samson seemed unusually alert too. He wondered if the dog sensed their state of mind or whether its own instinct for self-preservation had been aroused by the slaughter.

At the junction they turned and rode up the left fork. Because there were more trees along this fork and the undergrowth was exceptionally heavy near the water, much heavier than it had been up the right fork, they were unable to stick as close to the stream as they would have liked. They were forced to follow the path of least resistance, riding where the trees and brush were thin enough to permit their horses to pass without difficulty. Often they were dozens of yards from the gurgling fork, unable to note the location of beaver lodges and to plan where they would set their traps.

Nate's uneasiness had been eclipsed by constant razor-edged apprehension. He was jumpy and knew it, but he made no attempt to calm his jangled nerves. He well knew that when a man was on edge he was more aware of his surroundings and his reactions were quicker. And he might need that extra bit of wariness and speed should the beast come after them.

They had gone a quarter of a mile when Red Moon, who rarely spoke when they were on the trail, made an observation. "Few birds," he said. "Few squirrels and chipmunks."

Suddenly Nate realized a hush enveloped the forest through which they were passing. On the other fork there had been the continual twitter of birds and the chatter of squirrels and such. Now there was only an oppressive silence rarely broken by the normal forest sounds.

Where were all the small animals?

His mouth had gone dry and he worked his tongue back and forth, getting his saliva to flow again. He licked his lips and berated himself for being an idiot. By all rights he should be on his way to his cabin.

He came to a small clearing and bright sunlight stabbed into his eyes like a red-hot knife. The contrast between the gloomy forest and the clearing was startling. Squinting, he gazed at the trees, noting for the first time that the shadows were deeper and darker than they should be. He twisted in the saddle and peered upward at the regal mountain bordering the left fork on the opposite side of the stream. Over ten thousand feet high and rimmed with snow, the mountain was almost barren except along its lower slopes. It cast an enormous shadow over the entire left fork.

He looked closer. Much of the mountain between the low slopes and the snow consisted of a series of sheer cliffs rising to dizzying heights. Brilliant sunshine reflected off the tops of those cliffs. The lower portions, however, were obscured in inky shadow. He spied a circular patch of black below one cliff that might well be a cave, but the distance was too great for him to be certain.

Once across the clearing he paid attention to the undergrowth and trees hemming him in. If the creature sprang from concealment he would have a second or less to bring his weapons to bear. He must be ready at all times.

Hours went by. They didn't bother to stop for a noon rest. The sun climbed high into the sky, and not until late in the afternoon, when a meadow unfolded before them, did Nate halt and look at his companions.

"How about if we stop here for the night? It's still early, but we're all tired and the horses need a break."

"Fine with me," Milo said, arching his back. "I'd like to walk around and stretch my legs."

"We're awful far from the stream," Tom complained. "It must be two hundreds yards off."

Nate gazed at the intervening woods. Two hundred yards was a lot to cover when there might be an inhuman demon out there just waiting for an opportunity to pounce on one of them. "Since it's my idea to make camp here, I'll water the horses and fill our water bags," he offered.

"I will help you," Red Moon said.

They attended to their tasks with a minimum of conversation. After their saddles and supplies were stripped off their horses, Milo worked on their supper. Tom arranged their gear so it would be close at hand.

Nate took half of their animals and headed for the stream, Samson padding beside him. Red Moon, with the rest of the stock, came along.

The Crow kept looking through the trees toward the cliffs. "We do not need to worry until after the sun sets," he said. "Then the thing will begin to hunt."

"Maybe it ate its fill last night," Nate said. "Maybe it won't come out tonight."

"Maybe."

The dense brush necessitated hard work on their part before they pushed their way through to the water. Nate led his animals in first so Red Moon could stand guard.

Samson moved along the bank, sniffing the ground and testing the air.

"He knows," Red Moon said.

Nate was inclined to hurry the horses, but the animals had worked long and hard and deserved to drink their full. He stood in the stream, the water up to his ankles, and scanned the other side, bothered by a vague sensation of being watched. If the thing was there, he'd never know. The trees, high grass, and weeds presented an unbroken green wall extending for as far as the eye could see. There were also numerous thickets where a large animal could easily conceal itself. Spotting it would be a fluke.

Finally the last of Nate's animals raised its dripping muzzle and he took them onto the bank. Red Moon led the rest of the horses into the stream.

Nate watched the old Crow, thinking of the sacrifice the warrior was making to help his grandson. "My wife and I have some money put aside," he mentioned casually.

Red Moon glanced at him.

"If the worst should happen and we're driven out of the valley before we get enough hides, I'd be happy to give you the money you'll need to reach St. Louis."

The Crow lifted his rifle and became unusually interested in his ramrod. At length he replied in a husky voice. "Thank you, Grizzly Killer, I will keep it in mind."

Soon the horses were done and Nate took the lead back to the meadow. Milo was pouring coffee into a cup. Tom had gathered enough dead branches to last them a week and was still collecting more.

"See anything?" Milo asked.

"Peaceful as could be," Nate responded.

During the meal no one said a word. Each ate with his rifle in ready reach. The sun dipped below the western horizon and plunged the meadow into murky darkness.

Tom Sublette fed more limbs to the fire.

"Who wants first watch?" Nate inquired as the flames hissed and spit sparks into the cool air.

"Me," Milo promptly answered. "I doubt I can sleep much anyway."

"Me either," Tom said.

Nate took a sip from his fourth cup of coffee. He doubted whether he would sleep very much either. Somehow, he must. They all must. Fatigue made men careless, and a single mistake now could well cost any one of them his life.

It was then, as each man was lost in his own troubled thoughts, that a cry arose from the heights of the towering mountain beyond the stream, an eerie cry unlike that of any panther or other wild animal in existence, a drawn-out, wavering cry that rose in volume and diminished abruptly again and again without end.

"What the hell!" Tom blurted out at the first note, and grabbed for his rifle.

Nate stood and turned, his body tingling. It sounded more like a moan than a cry of rage, as if the creature making it was in acute misery.

"It's the thing," Milo said breathlessly.

"It is hurt," Red Moon stated.

On and on the cry lingered until, minutes later, it was replaced by the subtle rustling of the breeze in the trees.

Milo took two steps away from the fire. "That thing must be up there right this minute watching us. It knows we're here."

"That was just the wind," Tom said.

"You know better," Milo replied.

Rising, Tom nodded at the black bulk of the mountain that loomed above them like a menacing giant. "Get a grip on yourself. At times we've both heard the wind whistling through the high peaks. It can make all kinds of sounds."

"Not like that," Milo said.

"It's the wind," Tom insisted.

No one else believed him. Nate could see that. He also guessed that Tom didn't believe it himself. So why was Sublette being so stubborn? Couldn't he face the truth? Or was Tom simply afraid and unwilling to acknowledge his fear?

Red Moon drew a blanket over his shoulders. "It would be wise to have two men stay on guard at a time," he mentioned.

Nate agreed. If one should doze off the other could rouse him. "All right. Milo and Tom, take the first watch, then wake Red Moon and me." He finished the coffee, made himself comfortable in his blankets, and closed his eyes. Despite his weariness, he doubted he would sleep a wink. He couldn't, not with that thing up on the heights above them. Not in a million years.

A firm hand on his shoulder brought Nate around. He blinked and sat up, gazing in bewilderment at the low fire. "What is it?" he asked drowsily.

"The night is half done," Milo told him. "It's your turn to stand guard."

Half done? Nate tilted his head to see the stars in the heavens and recognized from the position of the Big Dipper that Benteen was right. He'd slept after all, for hours, but he felt no more refreshed than he had when he'd lain down. In fact, he felt worse. His muscles ached and his bladder was about to burst.

Red Moon was pouring coffee for both of them.

"The night has been quiet," Milo reported. "Once we thought we heard something moving through the brush to the north of us, but the crackling stopped."

Yawning, Nate rose. He swung his arms in circles and stamped his legs to get his blood flowing.

"Where's your dog, King?" Tom asked.

Pivoting, Nate searched the grass revealed in the flickering firelight but saw no sign of Samson. "I don't know," he said uncertainly. "I thought he was right at my side when I fell asleep."

"We noticed he was gone about an hour ago," Milo disclosed. "Didn't think too much of it at the time because he's always wandering off when the mood strikes him."

"But not at night," Nate said, anger flaring at their neglect in not letting him know sooner. "Why didn't you wake me?"

Milo shrugged. "We didn't think it was important. Sorry."

Nate inserted two fingers into his mouth and whistled shrilly, hoping the dog would return. He'd never had cause to whistle to it before so he didn't know what it would do. If he was lucky, the dog's previous owner had taught it to respond to whistling. He waited expectantly, hearing only the wind.

"Samson might be a mile off by now," Milo said. "Perhaps he didn't hear you."

Undaunted, Nate whistled again, even louder than the first time. Again he waited.

"Try once more," Milo urged after a while.

The whistle pierced the night, louder than the hoot of an owl or the screech of a bird of prey, carried by the wind across the valley to the steep slopes of the massive mountain. A minute went by. Then two.

Nate stooped to retrieve his Hawken. "Keep the fires going. I'll be back as soon as I find Samson."

"You're not going out there?" Milo asked in amazement.

Nodding, Nate took a stride, but the old Crow barred his path.

"It would be foolish, Grizzly Killer, to go into the forest before daylight. The thing that lurks in the dark might be waiting for one of us to make such a mistake. Samson can take care of himself."

Nate paused. Red Moon made sense, but he was loathe to stand idle when the dog might need him. He'd grown attached to the mutt over the past few weeks and he intended to take it back to the cabin and surprise Winona and Zach.

"Yeah," Tom chimed in. "I don't care much for the dog, but we can't stand to lose you. So stay here and wait for the mangy sack of fur."

Opening his mouth to issue a sharp retort, Nate froze when from the cliffs high above them there came a whistle in every respect exactly like his own.

Chapter Seventeen

"My God!" Milo exclaimed.

"It must be an echo," Tom said.

Spinning, Milo glared at his friend. "Damn your hide! You know what's up there as well as we do! It's not the wind, and it's not an echo."

"Has to be an echo," Tom stubbornly argued. "Since when do animals whistle like we do?"

Another whistle wafted down from the high elevations, distinct in the crisp mountain air, a perfect copy of Nate's own whistling only louder.

Milo faced the Crow warrior. "What the hell is up there?" he demanded in a strained voice. "What are we up against?"

"I wish I could tell you. No one has ever seen the beast and lived."

"You must know more. There must be something you're not telling us," Milo said, and jabbed a finger at the mountain. "How can a mere animal rout twenty

Blackfeet? How can an animal whistle like that?" He paused, his fists clenched, shaking from the intensity of his emotion. "What the hell *is* it?"

Red Moon bowed his head.

"I've had enough," Milo snapped, glancing at Sublette. "I don't care what you say. We're fools if we stay. Let's mount up and ride out before it's too late."

Tom stepped over and put a hand on Benteen's shoulder. "What's gotten into you? We have an agreement."

"To hell with the agreement!" Milo roared. "Didn't you see the bodies of those poor Blackfeet? Didn't you see their crushed skulls and busted limbs? Whatever killed them is a monster! A living, breathing monster that will do the same thing to us unless we leave this valley." He stared at the peaks, his eyes wide. "That's it! That's the answer! The thing calls this valley home and it doesn't like intruders. If we leave we'll be safe. It won't follow us. I know it."

"I'm not leaving," Tom said softly.

Milo whirled, his face creased in stark disbelief. "Weren't you listening to me? We must go."

"Listen to yourself," Tom said. "You were all set to fight it out with a Blackfoot war party when we were badly outnumbered, but now you're willing to turn tail, to turn your back on a fortune in prime pelts because of a lowly animal?"

"We don't know if it is an animal."

"What else, then? A ghost? Ghosts don't crush skulls and rip arms from bodies. This thing is flesh and blood like you and me, and like us it can be killed. All it takes is a well-placed ball in its head."

Nate saw Milo frown, saw sorrowful resignation in the man's eyes, and he felt sorry for him. Milo knew they were making the biggest mistake of their lives by staying, but he couldn't convince his best friend. And since they were good friends, Milo couldn't very well ride off and leave Sublette to face the creature alone. Milo was trapped by his friendship, just as Nate was committed because he had given his word and Red Moon because of his ailing grandson. All three wanted to leave. None of them could.

"If you say so," Milo said to Tom in a forlorn fashion. Stepping to his bedroll, he rolled out his blankets and turned in without another word, cradling his rifle in his arms.

Tom made a clucking noise in reproach, then also spread out his blankets. After lying on his back he placed his right forearm over his eyes, and within a minute he sound asleep.

Coffee was in order, Nate decided, savoring the stimulating taste, his gaze roving over the meadow. The horses were all at rest. Nothing moved in the trees. Although he listened intently, he did not hear the whistle repeated.

For the rest of the night Nate drank coffee to keep himself awake and paced around the camp, seldom standing still for more than a few seconds. Worry over Samson bothered him and he longed to see the big dog loping toward him from the forest.

Eventually dawn created a crimson blaze in the sky to the east. Normally, the birds would rouse to life and chirp gaily to greet the new day. But here, in the oppressive shadow of the sinister mountain, few did so. A robin here. A sparrow there. For the most part the forest was as silent as a tomb.

Nate woke up Benteen and Sublette. Neither was in a pleasant frame of mind. Milo grumbled a sour "Good morning." Tom scowled at the world in general. All four of them huddled around the fire to drink coffee and munch on jerked venison.

At last Milo said, "Do we continue up the stream or should we begin trapping right where we are?"

"We go upstream," Tom responded. "Why start here

when we're only about halfway up the fork? Think of all the beaver we'll lose."

"I'm thinking of staying alive," Milo said.

"Now don't start again."

Nate could see an argument blossoming. He held up a hand to draw their attention. "Why don't we compromise? We can use this spot as our base camp for a while and trap the stream in both directions. If all goes well, if we trap for a couple of days and the thing that killed the Blackfeet doesn't give us any trouble, we can press on to the end of the fork."

"I like the idea," Milo said.

"Well, I don't," Tom declared. "But I know better than to waste my breath trying to change your minds. If you promise me that we'll go up the fork once we've caught all the beaver there are in this stretch of the stream, I'll agree."

"I said we would," Nate reminded him.

"All right. Milo and I will lay our traps northwest of the camp. The Crow and you can lay yours to the southeast," Tom proposed.

Nate's temper flared. "The Crow, as you constantly refer to him, has a name."

"And we all know what it is, don't we?" Tom retorted. Upending his coffee cup over the fire as he rose, he glanced at Benteen. "Come on, Milo. I find the company here as stale as week-old bread." He walked off to the pile of trapping gear.

"Sorry, Nate," Milo said, and trailed his companion.

Nate waited until they departed, each burdened with six traps, before he put his cup down and opened the pack containing his Newhouses. He issued a half dozen to Red Moon, took six for himself, then remembered to completely extinguish the fire before making for the stream.

They emerged from the undergrowth close to a large beaver damn. Nate found a likely spot and placed his first Newhouse of the day. Sticking close to the water's edge, they hiked southeast and took turns positioning the rest of their traps. By the time they were done the sun was almost to the midday position. Not once had they seen or heard anything out of the ordinary.

Nate lent Red Moon a hand in climbing out of the frigid water after the Crow set the final one. "Let's go hunting after we reach camp," he suggested. "I'm tired of jerky, and since the beast knows we're here there's no reason not to fire our guns."

"Fresh elk meat would be nice."

About to agree, Nate gazed at the brush on the far side and spied movement in a thicket. Every muscle in his body tensed. He swung the Hawken to his shoulder, cocked the hammer, and took a bead on a dark form flitting through the vegetation toward the water.

"Don't shot," Red Moon said.

From between two pines near the water appeared Samson. He spotted them instantly and without hesitation plunged into the gently flowing water. His legs kicking in powerful strokes, he swam toward where they stood.

Relief made Nate smile. Dropping to one knee, he gestured for the dog to keep coming. "That's it, boy," he encouraged. "You're doing fine."

"Something follows the dog," Red Moon said.

Nate glanced at the forest rimming the opposite bank, his blood turning cold at the sight of the same thicket through which Samson had passed now swaying from side to side as something else moved through it. Standing, he clutched the Hawken and waited for whatever it was to show itself. But the thicket stopped moving and all was still.

"It watches us," Red Moon declared.

"Do you see it?"

"No. But I know."

Nate longed for a glimpse of the creature, just

enough to see what it was. He thought he saw a pine tree shake, but the motion ceased so abruptly he wasn't sure.

Splashing loudly, Samson reached the shore and clambered onto the bank. He paused to shake himself, spraying water in all directions.

Some drops spattered on Nate's face. He tore his eyes from the far bank so he could give the dog an affectionate rub under the chin. "Where have you been?" he demanded as if talking to an errant child. "I've been worried about you."

"We should leave, Grizzly Killer," Red Moon said.

Nate nodded. Benteen and Sublette should be told that the creature had descended from the heights and was in the area. He backed from the stream until he bumped against a tree, then spun and hurried for camp. Samson stayed close to him. Where *had* the dog gone? he wondered. Up the mountain? Why? Had it somehow trailed the creature by scent to its lair, and then the beast had followed Samson back down? No, that couldn't be. The creature would have killed Samson.

At length he saw the meadow through the trees and hastened his pace. He was still 20 yards off when he perceived that all was not well. First he noticed the horses. They were bunched together, their heads up, their ears pricked, their attention on the woods to the northwest. Then, through a gap in the trees, the camp itself came into view.

Nate halted in alarm. The contents of their packs lay all over the ground! He placed his right hand on a flintlock and broke into a run, bursting from the brush onto a scene of total, wanton destruction.

Every pack, every parflache, every pouch had been upended. The food had been trampled into the dust. Their clothes and blankets had been shredded and scattered about. The water bags had been torn apart and flung aside. Even worse, many of their pelts had been ripped in half. And an axe handle had been broken in two as a man might snap a twig.

"The beast did this," Red Moon said.

"How?" Nate responded in exasperation. "It was behind us. How did it do this?" He moved among the debris, seeking anything that could be salvaged. But the creature had done a thorough job of destroying every last article they possessed. Even the coffeepot had been smashed.

To the northwest there arose a crashing in the forest as something barreled through the brush toward their camp.

The thing! Nate's mind shrieked, and he whirled with the Hawken leveled. A running figure materialized, a figure in buckskins, and seconds later Milo Benteen dashed into the open. He took several paces, spotted them, and halted. His breath came in great gasps. There were thin cuts on his cheeks where the brush had lashed his face, and his hat was gone.

"Milo?" Nate said, running over to him. "What is it? What happened?" He looked into the forest. "Where's Tom?"

Benteen inhaled raggedly and tried to speak but failed. His features were pale, almost the color of milk. He motioned to his rear and croaked, "Gone. Tom is gone."

"What do you mean?" Nate asked, grasping the terrified man by the arm. "Tell us what happened!"

"The thing," Milo said, tears forming in his eyes. "The thing," he repeated softly, and sank to his knees, his head bowed.

Nate hefted his rifle and came to an immediate decision. "I'm going after Tom," he told Red Moon. "You stay here and try to bring Milo around."

"Be careful."

"You too. Keep an eye on the trees," Nate advised.

He leaned down and shook Milo. "Where did you see Tom last?"

Benteen stared blankly at the grass and didn't answer.

"How far up the stream did you go?" Nate persisted.

"He is in shock," Red Moon said.

"Damn," Nate muttered, and took off in the direction of the stream. He checked to verify Samson was tagging along, then ran all out, bounding over logs and skirting trees and thickets, the Hawken always gripped in both hands. He knew the thing was close by. He could feel it in his bones. A lapse of alertness now would spell his certain death.

He reached the fork and stopped. In the soft earth next to the stream were two sets of tracks, both moccasin prints. Tom and Milo had been moving upstream seeking places to put their traps.

In order to make better time, Nate jumped into the water and then ventured upstream. The undergrowth hugging the bank dipped low in many spots, nearly touching the surface, and he shied well clear of those points, wary of being jumped by the beast. Trailing the Pennsylvanians was simplicity itself. They'd made no effort to hide their tracks and there were many in evidence at the water's edge. He came to where they had placed their first trap, and halted.

Something had wrenched the stake from the earth, hauled the trap out, and bent the heavy steel as if it had been mere paper. The crumpled contraption now lay on the bank, completely useless. A partial print in the mud told the story.

Nate realized the creature had been shadowing the Pennsylvanians, observing them lay the trap line. After they had set this one and gone on, it had probably waited until they were out of sight and then slipped from concealment to do its dirty work. He studied the trap and discovered the jaws had been sprung prior to being twisted into so much useless metal. The beast must have used a stick to push the disk down and release the trigger.

He straightened in astonishment. There were many tales of wolves and wolverines that had raided trap lines and taken dead beaver off to eat, but in those instances the beaver were always torn from the traps and parts of their bodies were still held fast by the closed jaws. Never had he heard of an animal deliberately springing a trap. The creature must have done so to prevent the jaws from closing on it when it twisted the metal.

Nate stared at the forest, staggered by the discovery. This thing—this fiend—must be extraordinarily intelligent, far more intelligent than any animal he'd ever encountered. He dared not underestimate its intellect.

Samson began testing the air with his nose.

What did the dog smell? Nate surveyed the forest on both sides but saw no cause for concern. He headed up the stream again, his feet soaked to the ankles. In due course he found a second trap lying on the bank of a beaver pond. This trap had been accorded the same treatment as the first.

The tracks of Milo and Tom were still fresh. Apparently they'd had no idea they were being pursued. Now and then they'd position a Newhouse and go on. Exercising stealth and cunning the creature had closed in, gradually overtaking them.

Nate tramped for over three miles and spotted seven ruined traps. Then he rounded a bend and saw a tributary on his side of the stream, a narrow creek wending off among the trees. At the junction he stopped and scoured the ground.

The tracks told the story. Milo and Tom had halted and talked, and one of them had gone off up the tributary, perhaps to check for beaver. From the length of the stride and size of the footprints of the man who had gone to investigate the creek, Nate knew Tom had volunteered to handle the chore. Milo had continued up the stream, finished setting the traps, and returned. He'd promptly proceeded along the creek at a rapid clip, no doubt worried because Tom hadn't met him at the junction.

Nate gave Samson a pat on the head and jogged along the creek bank. The brush was thinner and he made good time. In a quarter of a mile he came to a beaver pond and saw a lodge out in the water. The tracks of Sublette and Benteen circled the pond so he did the same until he stood beside a damn where he halted to study the terrain.

Tom Sublette was straight ahead.

Nate stiffened on seeing the stocky form of the Pennsylvanian seated in front of a log near the water. Sublette's arms were draped casually at his sides, his rifle resting across his thighs. The shadow of a towering pine partially obscured Sublette's head and shoulders, and Nate couldn't tell in which direction the man was looking. "Tom!" he cried.

Sublette didn't move or acknowledge the hail.

Fearing the worst, Nate ran forward, covering almost the entire 30 feet before the awful truth drew him up short in unspeakable horror. He gaped, finally seeing the ragged flesh rimming the neck and the flies buzzing greedily about.

It was Tom Sublette, all right.

But just his body.

His head was gone.

Chapter Eighteen

Stunned, Nate cautiously advanced. Goose flesh broke out all over his body and his scalp tingled. Samson glided past him and sniffed Sublette's feet, then growled.

Evidently Tom had hiked this far and sat down to rest, his spine braced against the log, his back to the deep woods. How long he had sat there was impossible to gauge, but clearly long enough for the creature to slink out of hiding, creep up on the unsuspecting man, and tear Tom's head off. Strips of skin hung like tiny flaps over the collar of his buckskin shirt. Because of the copious blood that had spurted out when the head was ripped off, the shirt had been dyed a shade of pink.

Nate suppressed an impulse to be sick. He glanced at the log and slowly inched up to it. Beyond lay the missing head.

Tom's visage was oddly tranquil, as if death had

seized him before he was aware of the creature's horrid grip. Perhaps, Nate reasoned, the end had come
swiftly.

He noticed a hole in the top of the head and leaned
down for a closer examination. Again his stomach
heaved and he drew back, appalled to his core. The
top of Tom's head had been peeled back in the same
manner as an orange and the contents of his cranial
cavity scooped out. Nate looked for the brain but saw
no sign of it. A grisly idea occurred to him and he
shuddered.

At that moment, faint but audible, from the vicinity
of the meadow came the retort of a rifle.

The camp was under attack! Nate pivoted, darted
around the log, and raced off. Instead of following the
stream, which entailed taking a circuitous route, he
made a beeline for the meadow. He plowed through
heavy brush and thickets, using the Hawken to batter
a path where the vegetation was especially dense,
oblivious to the many tiny branches that bit into his
face and neck. All he could think of was Red Moon
and Milo. They were in dire danger and he must reach
them before the beast did to them what it had done
to Tom and the Blackfeet.

He thought of those unfortunate Blackfeet again, of
how a single creature had dispatched nearly the entire
war party, and he was troubled by an aspect to the
attack he felt he was overlooking. He couldn't isolate
the reason, but something bothered him.

The distance seemed unending. He fought his way
through tangled undergrowth time and again. Once
his leg was hooked by a low limb and he fell, jarring
his elbows in the process. He surged upright and raced
on, ignoring the pain.

No other gunshots sounded. He began to think he
was mistaken, that Red Moon had been out hunting
game for their supper and had downed a deer or an

elk. If the creature had attacked, surely the Crow and Milo would have gotten off more than one shot.

Over a mile from the creek he slowed, tuckered out, to conserve his breath and his energy. He thought of Samson, and glanced over his shoulder to see if the dog was still with him.

Samson had vanished.

Nate paused, but only for a second. His friends needed him. The dog could take care of itself and would show up when it was ready. Squaring his broad shoulders, he continued to run, pacing himself so he wouldn't be completely exhausted when he reached the meadow. If the creature was there he would need all of his strength and wits to dispatch it.

Sweat poured down his back and legs. He felt drops trickle down his cheek. His legs muscles protested the marathon but he forged ahead. Soon he would be there. Soon he would know.

It turned out he had miscalculated. The trees were to his rear and green grass was underfoot before he realized he'd emerged from the forest at the north end of the meadow instead of the south, where their camp was situated. He stopped, taking loud breaths, and saw with a sinking sensation in his gut that the horses were gone, every last one of them. They had yanked out their picket pins and galloped off.

Smoke curled skyward from the fire. He sprinted closer, seeking his companions. Their ruined supplies were still lying all over the place. Neither Red Moon nor Milo was anywhere in sight.

Nate stopped and wiped first one palm, then the other, on his leggings. "Red Moon?" he called, hoping against hope for a reply. "Milo? Where are you?"

Utter quiet prevailed in the meadow and the encircling forest.

"Red Moon?" Nate repeated, slowly stepping nearer to the fire, the stock of the Hawken flush with his shoulder. His thumb rested on the hammer, his finger lightly touched the trigger. "Red—" he began, and then beheld the body lying at the tree line to the south of the camp.

He surveyed the woods around him and drew abreast of the fire. To his left he saw Milo's long gun, the stock shattered, the heavy barrel bent.

In the forest to the west something snarled.

Nate stopped in mid-stride and swung around, expecting to see the beast charge from cover. Nothing happened, though, and he resumed walking to the body.

It was Milo, prone with his arms out flung. His face, twisted sideways, revealed a countenance locked in unparalleled fear. There were four fangs marks on his neck, blood still trickling from the punctures. From the unusual angle at which his head lay, it was easy to see his neck had been broken.

"Oh, Milo," Nate said softly. He studied the tracks, and read how Milo had been fleeing toward the trees when the creature overtook him from the rear. Poor Milo had not had a chance. In Milo's panic, he must have discarded his gun back near the fire.

Nate turned from side to side, seeking Red Moon. The Crow must be nearby, perhaps dead, perhaps wounded. Red Moon would not die easily, and that shot he'd heard must have been the warrior selling his life dearly. He moved along the tree line, searching for footprints. Ten yards from Milo's body he found moccasin prints leading into the forest. From the length of the stride, he concluded Red Moon had been running.

He peered into the gloomy woods, the gravity of his predicament hitting home. For all he knew, he was now alone. The horses were gone, leaving him stranded afoot hundreds of miles from his cabin. Even if he escaped from the valley he must cover a tremendous distance in a land teeming with grizzlies and wolves and panthers. Not to mention the Blackfeet. Few trappers left on foot lived to tell the tale. He would be lucky if he ever laid eyes on Winona and Zach again.

A moan issued from the forest, seeming to come from near a large pine 25 yards away.

Red Moon? Or the creature? Nate entered the woods, keeping low, stepping with extreme care to avoid twigs and branches that might break underfoot and give his position away. If the thing jumped him he would put up the fight of his life. He had the Hawken, the two flintlocks, and his butcher knife. There was plenty of ammunition in his ammo pouch and his powder horn was filled to the brim. He'd give a good account of himself before he died.

Every shadow seemed menacing. Any movement, no matter how slight, set his nerves on edge. If a leaf fluttered, he froze.

The oppressive silence gnawed at him, increasing his jumpiness. He recalled the Indian legends about the thing that lurked in the dark. Here it was broad daylight, and the beast was abroad and on the rampage. So much for the reliability of legends. Or had the Indians meant the dark of the forest and not the dark of night?

He shook his head, dispelling the foolish conjecture. If he allowed himself to be distracted the creature would find him easy pickings. Moving ever closer to the pine, he listened for another moan. When he was 15 feet off he heard one, low and brief. He thought it came from somewhere on his right and he headed in that direction. There were a number of trees growing quite near to one another with thick growth filling gaps among the trunks. On silent feet he slid in among them and stopped.

His head snapped up when he heard a peculiar

noise, a slight tap-tap-tap as if someone was rapping on a tree. He cocked his head, striving to pinpoint where the noise originated, and happened to spy a leaf lying on the ground. As his gaze fell on it a crimson drop fell from on high and hit the leaf, then another and another. This was the tapping he had heard.

Nate inched forward and looked into the tree above the leaf. An inarticulate cry passed from his lips and he rose, dazed, his mind whirling.

Red Moon hung six feet above the ground. He had been bodily lifted and impaled on a broken branch, and the bloody point of the branch protruded seven or eight inches from his chest. His arms and legs dangled limply. Blood flowed from the wound, down over his shirt and leggings, and dripped from the heel of his moccasins. His head sagged, his eyes were closed.

"No," Nate said. "Dear Lord, no."

The Crow's eyes flicked wide but it was a moment before he focused. He saw Nate and struggled to move his mouth until a word rasped out. "Run."

"I can't leave you," Nate said, touching Red Moon on the leg. "I'll try and get you down from there."

"No," the warrior said. "The beast has killed me. Save yourself. Get away before it comes."

"I won't desert you," Nate insisted.

Out of the depths of a thicket to the north came a piercing shriek of bestial rage and the thicket shook as if in a violent wind.

Nate's reaction was instinctive. He pivoted, took hasty aim, and fired into the center of the branches shaking the hardest. The shriek broke off and the underbrush crackled as something retreated through the forest.

"Run," Red Moon said.

"Save your breath," Nate responded, already beginning to reload. First he placed the butt of the rifle on the ground. Then his hands flew as he measured out the proper amount of black powder from his powder horn into his palm and fed the powder down the barrel. Next he took a ball from his ammo pouch and wrapped the ball in a wad. The ramrod came out easily, and after inserting the ball and wad into the end of the muzzle he used the ramrod to force both down on top of the powder. It took no time at all to replace the ramrod in its housing under the barrel. Turning, he looked up at his friend.

Red Moon had died. His eyes were open but blank, his mouth slack, a tinge of sadness lining his face.

"I won't let you down," Nate said softly. Facing due south, he ran. Ran as he had never run before. For the next hour and a half he maintained a grueling, steady pace that an Apache would have been proud of, a dogtrot that ate up the miles. He steeled his mind to the pain in his legs. All that mattered was putting distance between himself and the creature. If he traveled far enough, if he could get close to the valley entrance before weariness prevented him from going any further, he just might get out of the valley in one piece.

He thought often of his shot into the thicket, and consoled himself with the idea he'd wounded the beast. If so, like any animal it would go to its lair or seek an isolated place to hole up and lick the wound. Or so he hoped.

The afternoon sun climbed steadily higher, causing the temperature to rise. He sweated profusely and his soaked buckskins clung to his frame. When he came to where the forks merged he turned and followed the main stream. Here the going was easier and he stayed near the water so he could quench his thirst whenever the need became too overpowering.

Nate often scanned his back trail. As the hours elapsed and he continued to see no indication of pursuit he let himself relax a trifle. His legs were afire with pain. From his hips to the soles of his feet he was in constant discomfort. Years of living in the wilderness had bestowed remarkable endurance on him, but even superbly conditioned muscles possessed limits. When he could stand it no longer, he halted.

The stream beckoned invitingly. He shuffled over and sank to his knees, then splashed handfuls of the refreshing liquid on his face and neck. The water trickled under his shirt and down his chest, cooling his overheated body.

Nate touched his lips to the stream and drank sparingly. Too much water might sicken him. When a man was on the verge of exhaustion and had sweated practically every spare drop of moisture from his body, it was best to take small sips and slowly slake the craving for water. Later he could drink to his heart's content—provided he lived long enough.

He stood and stared northward. Where in the world was Samson? The dog had always been independent-minded, but it sure had picked a hell of a time to begin traipsing off wherever its whim led it. Samson's superior senses would come in handy right about now and he sorely missed the dog.

The sun drew his attention. There was no way he could reach the valley entrance before nightfall. If all went well he'd arrive there sometime tomorrow, about mid-morning. Which meant he must spend another anxious night in the domain of the wicked devil that would no doubt be stalking him once the sun dipped from sight.

He resumed running, but slowly to conserve his strength. In the few hours before twilight he could cover another four or five miles. Then he must find a place to make a stand.

Yet his options were limited. He could climb a tree and spend the night high in its branches, but he'd be unable to get a good night's rest and he badly needed rest if he wanted to flee the valley swiftly in the morning. He could dig a hole and crawl in, but for all he knew the creature tracked by scent and would find him without difficulty.

No, he needed another idea.

By the time he'd gone almost five miles and the sun had started its inexorable slide to the far side of the planet, he'd figured out what he would do. It was a simple plan, yet it might save his life.

He halted, drank some water, and stepped to the trees. There were plenty of broken limbs scattered around and he searched until he found three straight branches over five feet long, two of which had forked ends. Moving close to the stream again, he jammed the tapered end of one of the forked branches into the soil until it stood by itself, and then repeated the tactic with a second limb, placing it four feet from the first. Aligning the last limb in the forks of the uprights took but a moment.

Back to the forest he went to gather an arm-load of long, slender branches. These he leaned on the make-shift cross-beam to his lean-to in a neat row. Then he found smaller, even thinner branches, and weaved these among the longer branches to form a crude but serviceable wall facing to the north.

He collected more limbs and leaned these against the open end of the lean-to, leaving only a narrow space on either side to gain entry. This was deliberate. Should the beast hunt him down, it would have to tear the limbs aside to get at him. The noise was bound to awaken him and perhaps give him time to bring his guns to bear.

As an extra precaution he again ventured into the woods and gathered all the dry leaves and small dead twigs he could find. These he scattered in a wide circle around the lean-to until he had formed a carpet of crunchy material that would snap and crackle when stepped on.

Nate stood back and regarded his handiwork with satisfaction. The creature could not possibly reach him without making considerable noise, and a second or two of advance warning was all he needed to cock his rifle or pistols. It was the best he could do given the circumstances.

His stomach growled, but the sun was almost gone. He couldn't risk trying to find game. Instead, he eased to his hands and knees and crawled into the lean-to. Lying flat on his back so he could roll either way when the time came, he drew up his legs, rested the Hawken across his chest, and closed his eyes. His exertions had taken a terrible toll and fatigue washed over him from head to toe. He needed to sleep but doubted he could. Worry over the creature would keep him awake through the night. He thought of his dead friends and frowned. They never should have traveled to this vile valley, never should have let the lure of money eclipse their better judgment. He hoped Winona would forgive him if he never returned and hoped little Zach would retain some memory of his . . .

Nate opened his eyes with a start and held perfectly still, listening. He'd fallen asleep! For how long? He bent his head to see out the nearest opening. The night was pitch black except for the many stars dotting the sky, and a stiff wind from the northeast was bending the upper limbs of the trees. He had the feeling he'd dozed for hours but he couldn't be certain. His muscles ached, particularly those in his legs, and he still felt extremely tired. He was surprised he'd woken up at all.

Outside, dried leaves crunched.

Instantly Nate sat up, scarcely breathing, his fingers fumbling for the Hawken and closing on the barrel. Something was out there! He heard the stealthy pad of a step, heard more leaves crackle, and quickly cocked his rifle. The metallic click sounded loud enough to rouse a corpse. For a minute afterward the night was silent, then whatever was out there came closer to the lean-to.

Was it Samson? Nate hoped. Suddenly he could hear heavy breathing and knew it wasn't the dog. The creature had stalked him and was now out there, not more than a few feet away, perhaps baffled by the lean-to and trying to make sense of the structure. Nate peered at the opening opposite his feet.

The wind increased, whipping the trees, and the shaking leaves made enough noise to muffle the creature's steps.

A foul odor assailed Nate's nostrils, so rank it made him want to sneeze. He took his hand from the Hawken to pinch his nose tight, suppressing the impulse. In front of his eyes a great bulk loomed beyond the opening and a huge, hairy hand or paw reached inside. Dropping his hand to the rifle, he slanted the barrel at the beast and fired from the hip.

Flame and lead rent the darkness and a fierce howl filled the night. The looming bulk vanished, followed by the sound of something splashing across the stream.

Nate drew his right flintlock and moved to the opening. Near the far bank reared an enormous figure, well over seven feet in height, water spraying out from under its feet with every stride. It reached the far bank and disappeared in the undergrowth.

A second howl seemed to echo off the high cliffs above.

Elated, Nate commenced reloading the Hawken. The shot had driven the beast off! It could be killed just like any other animal. If he stayed awake he would be able to hold out until morning. He carefully poured black powder into his palm, having to guess at the proper amount by feel alone, and listened to a third howl from across the stream.

As if in response, from the forest close at hand came a shrill, bestial shriek.

A shiver rippled down Nate's spine and he glanced in that direction. There were two of the things! A high-pitched wail from off to the north indicated there were three, perhaps more. Shocked, he sat still while his mind raced. Now he understood how the Blackfeet had been wiped out. The creatures must have hit the war party from several directions all at once and slaughtered the confused braves before the Blackfeet could rally.

He continued reloading while pondering. If all three beasts attacked simultaneously, he'd be overrun and slain in moments. Oh, he might get one shot off, but the others would be on him before he could fire again. Creatures that size would be able to plow through the sides of the lean-to with no effort whatsoever.

Instead of feeling safe, he now felt boxed in. The lean-to was flimsy and his carpets of leaves wouldn't do much good if the creatures came in a concerted rush. His warning time would be next to nothing.

Nate finished reloading, then poked his head outside. The air was cool and invigorating, the night deceptively tranquil. Lurking somewhere out there were the beasts; they might be closing in already. He had a decision to make and he must make it swiftly.

Rising into a crouch, he tip-toed away from the lean-to, heading south along the stream. Maybe the things wouldn't notice, he told himself. Maybe they would think he was still inside. It might give him time to gain a substantial lead.

When he had gone 50 yards he straightened and ran full speed, heedless of the risk of stepping into a hole or tripping over an obstacle and seriously injuring himself. He had no intention of stopping for more than a brief rest until he reached the valley entrance. Once he was safely out the creatures might leave him alone.

The ammo pouch and powder horn slapped against his body as he ran, while the big knife smacked against his leg. He held the Hawken firmly in his left hand, swinging it at his side. Every so often he would press down on the flintlocks with his right hand, ensuring the pistols were snug under his wide leather belt.

He lost all track of time. After a mile or so his sore muscles loosened up and the stiffness went out of his joints. A minor pain intermittently flared in his chest but he disregarded it. Twice he stopped to gulp a mouthful of water and take a short breather.

A gray streak creased the eastern horizon when Nate spied, far ahead, the gap in the mountains that would grant him safety. He was winded again, so he halted and bent over, catching his breath.

Across the stream in the brush branches crackled as something moved about.

Straightening, Nate swung around and pressed the Hawken to his shoulder. A large, vague shape walked into the open and the creature seemed to be staring at him. He wondered if the things could see in the dark, like cats. If so, they had seen him sneak away from the lean-to.

A hint of sound to his rear made Nate whirl, his thumb pulling back on the hammer as he did. He saw a huge beast rushing at him, its arms outspread to envelop him in its crushing grip, its features veiled by the darkness except for its yellow fangs. Only a few yards separated them when Nate squeezed off a shot.

The ball took the creature low down, in the abdomen, the impact stopping it dead in its tracks. It doubled over, voiced a feral snarl, and leaped.

Nate tried to evade the thing's brawny arms but it clipped him on the right shoulder and knocked him to the earth. On hands and knees he glanced up at its great hairy bulk and saw it raise a fist overhead to pound him into the dirt. Another snarl sounded, only this one came from off to one side, and a black streak hurtled out of the night onto the creature.

Nate recognized that black streak and his resolve soared. Samson had come to his rescue! He saw the dog clamp its jaws on the beast's left wrist and the creature roared in primal fury, then swatted at Samson as a man might swat a fly. Nate heard the thud as the blow landed and imagined he heard the crack of Samson's ribs. Unless he came to the dog's aid, Samson would be slain.

He whipped both flintlocks out and up, cocking them as he drew. Pointing the left pistol at the creature's head, he fired. In the flash from the gun the beast's face was momentarily illuminated. Nate saw hairy, inhuman features dominated by a pair of dark, sinister eyes, eyes seemingly aflame with unbridled hatred, and then the flash was gone and the beast bellowed in agony and flung Samson to the hard ground.

The creature spun, both hands or paws clasped to its face, and bounded into the forest, crashing through the undergrowth as it fled.

Nate twisted and spied the beast across the stream advancing toward him. It was a third of the way into the water and taking strides that no man could hope to match. He aimed hastily and fired his other flintlock.

Jerking around, the creature staggered, then recovered and retreated, snarling and growling and rumbling in its barrel of a chest. Upon reaching the bank it bounded into the vegetation and fell silent.

Nate began reloading his guns, glancing in both directions in case the beasts came at him again. Samson rose, favoring a front leg, and limped over. His tongue flicked out and stroked Nate's cheek. "You pick a hell of a time to be affectionate," he muttered, his hands working feverishly.

Once all three weapons were ready, Nate jammed the pistols under his belt, grabbed the Hawken, and stood. Total quiet reigned in the woods on both sides of the stream, which meant nothing. The creatures might be skulking toward him at that very moment. Turning, he headed toward the gap at a slow gait so Samson could keep up without straining that injured leg too much. Splashes of red and yellow and orange colored the eastern sky. Soon the sun would rise.

They traveled half a mile when Nate glimpsed an indistinct form in the forest to his left. He halted and spun, dreading another onslaught but determined to fight until he dropped. Samson simply stood and stared, and Nate didn't understand why until a few seconds later when the thing in the trees came toward them.

Into the growing light stepped his stallion.

Epilogue

There were eight Crow women gathering berries on a low knoll less than a quarter of a mile from their village. They chatted as they worked, gossiping about the latest news of a raid the men had been on against the Utes.

Stiff Back Woman was the oldest in the group. She had gotten her name in childhood when an accident had rendered her incapable of bending over. A horse had kicked her squarely between the shoulder blades and she had never been the same. Still, she had led a good life. She'd married a handsome brave and borne him two children, both sons. Now, in her old age, she much enjoyed spending time with her granddaughters and their friends. They respected her years, as all Indian youths were taught to respect their elders, and they looked to her for guidance in womanly matters.

As her wrinkled fingers nimbly plucked the ripe red berries and deposited them in her basket, she kept a wary eye on the surrounding plain for enemies. One never knew when the Blackfeet might stage a raid, and there were always grizzlies to watch out for.

As alert as she was, she still didn't hear the rider approach, and had no idea they were no longer alone until she glanced up and saw the white man observing them. Although surprised that any white man could come up on them so quietly, she retained her composure. He was a big man on a fine black stallion, and nearby stood a great black dog. She stopped picking berries and greeted him in her tongue.

"Hello," the man said in the Crow language, and then he pointed at the village and used his hand in flawless sign language. "I seek Red Moon's people. Is that his village?"

"Yes," Stiff Back Woman responded. She saw no reason to lie to this man. He had an air of honorable character about him that impressed her. "But Red Moon is not there. He has not been seen in four or five moons."

"Is his grandson there?"

Stiff Back Woman frowned in sadness. "Little Sparrow died two moons ago. He was asking for his grandfather when he gave up the spirit."

The rider closed his eyes and seemed to tremble. When he opened his eyes again they were moist. "Thank you. Tell your people Red Moon is dead. Tell them he died bravely." With that the white man wheeled his horse and rode off, the dog keeping pace with the stallion.

"Wait!" Stiff Back Woman shouted, but it was no use. The rider went down the knoll and out across the prairie, and was soon lost in the dust raised by his mount.

BLACKFOOT MASSACRE

To Judy, Joshua, and Shane

Chapter One

The strapping young man in fringed buckskins sighted down the barrel of his heavy Hawken rifle, his striking green eyes narrowing as he aimed at the buffalo cow grazing contentedly 20 yards off. From his prone position on a grass-covered knoll he could see her great jaws moving as she munched and the flick of her short tail as she lazily swatted at circling flies. His thumb curled around the metal hammer and pulled it back until he heard a click.

What a stroke of luck! Nate King reflected. To have stumbled on a lone cow so soon after beginning his hunt meant he would be back with his wife and son much sooner than he had anticipated. He would have liked to bring the boy along, but the only time Zach got to mingle with their kin and frolic with other children was for three or four weeks each spring when the family visited the Shoshones and for a brief spell at the annual Rendezvous. So rather than interrupt his son's fun, he'd gone hunting alone.

Nate absently wondered why the cow was alone as he

prepared to squeeze the trigger. Ordinarily, buffalo congregated in large herds, and he had been following a clear trail left by hundreds of the dumb brutes when he spotted the cow. Perhaps she was lame. Or maybe she had simply wandered off from the main body. Whatever the case, he wasn't about to pass up this golden opportunity.

Although buffalo were notoriously difficult to dispatch with a single shot, at such short range he was confident of dropping her with one ball to the heart. Having butchered scores of buffalo since leaving New York City nine years ago for the rugged life of a free trapper in the majestic Rocky Mountains, he knew precisely where a buffalo's vital organs were located.

Nate grinned, thinking of how amazed Winona would be to see him back at the Shoshone village so soon, and lightly touched his forefinger to the trigger. Taking a breath, he steadied the Hawken, and was all set to fire when the high grass near the cow stirred and up stood a young calf.

Blinking in surprise, Nate watched the reddish calf wobble over to its mother's side and bawl to get her attention. It was a newborn! Now he understood why the cow was by herself. She must have stopped to deliver her offspring, and the herd had continued on to the south, leaving her behind. In a day or two, when the calf was strong enough, she would catch up with the main body.

Damn! Nate fumed in annoyance, lowering the gun. This changed everything. While there were some mountain men and any number of Shoshone warriors who would kill both mother and calf without hesitation, regarding both as nothing more than food on the hoof, shooting either now went against his grain. Others might laugh and call him soft, but he couldn't bring himself to slay a mother and her baby, even if they were only animals.

Carefully lowering the hammer, Nate observed the calf greedily sucking milk from the cow's teats. Then he eased backward on his elbows and knees and angled down the knoll until he could stand without being seen by the mother buffalo. His proximity to the calf might cause her to charge, forcing him to shoot her whether he wanted to or not.

Turning, Nate walked to his splendid stallion, a gift he had received at a recent rendezvous from the Nez Percé after he helped them fight the dreaded Blackfeet. Widely noted for their horsemanship, the Nez Percé were also regarded as the best horse breeders west of the broad Mississippi. Many frontiersmen would give a year's earnings just to own one of their outstanding animals. His stallion was typical of the breed; it sported black spots on a roan background, had white-rimmed eyes, and was further distinguished by white stripes over its hoofs.

He swung nimbly into the saddle, gripped the reins, and swung around, about to head northward in search of more buffalo. In the far distance, at the limits of his vision, something moved, a tiny black speck amidst the vastness of the unending prairie. Leaning forward, he placed his left hand over his eyes to block out the bright morning sun. Was it another buffalo? If so, he'd reach the Shoshone village by dark and spend all night with his wife. The appealing prospect brought a smile to his lips.

Playing it safe, Nate turned to the west and rode in a wide loop in the hope he would spot a low hill or another knoll from which he could spy on whatever it was. While he would much rather ride in a beeline and find out if it was indeed a bull so he could kill it and return to the village, prudence dictated otherwise. As he well knew, careless mountaineers did not survive long in the wilderness. One of the first laws of survival he had learned was to never take anything for granted. What if that moving dot was in reality a fierce grizzly or a hostile warrior? He must determine what it was before he made his presence known.

He hunched low over the saddle to blend his silhouette with that of the stallion's. From far off the horse would appear to be riderless, just one of the many wild animals roaming the plains. If that figure out there was indeed an enemy, a lone horse wouldn't arouse suspicion.

Nate held the Hawken in his right hand, the reins in his left. He could feel the twin flintlocks he invariably carried rubbing against his midsection. They were wedged tight under his brown leather belt, one on either side of the big buckle. In addition to the pistols, he had a butcher knife in a beaded sheath on his left hip and a tomahawk tucked under the belt above his right hip. Slanted across his broad chest were a bullet pouch and a powder horn. Moccasins covered his feet. In every respect his attire was typical of trappers, those hardy souls who had ventured into the remote vastness of the foreboding Rockies to make their living by securing beaver pelts for the lucrative Eastern and European markets.

Nate had never regretted his decision to come west. Not only had he found the love of his life in the beautiful person of Winona, he had also discovered the true meaning of a word he had never paid much attention to during the years he spent growing up in New York City, a word he now regarded as one of the most precious in the entire English language: freedom. To be able to live as he pleased without being accountable to any man meant as much to him as life itself. Back in New York, where he had bowed to his father's every whim and labored as an aspiring accountant under a spiteful taskmaster, he had been bound by invisible chains and never realized the fact. His behavior had been . . .

What was that?

Nate drew rein, listening to the mournful, wavering notes of an eerie howl that wafted on the cool breeze. He glanced toward the dot, squinting in an effort to see it better. The distance prevented him from being certain, but he had the impression the figure was walking on two legs. A man afoot? It must be an Indian since no white man in his right mind would dare be so foolhardy as to travel anywhere in the wilderness without a horse. There were too many dangers, from wild beasts and hostiles alike.

The howling was repeated, and to the east of the lone figure materialized a dozen or more low forms flowing over the ground in the figure's direction.

Nate straightened, the short hairs at the nape of his neck tingling. Those forms were wolves. Although they ordinarily gave humans a wide berth, they would attack if hungry enough or if they came on an injured man or woman incapable of offering much resistance. They did the same with buffalo. Wolves were Nature's way of gleaning the weak and the aged from the huge herds, of insuring only the fittest survived. Elk, deer, and smaller game also fell prey to the roaming packs.

"Let's go, Pegasus," Nate said, goading the stallion into a gallop. An avid reader, he had always been fond of the many tales about ancient Greek heroes. As a child he had delighted in the fantastic exploits of the winged steed Pegasus. So when the Nez Percé had presented the stallion to him, the finest horse he had ever seen, he had named it after the mythical mount of antiquity.

"Faster," Nate urged. He had fallen into the habit of talking to the horse as he often did to the family dog, Samson. Some of his trapper friends thought he was mad. Why get attached to an animal, they often argued, when one day he might have to eat it? A valid point, but he still regarded Pegasus and Samson more as loyal friends than mere domesticated beasts. The dog had many times proven itself by saving him and his loved ones, and the horse had yet to fail him in time of need.

Now Pegasus flew, its mane flying, its sleek body rippling with latent power. Nate rode expertly, his gaze on the wolves. He guessed they were still a quarter of a mile from the man. If he rode hard he might be able to intercept them.

The wolves of the western lands were particularly hardy specimens. While not quite as large as their kin in the Atlantic states, they were thickly made and endowed with tremendous stamina and strength. Their color was usually a gray or blackish-brown, although some were occasionally seen that were a cream-colored white. Working in concert, they could pull down a grown buffalo bull or an elk with deceptive ease.

Nate wondered why the wolves' quarry made no effort to run. Surely the man could hear the howling. As he drew nearer, he discovered he had been wrong about the figure's identity. It was a white man, not an Indian, dressed in black pants, a white shirt, and a black coat. He also noticed the man walked slowly, unsteadily, with head bowed, and figured the poor soul must be injured or ill, which explained why the pack had given chase.

He hefted the Hawken, calculating the range, certain he could down one or two if he was to stop and take careful aim. But the rest would probably press on and overwhelm the man. If he was to do any good, he must get between the wolves and their prey.

The man suddenly turned, saw the pack, and broke into an ungainly run, his right arm pressed to his chest as if he were in great pain. But instead of heading south, toward Nate, he raced westward in stark panic.

"Here!" Nate shouted. "This way!"

Looking around at the sound, the man spied Nate and instantly changed course, his legs pumping furiously. "Help!" he cried weakly. "Please help me!"

I'm trying to, Nate reflected grimly. Some of the wolves had seen him and stopped. Eight continued to close on their intended victim. In the lead was an enormous gray wolf bearing a black mark on its forehead.

The man glanced at his pursuers, failed to watch where

he was going, and tripped when his right boot snagged in a clump of grass. He stumbled and fell, landing on one knee, his right arm tight against his chest.

Snarling viciously, the lead wolf was almost upon him.

Nate let go of the reins and whipped the Hawken to his shoulder, using the pressure of his legs to stay astride Pegasus. He took a hasty bead, keenly aware of the consequences should he miss, and got off a shot just as the lead wolf leaped. Fate smiled on him, for the wolf reacted as if struck in the side by a mallet, twisting in midair and flopping over to crash onto the ground and lie still.

Undaunted, five of the pack were speeding forward. The rest had halted or were fleeing.

In a smooth gesture Nate drew his left flintlock, seized the reins in the same hand that held the Hawken, and came to an abrupt stop within a dozen feet of the man in black, who had slumped over in apparent exhaustion, head touching the ground. He vaulted from the saddle, faced the charging predators, and sighted on the foremost. The flintlock spat flame and smoke. Hit squarely between the eyes, the wolf was flipped onto its back by the impact.

The remainder had had enough. As one they veered sharply to the left and sped to the northwest.

Nate watched them go, jamming the spent flintlock under his belt so he could draw the second one. Only when he was convinced they were actually leaving did he step to the man's side and squat. "You're safe now. How bad off are you?"

Grunting, the man lifted his head and mustered a grin. He was in his late twenties or early thirties and wore his dark brown hair down to his shoulders. His eyes, also brown, conveyed his gratitude at being saved. "Thank you, brother," he said softly. "I was a goner if you hadn't come along."

Brother? Nate put a hand on the man's thin shoulder. "Can you stand? Where are you hurt?"

"I fell yesterday on some rocks but I'm not seriously injured," the man said, pushing off the ground with his left hand so he could stand. As he straightened, swaying from the effort, he revealed a book clutched in his right fist.

Nate saw the title as he rose. *The Holy Bible*. He figured the man must be extremely religious to have held onto the Scriptures when it would have been smarter to toss the bible aside in order to run faster.

"My name is John Burke. I apologize for any trouble I've put you to," the man said, smiling.

"How did you come to be in this fix?"

"My horse and pack animals were stolen by Indians three days ago and I haven't eaten or had a drop of water since." Burke indicated his right leg where the fabric had been torn and his skin split open. "After I fell, I bled for quite a while. The wolves must have picked up the scent."

Nate nodded in agreement and stuck the flintlock under his belt to free his hands for loading the Hawken. "I'm Nate King. If you're agreeable, I'll take you to a Shoshone village not very far from here."

"Shoshones? Are they friendly?"

"There are none friendlier. I've lived among them off and on for nine years. My wife is Shoshone."

"Oh," Burke said, and absently began chewing on his lower lip, evidently in deep thought. He did not appear pleased at the prospect.

Nate was about to inquire into the reason Burke had been traveling across the prairie all alone when a low growl from directly behind him chilled his blood and gave him goose flesh. He whirled in alarm. There, not six feet away, was the enormous gray wolf he had shot in the side, upright and crouching to spring.

Chapter Two

Living in the raw wild changed a man. He learned to rely on his natural instincts if he wanted to survive. Where a comfortable city life often dulled a man's senses and made him physically flabby, the wilderness tempered him like a forge tempered a steel blade, firming his muscles until they were rock hard and honing his reflexes until they were as sharp as the wild beasts he frequently confronted.

So it was that at the very moment Nate laid eyes on the crouching wolf, he released the Hawken and threw himself to the right while clawing at the flintlock he had just wedged under his belt. The wolf was incredibly quick, springing as his hand closed on the gun, and Nate realized in a flash that he would be unable to get off a shot before the beast was on him. In a twinkling he shifted his hand to his knife, and was drawing the weapon when the wolf slammed into him.

Nate was bowled over, landing on his back with the snarling wolf on top of his chest. Snapping jaws narrowly missed his face. He thrust a forearm under the wolf's jaw to keep it from biting again while simultaneously thrusting the butcher knife into the animal's ribs. Again he stabbed, trying to pierce the heart, but he only succeeded in arousing the wolf to a frenzied pitch of feral wrath. Razor teeth bit into his wrist, ripping the skin, and he felt the clammy sensation of blood flowing down his arm. Claws tore at the front of his buckskin shirt. In desperation Nate bunched both shoulders and heaved, hoping to fling the beast from him. But the wolf clung to his wrist, its teeth grinding deeper.

Twisting, Nate drove the blade into the wolf's throat. The animal recoiled, its teeth slipping from his arm. With a lunge Nate rose to his knees, the knife held close to his chest, ready to thrust again. Out of the corner of his eye he saw John Burke a yard away, motionless, making no move to come to his aid.

The wolf growled, blood spraying from the hole in its neck, and jumped.

Nate rose, meeting the beast halfway, his blade arcing into the base of the wolf's throat once more, impaling it to the hilt. He wrenched the knife free, then slid to the left, giving himself room to maneuver. As he did he grabbed his tomahawk, and when the wolf leaped yet again he employed both weapons at once, ramming the knife into the animal's neck and slamming the tomahawk down on the top of the wolf's skull.

Thudding to the ground, its head split open to expose its brains, a crimson geyser erupting from its throat wounds, the wolf thrashed violently and snapped at the empty air. Gradually its limbs quieted and its head slumped limply; then the beast gasped and expired.

Nate half expected it to rise again. If there was a single trait many kinds of animals shared, it was an abiding tenacity that would cling to life at all costs. This wolf had been a prime example. Mortally wounded, it had attacked again and again. As the trappers often said about the mighty grizzly bear, the wolf had been hard to die.

He wiped the back of his sleeve across his sweating brow and struggled to calm his pounding heart. A glance at his forearm showed the bite marks weren't as deep as he had feared. Another glance, at John Burke, demonstrated his anger. "Thanks for the help," he said bitterly.

"I'm sorry, brother, but there was nothing I could do."

"You could have kicked it. You could have beaten it with your bible. Hell, you could have done anything but just stand there like a bump on a log," Nate told him.

Burke's features drooped in regret. "No, I could not. It is against my beliefs to do harm to any of God's creatures."

"Even when one of those creatures is trying to tear you apart?"

John Burke nodded and gazed into Nate's eyes. "I should explain. I'm *Reverend* John Burke, a missionary."

"You don't say," Nate said to cover his embarrassment. In all his years in the wild he had only run into two other men of the cloth, both missionaries on their way to the Oregon country. They had stopped at the site of the last Rendezvous and mingled with the trappers and Indians on hand for the annual festivities. Their presence had created quite a stir. Ministers and priests were as rare as hen's teeth beyond the established frontier.

"I've come all the way from Rhode Island," Burke was saying. "The Lord wants me to minister to the heathens, to show them the light, to lead them to an understanding of our Savior, Jesus Christ."

"That's a pretty tall order," Nate commented. "Most of the Indians I know are happy with the religion they have."

"Indians have religion?" Burke responded skeptically. "I was under the impression they practice barbaric rites of self-torture under the guise of Nature worship."

"Do you know any Indians personally?"

"No, but I've talked to many men who have contacted the heathens and I know . . ." Burke broke off, touching a palm to his brow as he unexpectedly tottered. "Oh, my! I'm afraid everything is catching up with me."

"Are you faint?"

"I feel dizzy. So very dizzy," the reverend said. His eyelids fluttered and he groaned. Then, without warning, he pitched forward.

Nate caught Burke in his arms before the man could strike the earth. His wrist flared with pain, and he grimaced as he gently lowered Burke onto his back. Stepping to the stallion, he removed his bedroll and unfolded the blanket he used at night. Inside was a spare shirt courtesy of Winona, an extra ammo pouch, and an extra set of moccasins. Because his line of work entailed repeatedly wading into frigid streams to lay traps and collect dead beaver, those moccasins frequently came in handy when the pair he normally wore became soaked. Using his knife, he cut off a strip from the hem of his spare shirt, then washed his wrist with water from his water skin before bandaging the bite marks as best he could. He did a crude job, but he wasn't worried about infection setting in. By nightfall he would be back at the village where Winona would doctor him with herbal medicines that were every bit as effective as anything white physicians relied on. In many instances the herbs were even better.

Replacing the bedroll, he carried the water skin to Burke and knelt. The man was unconscious, breathing regularly, the bible still clasped in his right hand. He tilted Burke's head and carefully let the cool water trickle between the reverend's parted lips. After a bit Burke sputtered, coughed, and opened his eyes.

"I passed out, didn't I?"

"Yes," Nate confirmed, capping the bag.

"I'm sorry to be such a bother. Give me a little food

and I'll be as fit as a fiddle.''

"Quit apologizing," Nate said, standing and securing the water skin to the saddle. "You're holding up fine considering all you've been through." He tapped the sack that contained his grub. "I can offer you a few strips of fresh jerked venison. They'll have to tide you over until we reach the village. Trying to eat too much right now would only make you sick to your stomach.''

"I see. Jerky it is then.''

Nate selected an especially thick piece. "My wife smoked the meat herself," he said as he handed the salted venison over. "I can guarantee you've never tasted more delicious jerky anywhere.''

Burke cocked his head and regarded Nate with a puzzled expression. "You sound very proud of her.''

"I am.''

"You *like* being married to a squaw?''

Anger made Nate scowl. Had another trapper asked such an insulting question, he would have torn into the offender with his fists flying. But the minister's voice betrayed no hint of sarcasm, his features no trace of effrontery. Nate suppressed his resentment and replied in a calm tone. "Yes, I do, Reverend. Winona is a lovely woman." He paused. "And I'll thank you to never, ever refer to her as a *squaw* again. It's not the most flattering of terms.''

"Oh," Burke said. "I didn't realize. Folks back East call Indian women squaws all the time.''

"And do they ever mean it as a compliment?''

The thin man pondered for several seconds. "No, I suppose they don't. Most of our kind don't hold the red race in very high regard, which is to be expected when a superior culture clashes with an inferior one.''

"You sound like President Jackson," Nate said testily. Andrew Jackson, or Old Hickory as he was commonly called, was in his second term. When Jackson first ran for the office, he'd publicly declared his belief that Indians were an inferior race, and asserted the U.S. government had an obligation to reorganize them as it saw fit.

"I take it you disagree with his policies?" Burke asked.

"If you knew the Indian people as well as I do, you'd disagree with him too," Nate declared, and extended a hand. "Now why don't we get you on my horse? The sooner we get started, the sooner I'll have you resting and well fed in my lodge."

John Burke allowed himself to be helped to his feet and given a boost onto Pegasus. He sagged, nearly pitched off, and gripped the saddle to brace himself.

"Can you manage?" Nate asked.

"The Lord will sustain me."

Nate pointed at the bible. "Let me put that in my sack for the time being."

"No."

"You can't ride well using just one hand."

"I'll be all right," Burke insisted, and wagged the holy book. "This is the only bible I have left. The rest were stolen by the same band of heathens who took my horses. I'll need this when I begin my ministry, and I'm not letting it out of my sight."

Nate thought the man was being foolish, but dropped the matter. He began reloading his guns. As he worked he scoured the plain for the wolf pack, but saw no sign of them. "Did you get a look at the Indians who stole your animals and provisions?"

"A glimpse was all," Burke said. He bit off a small piece of jerky and chewed slowly. "I had made camp in a stand of trees and gone off a ways from my fire to heed Nature's call. The next thing I knew my horses were acting up, so I ran back in time to see five redskins escaping to the northeast with all my worldly possessions." He sadly shook his head. "I didn't mind losing my food and blankets half as much as I did the ten bibles I brought along.

I intended to present them to savages who would accept Jesus as their Savior.''

Though engrossed in pouring the proper amount of black powder down the barrel of his Hawken, Nate paused and glanced up. "You have your work cut out for you, Reverend Burke. Most Indians I know think the white man's religion is downright strange."

Burke straightened. "I'll show them otherwise, Mr. King. I'll open their eyes to the truth. I have to. God commanded me to do so in a dream."

Nate didn't quite know what to say to that. He busied himself reloading the flintlock, then wiped his knife and tomahawk on one of the dead wolves to remove the blood and gore. Once all his weapons except the rifle were snug under his belt, he shouldered the Hawken, took hold of the reins, and hiked westward.

For the next half an hour they traveled in silence. Burke ate three strips of venison and greedily drank from the water skin between each piece.

Shortly thereafter, tree-covered foothills appeared. Beyond them reared snowcapped peaks glistening bright in the golden sunlight.

"Are those the Rockies?" Burke asked in awe.

Nate nodded, recalling the very first time he beheld a section of the chain of magnificent rocky ramparts that extended from just north of Santa Fe all the way up into Canada. The stirring sight of those rugged summits towering thousands and thousands of feet into the azure sky had thrilled him to his core. Right then and there he had decided to stay, although he hadn't quite realized the fact at the time. The Rockies held an allure that attracted his soul like a magnet attracted iron. In his estimation they were the pinnacle of creation, so sublimely beautiful as to defy description. "You should see the range down near where I live," he commented. "The peaks are even higher than these."

"You don't live with the Shoshones?"

"We have a cabin about a two-week ride to the south, near Long's Peak," Nate disclosed, referring to an exceptionally high mountain named after Major Stephen Long, who had been searching for the source of the Platte River back in 1820 when he spied the peak that would subsequently bear his name. In the 17 years since then, only a score or so of white men had also seen the mountain, which was well off the beaten path, being far north of the Santa Fe Trail and far south of the prime beaver territory regularly crisscrossed by the trappers. "At least once a year we visit's my wife's people and spend a month or so with them."

"Could it have been Shoshones who stole my belongings?"

"No."

"How can you be so certain?"

"Two reasons. First, the Shoshones don't go in for stealing from whites like some of the tribes do. Second, if you were three days from here when it happened, you were in Cheyenne and Sioux country. If I had to make a wager, I'd bet it was a band from one or the other that hit you."

"Could it have been the Blackfeet?"

Nate looked at the minister. "You know about them?"

An enigmatic smile curled Burke's lips. "I've heard a little."

"Then you must know the Blackfeet are the most bloodthirsty devils alive. They're constantly raiding other tribes. And they hate whites. If a war party of Blackfeet had found your camp, you'd be minus your hide right about now."

Burke touched a hand to his lower back and arched his spine to relieve a cramp. "I suppose I'll never know for sure which tribe was responsible." He swiveled and gazed out over the prairie. "Then again, perhaps I will."

"What do you mean?"

The minister pointed to the east. "If I'm not mistaken, here comes the same band that raided my camp."

Nate spun in alarm, leveling the Hawken as he turned. Not five hundred yards away were five warriors riding straight toward them.

Chapter Three

Nate stepped between Pegasus and the oncoming braves, his thumb on the Hawken's hammer, and adopted a casual air. Indian men admired courage above all else. If he displayed any fear, the band might see fit to try and take his stallion. He could tell by the style in which they wore their braided hair, the fashion of their buckskin leggings, and the painted symbols on their mounts that they were indeed Cheyennes. One was leading a saddled horse and a pair of packhorses.

"Those are my animals," the minister declared.

"I figured as much," Nate said, forcing a smile. The warriors had not made any threatening gestures; their bows were slung over their shoulders, their knifes in their sheaths. Only one man held a lance, the tip pointed at the ground to show his intentions were friendly. Nate waited until the five were 20 feet away before tucking the Hawken under his right hand and using sign language to greet them. They promptly reined up. A stocky warrior bearing a scar on his right cheek kneed his pony forward a few paces and returned the greeting.

"I am Speckled Snake of the Cheyenne," the man went on. "We come in peace, white man."

Nate kept his eyes on the others as he lifted his hands. "I am Grizzly Killer," he responded, using the Indian name bestowed on him years ago by a noted Cheyenne warrior known as White Eagle. Now the Shoshones, Nez Percé, Crows, and Flatheads all called him by that name.

Murmuring broke out among the warriors. Speckled Snake cocked his head and studied Nate from head to toe. "You are known to me. They say you kill grizzlies as other men kill rabbits. They say you have counted many coup on your enemies."

"What they say is true," Nate acknowledged. He wasn't boasting so much as making it plain to the five warriors that he was a man to be reckoned with, and that if they started trouble they could count on a fight.

"They say you have even killed many Blackfeet."

"I have," Nate signed. In truth, he couldn't remember the exact number. But the Blackfeet had been a persistent thorn in his side ever since he came to the Rockies, There had been the time a war party attacked his wife's people, and the time another band kidnapped one of his best friends. Not quite a year ago he had tangled with them again when they raided the Nez Percé. It was rumored the Blackfeet wanted his scalp more than that of any other white man, which was why he made a point of going nowhere near their territory.

Speckled Snake nodded at the minister. "Is this man a friend of yours?"

"He is," Nate replied, deliberately keeping his answers short in case the Cheyennes were trying to deceive him and made a play for their weapons.

"We did not know that," Speckled Snake signed. He twisted to indicate the three spare horses. "These are his.

He is welcome to have them back.''

"I thank you."

The stocky warrior motioned, and the Cheyenne holding the lead brought the horses forward, then wheeled and moved back beside his companions.

John Burke cleared his throat. "I don't understand, King. Why are they giving my animals back? What did you do? Threaten to shoot them?''

"No. They're returning the horses of their own free will."

"I can't believe that. Everyone knows Indians are inveterate thieves."

Speckled Snake had been listening to the exchange with interest. He pointed at the reverend and asked in sign, "What did he say?"

"He also thanks you for giving his animals back," Nate lied in the interest of keeping the peace. If he translated the minister's exact words, the Cheyennes would be insulted. And unlike whites, Indian men never allowed an insult to go unchallenged.

"Does he want to know why we followed him?''

"He is curious," Nate signed, only because he was intensely curious himself. By all rights the five warriors should be back at their village, reveling in their spoils. It was unheard of for a raiding party to return the goods they took. The only reason he could think of for why the Cheyennes trailed Burke was to finish him off and take whatever the reverend had on him.

The stocky warrior squared his shoulders. "We wanted to find out why he does not carry any weapons."

Nate held his right hand at shoulder height, his palm outward, his fingers and thumb pointed upwards and slightly separated, and turned the hand by wrist action three times in succession. The gesture was an all-purpose sign that stood not only for "what," but also "why," "when," and "where," depending on the context in which it was used. In this instance he was asking Speckled Snake to repeat himself since he felt he might have misunderstood.

"The skinny white does not carry weapons," the Cheyenne signed, and elaborated. "There were no guns or knives on his animals. All we found was a small ax for chopping wood." He stared at Burke. "We had watched him for a whole day before we took his horses, so we knew he did not carry a weapon on his person. We believed we would find them in his packs, but we were wrong."

Nate pursed his lips. The warriors must have been terribly disappointed, since most would give their right arm to own a white man's rifle. Ordinarily, Indians received only inferior trade guns known as fusees. A warrior who owned a genuine Hawken or other fine rifle was highly esteemed. Among the Blackfeet, any warrior who took an enemy's rifle received the highest honors. In fact, the Blackfoot word for war honor was *namachkani*, which literally meant "a gun taken."

"Who is this man who is so brave he travels without any means of protecting himself?" Speckled Snake signed earnestly.

Nate almost grinned at the confused look on the Cheyenne's bronzed face. Some of the others appeared equally perplexed. He could readily appreciate why they were baffled since it was unheard of for a warrior to go about unarmed. Even in their villages they seldom strayed far from their bows and lances since an enemy war party might strike at any time. And they undoubtedly knew that white men were always armed to the teeth with flintlocks, rifles, knives, and tomahawks.

"What's happening?" John Burke inquired. "Why are they looking at me like that?"

"They're puzzled because you don't own any weapons."

"How extraordinary. Well, inform them I'm a man of

the cloth, that it is against my religious convictions to harm another human being, even simple savages such as themselves.''

Speckled Snake motioned. ''What are his words?''

Again Nate hedged. ''The reason he does not carry weapons is because he has devoted his life to the Great Medicine,'' he signed, using the term that stood for God in most Indian tongues. The literal translation of ''medicine'' was ''mysterious'' or ''unknown.'' So when someone mentioned the Great Medicine, they were referring to the Great Mystery. Some of the mountain men claimed the expression should be translated as the Great Spirit, but ''medicine'' was the word most used by the Indians themselves.

The Cheyenne's surprise was transparent. ''The skinny one is a medicine man?''

''Yes,'' Nate replied, and in a sense he was right. Medicine men were tribal clergymen and doctors combined, leading spirit ceremonies when the occasion demanded and healing illnesses that arose. In some tribes they were more like clergymen than doctors, while in other tribes the reverse was true. Many whites made light of the Indian holy men, but from his own experiences Nate knew they were often wise, caring, and dedicated to the welfare of their people. In all tribes the medicine men were as highly esteemed as the chiefs, perhaps more so. By telling these Cheyennes that Burke was a medicine man, he was insuring they would hold the reverend in the highest regard and never bother him again.

Turning, Speckled Snake began an animated conversation with his fellow warriors. At length he faced Nate and signed, ''What is his name?''

Nate had to think before responding. There were no sign gestures for proper names in the English language, which was why trappers who chose to live among the Indians always took an Indian name and used it in all their dealings with the various tribes. He must make one up for Burke, and it should be something appropriate. "Medicine Teacher," he answered, which sparked a new round of discussion.

"Tell him we did not know he was a medicine man when we took his horses," Speckled Snake said in due course. "Had we known, we would never have bothered him." He lowered his hands briefly. "Ask Medicine Teacher if he is angry with us. We do not want him to put bad medicine on our heads for our mistake."

John Burke leaned toward Nate. "What the dickens is this heathen babbling about now?"

"They're afraid you'll put a curse on them."

"By George, I should!" Burke bellowed, jabbing a finger at Speckled Snake. "I should call down the wrath of the Lord on you and your pathetic, ignorant people for what you've done to me! But I won't. And do you know why?" He glowered at the five Cheyennes, then quoted from Scripture. "The Lord is my defense, and my God is the rock of my refuge. And he shall bring upon them their own iniquity, and shall cut them off in their own wickedness. Yea, the Lord our God shall cut them off." Smiling fiercely, Burke straightened. "Your own wickedness will be your undoing, savages. I need not lift a finger against you."

The fiery outburst had agitated the Cheyennes, who began whispering among themselves.

"What did Medicine Teacher say?" Speckled Snake inquired. "He sounds displeased."

Nate hesitated, simmering with indignation. Here he was, trying his best to convince these warriors that Burke and he were as friendly as could be, and the good reverend was doing his damnedest to stir them up. Already one of the warriors was fingering the hilt of his knife. If Burke wasn't careful, he'd get the Cheyennes downright mad. And medicine man or not, they wouldn't stand still for being insulted. He smiled to reassure them, then signed, "Medicine Teacher is angry, but not at you. He is angry at himself because his medicine failed him. He ate something he should not have eaten, and that is why the Great Medicine did not keep his horses and possessions safe."

"I understand," Speckled Snake said gravely.

It paid to be familiar with Indian customs, Nate reflected. Among many tribes it was customary for young warriors to go on vision quests to obtain spiritual power. By going off by themselves and fasting until an extraordinary dream, or vision, presented itself, they hoped to gain supernatural powers that would protect them in battle. A warrior might see a red hawk in a dream, for instance, and paint it on his shield to ward off enemy arrows. But with their new power usually came taboos. In order for the hawk shield to be effective, the warrior might have to refrain from eating the brains of a buffalo or from letting a menstruating woman come near it. The taboos were endless and varied, depending on how the warriors interpreted their dreams.

In the same vein, medicine men often went on vision quests to obtain healing powers or other abilities. And like the warriors, they had to stick to certain rules or their powers would be useless.

"We will leave you in peace," Speckled Snake now signed. "And we will tell our people of this meeting so they may learn that white men do know of the Great Medicine. There are some who believe all whites are dead inside, like rotten trees that can never bear ripe fruit, and know nothing of spirit matters."

Nate made the signs for "Go in peace." He sighed in relief as the five Cheyennes galloped off to the northeast without looking back, and felt the tension drain from his body. "That was close," he remarked.

"Why? Did those devils threaten to harm us?"

"No, but if you had opened your mouth one more time they just might have."

"What is that supposed to mean?"

Nate pivoted. "It means, Reverend, you have a lot to learn if you want to survive out here. Indians will not abide insults. You can't treat them like you would your congregation back in the States."

"I'll speak to them as the spirit of the Lord moves me," Burke said gruffly. "If they're offended, so be it."

"If they're offended, they might just turn you into a pincushion."

Burke smiled. "I'm prepared to be a martyr if that's what it takes to get these primitives to see the light."

"Suit yourself," Nate said with a shrug. Suddenly he was sorry he had ever run into the man. There was no reasoning with someone like him, and the way Burke was going it wouldn't be long before he got his wish and wound up scalped. Nate didn't want to be around when it happened. He would probably lose his life trying to save Burke's, and he had a wife and son to think of, "Reckon you're fit enough to ride your own horse?" he asked.

"I believe I can, yes."

"Then let's go. I want to reach the Shoshone village before nightfall," Nate said. He stood to one side as the minister dismounted, then climbed on Pegasus. "If you have no objections, I'll handle your pack animals."

"Very well," Burke said, stepping to his bay and climbing slowly up. He patted the animal's neck. "I knew the Lord would provide for me. See how He watches over his children?"

Nate grabbed the lead rope and clucked the stallion into a trot. For over an hour they rode steadily westward until they reached the base of the foothills, where he drew rein to give the stallion a short breather before forging onward. To the north, well out of rifle range, was a small herd of black-tailed deer. To the south a bald eagle circled far above the gently waving prairie grass. He inhaled deeply, enjoying the fragrance of the nearby pines.

Burke had said nothing the whole time, but he now saw fit to speak. "I appreciate what you did for me back there, Brother King. You're quite a hand at dealing with Indians, aren't you?"

"I should be after living among them for so long," Nate replied, glancing at the reverend just as Burke's eyes became the size of saucers and his mouth drooped open in astonishment. Swiveling, Nate gazed in the same direction and saw an enormous grizzly bear emerging from the forest.

Chapter Four

Of all the animals in the wilderness, grizzlies were the most feared by whites and Indians alike. Tremendous in size, with extremely wide heads, massive shoulders, and prominent humps that set them apart from their black cousins, grizzlies were the masters of their domain. Even panthers and wolverines gave them a wide birth. Sometimes rising to over eight feet in height when they stood on their hind legs, grizzlies were endowed with terrible claws over four inches long. A single swipe could disembowel a grown moose or decapitate a man.

Nate felt his mouth go dry as the grizzly started out across the plain, its huge head swinging ponderously from side to side, lumbering clumsily along, giving no hint of the startling speed of which a grown bear was capable. It was 50 yards away and as yet had not noticed them. If they didn't move it might keep on going. Grizzlies had notoriously poor sight. Their sense of smell, however, was exceptional. Hopefully the wind wouldn't carry their scent to it.

The monster abruptly halted and sniffed.

"What do we do?" Burke whispered.

"Don't move and don't talk," Nate advised. He saw the bear look toward them and gulped. Burke's bay was swishing its tail. The grizzly was bound to notice. Sure enough, a second later the beast took a heavy stride in their direction while continuing to test the wind.

"The Lord preserve us!" Burke breathed.

"When I tell you to, ride like you've never ridden before," Nate directed. "Head westward and don't look back."

"What about you?"

"I'll try and get the bear to chase me. After I lose it, I'll fire shots so you can find me again."

"What if it catches you?"

"My wife's name is Winona. Follow the setting sun until you come to a lake. The Shoshone village is on the south side. Let her know what happened."

"Your sacrifice won't be necessary," Burke declared. "I have a better idea."

"Such as?" Nate asked, and was flabbergasted when the minister unexpectedly turned his horse toward the bear, held his bible aloft, and shouted at the top of his lungs.

"Begone, foul beast! In the name of Our Lord Jesus I command you to leave us be!"

The grizzly uttered a fearful roar and charged.

"Damn!" Nate snapped, and swiftly gave the bay's rump a solid smack that sent the horse racing into the trees with Reverend Burke clinging to the saddle for dear life. Clutching the rope lead, Nate angled to the northwest and waved the Hawken to attract the bear. "This way!" he yelled. "Come after me, you mangy varmint!"

Loping faster than a man could run, the grizzly bore down on the horses.

In a twinkling Nate was wending among fir and spruce trees, a wall of branches momentarily screening him from the attacking monster. Ordinarily Pegasus could handily outdistance one of the giant bruins, but now the pack animals were slowing the stallion down. Burdened as they were with more supplies than was practical for a horse to carry, the pair was doing their best but still going nowhere near fast enough to escape the pursuing behemoth.

A branch plucked at Nate's beaver hat as he skirted a pine and crossed a narrow clearing. To his rear arose the loud crackle of underbrush, telling him the grizzly had entered the trees. His only hope was to stay ahead of the beast for the next two or three hundred yards. Provided he succeeded, the grizzly would tire and give up the chase. If not . . .

The forest was a blur. Nate had to constantly change direction to avoid trunks, logs, and boulders. Once the tip of a limb snagged his chin but his beard spared him from being cut. The ground sloped uphill, so he bore to the right until he came to a dry wash between two hills. The level stretch enabled him to urge the horses to go even faster.

At the west end of the wash, where it broadened out into a lush valley, he galloped madly toward a stand of aspen, the nearest available cover. A quick glance showed the grizzly just bursting from the woods.

Did he dare risk a shot?

No, he decided, because the odds of killing a grizzly with a single ball were slim. No less a personage than the famous Meriwether Lewis, of Lewis and Clark fame, had first chronicled the difficulty of slaying grizzlies in the journal he kept on his trek to the Pacific Ocean in 1805. When the men of the expedition initially encountered the gigantic brutes, they treated the grizzlies much as they would black bears from the States. But the first bear they shot for its meat and oil took ten balls before it dropped—

five through the lungs. Another grizzly was shot eight times as it tried to chase down and slay some of the members of the expedition. From then on Lewis and Clark treated the monsters with cautious respect.

Nate reached the aspens and darted into them. The grizzly was still in heated pursuit, rumbling continuously deep in its immense chest. Nate battered branches aside with the Hawken as he made for a field beyond the stand. The foremost pack animal bumped into a tree and stopped, catching him unawares, and he was nearly pulled from the saddle. With a frantic jerk on the rope he got the horse moving again.

Puffing noisily as its great feet struck the ground in steady cadence, the bear barreled onward.

Past the aspens Nate gave the stallion its head. He was strongly tempted to let go of the lead so he could escape, but he held on, his arm straining almost beyond endurance. The grizzly crashed into the stand and Nate swore the ground shook. The bear roared in frustration, the tightly spaced trunks slowing it down as he had planned.

More forest lay 60 yards ahead. To the right of the woods was a boulder-strewn hill. He made for the woodland, and was halfway there when over the top of the hill rode two warriors who promptly stopped on spying him. There was no time to determine if they were friendly or not. Already the grizzly had exited the stand and resumed the chase with renewed vigor.

Nate was beginning to think he would have no choice but to halt and fire. He could see the pair of warriors moving down the slope to intercept him. Perhaps they were hostiles intent on picking him off while he was preoccupied. One of them held a bow, and in the hands of a skilled warrior an arrow could slay a foe from a hundred yards off. He heard the warriors commence whooping and hollering and slowed just enough for a good look.

They were Shoshones.

Elated, he saw them angling toward the bear, not toward him. An instant later he recognized the duo as Drags the Rope and Beaver Tail. The former he had met on the very day he'd met Winona, and he was a close friend. Beaver Tail was a younger man barely out of his teens who had yet to count coup on a foe.

What in the world were they doing? Nate wondered. Both were beaming and lashing their war ponies with their leather quirts, clearly trying to reach the grizzly before it could overtake him. He saw Drags the Rope nock an arrow to his bowstring and Beaver Tail heft a lance. With a start he realized they were going to try and slay the monster.

Nate looked over his right shoulder to discover the bear had heard their clamor, spied them, and halted. Nate was in the clear. All he had to do was keep on going and there was no way the grizzly could harm him. The Shoshones would keep it occupied, although in the process both of them might lose their lives. Hauling on the reins, he jumped down and hastily tied the lead rope to a bush, then remounted and raced back.

Already the warriors were clear of the hill and sweeping toward the waiting bear. The monster seemed to sense their intent. It growled and swung a stupendous paw as if inviting them to try their best.

Drags the Rope raised his bow, sighted, and let the shaft fly when 40 feet from the grizzly. Streaking true to his aim, the arrow sliced into the bear's shoulder below the neck, sinking in all the way to the eagle feather fletching.

The grizzly vented a roar of rage and twisted its head to snap at the protruding feathers. Its jaws closed shy of the shaft. Thwarted, growling ferociously, it glowered at the onrushing Shoshones, then charged.

The warriors continued to close. Riding expertly, horse and rider as one, Drags the Rope cut to the right and sent a second arrow into the slavering brute. The bear slanted toward him, covering the ground with astounding speed.

It appeared certain the grizzly would be on him in seconds.

Beaver Tail whooped and galloped straight at the monster. He whipped his arm overhead, straightened, and tensed to hurl his lance into the bear's side. But the beast heard the pounding of his mount's hoofs. It whirled to face him, its jaws wide, its glistening teeth exposed.

Swerve aside! Nate wanted to shout. Evidently the young warrior had no intention of doing so. He saw Beaver Tail grin, saw the lance leap from the Shoshone's hand and strike the grizzly in the chest, then watched in horror as the young warrior tried to turn his horse too late. The bear, ignoring the lance imbedded in its body, took two quick steps and arced its right forepaw into the horse's head.

Blood sprayed from the war pony's crushed skull as the animal staggered, then toppled, hitting the ground on its right side. At the last instant Beaver Tail tried to leap to safety but the horse came down on his leg, pinning him. He drew a knife and twisted to defend himself from the approaching bear.

The grizzly halted and cocked its head regarding the young warrior intently. It placed a front leg on the dead war pony and started to step over the horse to get at Beaver Tail.

Yipping like a coyote, Drags the Rope galloped in close and unleashed a shaft into the monster's neck. The bear spun and roared, then sprang at Drags the Rope's mount, its paw flashing. The horse was struck on the flank, lost its balance, and fell. Drags the Rope jumped clear, drawing another arrow from his quiver as he did. The grizzly, paying no attention to the war pony's wild thrashing as it tried to stand, moved toward him.

By then Nate was there, riding Indian fashion, using his legs to guide the stallion, the Hawken tucked tight against his right shoulder, the hammer cocked, his finger on the trigger. He came in at a gallop, and when only four yards separated Pegasus from the growling monster he fired, aiming at a point in front of the bear's right ear. The grizzly whirled and tried to rip open Pegasus with its great claws, but at a jerk of the reins and a jab of Nate's heels the stallion bounded aside.

Roaring hideously, the bear gave chase, traveling a dozen yards before it abruptly stopped and began shaking its huge head as if perplexed. It took a few lumbering steps, then tottered unsteadily, swiped a forepaw at the air a few times, and collapsed, sinking slowly to the grass with its front legs outstretched and its head coming to rest between them.

Nate turned Pegasus and drew his left flintlock. The bear was motionless but it might only be dazed. Of all the creatures in the wilderness, grizzlies were the hardest to kill. Single shots rarely sufficed, even in the head, because their brains were protected by exceptionally thick skulls plus two large muscles that covered the sides of the forehead and served to stop or deflect any shots. The common phrase ''hard to die'' had in fact been coined by Meriwether Lewis in regards to the fierce beasts.

He drew within ten feet, aimed the flintlock, and fired. The barrel belched smoke and lead, and he saw the ball smack into the bear's head near the ear. The mighty animal didn't budge. Nate cautiously rode nearer, tucking the spent pistol under his belt and drawing the second flintlock just in case. Sliding from the saddle, he warily stepped up to the monster and touched the barrel to its brow.

The grizzly was still motionless, its eyes open but unblinking, pink drool flowing from its partially open mouth. Blood trickled from the two holes in its head as well as from the arrow and lance wounds. There could be no doubt the bear was dead.

Nate exhaled and straightened. That had been too close for comfort. Had the bear been a shade faster, it would have knocked down Pegasus and had him at its mercy.

He heard footsteps and a hand clapped him on the back.

"Well done, Grizzly Killer! How many does this make now? Seven or eight?"

Turning, Nate looked at the smiling face of his close friend and smiled too, although not as broadly. By all rights he should be glad to be alive and savoring the thrill of triumph, but deep down he was bothered by the incident. He had never taken satisfaction in killing except when it was absolutely necessary, such as for food for his family, for clothing, or for beaver pelts to make a living. He wasn't one of those mountaineers who went around shooting animals for the sheer hell of it. And although he would kill in self-defense, he regretted having to take the life of a creature that was only acting according to its given nature. "Four," he said in perfect Shoshone. "I think this makes four."

"Wait until I tell everyone! No member of our tribe has ever killed so many brown bears and lived to talk about it. Touch the Clouds will be jealous."

"It was luck," Nate said. Touch the Clouds, the foremost Shoshone warrior, a giant of a man with muscles of steel, was another good friend. As with every Shoshone warrior, Touch the Clouds prided himself on the honors he earned on the battlefield or in fights with wild beasts, and had counted more coup than every Shoshone except their aged chief, Broken Paw. But the giant had only slain one grizzly, and even then had nearly lost his life when the bear tore his back open. It was well known among the tribe that Touch the Clouds was envious of Nate's widespread reputation as a slayer of grizzlies.

"You are too modest," Drags the Rope said, and nodded at the dead bear. "Only a man with courage and skill could have done as you did."

From off to the left came a shout. "If you are finished congratulating him, we have another visitor!" Beaver Tail interjected.

Nate glanced at the young warrior, who was still pinned under his horse, and saw Beaver Tail point to the south. Pivoting, he spied the reason for the Shoshone's concern. Standing at the edge of the trees was another bear.

Chapter Five

Nate's first thought was that the newcomer was the slain grizzly's mate. During courtship was the only time the bears traveled together; the rest of the time they were solitary in their habits. But he promptly realized this new bear was much smaller and darker than the monster he had shot. "It's a black bear," he said.

The animal watched them for a moment, then turned and hurried into the woods.

"It must have heard the roars and the shots and come to see what was happening," Drags the Rope guessed.

Nate nodded. Most animals were innately curious. Hopefully, Reverend John Burke had also heard the shots and would soon show up.

"I would go after it but I fear my horse is hurt," Drags the Rope said. "My family could use the meat."

"I'll share the meat from this brown bear with both of you," Nate proposed. "A third for each of us. What do you say?"

"We did nothing to earn it."

"You came to my aid when the bear was close behind me," Nate told him. "If not for you, I would be lying here and the beast would be feasting on my corpse." He motioned at Beaver Tail. "How about you? Does a third of the meat sound fair?"

"Very fair and generous," the young warrior replied. "And it is also fair that I help with the butchering, which I can not do while stuck under this stupid horse."

Drags the Rope laughed and nudged Nate. "Perhaps we should leave him there and divide the meat between ourselves. Any man foolish enough to let his own horse fall on him is not worth rescuing."

"And had I not put myself in a position where my horse could be slain, you would now be in the brown bear's belly," Beaver Tail countered indignantly.

Grinning, Nate walked over to help Drags the Rope free the younger Shoshone. When, years ago, he had first met the tribe, it had come as a considerable shock to him to learn that Indians possessed a wonderful sense of humor. Perhaps because of the grim image of Indians painted by the Eastern press, and the many insulting remarks about Indian behavior and intelligence made by the likes of President Jackson, he had always imagined Indians as stone-faced devils who never cracked a smile, let alone laughed. He had been delighted to learn otherwise, and he now thoroughly enjoyed the Shoshones' rough humor and horseplay.

Drags the Rope stood over the dead horse and scratched his chin. "What do you think, Grizzly Killer? Should we cut Beaver Tail's leg off at the knee to free him?"

"Just try," Beaver Tail retorted, wagging his knife, "and I will nail your tongue to the entrance of my lodge."

"Your father's lodge, you mean," Drags the Rope reminded him. "You have yet to take a wife, as I recall."

Nate saw the pinned warrior become beet-red. No warrior liked to be reminded of his youth and inexperience, so to prevent an argument Nate commented, "I would be willing to bet all the guns I own that when Beaver Tail does have his own lodge it will be one of the grandest in the village."

The young warrior blinked, then beamed and puffed out his chest. "Grizzly Killer is a wise man, just as everyone claims." He gave his dead war pony a whack with the flat of his hand. "Now would you please get this bag of skin and bones off me."

Stooping, Nate placed his hands under the animal's front shoulders while Drags the Rope imitated his example on the other side of Beaver Tail. "On the count of three," he said, and when Drags the Rope nodded, he began. "One. Two. Three." Together they lifted, each of them grunting and puffing, and succeeded in raising the top of the horse an inch or two, just high enough for Beaver Tail to slide his leg out with a supreme effort.

The young warrior pushed to his feet, then gave the horse a kick. "You failed me when I needed you the most. I will pick my next war pony more carefully."

Nate was inclined to blame Beaver Tail for the mount's death, but he said nothing. Indian men regarded their war horses almost as highly as they did their wives. Indeed, some warriors even took their war horses into their lodges at night if enemy raiding parties were believed to be in the vicinity of their village. And he knew of one man who regularly brought his steed inside on freezing cold winter nights and made his wife go sleep with her parents to make room for the horse. The attachment was understandable to one who understood the Indian way of life. Horses had become an essential part of Indian culture, as necessary for their survival as the limitless buffalo. Of all their animals, the highly trained and pampered war horse was the most highly esteemed because the warrior's life frequently depended on its performance. Quite an attachment developed between each warrior and his preferred stallion. When the horse failed in its duty, as Beaver Tail believed was the case here, it was as if a close personal friend had let the warrior down.

Drags the Rope was staring off at the pair of pack animals. "Are those yours, my friend?" he inquired.

"No," Nate answered, and briefly related his meeting with the minister.

"A white medicine man?" Drags the Rope remarked when Nate was done. "I have heard of such men but never met one. I look forward to talking with him." His eyes twinkled. "Perhaps he is not as strange as most whites."

Beaver Tail took the cue. "I too would like to meet this man. There must be one white somewhere who knows something about the Great Medicine."

"Persist in making fun of me and I will keep all the bear meat for myself," Nate threatened good-naturedly, and they all enjoyed a hearty laugh.

Next they examined Drags the Rope's chestnut. The bear's claws had left five slash marks, none of which were deeper than an inch. Otherwise, the horse was fine.

Nate took time to load his guns. He debated whether to fire more shots and decided to save the ammo, confident the minister would be able to find him.

Drawing their hunting knives, they set to work on the grizzly. After rolling the bear onto its side, they slit the hide on both hind legs, then cut a straight line from its tail to its chin. Nate slit the inside of the front legs. Exercising care, they peeled the pelt from the massive body, cutting ligaments and muscles where needed to part the hide from the carcass, always remembering to hold the edges of their knives toward the carcass and not the hide so as not to tear it. Their painstaking toil would eventually pay off, once the hide was cured, salted, soaked, fleshed, dehaired, and tanned by their women, in a heavy robe of excellent quality.

Nate stood and surveyed the surrounding forest. He had expected Reverend Burke to appear long before they were done removing the pelt, and he began to worry that in Burke's weakened state the minister might have suffered an accident. Bending down, he wiped his blade clean on the grass and looked at his companions. "Would the two of you watch those packhorses until I get back? I must go see what has happened to Medicine Teacher."

"We will not let anything happen to them," Drags the Rope promised.

Nate retrieved his Hawken, swung onto Pegasus, and headed southward. He was annoyed at himself for not firing more shots earlier to guide Burke along. The minister, after all, lacked Nate's wilderness savvy and might not be able to determine which direction the initial shots had come from.

He rode for a quarter of a mile, to the top of a high foothill, where he reined up to scour the countryside. The dense pines on the slopes and the thick vegetation in the valleys hindered his attempts to spot Burke. He did see a red hawk wheeling above timber to the southwest, a pair of ravens winging low over an adjacent valley, a lone bull elk grazing in a meadow, and far to the southeast, on the prairie, a small herd of buffalo. Squirrels chattered at him from the treetops and chipmunks scampered about seeking food. But there was no sign of another human being.

Drawing his left flintlock, he pointed the gun into the air and fired. While the echoes of the retort rolled among the hills and bounced off the steep sides of the mountains to the west, he reloaded the piece. For ten minutes or better he patiently waited, constantly scanning the open spaces, seeking the reverend.

His concern rising, Nate turned the stallion to the east and descended the hill. He pressed on until he reached the edge of the plain, then made for the spot where the grizzly had first appeared. Since gunshots weren't doing the trick, he would have to track Burke down. His years in the Rockies, where his very life and the lives of his loved ones often depended on his hunting skills, had turned him into a skilled tracker. He was confident he would find the minister before another hour went by.

Locating the point where they had separated proved easy enough. The hoofprints were clearly imbedded in the soil. He followed Burke's trail into the trees, able to determine by the length of the bay's stride and the depth of the tracks that Burke had been riding at a reckless speed. It wouldn't be surprising if he found the reverend sprawled out on the ground somewhere, his head caved in by a low limb.

Several hundred yards from the tree line the bay had slowed down. Burke, evidently, had finally gotten the animal under control. Inexplicably, the minister had also changed direction and was now traveling to the southwest. Puzzled, Nate trailed him. He had told Burke to go westward to find the Shoshone village. Why wasn't the man heeding his advice?

The forest gave way to a long, winding valley, a gently bubbling stream flowing down its center. The tracks led to the stream, where Burke had watered the bay, then proceeded up the valley in an erratic fashion. One second the trail would be close to the stream, the next veering off to a stand of trees or going close to a bordering hill. Then back to the stream again. It was as if Burke were taking a leisurely ride on a country estate back East, enjoying the sights as he went.

At last Nate spotted the bay, two hundred yards away, its head down as it cropped the sweet green grass in the shadow of a cluster of spruces. Where was Burke? His eyes narrowed as he spied a thin figure hunched low over the saddle, and with a flick of his feet he prodded the stallion into a trot.

The bay looked up at his approach, its ears pricked, its nostrils flaring. Burke was unconscious, a nasty welt on his forehead testifying to the cause.

"Whoa there, boy," Nate said softly to show the bay it had nothing to fear. "Remember me?" He leaned down to grasp its reins, then slid off Pegasus.

The reverend groaned.

Nate put a hand on Burke's shoulder. Other than the two-inch welt there were no other injuries that he could see. Evidently the minister had hit a tree limb after all, back in the forest, and the bay had taken it on itself to meander on a southwesterly course. "Reverend Burke?"

Uttering a short gasp, Burke sat bolt upright as his eyes snapped wide and he stared about him in confusion. "The trees!" he blurted. "The trees!" Then he noticed that the bay was standing still and saw Nate by his side. "You!" he said angrily. "I nearly lost my life when you gave my horse that whack. The contrary critter wouldn't stop no matter what I did."

"Would you rather have been caught by the grizzly?" Nate countered.

"No, of course not," Burke said, and gazed in all directions. "Where is the bear? And where the dickens am I? The last thing I remember is seeing a tree limb appear out of nowhere." He reached up and gingerly touched the welt. "Goodness. Now I know why my head is splitting."

Nate handed the reins up and mounted Pegasus. "The grizzly is dead. A couple of friends of mine showed up and gave me a hand when I needed it most."

"Fellow trappers?"

"Shoshones. They're watching your pack animals until we get back."

The minister frowned. "You're allowing a pair of heathens to guard my possessions? Isn't that like letting a fox guard the henhouse?"

"They won't steal anything, if that's what you're worried about."

"Unfortunately, Mr. King, I don't have your confidence

in these savages. At best they're like primitive children, and one should never place temptation before a child. They lack the self-discipline to behave properly.''

"One of them is a close friend," Nate noted, annoyed by Burke's attitude. The man didn't even know Drags the Rope or Beaver Tail, yet he had no qualms about branding them as thieves, or worse. "I know him as well as I do myself. He's an honorable warrior, a decent human being.''

Burke snorted. "I'm afraid you've been living among the heathens too long, brother. You see nobility in them where none exists. Tell me, is this friend of yours a Christian?''

"No, but—''

"Then I've made my point," Burke interrupted smugly. "Remember what the Good Book says about those who aren't Christian.'' He cleared his throat before quoting more Scripture. "Give not that which is holy unto the dogs, neither cast ye your pearls before swine, lest they trample them under their feet, and turn again and rend you.''

Nate's lips compressed in a thin line. For Burke to accuse the Shoshones of being thieves had been bad enough. To call them dogs and pigs was more than he would tolerate. They were his adopted people, and he had come to know them as fine, intelligent, caring men and women who deserved as much respect as any white who ever lived. "For your information, Reverend, your belongings will be safer among the Shoshones than they would be in certain parts of New York City or St. Louis. As for them not being Christian, it's hardly their fault since no one has ever taught them our religion.''

John Burke smiled. "Precisely. Which is why I'm here. God willing, I will lead the heathens to the true light. *I* will be the shining example that shows them the error of their savage ways. You just watch.''

Chapter Six

The barking of a number of village dogs toward sunset drew the attention of three warriors conversing at the east edge of the encampment to the approaching party, and at their shouts Shoshones flocked from all directions to see who was coming.

Nate walked in the forefront, the Hawken in his left hand, leading Pegasus by the reins. His mood was a reflection of the storm clouds gathering to the west. Drags the Rope and Beaver Tail walked behind him. The three of them had secured the bear hide and as much meat as they could wrap inside it onto Pegasus, then packed more meat onto Drags the Rope's war horse. There had still been some left, and Nate had proposed tying it onto Burke's bay in order not to let it go to waste, but the minister had stubbornly refused to let his mount be used to haul a "miserable load of bloody meat."

The more Nate saw of the reverend, the less he liked the man. And he felt guilty for doing so. Burke was a

man of the cloth. Nate had been reared to always respect
the clergy, to believe they were special because they had
devoted their lives to God. Yet Burke made a mockery of
that devotion by flaunting it, and by regarding anyone who
didn't believe as he did as inferior.

Maybe, Nate reflected, he was being too critical. Burke
had been through hell out on the prairie, enduring hardships that would unsettle any man. Perhaps all it would
take was a hot meal and a good night's sleep to put him
in a better—friendlier—frame of mind.

There was much gesticulating and pointing among the
assembling Shoshones. Just arriving on the scene were a
pair Nate knew well. Chief Broken Paw was a wise old
man whose gray hairs and many wrinkles attested to the
fact he had earned his wisdom the hard way. Beside him
walked a giant to rival the Biblical Goliath, a warrior
almost seven feet tall who had one of the most fitting Indian
names Nate had ever heard. Touch the Clouds. He was
the son of a venerable warrior named Spotted Bull, who
in turn was the husband of Winona's aunt.

The chief and the giant moved a few feet in front of the
main crowd.

"What is this, Grizzly Killer?" Touch the Clouds
called. "You rode off to hunt buffalo and come back
walking your horse and bringing a stranger into our village?"

"I killed a brown bear instead of a buffalo," Nate responded, nodding at the hide on his stallion, and nearly
laughed aloud at the giant's stupefied expression.

"*Another* brown bear?" Chief Broken Paw said, smiling. "Keep this up and soon there will not be any left."

Nate shrugged and feigned a yawn. "It would serve
them right if they are wiped out. Any animal so easy to
kill will not last forever."

Touch the Clouds regained his composure and came

forward to inspect the pelt. "It seems to have been a very small bear," he commented

"How true," Drags the Rope said. "I only had to sit on my horse instead of stand on it to touch the bear's chin."

"You should have seen Grizzly Killer," Beaver Tail added, clearly amused at the giant's expense. "The bear had killed my brave horse and was about to do the same to Drags the Rope when Grizzly Killer rode right up to it. With no thought to his own danger, he shot it in the head."

"Grizzly Killer is a brave man;" Touch the Clouds acknowledged in an odd tone.

By now the news had spread among the Shoshones and they were talking excitedly. Brown bears, as they called grizzlies, were the most formidable animals they knew, and they considered it a favorable omen, a sign of good medicine, when a tribal member killed one.

Nate's moment of glory was short-lived. He was about to relate the fight with the beast, as custom dictated, when John Burke rode up alongside him.

"What is all this jabbering about, brother? I'm on my last legs and these heathens are more interested in your flea-ridden hide."

Chief Broken Paw scrutinized the minister closely. "Who is this white man, Grizzly Killer? Why does he speak words that sting like bees?"

"His name is Medicine Teacher," Nate replied, and promptly wished he had thought to change the name to Rock Head. "I found him on the prairie. The Cheyennes had stolen his horses and left him to die."

The chief stared at Burke's bay and the two pack animals. "You got his horses back for him?"

"No. The Cheyennes returned them," Nate said, and detailed his encounter with the five warriors. The Shoshones listened attentively, some nodding, some whispering.

"This Medicine Teacher truly must be under the protection of the Everywhere Spirit,'' Chief Broken Paw remarked when Nate was done. ''It is unheard of for an enemy to return stolen horses, especially the Cheyennes, who are such expert horse thieves. It is the same as the Blackfeet sparing a life, something that is never done.'' He smiled at Burke. ''I would be honored if this great man would stay at my lodge during his time among our people.''

''Who is this codger?'' the minister asked. ''And why is he looking at me the way he is?''

Nate hoped his feelings toward Burke weren't showing as he said to Broken Paw, ''Medicine Teacher is grateful for your offer, but he has already agreed to stay at my lodge. Rest assured we will come visit you as soon as he is rested.''

''My lodge is always open to him.''

Neither Drags the Rope nor Beaver Tail made any comments, and Nate knew why. Although neither man spoke English, they had been able to tell by Burke's attitude earlier exactly what kind of man Burke was. They weren't fooled by the name Nate had given him.

There was a commotion at the back of the crowd. Some of the people parted to allow a raven-haired woman in a beaded buckskin dress and a muscular boy of eight wearing a typical Shoshone-style buckskin shirt and leggings to pass through.

Nate momentarily forget all about Reverend Burke in the heartfelt warm rush of seeing his loved ones again. ''Winona,'' he said softly, and took his wife into his arms, savoring the minty scent of her hip-length tresses and the feel of her soft but full body against his. Heedless of the other Shoshones, he kissed her. Normally, members of the tribe refrained from public displays of affection. Courting couples often stood under blankets together in the evenings, but by and large most of the men and women were shy about showing their feelings toward one another where all eyes could see. Most had long since become used to Nate's impulsive nature, laying the blame on his fiery white blood. A few of Winona's female friends had teased her about it, hinting that she must enjoy a lively blanket life of her own once the fire in their lodge was extinguished.

"Did I hear correctly, husband?" Winona asked in perfect English as she stepped back, her concerned brown eyes straying to the bear hide on Pegasus. "You had another run-in with a grizzly?"

"Afraid so," Nate replied. "And now you have a new robe."

The eight-year-old moved between them. "When will I get to kill a brown bear, Pa?"

Nate looked down into the hopeful face of his pride and joy, a spitting image of himself at that age but with the finer, more angular features of Winona's Shoshone ancestry mixed in. In keeping with the fact the boy had parents from two diverse cultures, two names had been bestowed on him at birth. Nate had picked Zachary, and both Winona and he had decided on Stalking Coyote for the child's Indian name. Except for a brief visit to St. Louis and the annual Rendezvous, the boy had never lived among white men. Now, at a distance, young Zach would pass for a full-blooded Shoshone. Only close up did it become apparent he was part white. "In due time, sprout," Nate answered. "A bird doesn't fly its first day in the nest. You're not quite old enough yet to tangle with a grizzly."

"Darn."

Reverend Burke coughed. "I take it this is your wife and son. How about introducing me, brother?"

"Certainly," Nate said, and proceeded to do so, noting how the minister gave Winona a cursory glance but studied Zach long and hard. He then explained that the minister would be staying at their lodge until fit to travel again.

"We will be honored to have you, Reverend," Winona graciously said.

"I must say, my dear, your English is excellent," Burke remarked.

"I've had an excellent teacher."

"Has your husband also taught you the Scriptures? Are you and your child Christians?"

"We do own a bible, Reverend. And Nate has told me much about the Lord God of your people. Still, there is much I do not understand."

Burke smiled. "Then it's good I have come. I'll be able to answer any questions you might have, and perhaps before I depart to minister to those I seek, I might have the pleasure of baptizing you and your son."

Nate glanced up, wondering what the minister meant by "those I seek," but before he could inquire the Shoshones clustered around them, some congratulating Nate on slaying the brown bear, some to get an account of the fight from Drags the Rope or Beaver Tail, and some to stare at the minister in frank curiosity. At length Nate was able to start toward his lodge. He let Zach lead Pegasus while he took the pack animals. Winona stayed close by his side.

Not all the Shoshones had congregated at the east side of the village. Small children scampered playfully about, frequently accompanied by frolicking dogs. Here and there women sat outdoors as they frequently did during the warmer months, either tanning hides, sewing clothes, repairing blankets, or doing any of the many domestic tasks they performed daily. Warriors were busy grooming their horses, sharpening knives, restringing bows, or doing other such activities regarded as fitting for a man. Among the Shoshones and other tribes there were clear-cut distinctions between the work performed by men and that performed by women, and it was exceedingly rare for a member of one sex to take up the crafts of the other.

Burke pointed at a circle of seated elderly warriors in

the middle of an argument. "What is that all about?" he inquired.

"They're gambling with dice made of buffalo bone," Nate disclosed, and saw the minister frown. "At the moment there is a dispute over a wager one of them made."

"I had no idea these heathens indulged in such wicked practices," Burke said, drawing a sharp glance from Winona. "Gambling is the earmark of the wicked and the playfellow of the lazy."

"My people have played at dice since the beginning of time," Winona responded. "It has not hurt us in any way."

"That's where you're wrong, I'm afraid. Gambling eats away at the soul like dry rot eats away the inside of trees. It's far better for men to turn to the Lord for their diversions than to take part in idle pursuits. Instead of rolling dice, those men would do better to spend their time giving thanks to God and praying for salvation."

More and more Nate was regretting his decision to bring Burke back to the village. It could only lead to trouble if the reverend didn't learn to keep quiet about matters that offended him. Nate had known many ministers during the years he spent growing up in New York City, but none had been like this man. His parents had taken him to church every Sunday without fail, and he had listened to countless sermons by various men of the cloth. Frequently, his mother had invited the ministers over for meals. He remembered them as serious but lighthearted men who enjoyed a fine cigar and a good laugh as much as the next person. None had been as exacting as Reverend John Burke. None had Burke's knack for rubbing folks the wrong way.

Ahead Nate spied their lodge, constructed by Winona and seven of her relatives and friends. The women had sewn together the buffalo-hide cover after he had collected the long, straight saplings needed for the frame and trimmed the trees of all their small branches. One of Winona's kin was a skilled lodge-maker, and under her supervision, with Winona providing plenty of food and the rest supplying plenty of gossip, the 12 hides used had been stitched together in under a day.

This had taken place three years ago. Until that time, whenever Nate and Winona visited the Shoshones, they had stayed with her aunt, Morning Dove, the wife of Spotted Bull. But Nate had tired of imposing on the kindness of her relatives, and had had the lodge built so his family could stay as long as they wanted in the privacy and comfort of their own dwelling. When it was time to leave for their log cabin near Long's Peak, they would dismantle the lodge and drag it home behind their pack animals on several travois.

Nate halted near the entrance and scanned the camp, seeking sign of their black dog, Samson, a mongrel brute capable of holding its own against a panther. As usual the dog was nowhere to be seen. It was the most independent-minded, contrary critter he had ever come across. More than likely it was off in the forest somewhere chasing rabbits or bothering the squirrels, its favorite pastime.

Burke reined up and sniffed. "Are we all staying in this puny wigwam? Won't it be terribly crowded?"

"A wigwam, Reverend, is the kind of lodge the Ottawas, Ojibwas, and other tribes back East live in," Nate corrected him. "These lodges are called teepees."

"Wigwam. Teepee. What difference does it make?" Burke asked, dismounting. "It still promises to be crowded." Bending over, he entered without so much as a by-your-leave.

Nate was about to follow him when Winona clutched his elbow and leaned over to whisper in his ear.

"Later, my husband, you have explaining to do. A *lot* of explaining."

Chapter Seven

As it turned out, his explanation had to wait. They unloaded the bear hide and meat, picketed the horses near their lodge, and were just settling in when a tremendous ruckus broke out on the west side of the village. Nate was the first out of the lodge, his Hawken in his right hand. The sun had dipped below the high mountains to the west, shrouding the Rockies in twilight except for vivid streaks of red and orange framing the horizon.

From harsh experience Nate knew that just before sunrise and right after sunset were the times most favored by roving war parties to conduct their raids. Before the sun came up few warriors were fully awake. After sunset most of the men were in their lodges awaiting their suppers, fatigued after a hard day of work. In particular the Blackfeet, those widely dreaded scourges of the plains and the mountains, liked to strike when their enemies were most vulnerable. So when he heard a Shoshone shouting that each man should arm himself, he figured the Blackfeet must be up to their old, nasty tricks.

Beaver Tail appeared to the north, running toward the source of the noise.

"Do you know what is happening?" Nate asked.

"Bloods," the young warrior replied.

Nate rested his free hand on a flintlock. The Bloods were almost as bad as the Blackfeet. Those two tribes, plus a third known as the Piegans, had formed a confederacy of sorts and were continually waging war against everyone else. He had started to go see for himself when Winona and Zach emerged.

"I heard that," she declared. "You be careful."

"I will," Nate vowed, and looked at his son. "You stay by your mother's side and keep your bow handy in case some of the Bloods sneak into the village while I'm gone."

"Don't worry none, Pa. I'll part their hair if they show their faces."

"And I will keep an eye on our guest," Winona added icily.

"Thanks," Nate said, glad Burke had curled up on a hide the moment he'd entered the lodge and fallen instantly asleep. As exhausted as the minister was, Nate expected him to slumber until morning or later. He sprinted toward a throng of Shoshones near the lake shore.

"Grizzly Killer! Wait for me!"

He looked over his shoulder to find Touch the Clouds close on his heels. The giant held an enormous bow made of ash and had a large brown quiver strapped to his broad back. Side by side they ran to the shore, where a lean warrior was being besieged by questions as everyone tried to talk at once.

"How many were there, Otter Eyes?" asked one man.

"Where did you see them?" wanted to know another.

"Were they on horseback or on foot?"

"Did they try to kill you?"

Touch the Clouds stepped forward. "One at a time! How can he tell us what happened with all of you jabbering like women?" He moved through the excited warriors, towering over every single one of them, his mere presence serving to calm them down. When he reached Otter Eyes, he motioned for complete silence. "Now then. Tell those of us who arrived late what took place."

"There is not much to tell," Otter Eyes said. "I was bringing my horses to water when I saw two men at the edge of those trees and yelled to them, thinking they were friends." He pointed at the forest 20 yards away. "Instead of answering me, they ran off. As they did, I saw by their hair that they were Bloods. So I gave the alarm."

Nate stared at the woods. The deepening darkness made a shadowy maze of the many trunks and thickets. It would be difficult to identify anyone, let alone tell the difference between Shoshones and Bloods. Not that he suspected Otter Eyes was lying. But it might be that the warrior had simply seen a pair of Shoshones going off for some reason and mistaken them for enemies. He saw Touch the Clouds gaze in the same direction, his forehead creased in thought, and figured the giant had reached the same conclusion.

"We should go after them!" Beaver Tail cried. "We must not let them spy on us and get away with it! What if they were part of a large war party? This minute they must be on their way back to tell their friends exactly where to find our village."

Cries of agreement erupted from a dozen throats. Weapons were waved overhead and war whoops cut the air. Several men headed for the forest, but a sharp command brought them all to a halt.

"Stop! Have you taken leave of your senses?" Touch the Clouds demanded. "If there is a war party out there and all of you go rushing off into the woods, who will protect our families and our horses if the war party gets past you?"

The sheepish expressions on some of the Shoshones' faces were so comical Nate had to suppress a grin.

"It will soon be too dark to see anything," Touch the Clouds went on. "I say we have men stand guard until morning, then look for tracks and follow them."

Deliberations ensued as the warriors debated the merits of the idea. Nate placed the stock of his Hawken on the ground and leaned on the barrel, idly listening. He agreed with Touch the Clouds and knew the rest would too, given five or ten minutes of squabbling. Unlike whites, whose armies had clearly defined chains of command and were models of military precision, Indians seldom obeyed any single leader and did as they pleased whether at war or not. It was, in his estimation, their single greatest weakness.

Nate knew how the tribes east of the Mississippi had been treated by his own kind. Those that hadn't been enslaved had been wiped out, and those that hadn't been wiped out had been forced to relocate to less desirable land when envious whites decided they wanted the choice parcels for themselves. Indians had been on the continent before the arrival of the first Europeans, yet the Europeans saw fit to deny the natives citizenship when they formed their governments and divided the land. As a result, the Indians became despised and belittled outcasts, treated more like animals than human beings.

One of Nate's biggest fears was that someday the same thing would happen to the tribes west of the Mississippi. The idea seemed preposterous, but a clash would be inevitable if the population of the United States kept growing at its current rate. Already there were settlers heading for the rich new lands in Oregon country.

He hoped he wouldn't live to see the day when towns and cities sprang up on the prairie and in the mountains. If they did, it would bring to an end the way of life he cherished so dearly and forever put a limit on the freedom he valued as much as life itself.

So far he knew of only two or three trappers who shared his concerns. One was his mentor and best friend, Shakespeare McNair. Shakespeare had lived in the Rockies longer than any white man and, until recently, had been remarkably active for a man of his advanced years. Lately, though, McNair had taken to spending all his time at his cabin in the company of his Flathead wife. Lord, how Nate missed him! He toyed with the notion of paying a visit on his way home, then abruptly realized Touch the Clouds was speaking.

"I will be one of the first to stand guard. Who else will volunteer? There should be at least ten if we are to protect our village properly." He paused. "How about you, Grizzly Killer? Are you with me?"

Nate hesitated. After being gone all day he wanted to spend time with his family. And he didn't like the thought of Winona and Zach being left alone with Reverend Burke. He knew very little about the man, and the little he did know did not inspire trust. The minister, though, should sleep the night through. And Nate's desire to be with his loved ones had to be weighed against the welfare of the entire tribe. There really was no choice. "All right," he responded. "I will gladly do my part."

Immediately other warriors offered to help, and Touch the Clouds picked those he needed. Chief Broken Paw stood close to the giant but made no effort to interfere. Touch the Clouds was the best warrior in the Shoshone village, and in matters of warfare his judgment usually prevailed.

Nate was thinking that he would like to stand guard several hundred yards to the east, to be nearer his lodge, when Touch the Clouds came over and leaned down so only he could hear.

"Thank you, my friend. I was afraid some of the others would object to my idea and we would argue for a long time.'' He glanced around to be certain no one was trying to eavesdrop. ''Crooked Antler had that look in his eyes.''

Nate understood. Crooked Antler was the second best warrior in the tribe, and he saw fit to constantly oppose Touch the Clouds. Whether sparked by jealousy or petty revenge because Touch the Clouds had counted more coup and received more honors, the one-sided feud had been going on for two years or better and everyone in the village was aware of it. Crooked Antler was spiteful but he wasn't stupid; he was always careful not to push the giant too far, not to step over that invisible line that would result in a personal challenge. In a fight to the death he wouldn't stand a chance and he knew it.

''I called on you first because your word carries great weight with our people,'' Touch the Clouds was saying. ''Even though you are white, you are considered a fearless warrior whose good medicine is better than anyone else's.''

Nate chuckled. ''Has some trapper sold you a bottle of whiskey?''

''I am serious, my friend,'' the giant asserted. ''Everyone knows of your battles with the Blackfeet and the Utes. And no man since time began has killed as many of the great brown bears as you have. Your good medicine is extremely powerful.'' He absently scratched his forehead. ''Which is very surprising since you do not even own a medicine bundle.''

''I have been lucky,'' Nate said, and meant it. Most of his narrow escapes and victories over his enemies had been the result of dumb luck. But he could see how the Shoshones regarded him as a man possessing mighty medicine. To them, a man made his own luck by appealing to the invisible spirits for good medicine that would protect him from harm and ill fortune. Many warriors owned what were called medicine bundles, consisting of ordinary objects such as feathers, pipes, tobacco, or something else they might have seen in a dream and believed would give them special powers such as warding off the arrows of their enemies or keeping them in good health forever. There were even tribal medicine bundles. He had heard the Arapahos revered a bundle containing a flat pipe that was kept in a special lodge and watched over by a devoted keeper who made sure the bundle was always hung in the exact center of the lodge and never, ever allowed it to touch the ground.

"I know better," Touch the Clouds said. "You are talking like a white man, not a Shoshone. Your medicine is very powerful, and if you ever make a medicine bundle you will grow very rich by selling some of your power."

That idea had never occurred to Nate. Sometimes, no matter how hard a warrior tried, he was unable to see any visions or have any significant dreams. In such instances the warrior often went to another man noted for having good medicine and bought some of the contents of the man's medicine bundle, or perhaps the entire bundle, so he would have his own good medicine.

Touch the Clouds turned and addressed the others, asking for warriors to volunteer to stand watch during the second half of the night.

Nate felt his stomach growl. He was very hungry, but he wouldn't get a chance to fill his belly until about midnight, when he would be relieved. Resigned to his fate, he waited as those warriors who were not standing guard on the first watch departed for their lodges.

The giant faced him. "If there are Bloods in the area, I doubt they will raid us before dawn. But if they do, our weakest points are here and a ways to the south where the forest is thickest. If you will stand guard here, I will take the other spot."

So much for a place closer to Winona and Zach! Nate wryly reflected. He sighed, then said, "As you wish."

Touch the Clouds had actually bestowed an honor on him by asking him to protect one of the two approaches a war party would be most likely to use. The request was, in effect, a public testimonial to his courage and reliability, as the eight warriors who were staring at him clearly recognized.

In pairs and one by one the others drifted toward their positions around the camp. The giant hiked southward, pausing once to smile and wave, his teeth white in the murky night.

Nate stretched and gazed up at the multitude of stars sparkling in the firmament. A cool breeze from the northwest fanned his cheeks. Water gently lapped at the edge of the lake shore not six feet from his moccasins. The nearest lodge was better than 40 feet to the south. About 20 yards in front of him loomed the inky wall of vegetation that might conceal lurking Bloods. If they should spring a surprise attack, he would be on his own until the Shoshones rallied to defend their village. Like Touch the Clouds, he doubted the Bloods would do anything before dawn. But he had to stay alert anyway. The life of every man, woman, and child was riding on his shoulders.

He moved nearer to the water and along the shore another five yards, then knelt. Now he was close enough to the trees to be able to detect anyone moving across the open space between the lake and the woods and sound the alarm. Or so he hoped. The Bloods were bound to be experts at snaking silently toward an enemy encampment. It was unlikely he would have much forewarning of their presence before he spotted them.

Both flintlocks were wedged under his belt and he had his knife and tomahawk with him. His buckskins and beaver hat would keep him warm, so except for his protesting stomach he would be comfortable while he waited for midnight and his relief. Boredom might be his biggest problem.

Suddenly, as if to prove him wrong, a twig cracked in the forest.

Chapter Eight

Nate froze, probing the forest for movement. He didn't have to look very hard. A shadowy form materialized, advancing from the trees and moving directly toward the lodges. As near as he could tell, there was only one man. Quietly placing the Hawken down, he drew his big butcher knife and slinked forward. If he could capture the Blood alive, the Shoshones might be able to wring important information from him, such as how many were in the raiding party and where they were.

The vague figure made no attempt to conceal himself. Cocky devil, Nate thought, easing onto all fours with the knife clutched tight in his right hand. He angled to one side of the warrior's line of travel, then flattened and tensed for the spring.

On came the Blood, armed with a lance that he was holding at waist height instead of ready to use in combat.

Nate was amazed at the man's careless attitude, but he had no time to dwell on it. In seconds the Blood was passing him, and he let the warrior take two strides before he surged upright and pounced, his left arm looping around the man's neck and clamping down hard so the Blood couldn't cry out even as he pressed the tip of his blade into the man's right cheek and growled in Shoshone, "Make one move and you are dead."

The warrior started to struggle and gurgled as if drowning.

"Do you understand?" Nate demanded, applying more pressure and digging the knife in deeper. Immediately the man dropped his lance and ceased resisting. Nate slowly turned, forcing the Blood to move with him, self-conscious about having his back to the woods when there undoubtedly were more Bloods somewhere in the vicinity. He scanned the tree line but saw nothing. Should he shout to bring the Shoshones on the run? Or was it wiser to keep quiet so the war party didn't realize one of their own had been captured?

He headed south, pushing the Blood before him, his left forearm locked on the man's throat, his knife providing incentive for the warrior to cooperate. For over a minute he walked, constantly scouring the forest, barely paying attention to his prisoner, more concerned over getting an arrow or lance in the back than over the man giving him any trouble.

From out of the darkness came a walking mountain. Touch the Clouds appeared like a wraith out of nowhere, making no sound whatsoever. "Grizzly Killer?" he whispered. "Is that you?"

"Yes," Nate confirmed. "And I have caught one."

The giant came closer, peered into the prisoner's face, and made a sound like a bull elk startled by a stalking panther. "Have you taken a good look at your captive?"

"No. Why?"

"Perhaps you should."

Nate relaxed the pressure on the warrior's throat Just

enough so he could lean forward and see the man's features. Recognition took a second in the dark, but when he saw who it was he lowered his arms and stepped back. "Beaver Tail!"

The young warrior rubbed his throat and glanced from the giant to Nate. "You are strong, Grizzly Killer. I feared you would snap my neck before you learned it was I."

"You're fortunate I didn't shoot you on sight or slit you from ear to ear," Nate said. "What were you doing out in the forest?"

"The forest?" Touch the Clouds repeated.

Beaver Tail fidgeted nervously. "Yes. I wanted to see if there were Bloods nearby, so when you were talking and everyone was busy listening I sneaked off into the trees."

"You young fool," Touch the Clouds said sternly. "What if there had been a war party out there? What chance would you have had all alone? You took a needless risk."

"Which is easy for you to say," Beaver Tail replied. "You have counted more coup than ten men. You have no need to prove yourself. But what about those of us who have yet to count our first coup?"

Nate slid his knife into its sheath. The young man's motive was perfectly logical given the intense competition among the warriors to see who could garner the most honors in battle. To count coup a warrior would do practically anything: rush headlong into enemy fire, fight against overwhelming odds, even stake himself to the ground so that he couldn't leave the battlefield before all his enemies had turned tail or were dead.

"Patience, my friend," Touch the Clouds advised, draping a hand on Beaver Tail's shoulder. "You must have patience. Your time to count coup will come soon enough. Losing your hair in the meantime because you are too rash for your own good will make your name a laughingstock instead of one our women will speak with pride." He patted Beaver Tail's arm. "When you have been in as many terrible fights as I have, when you have seen so many honorable men die horrible deaths, many of them your best friends, you will not be so thirsty for blood."

"I will not rest until I have counted more coup than any Shoshone who ever lived!" Beaver Tail declared. Pivoting, he hastened toward the lodges, his back stiff, his chin thrust defiantly outward.

Touch the Clouds watched him go. "I have often wondered why the Great Medicine saw fit to make men so ignorant and childish. By the time we are old enough to figure out the way of the world, we are ready for the grave."

Nate had no answer for that one. "I should get back to my post," he said, thinking of his rifle, and began to retrace his steps. Hindsight told him it had been a mistake to go off and leave his Hawken behind. Not that any of the Shoshones would steal it. Few of them liked to use guns. Most preferred using their traditional bows and arrows over the white man's weapon, with good reason since a skilled archer could fire anywhere from ten to 20 shafts in the time it took the average trapper to reload. Then too, he had carved his initials on the stock and would have no problem identifying his own rifle.

Just being separated from the Hawken made him feel uncomfortable. A man's rifle was as essential to his continued existence as breathing itself, more so than a brace of pistols. Flintlocks were fine for close-in fighting and for shooting small game at close range. But for dropping bigger animals like buffalo, elk, and deer, at great distances, and for keeping hostiles at bay, there was nothing like a dependable Hawken.

He made for the approximate spot where he had jumped Beaver Tail, then walked to where he had deposited the rifle. It wasn't there. Bending over so he could see the ground better, he searched to the right and the left. He wasn't worried. He had simply misjudged the proper spot by a few feet or so and would find the rifle any moment.

A minute elapsed and he saw no trace of it. Puzzled, he straightened near the water and put his hands on his hips as he tried to deduce where he was going wrong. How could he be so far off the mark? Had he been farther east or west when he set the weapon down? In the excitement of seeing a presumed enemy, he might not have been as observant as he should have been.

Chiding himself for being such a dunderhead, he angled to the west, stooped low to examine every square inch of grass and dirt. If he failed to find the weapon in another minute or two, he would go to the nearest lodge and ask the warrior inside for a burning brand from the cooking fire. Weaving back and forth, he went closer to the trees. When he turned toward the village, he finally found his Hawken. But not in the way he expected.

The patter of rushing feet made Nate uncoil and spin, his right hand swooping to his flintlock. He saw a stocky shape an instant before something slammed into his forehead with the force of a runaway ten-ton boulder. Bright pinpoints of light blossomed before his eyes. And then the darkness claimed more than the land. It claimed his mind.

The tantalizing odor of roasting deer meat was the first sensation Nate became conscious of. He lay still, taking stock, aware he was on his back on the ground and a rock was gouging him in the lower back. His arms rested on his chest, his wrists were bound. Gruff voices spoke in a tongue he didn't know, but which he suspected was the language of the Bloods. His head throbbed. It hurt just to think. Otherwise, he seemed to be fine.

Cracking his eyelids, he peered at a group of seven Blood warriors gathered around a crackling fire over which a haunch of venison was roasting. Trees ringed them, leading him to surmise they were in a clearing in the forest. Through the trunks he spied the sun rising above the far horizon. Apparently he had been out all night long and now a new day was dawning. He could hear birds chirping and the chattering of an irate squirrel.

One of the Bloods, an imposing figure who wore three eagle feathers in his long hair, rose and came toward him.

Nate closed his eyes and feigned being unconscious. He involuntarily flinched when a sharp object jabbed him in the side. The warrior spoke a few words, then jabbed him again, only harder. There was nothing to be gained by pretending any longer, so Nate opened his eyes and stared up into the Blood's impassive face.

In the warrior's right hand was a hunting knife. He slid it into a sheath on his right hip before addressing Nate again. A second warrior, shorter and with a cleft chin, came over.

Nate didn't understand a word. "Do you speak Shoshone?" he asked when the warrior fell silent.

Neither Blood responded.

"How about English?" Nate inquired in that language.

Again the Bloods showed no indication they comprehended. They conversed briefly in their own tongue, then the one wearing the eagle feathers lifted his hands. "If you speak sign, white man, nod once."

Nate nodded. The shorter Blood drew a knife and leaned down to slice the rope binding his wrists.

"If you try to escape we will kill you here and now," the taller warrior signed. "I am Eagle Claw of the Bloods. Who are you, white man? And what were you doing at the Shoshone camp?"

Slowly sitting up, Nate rubbed his wrists to restore the circulation, then noticed the rest of the war party approaching. Two held bows, arrows nocked and ready to fly. He must make no unwarranted moves or he would never see his wife and son again. "I am known as Grizzly Killer," he signed. "The Shoshones are my adopted people."

Eagle Claw and the one with the cleft chin talked in their tongue for a bit. Finally, Eagle Claw looked down at him and said, "Are you the same Grizzly Killer who slew Mad Dog and White Bear of the Blackfeet?"

Nate answered honestly. Lying would do no good since he was the only white man in the entire Rocky Mountains who was called by that name. Occasionally Indian men from different tribes had the same name, but there were so few whites in the mountains that every name applied to only one person. "I am," he said.

Eagle Claw frowned. "The Blackfeet are our brothers."

"I know."

"Their enemies are our enemies."

"So I have heard," Nate said. The confederacy between the Blackfeet, Bloods, and Piegans was loose-knit in that they rarely conducted raids together or combined their forces to wage war, but whoever aroused the anger of one tribe incurred the wrath of all three.

"Then you must also know that we will slay you."

"You will try."

Eagle Claw's eyes narrowed, then he clapped his hands and burst into hearty laughter. Some of the others Joined in, but not the warrior with the cleft chin. He glowered, insulted by Nate's audacity.

"You have courage, white man," Eagle Claw signed when the rough mirth subsided. "I will grant you that. But even brave men die."

"The measure of a man is how well he dies," Nate signed, choosing his words carefully, seeking to impress the Bloods and buy himself a fighting chance. "Cowards whine and cry. Brave men like us go to the spirit world with our heads held high." He paused, gazing at each of them in turn. "All I ask is a fair chance, and I believe you will give it to me because the Bloods are widely regarded as some of the fiercest fighters of all the tribes in this land. Surely you would not stake me out to die in the hot sun like the Comanches might do, or tie me and fill me with arrows like the Apaches. Such deaths give no honor to anyone. Let me run a gauntlet. Or have me fight as many of you as you wish using only knives or tomahawks. Just let me die with dignity.''

At a gesture from Eagle Claw, the Bloods stepped closer to the fire and began a lively discussion.

Had the plea worked? Nate wondered hopefully. Indian men regarded bravery as the highest of virtues, and they regarded dying in battle as the ideal way to give up the ghost. No warrior wanted to die a helpless victim. He tried to read their feelings by their expressions but it was impossible. Eagle Claw and the one with the cleft chin were arguing strenuously while the others listened.

He suddenly spotted his weapons lying in a pile to the right of the fire. The flintlocks were on top. If he took a half-dozen quick strides, he could snatch them up and cut loose. But he knew those two Bloods with bows would both put arrows into him before he got off a single shot. He would live longer if he did nothing for the time being.

Eagle Claw was coming toward him. ''Your eloquent words have touched our hearts, white man. All of us except Kicking Bird agree a man should have a fighting chance when he dies. Kicking Bird says that you are white and don't deserve to leave this world like a true man. He says you should die like a dog.''

Nate glanced at the warrior with the cleft chin, who gave him a look of pure murderous venom.

''So you will get your wish,'' Eagle Claw signed.

''How is it to be?'' Nate asked.

The leader of the war party grinned enigmatically. ''We want that to be a surprise.''

Chapter Nine

Nate didn't like the fact that most of the Bloods then laughed and one made motions suggestive of a body being ripped to shreds, which prompted more laughter. Even Kicking Bird smiled, which confirmed the manner of death they had chosen must be particularly fiendish.

"We are about to have our breakfast," Eagle Claw signed. "Would you care for some deer meat?"

Surprised by the unexpected generosity, Nate licked his lips and signed, "Yes, please."

"A wise decision. You will soon need all of your strength," Eagle Claw said, and went to the fire.

One of the Bloods carved large pieces off the roast and passed them out to the others. He also brought a fist-sized chunk to Nate. The warriors sat down to eat, the pair with bows taking their seats with their backs to the flames so they could keep their eyes on their captive.

Rather than uselessly dwell on his impending fate, Nate ate with relish. He was famished, the deer meat delicious.

His piece included a wide strip of fat which he chewed on greedily, savoring the tangy taste. In his estimation animal fat was even better than the meat itself. When he was done he licked his fingers clean and smacked his lips, Indian fashion, to show the meal had been a good one.

The Bloods appeared surprised by his casual attitude. They soon had something else to occupy their attention, however; they divided up his weapons among them. Eagle Claw took the Hawken, and the rest of the band drew lots to see who would get what. Kicking Bird ended up with one of the flintlocks. To antagonize Nate, he held the gun out where Nate could see it and repeatedly stroked the barrel while smirking smugly.

Nate wished he could find a way of taking that bastard with him when he went. The sun was well above the horizon, and his intuition told him it wouldn't be much longer before the Bloods sprang their little surprise.

Minutes later Eagle Claw stood. The fire was hurriedly extinguished, each man gathered up his weapons, and in single file they hiked to the northwest. Nate was forced to walk between Kicking Bird and one of the bowmen. Like the Blackfeet, the Bloods rarely rode horses when on raids. They preferred to travel afoot and strike swiftly and silently.

It was a beautiful morning. Sunlight streamed through the branches overhead, bathing the grass and wild flowers in golden radiance. Sparrows flitted about in the undergrowth. Jays flew from tree to tree seeking food. And, as always, chipmunks were everywhere, darting to and fro.

Nate's headache evaporated after they had gone a mile. The invigorating mountain air and the exercise cleared his head and primed his senses for the ordeal to come. He kept looking for a chance to bolt for freedom, but the Blood behind him was as vigilant as a hawk.

Almost an hour after leaving the clearing they entered a verdant valley and marched up it to an ominous bald mountain. Huge shadows from drifting clouds shaded the higher elevations. The lower portion consisted of sheer cliffs and jumbled boulder fields where nothing grew. Desolate and bleak, the mountain was a barren contrast to the sea of life swirling all around it.

Eagle Claw walked back to Nate. "Do you know this mountain, white man?"

"No," Nate signed.

"My people call it the Mountain Where Evil Spirits Dwell. A long time ago one of our warriors was catching eagles up near the top when a strange wind came up and blew him over a cliff. When his friends found his body, they discovered it had been split in half. Since then we never go up there."

Craning his neck, Nate gazed at the rocky heights and spied a lone eagle soaring regally on the currents. He had once helped a Ute gather eagle feathers, and knew firsthand how difficult the task was. The favored technique consisted in digging a hole for a man to hide in, then constructing a latticework cover of thin limbs camouflaged with clods of grass and dirt. A warrior would stake out the bait, usually a dead rabbit, next to the hole and climb in. When an eagle dived down for the kill, the man would quickly reach out and grab the big bird's legs with one hand, then rapidly pluck feathers with the other. The warrior had to work swiftly since it was impossible to hold the enraged bird for long. Occasionally a man would lose a finger or an eye, and all for a handful of the most prized feathers an Indian could own. It would be much easier to simply shoot an eagle, but to the Indian way of thinking that would be a terrible waste of life. "Let me guess," he signed. "You want me to climb up there so the wind will blow me off?"

"No," Eagle Claw said, grinning. "We have another end in mind for you." Again he took the lead and they wound into a narrow ravine.

Nate paused once to scan the steep stone sides, and felt the tip of an arrow poke him in the spine. He walked on, perplexed, unable to deduce their intent. The ground was too rocky to bear tracks, so he had no idea whether the Bloods had ever been up the ravine before or not. He got the impression, though, they knew exactly where they were going.

The ravine twisted and turned like a sidewinder, eventually broadening out at the base of a high cliff on the south side of the foreboding mountain. Boulders the size of log cabins flanked the cliff, obscuring the lower section from view.

Nate reluctantly let himself be led into the boulder field. A glint of white to his left made him glance around, and there in the dust lay the leg bone of an elk, the bone bearing numerous teeth marks. He hadn't gone ten feet when he spotted another one, this time the thigh bone. Farther on he saw the complete skeleton of a young mountain sheep, the skull lying several feet from the rib section. Most of the rib bones had been cracked off and gnawed on.

Budding apprehension flowed through Nate. Where there were this many bones, there must be the lair of a predator nearby. In this instance it was most likely a panther—or mountain lion as some called the big cats. Was that their destination? He hardly thought so. The panther was just as apt to attack them as him.

He saw Eagle Claw slow, then stop in the shelter of a huge boulder. A warrior armed with a lance moved stealthily forward and disappeared. The others waited in silence. "What is going on?" he inquired.

"You will see soon enough, white dog," Kicking Bird answered. "And when you do, perhaps you will change your mind about wanting a fighting chance. If so, if you admit you are a coward and not a true man, I will make your end swift and painless." He tapped the hilt of his knife, then drew a finger across his throat.

Nate resented being taunted. ''There is only one coward here and he goes by the name of Kicking Bird.'' He detected a blur of motion a fraction of a second before his own flintlock struck him flush on the jaw. Lanced with pain, suddenly dizzy, he tottered and sank to his knees. Dimly, he heard harsh words spoken in whispers. When his vision cleared he saw Eagle Claw and another warrior restraining a furious Kicking Bird, who had cocked the pistol and was trying to point the barrel in his direction.

Kicking Bird gradually regained his self-control. He let the hammer down and barked a few words. His arms were released and he shoved the flintlock under the top of his leggings. His countenance mirrored volcanic hatred of Nate.

Wondering why they were all whispering, Nate slowly stood. Were they so near the predator's lair that they risked being heard and attacked? And what manner of predator would make a band of otherwise fearless Bloods behave like timid children?

In strained silence the warriors waited for their companion with the lance to return. Five minutes later he did, speaking urgently but softly to Eagle Claw, who pursed his lips and gave Nate a long, searching look.

What were they up to? Nate asked himself yet again. Kicking Bird was grinning at him, as if at a private joke. Whatever they had in mind must be typically devious and especially gruesome. Indians shared few of the qualms white men possessed about inflicting truly barbarous deaths on their enemies. Indeed, Indians victorious in battle often inflicted the most appalling atrocities on their captives to see how well the unfortunates held up. It wasn't that Indians delighted in torture. Torture was simply a test of bravery. Those taken prisoner knew what to expect and would do the same if the situation was reversed.

Eagle Claw took the lead again, Nate's Hawken held firmly in his hands.

The band wound deeper into the field of mammoth boulders, winding ever nearer the base of the bald mountain. Nate saw more bones. Lots more. In vain he hunted for tracks, for any clue as to the identity of the creature responsible, but the rocky ground was a blank page.

After three minutes of travel the Bloods slowed. This time two warriors were sent ahead while the band waited.

"It will not be long now, Grizzly Killer," Kicking Bird signed with a sneer.

"Until what?" Nate responded.

"Be patient, white dog," Kicking Bird said, and added mockingly, "Are you still feeling brave? Or are you ready to admit that all your talk of dying bravely was the talk of a weakling stalling for time in the hope you could escape?"

"You will see how brave I am when the time comes," Nate signed, then grinned. Here he was, sparring words with the Blood just as a shoshone would. In some ways he was more Indian than he realized,

"You find this humorous?" Kicking Bird asked.

"I find you humorous," Nate answered. "Until I met you, I had no idea that Blood men like to work their mouths more than their brains. I am quite amazed the Blackfeet would accept your tribe as allies."

Kicking Bird bristled, his hand swooping to the flintlock. For a moment he was on the verge of drawing. But he checked himself with a visible effort and relaxed his grip. "The only reason I do not kill you here and now is because I know what is in store for you and I do not want to deprive myself of the satisfaction of hearing you scream and plead for your miserable life."

Eagle Claw walked up to them and signed to Nate. "Why do you persist in insulting him? Kicking Bird is noted for his fiery temper. If you are not careful, he will shoot you where you stand."

"This white dog wants me to," Kicking Bird signed

using sharp, angry gestures. "He hopes I will spare him from his deserved fate, but he will be disappointed. I want to watch him die in intense agony. I want to see his guts ripped from his body and hear the crunch of his bones as—"

"Enough!" Eagle Claw interrupted. "You will spoil our surprise."

"My apology," Kicking Bird said.

Nate couldn't resist the opening. "There is no need to apologize. We all understand how children like to make idle boasts."

A flinty gleam came into Kicking Bird's eyes. "I have never looked forward to the death of an enemy with so much anticipation as I look forward to yours."

At that juncture the two warriors returned on the run. The Bloods clustered together and exchanged whispered words for several minutes. Eventually the pair with bows took up positions behind Nate and Eagle Claw motioned for him to start walking.

High above them reared the stark, jagged mountain, shrouded in shadows from passing clouds. Nate guessed they were within 50 yards of a towering cliff scarred by deep cracks and broken sections, toward which they were evidently heading. The Bloods were exercising great care, halting behind each boulder to survey the route ahead and crossing open spaces swiftly. He could practically feel their anxious tension.

He glanced back at the grim bowmen, who had him covered with their shafts, and frowned. It had been a mistake not to attempt to escape sooner. Now he must either commit virtual suicide by making a bid for his freedom or accept the inevitable and face whatever lay ahead. There was always the slim chance he might be able to slay the creature and then effect his escape. The sight of more bones, this time those of a bear, gave him second thoughts. The size of the bear's partially crushed skull revealed it had been between two and four years of age, not a cub by any means, in the prime of its vigor and strength.

Nate licked his lips and rubbed his moist palms together. What was capable of slaying a grown bear? He began to wonder if the creature might be of an unknown species, one he had never encountered. All tribes had legends of monsters, many dating from the times of antiquity when the Indians first settled on the North American continent. Most involved tales of heroic warriors who fought and vanquished ferocious beasts unlike any currently alive. And too, he recalled his own harrowing experience not long ago in a hidden valley far to the north where he had nearly lost his life to The Thing That Lurks in the Dark, as the Crows called the mysterious denizen of that valley.

Suddenly his reflection was brought to an end; they emerged from the boulder field less than 30 yards from the base of the cliff. Between them and the rock face the ground sloped down to form a huge bowl. They stood on the rim, surveying the erosion-formed depression. In front of them and to the left the earth walls of the bowl were ten to 15 feet high. To the right was an earthen ramp extending from the top to the bottom. The opposite side was actually the cliff itself, and at its base was the entrance to a cave, a murky opening a dozen feet high and equally as wide.

Nate took all this in at a glance. His main attention was riveted on the scores of skeletons littering the bowl floor. He recognized bones from all sorts of animals. Whatever killed them must have an insatiable appetite. The cave, he realized with a start, had to be the creature's lair. He had started to take a step backwards away from the edge when a rough pair of hands rammed into his shoulder blades and he was brutally shoved over the brink.

Chapter Ten

Nate instinctively threw out his arms to balance himself as he fell. He felt fleeting surprise, and then the ground was rushing up to meet him and he had to concentrate on relaxing as he hit to better absorb the shock and save his legs from injury. Too late he saw the bones of an elk directly under him. He tried to slant to one side but his momentum was too great. The soles of his feet slammed down onto the elk's rib cage and he heard a loud crack as one of the ribs snapped off. Jarring pain shot up his left leg. In a twinkling he was pitched to the left, onto his side, and he landed hard on his left arm, jarring the elbow and causing his arm to go numb.

For a few seconds he lay there, gathering his wits. His blood raced in his veins, his heart pounded in his chest. Now he knew why Kicking Bird had looked forward to his death with such relish. The Bloods were counting on whatever lived in the cave to do the same to him as it had done to countless wild animals. They were giving him his fighting chance, all right, against a monster that killed for food.

Nate pushed to his knees and glanced at the cave mouth, expecting to see a hideous nightmare appear. But nothing moved in the lair. Perhaps it was nocturnal and slept during the day. If he moved quickly he could run up the ramp and get the hell out of there before the thing came out.

He pushed upright and winced as pain lanced his left ankle. Was it broken? Taking a few tentative steps, he concluded he had suffered a mild sprain, which was the least of his worries given the circumstances. He turned toward the ramp and broke into a shuffling run, covering five yards before he heard a buzzing sound and an arrow thudded into the dirt at his feet.

Nate looked up. The seven Bloods, all smiles, were still perched on the rim. Both warriors with bows were set to loose a shaft again should he attempt to use the ramp. They had him right where they wanted him, and now they were going to stand up there and watch as whatever lurked in the cave made a meal of him.

Kicking Bird's hands moved in sign language. "Do you still pretend to have courage, white dog?"

Twisting, Nate glanced at the ramp 20 feet off. So close, yet so far. And there was no other way out. He faced the Bloods again, clenching his fists in fury.

Eagle Claw was holding the Hawken in the crook of his left elbow. "We decided this would be a fitting end for you, Grizzly Killer. Do not worry. If you die well, we will tell our people and spread the word among the Blackfeet and the Piegans. Sooner or later the story will get back to the Shoshones and they will honor your passing." He gazed at the cave. "We have known of Silver Hair for many years. Those who came to this mountain for eagle feathers always gave him and his lair a wide berth."

Silver Hair? They had a name for the monster? Nate

pivoted so he could keep an eye on the cave.

"Silver Hair is the oldest of his kind," Eagle Claw continued in sign. "Some say he has lived forever. Some claim he can never be killed. It is most appropriate that he be the one who kills you."

Why was it so damned fitting? Nate mused, and cast about for a weapon. There were plenty of bones, some heavy thigh bones that would suffice as a club. He saw one that appeared to be sturdy and went over to pick it up.

Deep within the cave, something growled.

A ripple of fear coursed down Nate's back and he froze in the act of reaching for the thigh bone to stare at the cave in dread. Whatever dwelled in there was awake and might be coming out! He grabbed the bone and stepped back, his skin crawling. Low chortles from on high drew him up short. The Bloods were laughing at him! A surge of indignation replaced his fear. Mad at himself for letting abject fright get the better of him, he glared up at the band.

Kicking Bird's shoulders shook with glee.

Nate took a few steps to the left, seeking a spot to make his stand. The scattered bones offered nowhere to conceal himself, so he had no choice but to fight for his life. From out of the cave issued another, louder, growl. The creature was indeed emerging. He hefted the thigh bone, so heavy and yet so puny.

A third growl let him know the monster was close to the entrance.

Nate had rarely felt so helpless. He thought of Winona and Zach and felt profoundly sorry he had failed them. Since a woman was rarely able to live by herself in Indian society, Winona would be forced to find a new husband, even though she had many times asserted that should he die, she would never marry again. And young Zach would be deprived of a father's guidance when he needed it the most.

Something moved in the cave.

Crouching, Nate clutched the end of the thigh bone with both hands and waited, his eyes probing the gloomy confines of the passageway through which the monster was approaching. He could see an enormous bulk moving ponderously outward. It paused just shy of the sunlight and he heard it sniff several times. Then, with measured strides, it advanced into the open.

Nate wished the earth would open up and swallow him. In all his years in the Rockies, in all his run-ins with wild beasts, he had never beheld anything as huge as the stupendous grizzly that now stood and met his gawking gaze with a baleful stare of its own. A colossal creature, it was almost the size of a full-grown buffalo bull. Likewise remarkable was the color of its coat; while grizzlies could be any color from yellowish-brown to almost black, often with white-tipped hairs that gave them their grizzled aspect, this one was solid silver from the tip of its twitching black nose to the end of its stubby tail.

Now Nate understood why the Bloods kept insisting his end would be so appropriate. After all, what could be more fitting for someone named Grizzly Killer than to meet his end under the slashing claws of the biggest grizzly in existence? He glanced up at the rim, thinking the band would be enjoying more laughter at his expense, and was mildly surprised to see they had all flattened and were peeking over the edge to witness the outcome of his battle.

The grizzly had yet to make a threatening move. It was studying him, perhaps confused at finding a human so close to its lair. Nate knew it wouldn't stand still for long. The number of skeletons dotting the bowl and lying among the boulders disclosed this one was an inveterate meat eater, unlike a normal bear. All grizzlies ate meat from time to time, but most would rather dine on berries, fruit, insects, leaves, and twigs. Meat was not their staple. Even

when they slew trappers or Indians, they seldom consumed
the bodies.

This grizzly was a different story entirely. Sometimes
the great bears developed a craving for raw flesh and would
eat little else. They would even kill their own kind if
another bear strayed onto their territory. The gigantic creature before him was just such a carnivorous monster.

Nate held himself as rigid as a pole. He scarcely
breathed. He saw the grizzly sweep its head from side to
side, then tilt its head upward to better catch the air currents. There could be no doubt the thing had seen him.
So what was it waiting for?

The bear took five steps to its left, halted, and resumed
sniffing.

Mystified, Nate waited for the beast to charge. His club
might as well be a blade of grass for all the good it would
do him. A bear that size would be impervious to any and
all blows, except possibly on the face. Once it came at
him, he would go for its eyes. Perhaps, if he could temporarily blind it, he might be able to reach the ramp provided the Bloods didn't kill him first. A quick look at the
rim confirmed they were still there, seven heads all in a
row, most smirking at his expense. What he wouldn't give
to be able to turn the tables and have them in his place!

A crazy idea blossomed, a way of possibly diverting
the bear's attention from himself to the Bloods. It all depended on the grizzly. Would the beast charge at his slightest move, or would it hold off for ten or 20 seconds, giving
him time to put his harebrained scheme into effect?

So far the monster did not appear eager to devour him.
Still sniffing, Silver Hair moved to the right.

Nate suddenly had an insight. If the bear had lived in
that cave for many years, as the Bloods claimed, then it
must be getting on in years, an old-timer well past its
prime despite its tremendous size. If so, its eyesight must
be extremely poor. Throughout their lives, grizzlies relied

extensively on their sense of smell because their vision was inferior even to man's. Advancing years only compounded the problem.

There was a saying among the Shoshones that adequately described the bear's senses. "When a pine cone falls in the forest, the eagle sees it, the deer hears it, and the great brown bear smells it." So now he knew why the colossus was trying so hard to catch his scent. The brute couldn't see him clearly and wasn't quite certain what he was.

Could he use that to his advantage? Nate wondered. He searched the ground around him and saw a shattered skeleton of a deer a couple of yards away. Among the broken bones was a piece the size of his fist. It would be perfect.

Taking a deep breath, Nate darted to the piece and scooped it up. Spinning, his eyes on Silver Hair, he raced toward the wall directly below the Bloods. The grizzly had cocked its head and was regarding him intently. Sheer dread lent speed to Nate's feet. He intentionally avoided looking at the Bloods until the very last instant so they wouldn't guess his intent and scoot from sight to thwart him.

He saw Silver Hair take a step toward him, and then he was right where he wanted to be, 12 feet from the wall, which was as close as he could get due to the angle involved. Abruptly facing the Bloods, he whipped back his right hand and hurled the piece of bone with all the might in his powerful shoulders. Straight at Kicking Bird.

Years of practice tossing rocks and skimming flat stones on the surface of various ponds, rivers, and lakes now paid off. The bone projectile flew true to his aim, striking Kicking Bird full in the face. The startled warrior vented a yelp of pain, and without thinking pushed to his knees, his hands pressed to his bloody nose.

Nate dived, hitting the ground on his elbows and knees, and held himself still. He glanced at the grizzly and nearly laughed in delight. His strategy had worked!

Silver Hair had heard the yelp and was now gazing suspiciously at the rim where Kicking Bird's torso was silhouetted against the backdrop of daylight. The bear advanced a third of the way across the bowl, its nose working like a bellows at a blacksmith's shop.

Nate twisted his head and saw Kicking Bird frozen in place. The warrior was afraid to move for fear the movement would be all that was needed to bring the grizzly up the ramp after him. Nate heard the bear growl, and turned his attention to it just as the monster caught an airborne scent and voiced a roar that shook the walls.

Silver Hair was up and out of the depression in the time it took Nate to blink twice. He never would have suspected the great bear could move so fast. The Bloods were also taken by surprise, and they barely had time to leap to their feet and race for the boulder field before Silver Hair reached the spot where they had been lying. Roaring lustily, the grizzly pursued them.

Nate pushed upright and ran to the ramp. He owed his life to the freakish nature of air currents. In the bottom of the bowl, which the breeze could not reach, there had been no current to carry his scent to the bear. But the breeze *off* the rim had been another story, bringing the scent of the Bloods to Silver Hair's nostrils and arousing the temperamental beast to a state of primal fury at having its sanctuary invaded by hated humankind.

He reached the top of the ramp before he realized he still clasped the thigh bone and cast it aside. The Bloods were almost to the huge boulders, the grizzly hard on their heels. To his consternation, Silver Hair inexplicably stopped and watched the band disappear from view.

The next moment the bear wheeled and started back toward the bowl.

Nate was caught flat-footed. There was no cover between the ramp and the boulders. At any second Silver

Hair would spot him, and in its agitated state, the grizzly would charge whether it detected his scent or not. He turned to the cliff and saw numerous cracks and spots where the rock face had crumpled. Climbing the rock wall was his only hope.

Stepping closer, Nate reached up and inserted his fingers into a crack, then jabbed the toes of his left foot into a groove at waist height. He gripped a second crack with his other hand and pulled himself off the ground just as Silver Hair roared once more.

A look back showed the bear had seen him and was barreling forward, its lips curled back over teeth that could crush a man's bones as easily as a man's teeth could sheer through a slice of bread.

Nate frantically sought another crack, found a suitable one, and clawed upward. If he could get high enough, the grizzly wouldn't be able to get him. Wedging his fingers into a narrow cleft, he rose another few inches. He dared not glance over his shoulder again. The delay might cost him his life.

Five feet he climbed. Then seven. His fingers hurt, his toes too, but he couldn't slow down. A horizontal crack enabled him to gain another foot, but he was still far from safe. He expected to hear the monster closing on him, but heard nothing. Then, as he grabbed for a hole formed when some of the stone had eroded away, he heard a rumbling growl from directly below, and peering between his legs, Nate saw Silver Hair at the base of the cliff. That very instant, the bear lunged upward, its huge forepaw reaching up to rip him from his perch.

Chapter Eleven

For a heartbeat Nate clung to the wall as terror flooded through him. Self-preservation, that most basic of human instincts, came to his rescue just as the grizzly's claws nipped at his left heel. He glanced up, saw an inviting crack a foot above his head, and thrust with both hands, sticking his fingers in as far as they would go. His feet lost their purchase. His body swayed outward, and for several harrowing seconds he thought he would lose his grip and fall on top of the bear.

Silver Hair had put a paw on the cliff face. Snarling, it swiped at Nate's dangling legs but failed to connect.

Mustering all his energy, Nate yanked his feet up and tucked his knees against his stomach. The tormenting strain on his arms and shoulders caused him to grit his teeth. He looked right and left, found a mere bump of rock, and got one foot braced on top of it.

Growling in anger, Silver Hair swung and missed. Not once, but three times, and after the third futile swing the grizzly lowered itself to the earth and began pacing from side to side while staring hungrily upward.

Nate gulped and sought another handhold overhead. Should it occur to the bear to stand on its hind legs and straighten to its full height, he would soon be in the beast's belly. He spied a protruding ridge no more than an inch wide about ten inches above and to the right, and gauged whether he could grip it with a quick flick of his hand. As he girded himself for the attempt, he was stunned to hear sharp retorts of gunfire come from the boulder field, mingled with savage war whoops and frenzied yells.

The grizzly also heard and turned.

Maybe the bear would leave to investigate, Nate hoped. From the sound of things, the Bloods were embroiled in a running battle. But with whom? A likely answer occurred to him and he felt a surge of excitement. It might be his Shoshone friends! The Shoshones could have tracked the Bloods to the vicinity of the bald mountain, then conducted a search when the trail vanished into the ravine.

His joy transformed into horror when Silver Hair began walking toward the boulders. If his friends got past the Bloods, they would have to contend with the monster. "Where are you going?" he bellowed, and whistled shrilly in an effort to keep the bear's attention fixed on him.

The grizzly halted, then swung around.

"That's it, you ugly good-for-nothing!" Nate shouted. "Come after me!"

Silver Hair lumbered back to the bottom of the cliff.

"Don't go anywhere," Nate kept talking. "I want you to stay right there, you flea-ridden sorry excuse for an animal."

Growling hideously, Silver Hair placed both forepaws on the cliff.

"You're too fat to climb!" Nate taunted, and waved his right hand in the air. "You're nothing but a big, hairy pig!" The shooting and the whoops had died down and his friends might appear at any moment. He wanted them to spot the bear before it spotted them.

Silver Hair inched higher, saliva dripping from its jaw.

"If I had my knife I'd show you a thing or two," Nate boasted, continuing to wave his arm to further keep the grizzly distracted. He stared at the boulders, then stiffened as the edge of the crack under his left hand crumbled and his fingers slipped out. In desperation he clutched at the cliff face, but the damage was done. Downward he plummeted.

Nate envisioned falling into the grizzly's gaping maw. Instead, he slammed onto the bear's head, his elbow smashing into hard bone, and then he was falling again, rolling down the bear's back until he struck the ground. He kept rolling, knowing to lie still would result in certain death, trying to make himself a difficult target for the bear to hit. A single swipe of those wicked claws would open him up like an overripe melon.

He rolled and rolled. Oddly, he seemed to be going downhill. The awful truth hit him at the same instant he hit the skeleton of an elk, coming to a gut-wrenching stop, and he shoved to his feet in dismay to find himself once again at the bottom of the bowl. He had rolled back down the ramp!

Silver Hair materialized at the top, the picture of bestial rage.

Nate stumbled rearward. He looked for something he could use as a weapon. To his right was the skull of a white-tailed buck with one antler still attached. Beside it lay the other antler, broken into sections.

Roaring its challenge, the massive grizzly swooped down the incline toward him.

What happened next transpired in a blur of action. Nate didn't think as he moved; he reacted instinctively, automatically, grasping the deer skull and raising it into the air, then waiting, poised to throw, until the bear was almost upon him. He hurled the skull with all of his sinewy might, catching Silver Hair on the brow and bringing the beast to an abrupt halt, really a pause of two or three seconds, just long enough for him to grab part of the broken antler, a straight section six inches long that ended in a tapered point, and to spring in close, wielding the antler like a knife.

The bear saw him leap and opened its mouth wide to bite.

In the fraction of time before Silver Hair could chomp down, Nate speared the tip of the antler into the grizzly's left eye and jerked his arm back. The monster erupted in a volcanic tantrum, roaring and swinging its front paws as it reared onto its hind legs. He glimpsed a paw sweeping at his temple, and then a battering ram collided with his head and he was swatted like a helpless fly, sailing ten feet or more to crash onto his back among the scattered bones.

Dazed, Nate rose on an elbow to see the grizzly swiping at the antler imbedded in its eye. He spotted the leg bone of an elk, one end jagged where the bear had bitten it off to get at the juicy marrow, and scrambled to his feet. In two bounds he had the leg bone in his hands. Whirling, impelled by necessity, he committed an act any normal man would regard as insane. He either fought or he died; so he fought. He charged Silver Hair.

Blood flowed from the grizzly's ruptured eye. It growled and swung, missing by inches, its reflexes dulled by agony and age.

Nate had ducked under that blow. Like a man possessed, he lanced the bone into the grizzly's side but barely dented its thick hide. Sliding to the left, he drove his crude spear up into the underside of the bear's chin where the hide was softer, and this time split it open. He drew back the leg bone to try again, but a huge paw walloped him on the chest and he was knocked off his feet, dimly aware his buckskin shirt had been torn, his flesh cut, the clammy feel of blood on his skin.

He rose slowly this time. Silver Hair was on all fours, moving toward the cave entrance. Suddenly the bear staggered, then sagged onto its forepaws. A thick flow of crimson poured from the stabbed eye.

Nate saw the deer skull and picked it up. His chest smarting abominably, he dashed to the grizzly's side and slammed the skull down on top of Silver Hair's head, flailing away like a madman, striking again and again, pounding until his arms were so tired he couldn't lift the skull. Wearily, he tottered to the left and gaped in amazement at the monster lying in the dust.

Silver Hair was motionless.

"It can't be," Nate mumbled, thinking the bear was playing possum. He swung the skull a final time and it shattered on impact, splitting down the middle and falling apart in his hands. The grizzly displayed no reaction.

Finally convinced Silver Hair was dead, Nate shuffled toward the ramp. His body was caked with sweat. Pain stabbed his chest with every step. Glancing down, he found five gashes where the bear's claws had ripped into him.

From on top of the bowl came the patter of rushing feet and the sound of heavy breathing, then a low growl.

Startled, thinking that Silver Hair must have a mate and it was about to tear into him, Nate looked up. At the upper edge of the ramp stood another huge animal, but this one was an enormous black dog, not a grizzly. It rushed down the incline and right up to him, then reared as it whined in delight.

"No!" Nate said, trying to brush the mongrel aside. In its enthusiasm the dog paid no heed and its heavy paws smacked into his chest, causing him to stumble backwards and fall onto his posterior. He sat there, a lopsided grin curling his mouth, as the black dog stepped up and began licking his face, getting slobber all over his cheeks and chin. "You dumb cur," he muttered.

"Samson, you found him!"

At the youthful cry of joy, Nate again looked up, and was astonished to see his son running toward him. "Zach?" he said in disbelief, trying to rise but unable to do so because Samson was straddling his legs.

"Pa! Pa!" the boy shouted. "You're alive!"

Nate could only sit in dumbfounded amazement as Zach threw himself into his arms and hugged him tight.

"I was so scared the Bloods had killed you," Zach said in a strained tone. "Ma kept saying you could take care of yourself, but I was scared anyway."

"Your mother?" Nate said, and suddenly spied Winona jogging along the rim. She wasn't alone. Trailing her were Touch the Clouds and Drags the Rope, both armed with bows.

Zach straightened, his eyes brimming with tears. "We had to come, Pa. Samson won't listen to anyone else but us, and we needed him to follow your scent. Touch the Clouds said we could find you faster using Samson than we could if the warriors had to follow the tracks the Bloods left."

Nate absently nodded. "True," he mumbled, and got to his knees. Zach stepped close for another hug.

"I love you, Pa," the boy said softly.

Feeling constricted in his throat, Nate embraced his son and silently gave thanks for being alive. To his rear, Samson began snarling. He twisted and saw the dog warily sniffing at the dead grizzly, the hairs on Samson's neck bristling. As he faced front a pair of slender arms circled Zach and him and warm lips touched his brow.

"You had me very worried, husband," Winona said huskily.

"I was worried also," Nate responded with a grin. There were tears of joy in her eyes as well. She pressed her face to his shoulder and gave a squeeze.

A shadow fell over all three of them. Touch the Clouds was beaming as he spoke. "My heart is happy to find you alive, Grizzly Killer. When we learned you were missing, I was sure some Blood would have your hair decorating his lodge before too many sleeps went by. It is good to see you are still wearing it."

Reverting to the Shoshone tongue, Nate asked, "What about the Blood war party?"

"All dead," stated Drags the Rope, stepping into view. "We saw them running toward us and ambushed them among the boulders. They were so busy looking back over their shoulders that they never saw us." He paused. "Most strange."

"Just the two of you killed all of them?"

"There are ten more men with us," Drags the Rope revealed. "They are still stripping the Bloods and dividing the spoils. We came on ahead with Winona."

"I can never repay you," Nate said, glancing from one warrior to the other. "I will always be in your debt."

The giant shifted self-consciously. "We are brothers in the same tribe, are we not? We only did what was right to do, the same as would you if one of us had been taken."

"Maybe so," Nate said, "but if either of you are ever in need, you have only to come to me and I will do all in my power to help you."

Winona and Zach straightened and moved back, and only then did they all notice the deep cuts where the bear had slashed him. "You've been hurt," she stated in concern.

"It's nothing," Nate said, rising slowly, his legs threatening to buckle. "A few scratches, nothing more."

Touch the Clouds was gazing at Silver Hair in frank awe. "Let me guess. *You* killed it?"

"Old age did more than I did."

"Our people will be telling tales of your exploits for as long as the sun rules the sky," Touch the Clouds said, and sighed. "It is just my luck to be living at the same time as you. No matter how many coup I count, you will be the one future generations remember."

"As a killer of bears perhaps," Nate said, dutifully returning the compliment. "But when it comes to glory in battle, I believe your name will be talked about around Shoshone camp fires more than any warrior in our history." He moved toward the incline, grimacing at an acute pang in his right side.

"What about this silver bear?" Drags the Rope asked. "Do you plan to take the hide back?"

"All I want is to lie down in my lodge and not move for a week," Nate replied. "I do not care if I ever see another bear, dead or alive, for as long as I live."

"But you must take the hide with you," Touch the Clouds protested, nodding at Silver Hair. "You killed this great beast. Our people must be permitted to see its huge skin and to hear from your own lips how you defeated such a formidable creature. It is your duty as a warrior to so honor yourself and our tribe."

Nate knew it was customary for warriors to publicly relate their exploits, but he was too tired and too sore to care about anything other than rest and recuperation. Wiping his sleeve across his forehead, he turned and spotted the rest of the Shoshone band making their way toward the ramp.

"If you are weary, we will skin the bear ourselves," Drags the Rope offered. "Such a fine hide will bring much good medicine to its owner and to our people."

"Whatever you wish," Nate said in resignation. It was useless to quibble, not to mention rude after they had risked their lives to save his. He sat down at the bottom of the ramp and rested his chin in his hands. The moment he did, Samson came over and resumed giving his face a saliva bath.

"We brought a water skin," Winona informed him. "I

will get it and tend your wounds. You stay here.''

''I'm not going anywhere,'' Nate said, and tried to move his head away from his dog's drooling tongue, but Samson stepped closer and kept licking. Saliva dribbled down both cheeks and over his chin.

''Is there anything I can do, Pa?'' Zach asked in English.

''As a matter of fact, there is,'' Nate said solemnly. ''You can tie Samson's mouth shut for me.''

His son, thinking he was joking, threw back his head and laughed.

Chapter Twelve

The entire village came out to meet them.

Nate walked at the rear of the band with his wife and son. Thanks to Winona's tender ministrations, he felt well again. She had applied an herbal poultice to the cuts on his chest and they no longer stung. His side still ached once in a while, but the pain was bearable. Considering the ordeal he had been through, he was in fine shape.

His weapons had been returned, and he felt like a whole man again with his knife, tomahawk, twin flintlocks, and rifle at his disposal. The Shoshones had offered him a share of the spoils taken from the dead Bloods, but he had refused and told them to divide everything, including the scalps, as they saw fit.

In front of him were two warriors carrying Silver Hair's hide. The size of three ordinary bear pelts, it wasn't so much heavy as it was awkward for a single person to tote. The warriors were quite excited about the trophy and couldn't wait to show it off to the tribe.

Now they got their chance.

From all directions the men, women, and children of the village swarmed toward the band. The return of a successful war party—in this case a rescue party—was always a cause for celebration. There would be plenty of food and drink and dancing later that night, and the warriors who took part in the rescue would regale their rapt listeners with their escapades.

Nate found himself surrounded by curious friends and relatives, all wanting to know what had happened. When it was learned he had killed a great silver bear, every last Shoshone wanted to hear the tale from his own lips. He promised all of them he would relate the full story that night.

Although he would rather have mingled and chatted, he was eager to get to his lodge and see how Reverend John Burke was faring. Since the band had camped overnight in the forest adjacent to the bald mountain to give him a chance to rest, not starting for the village until shortly after daylight, the minister had been left to his own devices for nearly two days. He hoped Burke had done nothing to antagonize the Shoshones.

As he hurried along with Winona on his right, Zach on his left, and Samson trotting behind him, he was stunned to see another white man come around a lodge, a grizzled mountain man sporting shoulder-length hair, a beard, and a mustache, all as white as the mantle of snow capping some of the distant peaks. So stunned was Nate that, halting in midstride, he almost tripped over his own feet.

"How now, Horatio!" the old-timer declared, his lake-blue eyes twinkling. "You tremble and look pale. Is not this something more than fantasy? What think you on it?"

"Shakespeare!" Nate blurted out, running forward to clasp his best friend by the shoulders. "We haven't seen you for months. What happened? Did Blue Water Woman get tired of your griping and boot you out of your cabin?''

Shakespeare McNair stiffened in mock indignation. ''My wife, I'll have you know, worships the ground I walk on. She would no more kick me out of the house than your lovely missus would you.''

''I've been tempted many times,'' Winona said, joining them and giving McNair a light peck on his bewhiskered cheek.

''Uncle Shakespeare!'' Zach chimed in. ''Are you going to stay a while? I want to show you how well I can ride a horse.''

''I might be so inclined,'' Shakespeare responded. ''If you're pa can tolerate my snoring for a few days.''

''I'll stick wax in my ears,'' Nate quipped, thrilled at this turn of events. Next to his wife and son, here was the man he loved most in the world, the man who had taught him practically everything he knew about the wilderness, the man who was a legend among the trappers and Indians alike. McNair, who had been dubbed Shakespeare years ago because of his fondness for the Bard of Avon and his penchant for quoting the playwright at the drop of a hat, had lived in the Rocky Mountains longer than any white man alive. He knew every trail, every pass. He knew the habits of every animal. He knew where to find rare medicinal plants few others were aware existed. McNair was a living fount of knowledge and no white man was more widely respected by the various tribes.

Shakespeare adopted a serious expression. ''Actually, son, this isn't strictly a pleasure call. I had a reason for coming to see you. I needed your help. Little did I know I'd find what I was looking for right here in the village. In fact, in your very lodge.''

''I don't understand,'' Nate said.

''Let's talk as we walk,'' McNair suggested, and slid between Winona and Nate as they all started off. ''I should fill you in before we get to your lodge so you know what's going on." He ran his fingers through his long beard. "Now let's see. It was about a week and a half ago that some Flatheads showed up at my cabin. They were all kin to Blue Water Woman, and they'd found themselves a stray white man. A city man, no less."

"You're not joshing me?"

Shakespeare shook his head. "Seems they came on this gent wandering around the prairie near their village. He was as lost as could be. Thank goodness he stumbled on them first and not the Blackfeet." He idly surveyed the encampment. "As you know, I've lived among the Flatheads and taught a few of them our language, so they were able to question this white man and learn what he was doing in their country. It turns out he was looking for someone and he wanted the Flatheads to help him. But they had a better idea."

"They brought him to you," Nate deduced.

The mountain man nodded. "Sure enough. They figured that since I know most everyone in these parts, I'd be the one who could help this man out. Well, I knew I'd need some help so naturally I thought of you. Got here just a few hours ago and heard all about you being captured by the Bloods." He glanced at Nate and made a clucking noise. "Here I thought I taught you how to take care of yourself! If the word gets out, I'll be afraid to hold my head up in public."

"As I recollect, *you* got yourself caught by the Blackfeet a few years ago. I was just following your example."

McNair chuckled. "True enough," he said, then quoted from his namesake. "Thus far our fortune keeps an upward course, and we are graced with wreaths of victory. But, in the midst of this bright-shining day, I spy a black, suspicious threatening cloud, that will encounter with our glorious sun, ere he attain his easeful western bed."

"I don't follow you," Nate admitted.

"What do you think of the Reverend John Burke?"

"You've met him?"

"No. Answer the question."

"He's a man with a chip on his shoulder the size of Long's Peak," Nate replied. "He wants to teach the Indians about Christianity, but with his attitude all he'll do is get them riled up."

"Then I was told the truth," Shakespeare said, frowning. "Unfeeling fools can with such wrongs dispense. I know his eye doth homage otherwhere; or else what lets it but he would be here?"

"Would you stop quoting that long-winded cuss and speak plain English?"

Shakespeare halted and touched his palm to his chest as if shocked. "Old William S. long-winded? Why, that's near blasphemy in my book. His too," he said, and cackled merrily.

"Will you get to the point?"

"The impatience of youth," Shakespeare said mockingly. "Very well. The lost gentleman's name is George Burke."

"He's related to the minister?"

"They're brothers."

Nate gazed straight ahead but had yet to catch a glimpse of his lodge. "Reverend Burke never even mentioned he had one. Were they traveling together and they became separated?"

"No," Shakespeare replied. "The good reverend left St. Louis alone. Then George, who is the younger of the two, cut out after him to try and stop him from doing what he intends to do."

"Which is?"

"You won't believe it."

"Tell me," Nate said a tad gruffly, wishing his mentor would come right out and say it instead of drawing out the suspense. But that was McNair. The man loved to gab. And while such a trait was highly entertaining on those long nights when they were seated around a lonely camp-fire off in the remote wilds, at other times it could be downright aggravating.

Shakespeare looked Nate in the eyes. "Reverend Burke plans to try and convert the Blackfeet to Christianity."

Both Nate and Winona halted in astonishment.

"I felt the same way when I first heard the news," McNair said.

Of all the tribes west of the Mississippi River, the Blackfeet were the most warlike, the most bloodthirsty. Ever since an incident involving the Lewis and Clark expedition, when a Blackfoot warrior was slain and another gravely wounded while trying to steal rifles belonging to Meriwether Lewis and a few of his companions, the Blackfeet had viewed all whites with an implacable hatred. Trappers caught in their territory were tortured, killed, and scalped. Every mountaineer, even greenhorns, knew to stay away from the Blackfeet at all costs.

"There must be an explanation," Nate declared as he walked forward. "Maybe the reverend doesn't realize how dangerous the Blackfeet are."

"He knows," Shakespeare said. "George told me they had a nasty argument in St. Louis over John's plan. Despite all of George's protests, John refused to change his mind."

Nate spied his lodge. And standing in front of it were two men involved in a heated exchange. One was Reverend Burke, the other a husky man with brown hair. That they were brothers was self-evident; their facial features were remarkably similar. As he drew closer he overheard their dispute.

"... should never have come after me," the minister was saying. "I didn't ask you to. I'm perfectly capable of taking care of myself. Besides, the Lord will never let any true harm befall me."

"You're not our Savior, you know."

"Meaning what?"

"That you can't perform miracles. The Blackfeet will laugh in your face, then carve you into little pieces. I'm not making this up. I've talked with men who know all about them."

"The Blackfeet may be heathens, but they are also children of God and deserve to hear the good news of the Gospel. Mark my words, George. One day there will be men of the cloth ministering to all these tribes."

George Burke shook his head in exasperation, then encompassed the village with a sweep of his arm. "Why not begin your ministry to the Indians here, among the Shoshones? At least *they* are friendly."

"I have made up my mind. I'm going to bring the Blackfeet to an acceptance of the Lord God and Our Master, Jesus Christ."

"Damn you, John!" George snapped, and whirled to stalk off. As it happened, he turned toward Nate and his family, and at the sight of them and McNair he hurried to greet them, his face a mask of barely suppressed fury. "You must be Nathaniel King," he said as he offered his right hand.

"My pleasure, Mr. Burke," Nate responded, shaking. He introduced Winona and Zach. "We couldn't help but overhear," he mentioned, nodding toward the lodge where Reverend Burke still stood.

George glanced at his brother and scowled. "John has become a fool. He'll get himself butchered and there is nothing I can do to stop him."

"You came all this way just to try and stop him from entering Blackfoot country?" Nate inquired.

The younger Burke nodded. "I tried to stop him in St. Louis, but he slipped out of the city in the middle of the night. By the time I bought my supplies and pack animals and took off after him, he had almost a two-day start." His voice lowered. "I love him dearly, but what is a man to do when his own flesh and blood is driven to commit suicide?''

Nate had no answer for that.

''If you'll excuse me,'' George said, his voice breaking, ''I need to walk alone awhile. I'll stop by in an hour or so, if that's all right with you?''

''We'll be expecting you.''

With a curt nod, George headed south, his head bowed, his fists clenched.

''Why are these men so upset with each other if they're brothers?'' Zach asked. ''Don't you always say that a family should stick together through thick and thin? I know if I ever get a little brother, I'll never get mad at him.''

Shakespeare chuckled and put his hand on Zach's head. ''Suggest but truth to my divining thoughts,'' he quoted. ''This pretty lad will prove our country's bliss. His looks are full of peaceful majesty, his head by nature framed to wear a crown, his hand to wield a sceptre, and himself likely in time to bless a regal throne.''

''Huh?'' Zach said.

''Pay no attention to Uncle Shakespeare,'' Nate advised. ''He's doing his best to confuse everyone today.'' Hefting the Hawken, he strode up to the minister. ''I take it you're feeling much better.''

''I was until my brother showed up,'' Burke replied. ''Now I'll have him pestering me until I ride out.'' He squinted up at the sun. ''It's too late in the day to leave now. We can depart tomorrow at first light if you're up to it.''

''We?''

''Yes. I need a reliable guide. From what your friend McNair was telling me, you're one of the most respected trappers in these mountains. I feared the Bloods had killed you, but your presence here proves you have courage. So at dawn we'll be on our way.''

"And just where do you expect me to guide you?''

"I imagine you know where. Into Blackfoot country, of course.''

Chapter Thirteen

Few words were spoken during the evening meal.

Winona served up a delicious elk stew, courtesy of her aunt, who provided the meat. She also made tasty cakes to dip in the stew and a boiled flour pudding for desert. Hot coffee capped off the supper.

Nate ate in somber silence. Normally, meals were an occasion for conversation and laughter, but the two brothers had put a damper on this one. John and George Burke sat across from each another, John the perfect picture of resentment and George wearing his anger on his sleeve. Their attitudes affected even young Zach, who usually talked incessantly; this evening he ate quietly, occasionally giving the two men a timid quizzical glance.

When the meal was over and Winona was busily clearing away the tin pans and flat pieces of bark that had been used as plates, Nate shifted to adjust his crossed legs and regarded the brothers coldly. "I think it's time we cleared the air and settled a few things. Your personal affairs are none of my business, but since the reverend has asked me to help him, I have a right to speak my piece.''

"What's your decision?'' John Burke asked.

Nate raised his tin cup to his lips and swallowed a mouthful of coffee. He had put off the minister earlier by informing the older Burke he needed time to decide whether he would serve as an escort to Blackfoot territory. In reality he had wanted the time to think up a way to convince John Burke he was making the biggest mistake of his life.

"Well?'' the reverend prompted impatiently.

"I've given the matter a great deal of thought,'' Nate said. "And I have to be honest. I agree with your brother.''

Reverend Burke glowered, placed his hands on the ground, and began to rise. "I should have known.''

"Wait,'' Nate said. "Hear me out.''

"There is nothing you can say that will persuade me to change my mind,'' the minister responded, although he relaxed his arms and leaned back. "But out of courtesy I will listen to whatever it is.''

Nate glanced at Shakespeare, who was filling a pipe and appeared distinctly uninterested in the entire matter, then at the brothers. "If it was practically any other tribe, Reverend, I would take you to them without hesitation. The Nez Percé, the Flatheads, the Bannocks, the Sioux, they are all reasonably friendly to whites. They would hear you out, and they'd allow you to leave in peace whenever you wanted.'' He tapped his coffee cup with a forefinger. "The Blackfeet will kill you before you can open your mouth.''

"You can't be certain of that.''

"But I can. More white men have lost their lives to the Blackfeet than to all the other tribes combined. You will be dead five minutes after you run into them unless they're of a mind to torture you first to see how brave you are. In that case you'll live a bit longer.''

"The Lord is my rock, and my fortress, and my deliverer; my God, my strength in whom I trust, my buckler, and the horn of my salvation, and my high tower," Burke said, quoting Scripture. "I have nothing to fear."

Nate tried another argument. "All right then. Let's suppose you do meet up with the Blackfeet. How will you teach them about God and Jesus when none of them, to my knowledge, speak English? Do you know sign language?"

"No."

"Do you know the Blackfoot tongue?"

"Of course not."

"Then how will you teach them?"

"Where there is a will, there is a way," Reverend Burke said. "I trust in the Lord. He will guide me."

"If you don't mind my saying so, I don't think you're being very realistic," Nate commented.

"I do mind," Reverend Burke stated, and stood. "Thank you for an excellent meal, Mrs. King. And I want to thank both of you for the gracious hospitality you've shown me. You'll be glad to hear that I won't be a burden to you much longer." Wheeling, he stepped to the flap.

"Wait," Nate said, but the minister paid no heed. The flap closed and John Burke was gone.

"He will never listen to reason," George said bitterly. "My brother is the world's biggest fool."

Shakespeare, who until that moment had been uncommonly reticent, not uttering so much as a syllable, now grunted and said, "All places that the eye of heaven visits are to a wise man ports and happy havens. Teach thy necessity to reason thus; there is no virtue like necessity."

George gave the mountain man a sharp look. "Are you saying you agree with his insanity?"

"Not at all," Shakespeare said. "I merely made an

observation written years ago by old William S.''

"Explain what you meant. I don't follow you."

"No one ever does," Nate joked, leaning forward. He cradled the coffee cup in his hands and swirled the dark brew a few times. "George, what will John do now that I've turned him down? Will he give up and go back to St. Louis?"

"Never. Not him. He's too pigheaded."

"But without a guide his chances of finding a Blackfoot village are slim."

"That won't stop him," George said, his shoulders sagging. "You see, there's more to this notion of his than you know."

"Enlighten us," Shakespeare said.

The younger Burke sighed, his brow furrowed in deep contemplation. After a while he glanced at them and bobbed his chin. "Very well. By all rights John should be telling you this, but he won't ever tell a soul." He ran a hand through his hair. "You see, my brother wasn't always as stubborn as he is today. Once he was the kindest, most tolerant man you would ever want to meet. He tried his utmost to live the Golden Rule, to love everyone, to do unto others as he would have them do to him. He was highly respected and his church services were usually filled to overflowing."

Outside arose a few shouts and loud laughter. The Shoshones were gathering for the night's festivities.

"John had a lovely wife named Pearl," George went on, "and they were the proud parents of a six-year-old boy they named Solomon. They were loving, caring parents. You would have marveled to see them."

"It hardly sounds like the same man," Nate said.

"True," George said sadly. "And with good reason." He inhaled loudly. "Not quite a year ago John took his family from our hometown in Rhode Island to St. Louis. He'd heard about the rowdy, godless types who inhabit that city, and he figured there was a great spiritual need he could fill. Very few ministers venture anywhere near the frontier. He wanted to be one of the first."

"Where are his wife and son now?" Nate asked.

"Bear with me," George said. "About six months after John began his new ministry, I received a letter from him. It turned out that the trappers, mountain men, and traders in his flock had filled his head with tales about the many Indian tribes living on the plains and in the mountains. And do you know what impressed him the most? The fact the Indians were all heathens. He saw an even greater need than in St. Louis. So earlier this year he started out with Pearl and Solomon for the Rockies."

Shakespeare's head shot up. "All by themselves?"

"Yes. I wrote him and tried to convince him that he was putting his family at great risk, but he never answered me. After all the stories I had read in the newspapers about trappers and other travelers who had run-ins with the Indians, I was extremely worried. I suggested he find another party heading west and travel with them." George closed his eyes and touched a hand to his brow.

No comments were necessary. Nate solemnly waited for the younger Burke to continue, certain he knew how the account would end.

"The next thing, about a month and a half after my brother departed St. Louis, I received a letter from a man who was a former member of my brother's congregation there. It turned out that John had been back for two or three weeks and never let me know. The man kindly told me there had been a terrible tragedy, that both Pearl and Solomon had been slain. John was distraught, and the man felt I might be able to comfort him. So I left immediately for St. Louis."

All eyes were on George as he took a hasty sip of coffee.

"I found him easily enough, and I couldn't believe the

change that had come over him. He wasn't the brother I remembered. His whole personality was different. Where before he had been kind and considerate, now he was bitter and rude. And nothing I said or did would bring him around.''

"What happened to his family, sir?" Zachary inquired.

George licked his lips. "They were killed by Indians. John refused to talk about it, but I was able to find the three trappers who had found him and brought him all the way back to St. Louis. They told me John and his family camped in a stand of trees beside a small stream. Apparently, a band of Indians spotted them and that night closed in. John was at the stream, bending down to fill a bucket with water when he was hit over the head, struck from behind with a tomahawk. The Indians must have figured they'd split his skull because they left him there and went after Pearl and Solomon.''

"You don't need to finish," Nate said softly. "We can guess what happened."

"No, I don't mind," George said. "You might as well know. It will help you to understand why my brother is acting the way he is." He took another deep breath. "From the tracks at the scene, the trappers believed Solomon had tried to go to John's aid and was stabbed in the chest, then scalped. Pearl was stripped naked, ravaged, and had her throat slit. They probably would have scalped John too, but they must have seen the trappers approaching the camp fire and left.''

In the profound silence that ensued, the laughter and happy voices of the Shoshones outside seemed grossly inappropriate.

"Did the trappers know which tribe was responsible?" Shakespeare asked.

George shook his head. "They scoured the area but all they found were a few moccasin prints and hoof tracks. The Indians didn't leave any solid clues behind." He coughed. "The oldest trapper thought a band of Kiowas might have done the deed based on the stitching of the moccasins."

Nate frowned. It was indeed possible to note the stitching pattern if a footprint was left in soft soil, such as at the edge of a stream. And the Kiowas, while not as widely feared as the Blackfeet, were formidably ruthless in their own right and prone to exterminating any whites they encountered.

"John was beside himself when the trappers revived him. He refused to eat for days and came near dying himself. By the time they reached St. Louis he was a skeleton. He's still thinner than he ever was in his whole life. I doubt he eats regularly. His guilt is gnawing away at his soul, and if he keeps on as he's doing he'll eventually waste away to nothing." George paused. "But he doesn't intend to let it get that far."

"No," Shakespeare said, and launched into another quote. "Methink I am a prophet new inspired and thus expiring do foretell of him: His rash fierce blaze of riot cannot last, for violent fires soon burn out themselves; small showers last long, but sudden storms are short; he tires betimes that spurs too fast betimes; with eager feeding food doth choke the feeder: Light vanity, insatiate cormorant, consuming means, soon preys upon itself."

"When did he get this crazy notion of ministering to the Blackfeet?" Nate inquired.

"About six or seven weeks ago, when he was talking to the same trappers who had saved him. They told him that converting the Indians was impossible, that his heart had been in the right place but he was wrong in thinking the Indians would be remotely interested in the white man's religion. I was there. I saw the look on his face when the oldest trapper mentioned that some tribes were decent while others were devils incarnate."

"And this trapper mentioned the Blackfeet by name," Shakespeare said.

"Yes. He went on about them at length, how they are the worst of the lot, fiends who delight in inflicting pain and seeing others suffer."

Nate shared a melancholy look with Winona. They both understood John Burke now. Nate, in particular, could identify with how the minister must be feeling. Should anything ever happen to his wife or Zach he would probably react in the same way.

"I had no intention of becoming involved in this," Shakespeare said. "But now I guess it's my duty to sit down with your brother, George, and explain the facts of frontier existence to him."

George mustered a wan smile. "I appreciate the offer but it won't do any good. John has his mind made up. Nothing we can do will change it."

"With time maybe we can change it," Nate said confidently. "And we'll buy that time by taking his horses and supplies over to Touch the Cloud's lodge and asking Touch the Clouds to keep them there until we fetch them. John can't go anywhere on foot and without provisions. If we do our best, in three or four days he might see reason."

"I don't know," George said uncertainly.

"What have we got to lose?" Nate responded. "Touch the Clouds will be busy at the celebration tonight, so first thing in the morning, before your brother wakes up, I'll sneak everything over. John will have no choice but to hear us all out if he wants to get his effects back."

"I suppose you're right," George said. "But you don't know my brother like I do. When he sets his mind to something, watch out. If there's a way to foil us, he'll think of it."

"Relax. Everything will be fine," Nate assured him.

"For the time being let's enjoy the celebration and forget all about it."

Not twelve hours later he was to deeply regret those words.

Chapter Fourteen

Dimly Nate became aware of a hand roughly shaking his right shoulder. He instantly sat bolt upright, blinking to focus while trying to clear lingering tendrils of sleep from his mind. The interior of the lodge was dark except for burning embers in the fire. The acrid scent of smoke tingled his nostrils. To his right lay Winona, sound asleep. Also asleep were Zach and George Burke. Beside him squatted Shakespeare wearing a pensive expression.

"Sorry to wake you," McNair whispered, "but I figured you should know that the minister is gone."

"Gone?" Nate repeated, and again gazed around the lodge. "Maybe he's out watering the grass."

"What do you think I was just doing?" Shakespeare said. "That's when I noticed his horses were missing. So are all of his supplies."

Suddenly Nate was completely awake. He rose and glanced at the vacant spot where John Burke's provisions had been piled. "Damn," he muttered, hastening outdoors. A faint pink tinge lined the eastern horizon, signifying dawn was an hour or so off. Dashing around to the rear of the lodge, he saw Pegasus and his other animals, Shakespeare's white mare, and the two horses belonging to George Burke. Nowhere was there any sign of the minister's bay and pair of pack animals.

"I figure the reverend skunked us but good," Shakespeare said at his elbow. "He lit out last night while all of us were at the celebration."

Nate turned. Could it be true? Come to think of it, he didn't recall seeing John at the festivities, nor had he seen him when they all returned to the lodge shortly after midnight. He hadn't thought much of it at the time, assuming John was still mad at George and had gone off somewhere to pray or simply to be by himself.

"Either he overheard our talk about taking his horses and supplies, or he just wanted to put as much distance as he could between his brother and him so George couldn't stop him from riding into Blackfoot country," Shakespeare speculated.

"We have to go after him," Nate declared, staring at the eastern sky. If they left at first light they might be able to overtake the reverend by noon.

"We might be wasting our time," Shakespeare said. "What if we catch up with him and he doesn't want to come back? Do we truss him up and haul him back here anyway?"

Nate shrugged. "We'll cross that bridge when we come to it. All I know is we can't let him go off and kill himself. He's throwing his life away for nothing."

"Maybe he doesn't see it that way."

"I'll never be able to live with myself if we don't try," Nate said, and hastened inside.

George Burke was propped on his elbows. "What's going on?" he asked with a yawn. "I saw Shakespeare and you whispering, then you both ran outside. Is something wrong?''

Nate would much rather go in pursuit with only Shakespeare at his side. George was a greenhorn who knew next to nothing about wilderness survival and inevitably would slow then down. But George was the minister's kin, and as such Nate had no right to refuse him. ''Your brother has run off.''

''What?'' George exclaimed loud enough to rouse a bear from hibernation, and came off his blanket as if he'd been shot from a cannon. ''When?''

''We think he left last night sometime before we got back,'' Nate disclosed, shifting to see both Winona and Zach now awake and sitting up.

''Then we must go after him right away,'' George declared, stooping to grab his boots. ''We can't let him reach Blackfoot territory.''

''I know,'' Nate said, ''but we can't go off half-cocked either. We'll have breakfast, pack some jerky and whatever else we'll require on the trail, and ride out as soon as the sun rises. We'll need the light to follow his tracks.''

''All right,'' George said sourly. ''You know best.''

I thought I did, Nate thought to himself, and went over to his loved ones.

A few tiny clouds, like balls of cotton adrift in an azure sea, were the only things moving in the morning sky when Nate, Shakespeare, and George Burke rode out of the Shoshone village, heading to the northeast. Nate had asked Winona's aunt and her husband to keep an eye on his family while he was gone. Spotted Bull, Touch the Clouds, and Drags the Rope had all offered to help, but Nate had declined their generosity.

This was his problem. Since he had been the one who brought Reverend Burke to the village, and since his lapse in judgment had enabled the minister to get such a substantial head start, he felt directly responsible for John Burke's welfare. In addition, he was annoyed at himself for not taking the man's horses and supplies over to Touch the Clouds before leaving for the celebration. If he had, Burke could never have given them the slip.

They found the tracks left by the minister's three animals right away. Reverend Burke had hugged the shore of the lake, leaving clear prints the whole time, until he reached the north end, at which point he turned into the forest.

Shakespeare leaned down to study the trail. "He was moving fast," he remarked.

"Can he elude us?" George asked.

"Not in a million years. He's leading two packhorses while we have our grub in our parfleches," Nate said, giving the rawhide pouches draped behind his saddle a pat. Parfleches were the Indian equivalent of saddlebags, and his were crammed with enough jerked venison and pemmican to last him two weeks. "We can go faster than he can. It's only a matter of time until we overtake him."

"I hope you're right," George said.

For the next ten miles they traversed dense woodland. Then the tracks slanted almost due east for a mile along a winding valley before turning to the northeast once more. Minutes later they found themselves at the top of a bald hill.

"He stopped here for a bit," Shakespeare noted as he read the hoofprints.

"Why?" George wondered.

"He was getting his bearings," Nate said. "My guess is he hoped to spot the prairie from here but he wasn't quite close enough yet."

George gazed eastward at the sprawling vista of tree-covered foothills. "What significance does the prairie hold?"

"He can make better time on the plains and spot others coming a long way off. Too, he probably knows the Blackfeet have their villages on the plains to the east of the Rockies, but north of here. All he has to do is continue north and in a week or so he'll be in the middle of their country."

"If he doesn't run into one of their roving war parties before that, or something worse," Shakespeare said.

"What could be worse?" George asked anxiously.

"All sorts of nasty fates await men who presume to tackle the wilderness on their own terms instead of learning Nature's habits and acting accordingly."

"Is that more from William Shakespeare?"

McNair chuckled. "Good Lord, no. That was original. But I know what I'm talking about, son. I've lived in the Rockies for more years than Nate and you have lived combined, and I know the dangers better than anyone." He clucked his white horse into motion and took the lead.

Nate fell in behind George Burke. Since Shakespeare was preoccupied with following the tracks, he had to keep alert for hostiles, grizzlies, and whatnot. One of them had to be on the watch at all times, or they might blunder into an ambush or a lurking bear.

In a way, they were lucky. Reverend Burke's pack animals were heavily burdened and left deep impressions. If Burke was on foot, tracking him would be impossible from horseback because they would need to get close to the ground to properly read the telltale smudges, crushed blades of grass, and partial prints that walking men made. That was why the Shoshones who came to his rescue had not used their horses; the Bloods had all been on foot.

Another hour brought them to a valley leading due north. Nate was puzzled when the trail led up it. If Reverend Burke was heading for the plains, as he surmised, then the tracks should continue on eastward. Why this new change of direction?

The air was crystal clear. A bald eagle glided high up, seeking prey. A marmot squatting beside its burrow near a cluster of boulders spotted them, vented a shrill whistle, and disappeared in a flash into the security of its den.

As always, Nate drank in the magnificent splendor of the untamed land. Shakespeare was of the opinion that one day, far in the future, the West would be just like the East: overrun with people, crowded with towns and cities, the wild creatures reduced to small populations or killed off completely. They had discussed this bleak outlook on several occasions, and Nate fervently hoped his mentor was wrong. To have the unspoiled wonder of the rolling prairie and the lofty Rockies reduced to mere stepping-stones on man's relentless trek to the Pacific was a travesty of progress and an affront against Nature. Why, if humankind kept on as they had been doing, one day the whole world would be filled to overflowing with more people than the planet could handle. What then? Where would the people of the future go to enjoy the natural beauty now so abundant once the wilderness was gone?

Movement in trees high on a foothill brought his reflection to an end and he squinted up at the pines. Shortly a large bull elk stepped into a clearing and gazed down at them. It was alone. Later in the year, during the mating season, the bull would congregate with others of its kind and battle other bulls for the attentions of the cows. Nate had witnessed the spectacle many times. The bulls would challenge one another with their distinctive bugling cries, then rush at each other, their racks clashing with a crash that could be heard a hundred yards away. Rarely was one killed. Those bulls that proved stronger gathered harems that would make a sheik of Arabia jealous, sometimes numbering 50 or more.

They came on a stream and halted to water their mounts. Shakespeare dismounted to squat and examine the ground. "The reverend stopped here too. Not long, though. He was still in a hurry."

"He knows I'll come after him," George said. "He's

counting on outrunning me.''

"Have you given some thought to what you'll do when we catch him?'' Shakespeare asked.

"Not really,'' George answered. "I figure I'll try to talk him out of carrying through with this foolishness. What else can I do?''

"Tie him up and lug him back to the village.''

"Bind my own brother? A man of the cloth?''

Shakespeare rose. "He's already proven he won't listen to reason. And I, for one, don't intend to sit around a camp fire close to Blackfoot territory for two or three days while you try to persuade him. It would be safer to take him back whether he wants to go or not.''

George bit his lower lip. "I don't know if I could do that to my own flesh and blood.''

"Your choice. Just bear in mind he won't have flesh or blood if the Blackfeet get ahold of him.''

Soon they were on their way, riding to the end of the valley where the tracks headed up and over another foot-hill.

"He's scouring the country again,'' Nate commented when they were at the top.

From the hill, the minister had traveled due east, keeping to the low ground to make better time.

"Thank goodness he's not sticking to the high ground,'' Shakespeare remarked. "A man stands out like a sore thumb up there.''

A small pond was their next stop. In the soil at the water's edge were the reverend's boot tracks and a single hand print where he had leaned down to drink.

"Your brother must not be feeling up to snuff,'' Shakespeare told George. "There's no need for him to be stopping to drink as often as he does.''

"He's not fully recovered from what happened on the plains,'' George said. "If he's not careful he'll have a relapse.''

"Could be," Shakespeare said, "and if he collapses out here with no one to tend him, he's in big trouble."

Reverend Burke, inexplicably, had borne to the northeast once he left the pond, into dense forest of large fir and spruce. They followed the hoof tracks, passing under trees in which squirrels scooted about and birds sang. Periodically frightened rabbits would bound from their path in prodigious leaps.

George twisted to see Nate. "Is it always like this, always so indescribably beautiful?"

"Always," Nate said.

"I think I understand why you stay in these mountains instead of going back to civilization," George said wistfully. "In the States there are a lot of people who believe men like McNair and you are crazy. Now I know better."

Nate gazed around and smiled. "It does grow on a man. I never planned on becoming a free trapper, but once I'd been out here a spell I knew I'd never be able to go back and live in the States again. Give me the wide open spaces and freedom over a crowded city and a hectic life any day."

The forest thinned out and they rode out onto a spacious meadow. They'd only gone a dozen yards when Shakespeare abruptly reined up and jumped down.

"What is it?" George asked.

"Your brother has company. Four Indians are following him now."

Chapter Fifteen

Nate was promptly at Shakespeare's side, bending low to read the spoor. Sure enough, he saw where four sets of hoofprints, all unshod horses, had come out of the woods and fallen into a line as they stalked Reverend Burke.

"What kind of Indians are they?" George inquired, his anxiety as plain as the nose on his face.

"Can't tell from the tracks," Nate replied. "They could be Bannocks who are just curious."

"Bannocks are friendly to whites?"

"Sometimes they are, sometimes they aren't. All depends on their mood at the time," Nate said, and when the younger Burke blanched he added as reassurance, "They have close ties with the Shoshones and some of their bands are just as friendly."

"What other tribes frequent this area?"

Nate rested the stock of the Hawken on the ground. "Oh, the Crows, Arapahos, even the Cheyennes."

"Don't forget the Blackfeet," Shakespeare interjected.

"But since they go about mostly on foot, these Indians are probably from one of the tribes you mentioned."

George gestured impatiently. "Let's quit wasting time. My brother could be at death's door as we speak."

"Don't get yourself in an uproar," Shakespeare cautioned, stepping to his mare. "Whoever these Indians are, they came on your brother's trail quite a spell after he went by. Their tracks are so fresh I'd guess they're not more than half an hour ahead of us."

"Then what are we waiting for?" George demanded, moving out ahead of them.

"Uh-oh," Shakespeare said softly as he swung up. "Here's Agamemnon, an honest fellow enough and one that loves quails; but he has not so much brain as earwax." He urged the mare into a gallop.

As before, Nate brought up the rear. He followed his companions and kept a constant eye on the surrounding hills. Miles to the west reared the first line of jagged peaks denoting the mountains proper, peaks glistening bright with snow. Miles to the east, but out of sight, lay the grass-carpeted prairie.

He hoped the four Indians were Crows. Like the Shoshones and the Nez Percé, the Crows were invariably friendly to whites. There had been an incident a few years ago at a Rendezvous when a couple of thoughtless trappers had gotten an old Crow drunk. An irate band of young warriors had threatened to beat the fools within an inch of their lives, and had only been dissuaded by trappers they respected. The Crows hated the white man's fool water, as they called distilled spirits of any kind. They believed that once a Crow drank liquor, he ceased to be a Crow and became a stupid animal. Trying to sell spirits to a Crow was as chancy as trying to feed raw meat to a panther.

An hour and a half went by. From the evidence presented by the tracks, the Indians made no attempt to narrow the gap between them and Reverend Burke, who stuck to valley after valley.

George pressed on ahead, able to follow the trail himself since the trampled grass and gouged earth was now so easy to read.

As they were passing a bluff on their right, Shakespeare called sternly, "You can slow down, son. Wearing out our horses will only delay us."

"I'm not slowing down until my brother is safe."

Shakespeare moved up beside him. "I wasn't asking you, George. As much as I share your concern, the horses come first. Do as I say or I'll make you walk."

Nate had opened his mouth to agree with McNair when he happened to glance at the bluff and detected a glint of sunlight at the top. The distance, close to two hundred yards, prevented him from seeing the cause. But he dared not ignore it. "Keep acting normally and don't look at the bluff," he warned the others. "There's someone up there."

"What did you see?" Shakespeare asked.

"Might have been sun on a rifle barrel."

Forgetting Nate's advice, George started to turn toward the bluff, but was stopped by a smack on the arm from Shakespeare.

"We don't want whoever it is to know we know he's watching us," the mountain man said.

"But what if it's a hostile and he takes it into his head to shoot at us?"

"We're a hundred and fifty yards off if we're a yard," Shakespeare responded. "He'd have to be a damn fine shot, and he knows that even if he bagged one of us the other two can reach the trees before he reloads and then go after him."

"There might be more than one," George argued, convinced they were in mortal jeopardy.

"We'll find out soon enough," Nate said. "I aim to ride up and have a look."

"We could all go," Shakespeare said.

"And make three times as much noise," Nate replied. "No, I'll go by myself. You know what to do."

"We'll be waiting," Shakespeare said, and grinned at him. "Shoot sharp's the word."

"What?" George asked.

"That's trapper lingo for good luck."

"Oh."

Waiting until the valley curved to the right and a projecting arm of pines blocked the bluff from view, Nate yanked on the reins and rode rapidly into the forest. Bending low over the saddle, the Hawken clutched in his left hand, he headed for the north base of the bluff. If whoever was up there was still watching, it would be a minute before Shakespeare and Burke rode into sight. By the time the person figured out Nate was no longer with them, he would be at the bluff.

Thick undergrowth enabled him to reach his goal without mishap. Straightening, he held Pegasus to a walk and moved eastward along the base. The front of the bluff consisted of a gently sloping hill covered with high grass, scattered pines, and infrequent boulders. He drew rein under a spruce to scan the hill carefully, and was rewarded by spying a ground-hitched, saddled roan halfway up the slope.

He moved toward it. A saddle meant a white man. Who did he know who might be roaming through this region? He could think of no one, and since it wasn't wise to ride right up to a man who might not want to be found, he dismounted next to the roan and grounded the stallion's reins. Then, his Hawken at the ready, he slowly climbed the hill.

The bluff leveled off near the top. Nate glided silently, his footfalls muffled by the grass underfoot, using all available cover, moving from boulder to tree to clump of weeds like a buckskin-clad ghost. He had learned his lessons well, and few were the warriors who could move more quietly.

Someone coughed above him and to the left.

Nate crouched, the grass swishing lightly against his moccasins as he advanced. There was a row of small boulders near the rim and a solitary stunted pine. Suddenly a shadow separated itself from the trunk and inched closer to the rim. His thumb on the hammer, Nate crept forward until behind one of the boulders. Tensing, he stood upright and trained his rifle on the figure squatting in the open. "Howdy, friend."

The man whirled, his face showing astonishment. A lanky frontiersman in typical buckskins and moccasins, he had oily black hair worn well past his shoulders and a greased mustache but no beard. His eyes were brown, his tanned skin the result of spending all his time in the outdoors. "Tarnation, mister!" he declared. "You plumb scared me half to death!"

Nate saw a telescope clutched in the man's right hand. So that explained the glint of sunlight he had seen. A sizeable number of mountaineers, including the redoubtable Jim Bridger, relied on telescopes when scouting the country around them. As Bridger had once joked in Nate's presence, "It's easier to give a band of hostiles out for scalps the slip when you see them coming a mile off than when they pop up out of a ravine right in front of you."

"Why'd you sneak up on me anyway?" the frontiersman demanded, regaining his composure.

"I like to know who's spying on me," Nate replied. "What's your name?"

"Allen. Henry Allen, from Tennessee. And who might you be?"

"Nate King. Some folks know me better as Grizzly Killer," Nate answered, stepping around the boulder and slowly lowering his Hawken. He noticed Allen's rifle propped against the stunted pine. Allen also had a belt knife and a single flintlock.

"I saw you at the last Rendezvous but never got a chance to talk to you. You're Shakespeare McNair's close friend, as I recollect."

"I am," Nate allowed, suppressing a smile. For all his fame as a killer of bears, Shakespeare had him beat hands down. McNair was a truly legendary figure among trappers and Indians alike, more widely recognized than Bridger himself.

"Was that him I saw you with down yonder?"

Nodding, Nate moved forward and offered his right hand. "I apologize for spooking you. But as you must know, a man doesn't live long out here by being careless."

Allen grinned. "Believe you me, I know. I've been trapping for pretty near two years."

"What are you doing in this neck of the woods?"

Allen closed his collapsible telescope, then gestured to the northwest. "I've been living with some Crows for the better part of ten months. Have me a Crow wife and a sprout on the way come fall." He stepped to the tree to reclaim his long rifle, a Kentucky in fine condition. "Their village is about four days' ride from here. My wife has been nagging me about needing a new buffalo robe, so I'm on my way to the plains. I stopped to rest my horse and while I was sitting up here keeping my eyes peeled for hostiles, who should I see but four Arapahos heading north."

"Arapahos?" Nate repeated, worried for the minister. Or more precisely, the minister's horses and possessions. Arapahos were not inherently warlike, as were the Blackfeet, but they would steal a man's belongings if they felt they could get away with it.

"Why are you so concerned?" Allen asked. "They went by forty minutes ago or more."

Briefly, Nate told Henry Allen about Reverend John Burke and the reverend's plan to try and convert the Blackfeet to Christianity.

"Is the man touched in the head?'

"In a sense," Nate said, sighing. He related the fate of John Burke's family.

"My. That's sure a pity," Allen said at the conclusion of the story. "A man of the cloth, no less. I guess it can happen to the best of us." He hefted his Kentucky. "Tell you what, friend. If you have no objections, I'd like to tag along and lend a hand. Some folks say I'm a fair shot, and I know this country hereabouts better than most because I hunt and trap it all the time."

"We'd be happy to have you," Nate said gratefully. When confronting Indians, there was always greater safety in numbers. Most warriors would think twice about tackling a superior force of whites, but wouldn't hesitate a second if they outnumbered their intended victims.

"Lead the way," Allen said, and when they had gone a few feet added, "I heard tell that you have a Shoshone wife and a young'un."

"I do."

"And that you kill grizzlies with a swat of your hand."

Nate laughed. "I wish it was so easy."

"Killed any lately?"

"Two within the past few days."

Allen broke stride, then quickly recovered. "Oh. Is that *all*? Maybe sometime you'll share the secret of your success. I for one go in the opposite direction when I see a grizzly coming."

"My secret is no mystery. It's called bad luck."

"How can killing grizzlies right and left be bad? Would you rather they killed *you*?"

"It's not the killing, it's running into the blamed things in the first place."

"Never thought of it that way."

Once on their mounts, Nate led his newfound acquaintance down to the base of the bluff and into the forest. Now if they could only overtake the Arapahos before the Arapahos overtook John Burke, they might be able to avert serious trouble. Speed was of the essence.

He found Shakespeare and George a quarter of a mile from the point where he had left them, waiting in the shade at the edge of the trees. Once introductions were over and Nate disclosed the identity of the four warriors, he assumed the lead and pressed Pegasus into a gallop. None of the others spoke; they all appreciated the gravity of the situation.

The reverend's trail took them on a winding course among the foothills instead of making for the prairie as Nate had guessed would be the case. Nate got the impression John Burke had been looking for something. But what? A place to camp? More water? Rounding a low hill, he suddenly reined up, his gaze fastened on a thin column of white smoke spiraling skyward half a mile distant.

"My brother has stopped!" George exclaimed, and raced ahead, lashing his steed with the ends of his reins.

"Hold up!" Nate cried, but was ignored. He gave chase, seeking some sign of the Arapahos, afraid George would recklessly rush into an ambush. To his rear thundered Shakespeare's and Allen's horses. They covered a quarter of a mile before Nate was able to draw abreast of George. "Slow down!" he bellowed. "You're putting all our lives at risk."

"My brother might need us! I'm not halting until we're there!"

"Yes, you are," Nate retorted angrily. Lunging to the right, he grabbed George's reins and wrenched them from the unsuspecting man's grasp, forcing George to grab onto his saddle and cling to it to keep from being spilled onto the ground. Nate brought Pegasus and Burke's animal to a gradual stop, and was about to give George a tongue-lashing when from the vicinity of the smoke arose a series of shrill war whoops.

Chapter Sixteen

"Damn!" Nate snapped, flinging George's reins down. Digging his heels into Pegasus, he flew toward the smoke, the fringe on his buckskins flapping in the wind. Reverend Burke had made camp in a stand of firs through which a narrow creek flowed. Until Nate reached the trees, he couldn't see what was happening. But as he dove in among the trunks he glimpsed a number of horses on the east bank and several figures moving about near a fire.

His arrival took the Arapahos by surprise. They were in the act of plundering the minister's supplies, whooping and venting cries of delight at their finds, and consequently didn't hear him coming until he was among them. He burst from cover into the clearing in which the camp was situated just as a tall warrior held aloft a spare pair of long underwear and crowed loudly.

Three of the band were by the crackling fire, the fourth standing near the prone form of Reverend Burke. They all spun, and the tall one dropped the long underwear and grabbed for a tomahawk at his waist.

Nate reined up with one hand as he jammed the Hawken to his shoulder with the other and trained the barrel on the tall warrior. The Arapaho recoiled backwards anticipating a ball in the chest. But Nate held his fire. His meaning was clear. If any of them pulled a weapon on him, he would shoot.

For a moment the outcome hung in the balance, the warriors frozen in indecision, Nate doing his best to keep the Hawken trained on the tall Arapaho despite the fidgeting of his stallion. And then Shakespeare, Allen, and George arrived, the first two with their rifles leveled.

The younger Burke took one look at his brother and leaped to the ground. He started to run over when a harsh command from Nate halted him in his tracks.

"Not yet! Don't get between us and these Indians or you might be caught in the cross fire if they decide to put up a fight!"

"But John—"

"Will have to wait," Nate ordered. He slid off of Pegasus and warily approached the tall warrior, lowering his Hawken to waist height but kept the man covered. "Do you speak their tongue, Shakespeare?" he asked without taking his eyes off the Arapaho. So far as he knew, his friend was fluent in four Indian languages, spoke three others passably well, and might know more. McNair wasn't the type to brag about his accomplishments.

"Can't say as I do," Shakespeare answered. "Always wanted to but somehow or other I never got around to it. Once I hit seventy I started to slow down. No excuse for it other than outright laziness, I reckon."

"Watch them like a hawk," Nate cautioned, and tucked the Hawken under his left arm to free his hands. "I am Grizzly Killer of the Shoshone," he signed, then pointed at the minister. "This man is my friend. Have you killed him?"

"I am Running Antelope of the Arapaho," the tall warrior responded. "Do not blame me or my friends for his condition."

"Then why is he lying there?"

Running Antelope glanced up at Shakespeare, then at Shakespeare's rifle. "I do not know. We were following him, waiting for a chance to steal his horses, when he made his camp at this spot. We watched him build his fire, walk to the stream, and drink some water. As he moved toward his horses he suddenly put a hand to his forehead and fell. We did not touch him."

Nate believed him. While Arapahos might be horse thieves and occasionally cold-hearted killers, they were no worse in their dealings with whites than any other tribe, not counting the Blackfeet and their confederates. And the Arapahos certainly weren't liars. Few warriors in any of the tribes made lying a regular practice because of the scorn that would be heaped on them if they were caught. By and large, Indians in general were much more honest than their white counterparts.

He sidled over to the minister and dropped to one knee to touch his hand to John Burke's cheek. It was as hot as the nearby fire. Pressing his palm to Burke's brow confirmed the reverend was burning up with fever.

"Is he—?" George asked, unable to finish the question.

"He's alive," Nate said, "but he's as sick as a dog. All that gallivanting in his weakened state only made matters worse."

"Can I help him now?"

"Go right ahead," Nate said, rising. He stood aside as George rushed to John's aid, then addressed Running Antelope. "I believe you did not harm our friend. But you were all too eager to take his possessions when he was helpless, and this I hold against you. Neither I or my friends have ever sought trouble with your people. We deserve to be treated better than this." He tactfully did not mention the run-in he once had with a war party of five Arapahos who had kidnapped Winona. Fortunately, none of the five made it back to their village to report the clash.

Running Antelope appeared bewildered by the statements. He stared at the minister and the minister's packhorses. "Perhaps we were wrong in thinking this man was our enemy and that we had every right to take his things, but our people have not had many dealings with whites. No one has ever told us the whites are our friends."

"My people have a saying," Nate signed. "Always do to others as you would have them do to you."

"A wise saying," Running Antelope conceded after a bit. "I will be sure to tell everyone I know that your people are not as bad as we think if you allow us to leave in peace."

Nate nodded at their war ponies. "You are free to go now. We have no wish to kill you'."

At a gesture from Running Antelope, the Arapahos climbed on their horses and turned their mounts to the south. Running Antelope paused to look at Nate. "You have spared us and we are in your debt. In return, I will warn you that two sleeps ago we came on the sign left by a large war party of Blackfeet. They are roaming in this area."

"I thank you," Nate said, disturbed by the news. If the war party found them, there would be hell to pay. They had to get the reverend back to the Shoshone villages quickly.

Uttering a loud yip, Running Antelope led his fellow warriors southward at a trot. They never looked back, and were soon out of sight.

"Well done, son. You averted bloodshed," Shakespeare stated. "The youngest son of Priam, a true knight, not yet mature, yet matchless, firm of word, speaking in deeds and deedless in his tongue, not soon provoked nor being provoked soon calmed; his heart and hand both open and both free.''

Allen cast an incredulous glance at the mountain man. ''What did you just say?''

''Pay him no mind,'' Nate threw in. ''His brain stopped working a decade ago.''

''You pierce me to the quick, young sire,'' Shakespeare said.

George Burke, who had been carefully examining his brother, turned on them. ''I'm glad you can find the time to joke around while poor John lies at death's door. He's ill, terribly ill, and I don't know what to do.''

Shakespeare slid off his mare. ''Allow me. I've picked up a little medical know-how from the Indians over the years and I might be able to do some good.'' He knelt next to the minister.

''Those Arapahos told us there's a band of Blackfeet in this area,'' Nate informed George. ''No matter how bad off your brother is, we have to head back within the hour. If they caught us here we wouldn't stand a chance.''

''John is in no shape to ride,'' George said.

''Then we'll rig a travois and haul him behind his pack animals,'' Nate proposed.

''Do you really think that will work?'' Allen asked. ''Those horses aren't accustomed to pulling a travois. They might buck or kick or drag Reverend Burke off into the brush before we could stop them.''

''I know,'' Nate said. ''We'll just have to keep them under control until we're satisfied they won't give us any trouble.''

''It sounds too risky to me,'' George said. ''What if I refuse to allow it?''

''Would you rather wind up in the hands of the Black-feet?'' Nate said, and glanced at the fire. That column of smoke was a certain giveaway of their location, and it would draw a hostile war party like a flame drew moths.

He saw a tin pan the minister had unpacked, apparently in preparation for making a meal, and quickly picked it up and went to the creek. Three trips were needed before he completely doused the flames. He stood back as the last tendrils of smoke climbed upward, then stamped on a few lingering embers.

"We have a problem," Shakespeare announced, standing, his features set in grave lines.

"What is it?" Nate asked, although deep down he had a feeling he already knew.

"Reverend Burke is in bad shape, so bad he won't survive a journey to the Shoshone village even on a travois. I don't know whether the hardships he went through on the plains finally caught up with him or whether he's come down with a sickness. But his fever is burning him up and he's as weak as a newborn kitten." Shakespeare gazed down at the minister and shook his head. "In his weakened state he should never have taken off from the village. He needed another week, at least, to recuperate."

"What do you think we should do then?" Nate inquired.

"Stay here overnight. Give him a chance to get some of his strength back. If we keep him warm and get a lot of liquids into him, he might come around enough to be able to make the trip on a travois."

George squatted and rested a hand on his brother's chest. "I don't care what the rest of you decide, but I'm doing as Mr. McNair says. You can all go back if you want. I'll take care of John."

"We're not about to abandon the two of you," Nate declared. "We'll stay here until morning and see how John is faring."

Allen rested his rifle across his saddle. "The closest hill is west of here," he mentioned, and jabbed a finger at the tree-covered crown visible over the tops of the trees on the other side of the creek. "How about if I ride up there and take a gander at the countryside. If those Blackfeet are skulking about, I might spot them."

"Good idea," Nate said, "Have at it." He watched the trapper ford the creek, then devoted himself to watering and tying their horses while Shakespeare and George did their utmost to make John as comfortable as they could, wrapping the minister in blankets and placing a wet cloth on his brow to cool his perspiring forehead.

George looked around as Nate joined them. "I appreciate you staying," he said, his eyes going past Nate to their mounts. "Say, you didn't unsaddle our horses. Why not?"

"If we have to leave in a hurry there won't be time to spare to saddle up."

"Oh. I hope it doesn't come to that."

"So do I."

Shakespeare was poking a stick among the wet remains of the minister's fire. "I hate to say it, but we'll need a new fire if we're to boil some broth. I'll chop up some jerky and see what else I can find to throw in." He headed into the trees.

"Leave the fire to me," Nate said. "I was the one who put it out in the first place." He walked into the trees and gathered broken limbs he could break down to suitable lengths. The older the limb, the better. As he came into the clearing he saw George holding John's hand and fighting back tears. The two of them must have been very close before the loss of John's wife and son changed John's outlook on life and caused the rift between them.

"Do you have a family in the States?" George asked as Nate walked up.

"Yes."

"Ever miss them?"

"Of course," Nate said, controlling his annoyance at being reminded of them.

"I don't see how you do it," George said earnestly. "I could never sever all my ties with my relatives just to head off for somewhere unknown." He stared at the gurgling creek. "I could never live in these mountains, no matter how splendid they are, knowing I might never see my parents again."

"Seldom does a day go by that I don't think of my folks and the rest of my kin," Nate said, bending over to deposit the branches on the grass. "We were a close-knit family, and naturally it pained me to leave them." He straightened. "At the time I figured on going back, but things never worked out that way. Now my father and mother are both dead and I'll never be able to look into their faces and tell them how much I truly cared."

George was studying Nate's own face. "I'm sorry. It was thoughtless of me to bring the subject up. I should have realized you'd have regrets."

"Regrets?" Nate said, and sighed. "If you only knew. But there comes a time in a person's life when they have to weigh their personal happiness against the blood ties of their childhood. Sometimes, as in my case, a person finds the mate of their dreams and the land of their heart's desire far from the home they knew and loved, and they have to make the hardest decision of their lives. Do they go off on their own to start anew or return to the old life? Do they stand on their own two feet and do what is best for them or do they do what might be best for their parents?"

"You sound as if—" George began, and stopped abruptly when a tremendous crackling and crashing in the undergrowth on the west bank heralded the sudden arrival of Henry Allen, who galloped into the open and reined up sharply.

"Blackfeet!" Allen cried, pointing to the south. "Heading this way!"

Chapter Seventeen

Hawken in hand, Nate sprinted southward along the edge of the creek where there was scant vegetation and he could make better time. "Stay with your brother," he directed George over his left shoulder. Allen, he saw, had reached their side of the creek and was vaulting to the ground.

Where was Shakespeare?

He couldn't see his mentor anywhere, and he fervently hoped McNair wasn't out in the open where the Blackfeet could see him. Ten feet from the end of the stand of trees he slowed and moved into the pines, doubled at the waist as he glided from trunk to trunk until he could view the approach to the south.

Over a quarter of a mile off was a band of five Blackfeet, hiking northward.

Nate's thumb touched the hammer of his rifle. Between the Hawken and his flintlocks he should be able to drop three of them once they were close enough, but he would rather avoid a conflict if he could. The Blackfeet were concentrating on the ground, reading the sign, and the shod hoof tracks would tell them there were white scalps to be had if they could find where the riders had stopped.

Why were there only five? Nate wondered. The Arapahos had claimed there was a large party. Where were the rest? And speaking of the Arapahos—what had happened to them? Had Running Antelope and his fellows blundered into the Blackfoot war party? Had these five backtracked to determine where the Arapahos came from and stumbled on the tracks left by his party? It hardly seemed possible there had been time for the Blackfeet to kill the four Arapahos. But then he realized 15 to 20 minutes had gone by since the Arapahos had departed, which was plenty of time. In the wilderness death often claimed men and animals alike with astonishing swiftness.

He doubted whether he would ever know the truth. The Blackfeet weren't about to tell him. If he showed himself, they would descend on the stand at a run, thirsting for his blood. At that moment, muffled footsteps to his right let him know he was no longer alone.

"I was only partway up the hill when I saw them through my telescope," Allen disclosed as he crouched behind a fir. "So I came back right away."

"Were these the only ones you saw?" Nate asked.

Allen nodded.

"Did you happen to see Shakespeare?"

"No."

Nate focused on the Blackfeet and came to a decision. "If they come this far we should try to kill them quietly so as not to alert the rest of their war party."

"Two against five? I'm a fair hand with a knife but you're asking the impossible. These are Blackfeet, not Diggers."

The reference was appropriate. Digger Indians were a branch of the Snake tribe to which the Shoshones belonged, but they were as different from the Shoshones as night was from day. While the Shoshones lived much like the other tribes on the plains, the Diggers lived in primitive fashion, going about near naked and subsisting on roots, pine nuts, rice grass, and small game. Most plains tribes held the Diggers in contempt; their fighting prowess was laughed at.

"Even so," Nate said, "if we fire our guns the rest of the war party might hear." He leaned forward, trying to see if the five warriors were carrying firearms. They were still too far off to tell.

"King, look!" Allen suddenly declared, his hand extending to the southeast.

Nate swiveled and felt his pulse quicken. Shakespeare had emerged from another group of trees two hundred yards away and was strolling toward them, his rifle in the crook of his left elbow, his back to the oncoming Blackfeet, oblivious to the danger.

"They see him!" Allen said.

Nate saw that for himself. One of the warriors had excitedly jabbed an arm the second Shakespeare appeared, and now all five were bounding like black-tailed bucks toward the unsuspecting mountain man. They were as far from McNair as he was from the stand, and they were bound to catch him before he reached safety even if he started to run. Nate leaped up and dashed into the open, waving his arms as he did. "Shakespeare! Behind you!" he yelled. "Look behind you!"

The grizzled mountaineer turned. Instead of dashing for the stand, he stuffed something he was holding in his right hand into his ammo pouch, then raised his Hawken and took a bead on the charging Blackfeet.

"He can't hit one at that range," Allen said. "He'll waste the lead."

Nate watched with bated breath. McNair seemed to take forever to aim. At last the Hawken cracked and belched smoke. Down the valley the foremost Blackfoot grabbed

at his chest, staggered, then toppled. The rest halted. One
of them lifted a rifle. Shakespeare was already sprinting
toward the stand, running a zigzag pattern to throw off
the warrior's aim.

"He should go to ground," Allen said. "That red devil
might get lucky."

The same worry afflicted Nate. He heard a pop when
the Blackfoot fired and glanced at Shakespeare, afraid his
friend would be hit. Evidently the shot had missed because
McNair never slowed. "Keep coming!" Nate called,
beckoning his mentor onward.

None of the Blackfeet were in pursuit. All four were
gathered around their fallen companion and two of them
were assisting the man to his feet. Moments later the pair
hastened to the south with their burden as rapidly as they
could while the remaining two pivoted and made for the
stand.

"They'll try to pin us down here until the rest show
up," Allen predicted.

"We can't stay no matter how bad off the minister is,"
Nate said grimly. As much as he wanted to help John
Burke, it was pointless to sacrifice all of their lives in the
process. "You go back and set to work on making a travois
while I stay and cover Shakespeare."

"George won't like it."

"Tell him that unless we head out in the next ten minutes, we risk being overrun by the Blackfeet."

"All right, but it won't make a difference to him,"
Allen said, and dashed off.

Nate remained where he was. The two warriors, unwilling to suffer the same fate as their comrade, kept up
a halfhearted chase until Shakespeare, panting heavily,
reached the trees. Then one bore to the right, the other
the left, and they vanished in the high grass and weeds.
"Enjoy your stroll?" Nate quipped.

"You have too courtly a wit for me," McNair said,

and grew serious. "Thanks for the warning. I was so busy thinking about how best to help the reverend that I failed to pay attention to what was going on around me." He tapped his temple. " 'Tis gone, you see."

"What is?"

"My brain."

"Quit prattling," Nate said, scanning the valley. "The Blackfeet will be on us soon. Allen is putting together a travois, Why don't you lend him a hand while I keep watch?"

"If we leave now, John Burke will die."

"If we don't, *we'll* die."

"Son, I have an herb that will help him," Shakespeare said, tapping his ammo pouch. "Give me fifteen minutes to get the medicine ready, then we can go."

"And what if the Blackfeet get here before you're done?" Nate responded while backing slowly into the firs. He alertly scoured the grass for sign of the two warriors who were in hiding. One had been armed with a lance, the second a bow, and it was the bowman who most concerned him. The Blackfoot might sneak close enough to put a shaft into him or one of the others.

McNair also backed into the shelter of the pines. "Bear with me," he said when they were temporarily safe. "I found some crawley over yonder, and there's nothing better for fighting high fevers. I can't feed it to Burke as it is because he's too weak to chew. And tea alone won't do the job because he needs something more substantial in his belly. So I'll heat some water, chop up some jerky into tiny pieces for flavoring, add a smidgen of flour, and throw in bits of the root. Just one dose of my broth should have him back on his feet within ten to twelve hours."

Nate knew how effective herbal remedies could be. And Shakespeare knew more about herbs and wild plants in general than any white man alive. "Do what you have to," he said. "I'll stay and keep watch for the war party."

"Thanks," Shakespeare said, giving Nate's arm a squeeze. "I'll fetch you when we're ready." He started to leave.

"Frankly, I never thought you cared that much for ministers," Nate commented. "Some of the remarks you've made led me to believe you hold them in low regard."

The mountain man seemed shocked. "I gave you that impression?" He frowned. "Yes, I suppose I do criticize their profession from time to time, but I have my reasons." Turning, he again began to stride off, then paused and glanced back. "My father was a minister."

"Your father?" Nate blurted out, but Shakespeare was gone, trotting toward the camp. It abruptly dawned on Nate that Shakespeare had never talked about his parents in all the years they had been close friends, had never so much as mentioned their names. Nate did recall a few comments that hinted at a hard childhood and a strict upbringing, but he wouldn't have guessed in a million years that Shakespeare's father had been a man of the cloth.

He leaned against a trunk and scoured the valley. There would be ample opportunity later to probe further into his mentor's background. For now there were the Blackfeet to worry about. Would the entire war party approach from the south, or would they split up and come at the stand from different directions? Should he stay in one spot or rove around the edge of the stand to better safeguard against a surprise attack?

Nate decided to compromise. He moved to a position at the southeast corner where he could see both the southern and eastern approaches. Still not completely satisfied, wishing he had thought to ask Allen for the telescope, he selected a pine and climbed ten feet. His elevated perch gave him a better view of the high grass should the Blackfeet attempt to crawl through it.

Almost immediately he spied the warrior armed with

the lance, lying on his stomach 40 yards out. The bowman, though, was too well concealed.

The minutes elapsed at a snail-like, nerve-racking pace. He heard someone chopping wood at the camp, and figured it was Allen acquiring the poles used to form the framework of the travois. Glancing back, he glimpsed the flickering flames of a fire and Shakespeare kneeling beside it.

More time went by. Nate fidgeted and searched the grass once more. The Blackfoot with the lance had not moved. Nor had the bowman given his location away. They were content to lie there and wait. Nate knew why.

When a half-hour passed and nothing happened, Nate eased toward the ground. He would check to see how the others were doing. The travois should have been put together and the minister fed the broth by now. They should be all set to ride out.

Movement at the south end of the valley made him stop and look. He counted six warriors spread out in a line, coming on at a dogtrot. Only six? He had expected more. Gripping a branch below him, he had started to drop to the earth when he saw additional figures to the east, five of them again spaced at regular intervals as they advanced.

The Blackfeet had split up!

Nate let go and landed hard on his heels. Spinning, he dashed through the trees to the north until the north end of the valley unfolded before his probing gaze. To his consternation, six more Blackfeet were moving toward the stand from that direction. And it was a safe bet there were more warriors coming from the west. Their strategy was obvious; they had the stand hemmed in on all sides, blocking any escape, and they could wage the battle on their own terms.

He raced toward the fire. Shakespeare and Allen were near the horses, talking. One of the pack animals had been fitted with a crude travois consisting of two long poles tied crosswise above the animal's neck and a blanket lashed to the poles dragging on the ground behind it. Lying on that blanket was John Burke, unconscious. George was at the creek, drinking.

All three glanced up as Nate appeared. "We're in for it now," he declared. "The Blackfeet have us surrounded."

Henry Allen cursed. "I knew we were taking too long!" He stared at McNair. "Why didn't you hurry like I wanted?"

"When a man has a job to do, he should do it right," Shakespeare said. "If we rushed building the travois it would fall apart before we went a mile."

George rose, water dripping from his chin. "What do we do?" he asked nervously. "You're the experts. I don't know a thing about Indian fighting."

"We can try to break through their lines, but it won't be easy hauling a travois," Nate said. He addressed his mentor, doing his best to keep any hint of reproach out of his voice. "I trust you fed the broth to the reverend?"

McNair nodded and touched the travois. "He'll pull through, given time."

"Provided we get out of this with our lives," Allen amended, holding his Kentucky in both hands as he peered through the trees. "How many Blackfeet are there anyhow?"

Nate performed a few mental calculations, "Seventeen that I saw, but there are probably more to the west."

"Sweet Jesus!" George Burke exclaimed.

"When this ole boy offered to help you, he didn't count on being killed by a pack of mangy Blackfeet," Allen said.

"We have to stay calm," Shakespeare said. "If we keep our wits about us, we can save our hides." He motioned at the pines on the west side of the creek. "This stand is too big for us to be able to defend the whole thing, so we'll have to pull back into these trees on the east side and hunker down for a battle.''

''How soon before they attack?'' George asked.

''There's no way of telling,'' Nate replied. ''But you'll know it when they do.''

''How?''

As if in response, from all points of the compass erupted a savage chorus of bloodcurdling cries.

Chapter Eighteen

"Here they come!" Allen cried.

"You cover George while he takes the horses into the trees!" Shakespeare directed the trapper. "Nate, you head north and I'll go south. Keep moving and make every shot count." With that, he whirled and ran southward.

Nate streaked toward the northeast corner as fast as his legs would carry him. He saw the rows of onrushing Blackfeet before he stopped behind a tree and whipped the Hawken to his shoulder. A strapping warrior waving a huge war club proved a tempting target, and he sent a ball into the man's chest. In a smooth motion he drew his right flintlock, extended it, and fired at a young Blackfoot to the east. The warrior fell, venting a gurgling shriek.

The rest instantly sought cover, diving into the grass.

Crouching, Nate swiftly reloaded, his eyes constantly darting to the north and east. To the south Shakespeare's Hawken boomed, and seconds later Allen's Kentucky thundered close by the creek. Despite the overwhelming

odds, they stood a slim chance if they could keep the
Blackfeet at bay. Once the warriors got into the pines, the
contest would soon be over.

Another factor worked in their favor. Successful war
parties were judged not only by how much booty the par-
ticipating warriors brought back to their village, but by
how few men were lost along the way. If a band stole a
hundred horses from another tribe, but lost one man in the
bargain, that raid was rated a failure and the warrior responsible for leading it was judged to have bad medicine.
But if a band stole only ten horses yet didn't lose a single
life, that raid was considered a great triumph.

Nate had downed two of the Blackfeet, and they would
be averse to losing more. They would try every trick they
knew, but they wouldn't recklessly expose themselves
again unless certain of slaying him when they did.

Silence prevailed on all sides. He wondered how Shakespeare and Allen had fared. Twisting to scan the stand,
he heard a buzzing noise, and threw himself to the right
as an arrow streaked past his head and thudded into a fir.
He lay on his stomach, his heart drumming, and tried to
spot the archer. The high grass taunted him with its seeming emptiness.

Nate crawled backwards until he was next to the wide
bole of a tall pine, then rose to his knees. A rifle blasted
to the east and a ball smacked into the tree within inches
of his face, showering wood slivers on his cheeks and
forehead. Dropping flat, he shifted in the hope of spying
the warrior, but all he saw was grass.

So that was their game! The Blackfeet were going to
lie out there and pick him and his companions off at their
convenience. Or worse yet, the Blackfeet would pour arrows and lead into the stand in order to slay the horses,
sealing the trap.

A bunch of weeds 20 yards to the north fluttered and a
painted face poked out. Nate quickly pointed the Hawken,

cocked the hammer, and squeezed the trigger. The Black-foot's head jerked as if kicked by an invisible foot; then the man slumped from sight.

In retaliation three arrows penetrated the stand, all missing by a wide margin.

Nate snaked to the left, convinced only a few of them knew his approximate position. The rest were shooting at random. He sat up behind a fir and hastily reloaded the rifle. As he was sliding the ramrod home, the brush to his rear rustled and George Burke, armed with a flintlock and a knife, stepped from cover. "Get down!" Nate hissed.

George halted, then obeyed, and as he did an arrow flashed through the very space his chest had occupied a second before.

"Stay low!" Nate instructed him.

Nodding, George crawled to the tree. "Shakespeare sent me," he whispered. "He wants to see you. I'll keep watch here."

"Has anyone been hit?"

"Not yet. An Indian almost got me but Allen shot him dead," George said, and smiled. "The really good news is that my brother has revived."

"So soon?"

"The travois bumped into a tree or two when I was getting the horses under cover and all the bouncing around woke him up."

"I'll go see what Shakespeare wants," Nate said. He hesitated, then held out the Hawken. "Take this until I get back. But don't shoot unless you're sure you can score."

"Thanks. I left mine back at the village."

Greenhorns! Nate reflected sourly as he angled through the trees until he came on a small clear space where the horses had been bunched. Shakespeare stood near the travois. "Where's Allen?" Nate inquired.

"On the south side," the mountain man said.

Reverend Burke's eyes were open but they were dull and his eyelids drooped. "Brother King," he said weakly, the words slurred. "How bad off are we? McNair won't tell me."

"Bad enough," Nate said.

"It's all my fault. If I hadn't been so pigheaded—"

"You should rest, Reverend," Nate told him. "You'll need all your strength when we make our escape."

Shakespeare squinted up at the sun. "I reckon we have six hours of daylight left, maybe a little more. Since Blackfeet don't like to fight at night, they'll spend all afternoon trying to kill us one by one, then rush those of us who are left right before dark."

"We'll mount up and be ready to ride when the sun touches the mountains," Nate proposed. "One of us can create a diversion while the rest try to bust through the Blackfoot ring."

"I'll do it."

"No, I will."

"Why you?"

"I have the best horse. Pegasus can move like lightning. They'll never lay a hand on me."

Reverend Burke coughed. "How exactly will you go about diverting their attention?" he asked.

"I don't rightly know yet, but I'll think of something," Nate said, wishing he felt as confident as he sounded. Short of charging the Blackfeet, nothing he could do would occupy their attention long enough for Shakespeare and the rest to flee.

"I wouldn't want your death on my conscience," the minister said. "You're in this fix because of me and it's my responsibility to see to it that all of you get out safely."

"You just lie there and rest," Nate reiterated, puzzled by the reverend's newfound interest in their welfare. It was a trifle late, in his opinion, for Burke to be thinking of them.

From the north came the retort of a rifle.

"George!" Nate declared. "I'll go see why he fired." He was off in a flash, weaving among the trunks, drawing both flintlocks on the run so he would be ready in case the unpredictable Blackfeet had launched a full-scale assault. He saw a commotion under the tree where he had left George, and rounding a thicket discovered the younger Burke in brutal combat with a sturdy Blackfoot. Each had his hands clamped on the other's throat. Nearby lay the Hawken and a lance.

Nate was almost on them before the Blackfoot reacted to his arrival and looked up. The warrior, snarling like an enraged panther, pushed George away and clawed at a big knife in a beaded sheath on his right hip. All Nate had to do was extend his left pistol and fire.

Struck between the eyes, the Blackfoot stiffened, twirled, and pitched forward, striking the tree with a dull thump as he fell.

George put his hands on the ground and started to rise.

"No!" Nate said, crouching and surveying the trees and the valley beyond. "Keep low unless you want an arrow in the back."

"This one nearly had me," George said breathlessly, his face red from his exertions. "I was watching the grass when I heard a faint sound behind me, and there he was."

Nate glanced at the dead warrior. "He was eager to count coup, I reckon."

"Odd thing, though," George whispered. "He didn't try to kill me when he had the chance. My back was to him and he could easily have run me through with his lance, but instead he jumped me and tried to pin me down. Why would he do that?"

"Perhaps he wanted to take you alive. The Blackfeet take particular delight in torturing whites."

George swallowed hard. "I see." He moved to the Hawken and picked it up. "I had the gun cocked when he leaped on me and I'm afraid I accidentally squeezed the trigger.''

"No harm done. I have plenty of black powder and balls,'' Nate said. Satisfied there were no more Blackfeet lurking close by, he reloaded both the rifle and the pistol. George watched him attentively.

"How can you do that so fast? It would take me two minutes just to measure out the right amount of powder.''

"When you load a gun often enough, you learn short-cuts. You learn how to judge the right amount of powder by sight alone. You always stick the patch between your front teeth until you're done pouring the powder so you can wrap it around the ball that much quicker. And you always start the patch and ball down the barrel with your thumb, then use the ramrod. Shaving a few seconds here and there comes in handy when hostiles are out for your hair.''

George rested a hand on the flintlock tucked under his belt. "I never have been much good with these. Our mother wouldn't allow guns in the house, so I never learned how to properly use them. A friend took me hunting a few times, but I never bagged a deer.''

"If we get out of this, I'll teach you all you need to know,'' Nate said with a smile. "You'll go back to Rhode Island and bag the biggest buck in the state.''

"That would be something,'' George said. He glanced toward the clearing where his brother rested on the travois. "Do you need me further? I'd like to check on John.''

"Go right ahead,'' Nate said, and waited until the younger Burke was gone before he dashed to another tree ten feet away and knelt behind it. To prevent the Blackfeet from pinpointing his position, he could not stay in any one spot too long.

A profoundly disturbing silence enveloped the stand.

Nate listened, but didn't hear so much as a bird. The wildlife had all sought shelter or fled the vicinity. And the breeze had died down so even the high grass was still. He scoured the open tracts and saw nothing. But the Blackfeet were out there, waiting their chance. One mistake and he would pay for it with his life.

Easing onto his stomach, Nate crawled to the west until he could see the creek. The gently flowing, softly bubbling water lent a deceptively tranquil atmosphere to the setting. Sooner or later the Blackfeet would get around to sneaking up on them through the firs on the west side. There were undoubtedly a few concealed in the undergrowth already. If only he could spot one!

Glancing to his left, he spied Henry Allen coming toward him. The trapper moved with fluid grace, like a panther on the prowl, adept at woodland travel, using all available cover.

"I ran into George and he told me you got one of the bastards," Allen whispered as he went prone in the shadow of a thicket.

"Four so far," Nate said.

"Shakespeare has dropped two and I winged one. No wonder they're in no rush to slaughter us." Allen craned his neck upward. "That will change, though, once the sun starts to set."

"We're riding out before they can overwhelm us."

"I know. McNair told me your plan," Allen said, and looked at him. "Listen, friend. I would be grateful if you'll take word to my wife should something happen to me. You can find the Crow village easy enough. Ride for four days due northwest and keep a lookout for a mountain with twin peaks, both covered with snow. There will be a river to the south of that mountain. The Crows are camped beside it."

"Let's pray I won't have to," Nate said.

Branches in the upper half of a pine across the creek suddenly swayed and a bronzed arm appeared, looped over a limb.

"Do you see what I see?" Allen asked, and snickered.
"I do."

"Allow me the honor," Allen said, pressing the Kentucky to his shoulder. He grinned as he cocked the hammer.

Nate saw the arm but no other part of the warrior. From the angle the arm was being held, he figured the Blackfoot was lying on the limb. Allen apparently figured the same way, because the next moment the Kentucky boomed and a warrior abruptly sat upright, a hand clutching his side. Grimacing in pain, the Blackfoot doubled over, lost his hold on the limb, and leaned precariously outward.

"Put a ball into him," Allen urged. "Finish him off."

Before Nate could do so, the warrior made a frantic grab at the limb, lost his perch, and plummeted. A high-pitched shriek ended when the Blackfoot slammed into the earth with a sickening crunch.

"That will teach the varmints!" Allen gloated.

As if to prove him wrong, a rifle cracked and a flight of arrows streaked above the creek and into the trees around them, smacking into trunks and limbs. One shaft thumped into the soil within inches of Nate's foot.

Allen laughed. "We've got them riled now!"

The humor was lost on Nate. A second flight of arrows buzzed through the air like angry hornets, and he scooted next to a tree for protection. A shaft hit the front of the trunk, shattering instead of imbedding itself.

"Show yourselves, you yellow-bellies," Allen growled as he fed black powder into his rifle. "I want another shot. Just one is all I ask."

Nate saw a third swarm of arrows speed toward them. He had turned to say that the thicket was a poor shield, and to advise the trapper to find better shelter, when suddenly a shaft sped true.

Henry Allen was hit.

Chapter Nineteen

The arrow caught the trapper on the right side above the thigh, piercing him from front to back, the impact twisting him around. Allen grunted, grabbed the shaft, and sprawled onto his side, his features contorted in agony.

"Hang on!" Nate said, reaching Allen in two bounds and stepping over the lanky frontiersman to grasp him under the arms. Digging in his heels, he heaved, and dragged Allen away from the thicket as more shafts sought them. Several tightly spaced pines afforded sanctuary.

"It hurts like the dickens," Allen rasped after Nate lowered him to the ground. Although in torment, he had held onto the Kentucky, which he now put beside him. "Damn them all to hell."

Nate sank on one knee. Thankfully, the arrow had penetrated skin and flesh but missed the lower ribs. The barbed arrowhead jutted six inches from the exit wound, which in itself was a stroke of luck. Indians sometimes applied snake venom or other poisons to the tips of their shafts, and an arrowhead left in the body for any length of time could result in death even though it missed vital organs. Another reason trappers had to dig out arrowheads quickly was that the glue holding the arrowheads on the shafts often dissolved after 20 or 30 minutes. If a man didn't get the head out before it came off, he would be forced to dig around inside with a knife or a special pair of thin pliers many trappers carried for just such an emergency.

"You know what to do," Allen said, and bit his lower lip.

"First things first," Nate said, and peered past the pines. The Blackfeet had vented their anger and were holding their fire. None were visible. Shifting, he searched around until he located a piece of broken branch as long as his middle finger and as thick as his thumb. This he gave to Allen.

"If I pass out I'll never stand the shame," the trapper said. He stuck the piece in his mouth and clamped down.

"Here we go," Nate said, gripping the shaft below the arrowhead and bracing his other hand against Allen's back over the exit wound, his finger curled over the arrow. Allen nodded once. Nate bunched his shoulder muscles, then wrenched with all his might.

The arrow broke with a loud snap.

Nate tossed the barbed tip aside and moved in front of the trapper. Allen's brow was beaded with perspiration and saliva flecked his lips. "Can you take it?" Nate asked.

Brief anger animated Allen's eyes. Free trappers prided themselves on their fortitude and their ability to endure pain without complaint. There were cases where men had been terribly mauled by grizzlies or been severely hurt battling hostiles, yet they'd never voiced a single complaint. Some, who hadn't been able to extract a deeply imbedded arrowhead, carried the grisly memento inside of them for years before they came on someone with enough surgical skill to remove it. Allen impatiently motioned for Nate to proceed.

"Hold on," Nate said, and again checked the trees across the creek for signs of the Blackfeet. He also scanned the north and east perimeter. The war party was still biding its time. Kneeling, he grasped the shaft next to Allen's buckskin shirt, then pulled. While arrows frequently came out easily, on other occasions they were as hard to remove as a contrary wisdom tooth. This shaft was difficult to budge. He had to twist it slightly to work it loose, and keep twisting to get it to continue sliding out inch by slow inch.

Allen's body shook, his teeth digging into the branch, his fists clenched on his lap.

"It's coming," Nate said, trying not to think of the fact his back was to the edge of the trees, and trying not to imagine what would happen should a Blackfoot spot him. He would be a sitting duck. The hair at the nape of his neck tingled the whole time he tugged on the arrow. When, at long last, the shaft popped free, blood dripping from the broken end, he promptly turned to look for hostiles. He saw only firs and brush.

Henry Allen spat out the branch, which had nearly been bitten in two, and gingerly touched his right side. "Thanks," he said. He inhaled deeply and mopped his forehead.

"We should get you to the clearing," Nate proposed, retrieving his Hawken.

"I can manage by my lonesome. You stay here in case those varmints try something."

"Are you sure?"

"Quit babying me, King. I'm a growed man, not a kid," Allen said, rising until he was stooped over, the Kentucky in his right hand. "Damned if you don't act like a mother hen sometimes." Chuckling, he made his way to the south.

Nate found himself liking the trapper a lot. Once they escaped—if they did—he intended to invite Allen and Allen's wife to the Shoshone village. The Crows and the Shoshones got along tolerably well so there shouldn't be a problem in that regard.

He crept to within eight feet of the tree line. Propped on his elbows, he surveyed the valley. What if the Blackfeet didn't wait until sunset? What if they sprang their trap sooner? Getting the reverend to safety would be a hopeless task; simply staying alive would be a chore. But if he was to mount Pegasus right then and there and cut out at a full gallop, he'd more than likely make it through the Blackfeet. There was only one problem. He would have to leave the others behind, and he would never, ever desert friends in a time of dire need.

For the next two hours Nate patrolled the north end of the stand, going from east to west and back again, stealthily slipping from tree to tree, always alert, always ready to fire should a Blackfoot appear. He felt disappointed when none did.

The sun arced on its downward course through the blue vault of the sky.

Nate was trying to determine if a dark patch off in the grass was a weed or a warrior when someone came through the brush to his rear and whispered urgently.

"King! Shakespeare wants all of us at the clearing."

Glancing over a shoulder, Nate saw the younger Burke. George was a bundle of nervous energy, and kept transferring his weight from one foot to the other while wagging the flintlock he held as if swatting at flies. "Why? What's wrong?" Nate asked.

"We're pulling out now instead of waiting for sunset."

Surprised, Nate cautiously retreated until he stood by Burke's side. "Why the change in plans?"

"Talk to Shakespeare. He told me the Blackfeet are up to something but he didn't say what."

Alarmed, Nate hastened to the clearing. All the horses were facing due south and Henry Allen was astride the roan, holding the leads to the pack animals. McNair was adjusting the bridle on his white mare. Reverend Burke, amazingly, was sitting up, a bible in his left hand. "How are you faring?" Nate inquired.

"As well as can be expected. Don't fret over me, brother. The Lord will preserve me."

Nate stepped to the mare. "Why the rush to get out of here? I thought we were waiting until near dark."

"I took Henry's telescope and climbed a tree," Shakespeare answered. "Spotted six warriors sneaking to the west to reinforce those already there. The way I see it, they're getting set to mount an attack. If they come at us through the trees on the other side of the creek, they'll force us out into the grass where the rest can kill us or take us prisoner."

"Damn," Nate muttered, although he admired the wily strategy. When would he learn to never underestimate the Blackfeet? When would he learn to always expect them to do the unexpected? How often must he remind himself they were the scourge of the northern plains and Rockies with good reason?

"If most of the warriors are west of us, their lines in the grass will be thin," Shakespeare was saying. "We should be able to fight our way out." He finished with the bridle. "We need to leave now, before they can spring their surprise. I'll go first to draw their fire. Allen will handle the pack animals. George will stick close to the travois so he can keep an eye on his brother. You bring up the rear."

"I should be the one who draws their fire," Nate objected. "I can—" He stopped speaking as a series of savage whoops arose west of the creek.

"They're attacking!" Allen cried. "And they'll be on us before we can get out of the stand!"

"I'll hold them off!" Nate said, whirling. He ran toward the creek, cocking the Hawken as he did, and probed the trees for movement. If he could delay the Blackfeet, if he could halt the charge for even a few minutes, it would give the others the time they needed to escape. The ribbon of water came into view, and so did a dozen or more Blackfeet who had already crossed it and were entering the pines on the east side. Stopping, he jammed the stock to his shoulder, sighted, and stroked the trigger.

The Hawken spat lead and smoke. A tall Blackfoot who seemed to be leading the attack crumpled. Immediately, the rest sought cover, some diving to the ground, others dashing behind trees. But a few never made it.

To the left of Nate guns cracked, three in swift succession, and he turned to see Shakespeare, Allen, and George, smoke curling from the barrels of their weapons. "What the—!" he blurted out, and saw a warrior coming straight at him bearing an upraised war club. In the blink of an eye the right flintlock was in his hand, and he fired when the onrushing Blackfoot was no more than seven feet away. The ball took the warrior in the throat, stopping him in his tracks as if he had slammed into a stone wall. Then the Blackfoot staggered and fell to his knees, his hands clamped to the wound in a futile attempt to staunch the crimson geyser spraying forth.

Nate would have liked to finish the warrior off, but if he used the second flintlock he would have to rely on his knife or tomahawk should another Blackfoot try to slay him. So he backed up, sticking the expended pistol under his belt and drawing the loaded one.

To the left more guns boomed. Shakespeare and Allen fired pistols simultaneously while retreating into the brush.

Suddenly someone screamed.

Pivoting, Nate beheld George Burke on his side on the ground, an arrow through his chest. Nate took a step, intending to drag Burke to safety, when two more shafts sped out of the greenery and sliced into Burke's chest within a hand's width of the first.

George swiveled his head and spied Nate. His eyes were wide in shock and disbelief. Then, blubbering red spittle, he collapsed and expired with a sigh.

Pausing behind a fir, Nate scanned the stand. The Blackfeet were all in hiding. Temporarily, at least, the charge had been broken. Both Shakespeare and Allen were behind trunks, reloading. Crouching low, he burst from concealment, racing toward McNair. A rifle thundered and something tugged at his beaver hat. An arrow missed his head by a hair. And then he was there, the trunk sheltering him.

"Trying to get yourself killed, Horatio?" Shakespeare whispered while wedging a ball and patch into his rifle.

"What the hell are you doing? You were supposed to cut out with the others."

"Does your wife know you use such foul language?"

"Damn it, this is no time to be making jokes."

"Why, how now, Adam! no greater heart in thee? Live a little; comfort a little; cheer thyself a little."

"Shakespeare!"

The mountain man grinned and peeked around the pine. "All right. All right. Don't throw a fit." He glanced at Nate. "Did you really and truly think I would run off and leave you to be butchered? I knew what you were trying to do, but one man couldn't stem their charge. So we joined in. Now, if they don't press us, we can sneak back to the horses and light out." He gazed into the trees. "Where's George?"

"He's dead."

"Drat. I liked the lad." Shakespeare leaned the rifle against the trunk and began reloading his pistol. "You'd better reload your pieces, Horatio, unless you're fixing on fighting the Blackfeet tooth and claw."

Exasperated, Nate opened his powder horn. "I don't need you to remind me what to do. And I'll thank you to stop calling me Horatio. It's not my name.''

"What's in a name? That which we call a rose by any other name would smell as sweet.''

"Sometimes I think you're a lunatic,'' Nate muttered. He repeatedly glanced at the surrounding pines, anticipating a second assault.

"We'll let them try again,'' Shakespeare whispered loud enough for Allen to hear. "When they hunt their holes, we get back to the horses and show these Blackfeet how fast white men can ride when they have to.''

"We can't go fast hauling that travois,'' Nate reminded him. "The Blackfeet will be on us like wolves on snowbound deer.''

"We are not the first who with best meaning have incurred the worst.''

"Here they come!'' Allen warned.

Flitting like painted specters from spot to spot, yipping and yelling like demented furies, the warriors were closing in, some sweeping to the right, some to the left, executing a pincer movement to outflank their foes.

"Fire, men, fire!'' Shakespeare bellowed, doing just that. About 30 feet out a Blackfoot toppled, a hole where his nose had been.

Nate heard Allen join the fray as he picked up the loaded flintlock, trained it at an onrushing figure, and shot. A feather in the warrior's hair leaped from the man's head, but the Blackfoot himself, untouched, dove for safety.

"Now!'' Shakespeare shouted, backing into the undergrowth.

All of Nate's guns were empty and taking the precious time necessary to reload them would be certain suicide; the Blackfeet would be on him before he could do it, So he sprinted for the clearing, dodging and weaving like a man possessed, deadly shafts tipped with their terrible barbed points raining down on all sides. Shakespeare was ahead of him. Allen, because of his wound, was in the rear but moving as if his heels were on fire.

Nate saw Shakespeare break from the vegetation into the clearing, and a second later did likewise, only to halt in astonishment and gap in stupefied shock at finding their horses gone. Every last animal. Even the packhorses and the travois. "How?" he blurted.

"There!" McNair declared, pointing to the south.

Nate, bewildered, sprang forward. Outlined against the firs, standing at the boundary of the stand and the tall grass, were all the animals including Pegasus. How had they gotten there? Was the reverend responsible? To the west the Blackfeet whooped in murderous rage as they closed in.

The travois was empty.

In startled bewilderment Nate noticed the vacant blanket and feared the Blackfeet had seized the minister, until his gaze lifted and he spied Reverend John Burke walking into the grass. "Reverend!" he yelled, but Burke paid no heed. The minister, walked with firm tread, his shoulders squared, his bible held aloft in his right hand.

Nate stopped beside Pegasus and surveyed the valley. The Blackfeet in the grass had yet to show themselves. Their attention was undoubtedly on the reverend, who suddenly started quoting Scripture at the top of his lungs.

"The Lord is my shepherd, I shall not want. He maketh me to lie down in green pastures, he leadeth me beside the still waters."

"Come back!" Nate cried. He took a step to go after Burke, but a firm restraining hand on his arm checked his advance.

"No!" Shakespeare said. "Mount and ride. We'll get him on the fly."

Nate spun and vaulted onto his stallion. Out in the open the minister boldly walked deeper into the grass, reciting all the while.

"He restoreth my soul. He leadeth me in the paths of

righteousness for his name's sake. Yea, though I walk through the valley of the shadow of death, I will fear no evil for thou art with me. Thy rod and thy staff they comfort me.''

Jabbing his heels into Pegasus, Nate galloped toward John Burke. A Blackfoot popped up off to the right, an arrow nocked to a taut bowstring, and aimed at the too tempting target. ''Try me!'' Nate shouted, but the warrior loosed the shaft a heartbeat later, and in helpless horror Nate witnessed the flight of the glittering arrow as it flew true, striking the reverend high on the chest.

John Burke staggered and almost fell. Miraculously, he regained his balance, held the bible higher, and walked onward. ''Thou preparest a table before me in the presence of mine enemies,'' he thundered as if from a pulpit. ''Thou anointest my head with oil; my cup runneth over.''

Nate was halfway to the minister. He saw the Blackfoot nock another shaft, and nearly laughed with glee when Henry Allen's Kentucky cracked and the warrior dropped like a stone. His elation was short-lived, however.

Another Blackfoot rose, his right arm sweeping back to throw a lance.

This time it was Shakespeare who fired. The warrior was lifted from his feet and crashed from sight in the grass.

''Reverend Burke!'' Nate called, hunching over, bracing to grab the minister under an arm and heave him over the saddle. Vaguely he was aware of Blackfeet in the trees behind them and a few Blackfeet on both sides.

''Surely goodness and mercy shall follow me all the days of my life,'' the minister roared, ''and I will dwell in the house of the Lord forever!'' Stopping, he turned, his eyes alighting on Nate, each twinkling with a gleaming spark of inner victory. He beamed proudly. ''Did you see, brother?'' he yelled. ''Did you see?''

See what? Nate wondered, reaching out with his left hand. He was nearly there—ten feet or less to go and he

could grasp the reverend's arm—when another arrow
transfixed John Burke from back to front, the tip exploding
out Burke's chest. The reverend took a halting step,
gawked at the barbed point coated red with his blood, and
then collapsed, falling straight down in a disjointed heap.

"No!" Nate bellowed, slowing, thinking there still
might be hope, that John Burke might still be alive, until
a glimpse of the minister's blank eyes and parted lips
convinced him otherwise. Glancing up, he spotted the
warrior responsible whipping another arrow from a quiver.
Rage seized him, and without realizing what he was doing
he goaded Pegasus into a full gallop and angled toward
the bowman.

The Blackfoot nocked the arrow and elevated the bow,
his actions precise and rapid, a seasoned warrior who knew
enough not to waste motion when in combat. He made no
effort to move out of the way until the absolute last moment.

Nate's gaze was locked on his adversary. When the
arrow leaped toward him he was rigid in the saddle, aflame
with a burning desire to revenge John Burke. He scarcely
felt the shaft as it shot under his left arm, clipping fringe
as it passed. But he did feel the impact when Pegasus
plowed into the Blackfoot like a living battering ram and
sent the warrior flying. The bow sailed into the grass. Nate
wheeled his stallion, holding the Hawken and the reins in
one hand, and drew his tomahawk. Somewhere, someone
was shouting. He didn't care who or why. All he cared
about was satisfying his craving for vengeance.

The stallion pounded toward the warrior once more.
Dazed but game, the Blackfoot was standing, pulling a
sheath knife as he straightened. He never had the opportunity to use it.

Nate swooped down on the warrior, his tomahawk shining in the sunlight as he swung it on high, then buried the
edge in the top of the Blackfoot's skull. He let go of the

handle and swept on past, making for the south end of the valley, hearing rifles blast and the frenzied cries of the war party.

Somehow, Shakespeare and Allen had gotten ahead of him and were beckoning him on.

He raced after them, listening to the buzz of arrows and balls, hoping Pegasus would be spared. A glance showed him ten or so Blackfeet pouring from the pines. He wasn't worried. Not even the fleetest of men could hope to overtake a robust stallion in the prime of its life.

Shortly the arrows and balls ceased cleaving the air and Nate slowed Pegasus to a trot. A hundred yards distant awaited his friends. Twisting, he saw a crowing Blackfoot next to John Burke, waving the minister's scalp in small circles. Had the Hawken been loaded he would have shot the warrior dead. He watched others dance in glee around the body and strike it with their clubs and tomahawks. Still others had hold of the packhorses and the animals belonging to the Burke brothers, but they were making no attempt to give chase. Evidently the Blackfeet were satisfied with their spoils, or else they simply didn't care to lose any more men.

"I thought for a bit there you were a goner, King."

Facing front, Nate thoughtfully regarded the trapper and fell in between Allen and McNair as they started homeward. "It would have served me right if I was." He sighed and sadly shook his head. "I came so close. So damn close."

"Don't talk nonsense, Horatio," Shakespeare said. "We did all we could for the good reverend, and then some. He made the choice. There was nothing we could do."

"What choice?" Allen asked. "Do you mean he wanted to get himself killed? He deliberately walked on out there knowing what would happen?"

"Stranger things have happened."

Nate breathed the sweet mountain air and watched a butterfly flutter over the grass. "I'll find a way to send word to the Burke family in Rhode Island. It's the least I can do." He looked toward the Blackfeet again, to be certain none were in pursuit. The war party was moving into the stand, taking Burke's body with them.

Henry Allen was also gazing back at the trees. "I still don't understand. Why did Reverend Burke do it?"

"Old William S. had the answer to that one," McNair responded soberly. "All the world's a stage, and all the men and women merely players. They have their exits and their entrances. And one man in his time plays many parts." He gave the mare a pat. "I just pray, when my times comes, I play my part as well as John Burke did."

 **David Thompson**

Follow the adventures of mountain man Nate King, as he struggles to survive in America's untamed West.

Wilderness #20: Wolf Pack. Nathaniel King is forever on the lookout for possible dangers, and he is always ready to match death with death. But when a marauding band of killers and thieves kidnaps his wife and children, Nate has finally run into enemies who push his skill and cunning to the limit. And it will only take one wrong move for him to lose his family—and his only reason for living.

_3729-7 $3.99 US/$4.99 CAN

Wilderness #21: Black Powder. In the great unsettled Rocky Mountains, a man has to struggle every waking hour to scratch a home from the land. When mountain man Nathaniel King and his family are threatened by a band of bloodthirsty slavers, they face enemies like none they've ever battled. But the sun hasn't risen on the day when the mighty Nate King will let his kin be taken captive without a fight to the death.

_3820-X $3.99 US/$4.99 CAN

Wilderness #22: Trail's End. In the savage Rockies, trouble is always brewing. Strong mountain men like Nate King risk everything to carve a new world from the frontier, and they aren't about to give it up without a fight. But when some friendly Crows ask Nate to help them rescue a missing girl from a band of murderous Lakota, he sets off on a journey that will take him to the end of the trail—and possibly the end of his life.

3849-8 $3.99 US/$4.99 CAN

CHEYENNE

DOUBLE EDITION
JUDD COLE

One man's heroic search for a world he can call his own.

Arrow Keeper. A Cheyenne raised among pioneers, Matthew Hanchon has never known anything but distrust. The settlers brand him a savage, and when Matthew realizes that his adopted parents will suffer for his sake, he flees into the wilderness—where he'll need a warrior's courage if he hopes to survive.

And in the same volume...

Death Chant. When Matthew returns to the Cheyenne, he doesn't find the acceptance he seeks. The Cheyenne can't fully trust any who were raised in the ways of the white man. Forced to prove his loyalty, Matthew faces the greatest challenge he has ever known.

___4280-0 $4.99 US/$5.99 CAN

DOUBLE EDITION
Blood Bounty/The Trackers
Jake McMasters

Blood Bounty. The settlers believe Clay Taggart is a ruthless desperado. The army says he should be left to rot under the desert sun. But Taggart is an innocent man with a bounty on his hide. With a motley band of Apaches, he roams the vast Southwest, waiting for the day he can clear his name, fighting any bounty hunter foolish enough to take him on.

And in the same action-packed volume...

The Trackers. When a bloodthirsty trio comes after the White Apache and his followers, prepared to slaughter them like sheep, they don't know that Clay Taggart isn't about to let anyone kill him.

___4318-1 $4.99 US/$5.99 CAN

Dorchester Publishing Co., Inc.
P.O. Box 6640
Wayne, PA 19087-8640

Please add $1.75 for shipping and handling for the first book and $.50 for each book thereafter. NY, NYC, and PA residents, please add appropriate sales tax. No cash, stamps, or C.O.D.s. All orders shipped within 6 weeks via postal service book rate. Canadian orders require $2.00 extra postage and must be paid in U.S. dollars through a U.S. banking facility.

Name_____
Address_____
City_____ State_____ Zip_____
I have enclosed $_____ in payment for the checked book(s).
Payment <u>must</u> accompany all orders. ☐ Please send a free catalog.